BACHELOR GIRL

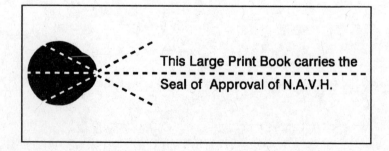

This Large Print Book carries the
Seal of Approval of N.A.V.H.

BACHELOR GIRL

KIM VAN ALKEMADE

THORNDIKE PRESS
A part of Gale, a Cengage Company

Farmington Hills, Mich • San Francisco • New York • Waterville, Maine
Meriden, Conn • Mason, Ohio • Chicago

LIBRARY OF CONGRESS CIP DATA ON FILE.
CATALOGUING IN PUBLICATION FOR THIS BOOK
IS AVAILABLE FROM THE LIBRARY OF CONGRESS.

ISBN-13: 978-1-4328-4774-6 (hardcover)

Published in 2018 by arrangement with Touchstone, an imprint of Simon & Schuster, Inc.

Printed in the United States of America
1 2 3 4 5 6 7 22 21 20 19 18

*To the memory of my grandmother
Florence Ferster Berger,
1918–2017*

PROLOGUE:
JANUARY 20, 1939

Steam heat fogged the tall windows as Albert and I joined the crowd assembled in the lawyer's office. A clerk with a clipboard ran around, establishing that everyone listed in the will was in attendance. "Helen Winthrope?" he asked. I nodded. It felt strange to see him check off my name. I hadn't expected Jake to leave me anything, not after all he'd done for me while he was alive.

Chairs had been arranged as in a small classroom. Albert and I exchanged somber nods of recognition with the members of Jake's household staff as we found seats in the back row. Ahead of us sat managers from the brewery and the realty company and the baseball team. Representatives from Lenox Hill Hospital and the Metropolitan Museum, anticipating major gifts, tried not to look too eager. Up front, Jake's brother, George, sat with his sons and nephews, black bands fitted around the sleeves of their jackets. I assumed the women, swathed in black crepe with starling feathers bristling from their hats, were Jake's sister and his nieces. I'd never been in the same room with them before.

It took a while for the lawyer to read through all the small bequests, gifts of five hundred or a thousand dollars to the many people who'd served Colonel Jacob Ruppert so well. Besides his chauffeur, he'd made provision for his laundress and his cook, for the brewmaster who was his oldest employee, and for the zookeeper who'd cared for his many animals. Jake had disbanded his kennel of Saint Bernards years ago, selling off the breeding stock and retaining only a few aging show dogs as pets. The peacocks would be left to wander Eagle's Rest, I supposed, the next owners of the estate forced to take them on. The monkeys would be going to the Bronx Zoo, I learned. Thinking of them reminded me of when my little dog Pip died. I'd wrapped his body in a blanket and rushed up the Hudson to Eagle's Rest to show his corpse to the rhesus female who loved him so. I knew she'd never stop pestering me if she didn't understand in her own way that he was dead. She'd reached through the bars of her cage and taken my limp Pip in her arms, mourning him like a lost infant.

I returned my attention to the proceedings at the lawyer's office. Jake left his collection of Chinese vases and jade carvings to the Metropolitan Museum, as expected. The bequest of one hundred thousand dollars to Lenox Hill Hospital seemed unaccountably large, I thought, given their failure to cure the phlebitis that killed him. Mr. Nakamura was recognized with a bequest of five thousand dollars, a handsome sum for a butler. When the lawyer announced that Albert had been left ten thousand dollars I took his hand, delighted that his years of loyal service as Jake's personal secretary had been so generously acknowledged. A man could buy a comfortable house on Long Island for less than that. My mind wandered as I pictured myself helping Albert pick out curtains and carpets. Perhaps we could plant a garden. I imagined a patch of grass bordered with tiger lilies and black-eyed Susans, an apple tree that would flower in spring and fruit in the fall.

"To Miss Helen Winthrope —" The sound of my name pulled me back to the present. "I bequeath my estate known as Eagle's Rest, along with all associated properties and contents."

My fantasy about a brick bungalow on

Long Island evaporated as I tried to absorb the idea that Eagle's Rest was mine. I couldn't understand why Jake had picked me for such an extravagant inheritance. I thought back to that day we'd first seen the property, Jake telling me how he wanted a house of his own where he could be himself with his family and friends. A lifelong bachelor who'd outlived three of his siblings, he didn't have much family, but Albert and I had tried to make up for it. I remembered standing beside Jake on the widow's walk of the old Victorian he'd torn down to make way for his new mansion. That's where we saw that eagle carry off its prey. We'd been speaking of my father's death — it was coming back to me now — and I'd been so relieved to learn he hadn't died alone. I supposed that was what Jake wanted me to think of, because it could only be symbolic, this gift. How could a single woman possibly fill fifteen bedrooms? Besides, there was no way I could afford the upkeep. I supposed I'd have to sell it, peacocks and all, though who'd buy an estate like that in this Depression I had no idea. Since the Crash, the market was glutted with the abandoned mansions of impoverished millionaires. In the end, my inheritance might not amount to much more than Albert's.

"— the sum of three hundred thousand dollars."

A collective gasp sucked the air out of the room. I leaned over to Albert, my voice a whisper. "What did he say?"

"Three hundred thousand dollars."

"Oh, who was that for?" I'd thought the museum and the hospital had been the biggest legacies.

Albert searched my face as if some secret message were written on my skin. "You, Helen. It's for you."

All the heads of all the people in all the chairs turned toward me. The room began to blur. I shut my eyes tight and yanked them open again, testing to see if I were in a dream.

The lawyer cleared his throat, his mouth giving voice to Jake's words. "As to the remainder of my holdings, including all my various enterprises, as detailed below" — his eyes swept down the document until they landed again on solid ground — "and in particular the New York Yankees baseball team, of which I have been sole owner since 1923, I direct it be divided between my nieces —" He paused to indicate two women, both married now and known only by their husband's names. I shifted in my seat, assuming we'd reached the end of the

11

will. But he had one more name to read. "— and Miss Helen Winthrope, in three equal shares." He lifted his head and scanned the room. "Thus concludes the reading of Jacob Ruppert's will. Bequests shall be distributed once the will has been accepted by the probate court. If you would be so good as to make sure my clerk has your correct address on your way out?"

I would have fled the room right then but Albert pulled down on my arm. I hadn't realized I was still holding his hand, squeezing it, really. I was afraid his knuckles might have cracked. I stretched open my fingers and saw that they were shaking.

"If the principal beneficiaries could remain." The lawyer raised his voice over the hum of conversation. "There are some matters to discuss."

Jake's black-clad relatives huddled around the lawyer's desk. They must have thought I was a gold-digging hussy, this unrelated woman who'd usurped their inheritance. Who would believe, now, that I was simply Jake's friend? My stomach churned. "Albert, I don't think I can spend another second in this room." I asked him to stay for me and find out what they wanted; people were so used to seeing the two of us together, I figured we were interchangeable.

I must have gone white as marble to have inspired his look of panic. "Of course, Helen, let's get you home. I'll come by after it's all settled."

I didn't even notice Albert putting my coat over my shoulders or leading me out to the sidewalk. The next thing I knew, I was dropping into the backseat of a cab, my knees watery. I grabbed his lapel before he could close the door. "Did you know?"

"No, Helen. I promise, I had no idea."

"Come over as soon as you can." I lifted my chin for a kiss, his lips quick on my mouth. I was halfway across Manhattan before it occurred to me I couldn't feel my toes. Looking down at my feet, I saw from the state of my shoes that I must have carelessly stood in a puddle of slush, though I had no memory of even stepping off the curb. By the time I got home, the cold had risen up my legs until even my neck was stiff.

I hoped Clarence would be in the lobby, but he was nowhere in sight. I went up to the apartment I still shared with my mother, even after all these years. She was waiting in the doorway. At the sight of my shocked face, she asked, "What is it, Helen? Didn't he leave you anything?"

I hugged my mother tight, bracing her for

the astonishing news that her spinster daughter had been transformed into an heiress.

■ ■ ■ ■ ■

1918

■ ■ ■ ■

CHAPTER 1

I was in my bedroom getting dressed when I heard the telephone ring. Disinterested, I finished hooking the buttons on my shoes. Let my mother get it, I thought. No one had called for me in ages, the drama agency that used to book me having apparently forgotten I existed in the months I'd been off the stage. It rang again. Realizing my mother must not be home, I went to answer it, my heel catching on the sports pages of the newspaper my little brother, Rex, had left strewn across the living room floor. I'd always wondered at the extravagance of having our own telephone when my mother was otherwise so careful to budget within the limits of the life insurance checks. Most of our neighbors in the building made do with the shared telephone in the lobby, where one of the custodian's children was always alert for its ring. Tenants tipped a penny to have their messages delivered, the child's pink palm eager for the bright coin, while my mother was billed five cents for every call.

Reaching for the telephone, I wondered if it might be Harrison calling. My heart jumped at the thought. I hadn't heard his voice since he'd found me burning with fever on the floor of my dressing room at the Olde Playhouse. The last thing I remembered from that night was Harrison cradling my neck in his huge hand as he shouted for someone to call an ambulance. My next memory was opening my eyes to see my mother's face hovering over the hospital bed. I was stunned when she told me that between those two moments more than a month had passed, the Christmas tree my brother and I had draped with tinsel long since tossed to the curb.

I didn't blame Harrison for not visiting me in the hospital. With me so suddenly out of the lead, he had his hands full directing the play. He did send cards — for the first few weeks, at least. I'd hoped he'd come see me once I was back home, but then the pneumonia developed, plunging me into a fight for my life. Every inhalation was a skirmish in a battle that raged through the winter and into the spring. Even if my mother had allowed me visitors, I wouldn't have had the breath to speak to them. Yet here I was, recovered at last, about to answer Harrison's call in my own clear voice. My hand shook as I lifted the earpiece and said hello.

"Hello, Teresa?"

I dropped into the seat beside the telephone, disappointment taking me out at the knees. "I'm sorry, my mother's not home."

There was a pause so long I wondered if we were still connected. "This must be Helen." The man pronounced it "zeese" so it rhymed with "geese," and I wondered what accent it was. "I'm glad to know you're up and out of bed, Helen. Are you feeling that much better?"

"Yes, I am better, thank you." I thought he might be a tradesman — my mother had been keeping everyone in the neighborhood apprised of my progress — but I didn't have a chance to ask to whom I was speaking before he started up again.

"You gave us a scare. Appendicitis is a serious thing. My dear sister Cornelia died of it. You shouldn't have ignored the pain, no matter how much you wanted to play that part."

German, I decided ("zee pain," "zat part"), though I had to listen carefully to pick it up. Perhaps the butcher on Ninth

19

Avenue where we got our pork chops? He always had been a busybody. "Don't blame my appendix. If it had just been the surgery, I would've been better months ago."

"Yes, of course, the pneumonia was an awful blow. Such a terrible time for your mother."

"It was a terrible time for *me.*" I blurted out the petulant words before I could stop myself.

"Of course it was, Helen. You've come through quite an ordeal."

I had, but I didn't want to talk to the butcher about it. "Shall I take a message?"

"Don't bother, I will call again." The warm hum in the line disappeared as the connection ended.

I hung up with a shrug and glanced around the room, wondering what to do with myself. Though the doctor had declared me cured, my mother didn't want me so much as taking the elevator to the lobby without the hired nurse holding my arm. I'd needed her help on those first forays outside, my limbs weak from disuse. As I'd gotten stronger, though, the constant fussing began to fray my nerves. It had been only a week since I'd convinced the nurse to stop coming by every day. And now my mother was out, too. Harrison may not have

20

called me, but my heart sped back up at the realization there was no one to stop me from going to see him.

I regretted my outfit, an old shirtwaist tucked into a gray skirt, but I didn't want to risk taking the time to change into something more flattering. Heading for the door, I glanced at the mirror in the hallway. What I saw was a far cry from the glamorous portrait I'd had done a year ago for the drama agency. The photographer had emphasized my eyes with mascara to balance my thin mouth and heavy chin. The result had been compelling, if not exactly beautiful. But so what if I didn't have the face of a Gibson girl? I didn't aspire to be a nameless beauty in some chorus line. Fascinating and full of character, like Sarah Bernhardt or Charlotte Cushman: that was the kind of actress I'd wanted to be. Still did, if I could find a way to get back on the stage. Grabbing my jacket and pinning on a hat, I let myself out of the apartment.

I expected to see Clarence downstairs, but he wasn't on the stool by the door where he usually perched, ready to welcome a tenant or receive a package. When we were both kids, our routines used to match so perfectly that any hour we weren't in a classroom I could find him in the lobby, but his schedule

21

had become unpredictable now that he was in college. It was just as well he wasn't around. Clarence had been so worried about me these past few months, I knew he wouldn't approve of me going out on my own.

Anxious to avoid running into my mother, I took fast steps up the block, stopping at the corner of Broadway to catch my breath. After the isolation of my sickbed, it felt good to be soaking in the life of the city again. The subway rumbled beneath my feet as I navigated the tide of people rushing along the sidewalk. A blinkered dray horse harnessed to a milk cart whinnied and stomped while the traffic cop's whistle tried to control the chaos of streetcars and automobiles in the road. On every corner, newsies shouted out the day's headlines: Germany Bombards Paris! American Troops Arrive on British Front! Liberty Bond Campaign Raises Millions! But I didn't want to think about the war or gas attacks or ship sinkings. Avoiding the newsstand, I turned down one of the streets off Times Square.

I walked the long blocks until I crossed Tenth Avenue and there it was, the Olde Playhouse. I'd read in the paper that Harrison had a new play opening in a couple of weeks, but the last show hadn't closed yet, which meant they'd still be in morning rehearsals. I anticipated the look of delight and surprise on his face as I appeared backstage. Maybe seeing me again would make him realize what a mistake it had been to end things between us. I'd be less shy this time around, I told myself, and more careful, too, if only he'd give me a second chance.

The marquee lights were off and the main entrance closed, but the side door was usually left unlocked during rehearsals. I tugged on the handle and it swung open with a familiar groan. In daylight, the lobby looked shabby, the Italian marble dull from decades of scrubbing, the flocked wallpaper worn thin, the velvet curtains threadbare. Come evening, though, when the lighting was right, it would glow with the promise of sophisticated entertainment. I'd been impressed when I came here last fall to audition, hoping to land a small part in Joseph Harrison's latest play. I was crestfallen when the great director assessed my performance as too subtle for the role of the sister and too restrained for the maid. Harrison chewed on an unlit pipe and considered my fate while I stood stranded at center stage. When he proclaimed he'd found his leading lady, I'd nearly fainted with elation. I couldn't believe it had finally paid off — the years of living at home to economize, the dead-end jobs after high school to pay for acting classes, the endless auditions, the inevitable rejections. I had no idea, that day, how fleeting it all would be.

Richard Martin, the Olde Playhouse's venerable owner, was behind the ticket window sifting through a pile of paperwork. He spotted me and stuck his head out, his reading glasses sliding off the end of his nose and swinging from the chain around his neck. "Helen Winthrope, what a sight for sore eyes! I thought you were in a sanatorium out in New Mexico."

I'd wondered what people were saying about me; the rumors had obviously taken on a life of their own. "No, I was right here in Manhattan. How's everything with you?"

"Oh, the usual, on the brink of disaster, but that's the theater for you. I should have sold out decades ago." Sighing heavily, he wiped his forehead with a crumpled handkerchief.

Having been an invalid so recently myself, I recognized his exhaustion. "Aren't you well, Richard?"

"I haven't been exactly well for years, but what can I do? This place would fall apart without me."

I told him he was the heart and soul of the Playhouse, but that he really should take care of himself. He waved away my concern as we fell into gossip about the closing of the current play and the opening of the next. I said I was surprised that he'd brought Harrison back to direct again.

Richard rolled his eyes. "He's a brute, of course, but the man's a genius. It wasn't his fault his last production ended its run in the red. Jessica couldn't carry the part the way you would have." A painful expression clouded his face. "You do know his new play's been cast already?"

I pointed to a poster on the wall. "I see he's given Jessica the lead again."

"The man doesn't always think with his brains, if you know what I mean." Richard gave my hand a squeeze and settled his glasses on his nose, turning his attention back to his paperwork. I tried to sound casual as I asked if Harrison was backstage, but Richard said he hadn't arrived yet. How typical for him to be running late; he'd always hated morning rehearsals.

I went into the empty house and sat in the back row, shifting uncomfortably on the lumpy horsehair seat. The Olde Playhouse was an intimate space, without a balcony or boxes, the tin ceiling still darkened by smoke from before the gaslights had been converted to electric. Compared to the moving picture palaces that were going up all over Manhattan it was downright cramped, but I loved its old-fashioned charm. Not that it couldn't do with a few improvements, new seats being at the top of a long list.

Behind me, a waft of air from the lobby stirred the curtains as Harrison strode into the house. I drew an excited breath — then held it as I saw Jessica Kingston clinging to his arm. Jessica Kingston my foot, I thought. When we'd first met in acting class, her name was still Jadwiga Kwiatkowska.

I forced myself to exhale. "Harrison."

He stopped and turned. "Helen, my God. We heard you'd gone to Colorado for the cure." He shook Jadwiga off his arm. "Jessica, go on, I'll be right behind you."

"Don't be long, Harrison, we're late as it is." She gave me a hard stare. "Nice to see you again, Helen."

I moved over so he could sit beside me, his bulk making the seat groan. Joseph Harrison was one of those men whose confidence in his own genius generated a kind of magnetic field that drew women to him, despite his sour odor and bulging gut. I couldn't resist the thrill I felt at his proximity as he stretched a heavy arm behind my shoulders. I asked what gave him the idea I was out west. Turned out, I had my mother to blame, not him. He'd tried to see me but she'd told him I was off recovering in a sanatorium. He assumed I had tuberculosis.

"No, I developed pneumonia after the appendectomy. My mother took care of me at home."

He turned the full force of his gaze on me. "She must be a good nurse. You're looking wonderful, Helen."

Fast as the flash people see when their lives are in danger, the entirety of our relationship played out in my mind. I remembered how, despite his initial enthusiasm at casting me, he became frustrated with my performance as rehearsals commenced. He invited me out for a late supper one night so we could discuss the role. Over glasses of wine, he urged me to draw on my experience of passion to fully inhabit the part. My blank look prompted him to ask if I was still a virgin. The blush on my cheeks gave him his answer. "That's the problem, then. Your lack of sex experience is inhibiting you as an artist." He himself was an advocate of free relations, he explained. He believed in love given and taken without obligation or expectation. He would never ask a woman to sacrifice her individuality or her career on his behalf — as he himself would refuse to sacrifice either for a woman's sake. Didn't I agree, he asked, in freedom for women equal to the freedom enjoyed by men? Overwhelmed by his words and the wine, I nodded. "Don't you see, Helen? To be a great actress, you need to have a complete experience of life, including the physical act of love."

I felt ridiculously naive in that moment to think that the only kisses I'd known were staged ones in acting class. Except, of course, for my first kiss on the fire escape with Clarence. But we were only fourteen then, still kids really. If I'd felt any stirrings of passion they'd been knocked out of me by the sting of my mother's slap across my face. Her reaction had shocked me. Lots of my friends in eighth grade were kissing boys, I argued. That may be true, my mother said as she washed my mouth out with soap, but she was damn sure none of those boys were Negroes.

On my next date with Harrison, a cold supper with chilled champagne in his apartment, I boldly asked him to provide me with the experience I so obviously lacked. It wasn't the romantic scene I'd imagined, which in my mind had culminated in being carried to a bedroom discreetly offstage. I hadn't anticipated the fleshy reality of his nakedness, thick hair matted to his pasty skin and pimples scattered across his back like bread crumbs for pigeons. As his sweat dripped into my eyes, I wondered what aspect of the sex experience was supposed to leave me feeling more complete. But afterward, as he stroked my hair and called me his dear girl, his tenderness unhinged my heart. Having already been broken in childhood by my father's death, it didn't take much to crack it open. And oh, what a hungry heart mine was.

When the affair came to an abrupt end, I blamed myself for being too inept to hold his interest. If we'd continued, I was sure I'd have learned to give him more variety, even to take pleasure in it myself. But there never seemed much for me to do once he'd removed my clothes and directed me to recline on the bed. When his wandering eye turned to Jessica, Harrison set me adrift to interpret the role on my own. Though our affair had lasted mere weeks, heartbreak was the only word for the ache in my chest as I watched them go off together. My foray into free love hadn't helped me understand the character I was playing, but competing for Harrison's attention onstage did intensify my performance. I consoled myself that his praise of my acting was more important than who went home with him once the curtain fell. By the time I understood the trouble I was in, it seemed too late to turn to him for help.

I came back to the present moment, in which Harrison's meaty hand had found its way to the back of my neck. "I was worried sick about you, Helen."

"But you managed without me, I see."

"Oh, well, the show must go on and all that. Are you interested in auditioning? This play's been cast, but I do have a new project coming up."

I stared into his eyes, all their sapphire intensity seemingly focused on me. Except I could sense his distraction as he thought of the actors waiting for him to begin rehearsal. As he assessed whether it would be worth his while to break it off with Jessica and take up with me again. As he wondered whether he should have supper at the little restaurant we used to go to. He'd forgotten about that place, I imagined him thinking, but seeing me reminded him how much he liked the steaks there.

Suddenly I could see him clearly: a genius, yes, but a selfish glutton, too, incapable of returning the feelings he'd stirred in me. I felt foolish for coming to see him. Suddenly I wanted nothing more than to get as far from him as I could. "No, I can't think about acting yet. I still haven't recovered my full strength." I shrugged his hand off and stood. "Best of luck with the new production."

"You know better than to jinx me like that, Helen." He hoisted himself to his feet. I dodged the wet kiss he tried to plant on my cheek and hurried up the aisle. In the lobby, my conflicted emotions got the better of me. Light-headed, I sank onto an upholstered bench, inhaling deeply and exhaling slowly, a lung exercise the hired nurse had made me practice.

Richard appeared with a glass of water. "You're better off without him, Helen. You must know that."

I accepted the water gratefully. "You're right, I know. I wasn't hoping to get him back, I just wanted to tell him something."

"Did you?"

"No, but it doesn't matter anymore."

He took back the empty glass. "Listen, Helen, if you're looking for something to do, I could use your help sorting through the papers here. I haven't been able to keep up with things as well as I should and I've dug myself into something of a hole. It

31

shouldn't be a difficult job, and I'd pay you, of course. Maybe you could come by tomorrow? After rehearsals, so you won't run into Harrison."

I wasn't sure I was strong enough to take on a job, even one as easy as sorting paperwork, but Richard seemed so desperate I agreed. At least it would give me a reason to get out of the house, I thought, as I walked back toward Broadway. I wanted to get back on the stage, of course, but it would be a while before I had the stamina for eight shows a week. In the meantime, I could use the money I earned to pay for an acting class. It would do me good to practice my craft before asking the drama agency to start sending me out on auditions again.

I'd been sick for so long I'd forgotten what it felt like to think about tomorrow, but why shouldn't I? I was only twenty-one. I had my whole life ahead of me. I put Harrison and the past out of my mind as I set my sights on the future.

CHAPTER 2

"Be careful you don't break your neck, Mr. Kramer!" my landlady exclaimed. She was washing the stoop and in my haste that morning, I'd nearly kicked over her scrub bucket.

"Sorry about hat, Mrs. Santalucia," I called back as I rushed down the steps. In Washington Square Park, I ran past children playing by the fountain and old men scattering bread for pigeons without so much as a glance at the soldiers loitering under the Arch. After waiting impatiently for the traffic cop's whistle, I dashed across Astor Place to the Third Avenue El, taking the stairs two at a time. Out on the platform I looked down toward the Bowery, the track stretching away like a flattened roller coaster, as if my gaze could draw the train any faster. When the vibration in the wooden boards beneath my feet announced the train's arrival, I checked my wristwatch and finally relaxed. I'd been late only once since becoming Jacob Ruppert's personal secretary, but a single experience of his withering disapproval had been enough.

Dropping into an empty seat, I pulled my hat down over my eyes. I'd stayed out too late the night before and was hoping to get some rest as we continued uptown, but more commuters crowded on at every stop until the aisle was thick with straphangers, their briefcases and bags bumping my shoulder. When we lurched away from 76th Street, the man standing in front of me lost his footing and stumbled, his shin wedged between my knees. He righted himself and caught my eye to mutter an apology before looking down at the newspaper in his hand. He was handsome, a masculine type, with dark hair and strong features. I was still looking up at him when his eyes swung back to me and lingered for a moment before sliding away again.

I knew what I would have done if we'd been on the street and he glanced back at me like that: put a cigarette between my lips and ask for a light. It was the easiest way. Any man in the city would stop to give a fellow a light, packs of matches ubiquitous in men's pockets. He'd strike the match and cup his hands as I lowered the tip of my cigarette to the offered flame. A man who wasn't interested in my sort would keep his eyes on the glowing tip of the cigarette and wave out the match as soon as the tobacco started to burn. But a man like me (or rather, a man who liked men like me) would lift his eyes from the burning match to find me staring up at him. He'd hold my gaze until, perhaps, the match burned his fingers. He'd toss it away, cursing, and I'd offer to buy him a drink to make up for it — there was hardly a block in Manhattan where two men couldn't step in off the street for a friendly drink. If he said yes, well, it wouldn't be long before I knew whether or not we were part of the same world.

But smoking wasn't permitted on the train, and anyway (I discovered as I patted my shirt pocket), I'd left mine on the nightstand in my hurry to get dressed. What I did have in my pocket were the ballet tickets Paul had given me for Sunday night. I could use them, I decided. I'd done it before with opera tickets, the question "Do you like the opera?" dropped casually into conversation with an attractive stranger. If the fellow said he did, I'd follow with a story about being stuck with an extra ticket and how I was looking to give it to someone who appreciated that sort of thing. A few days later we'd meet up at the performance and if, as the lights went down, our knees began to touch, then I'd know how our night might end.

What I needed, I realized, as the train stopped at 84th Street, was for some old crone to hobble on to whom I could gallantly offer my seat, leaving me no choice but to grab the strap next to the man who'd stumbled into me. Then, as the train lurched away from the platform, I could sway into him, apologize for my clumsiness, and strike up a conversation.

But no old crones did get on and the next stop was mine. I looked up at the man again, hoping to catch his eye, but he was still staring at his paper. As the train applied its brakes I readied myself to get off, piqued over the missed opportunity. Just as I stood up, however, a heavily pregnant woman waddled on. I waved her to my seat and grabbed a strap, pretending that had been my intention all along. As the doors closed, I checked my wristwatch. There was only enough time to ride to the next stop. I'd have to talk fast.

The train pulled out and I readied an apology as I swayed — into nothing. No one was beside me. I looked over my shoulder and saw that the man had taken an empty seat across the car. He lifted his eyes, saw

36

me looking at him, and snapped his paper open, ducking his head behind the newsprint.

I felt a fool hanging there as the train chugged past my workplace. As soon as the doors opened at 99th Street I ran across the platform, through the waiting room, and down the stairs. I decided riding back would be faster than walking, so I dodged traffic to cross Third Avenue, panicking as I heard a train rumble above my head until I realized it was the express. I raced up the stairs to the downtown side of the El and dropped my second nickel of the morning into the turnstile. Through the stained-glass windows of the waiting room I saw a thin crowd milling on the platform. Pausing to catch my breath, I put my hand to my chest and felt my heart beat its irregular rhythm. When the train came along, the car was jammed and I had to shove my way on, the door closing practically on my nose. Pressed up against the glass, I looked directly into the upper windows of passing apartments, men swilling coffee and women nursing babies an arm's length away.

In a couple of blocks, the residential buildings gave way to industry, and soon everything I could see belonged to Colonel Ruppert: the ice factory and the grain silo, the train spur and the warehouse, the new garage and the old stable, and finally, through the massive windows of the brewery itself, the gleaming copper kettles that had made his fortune.

I got off at 89th Street, shaking my head over my misadventure. At the newsstand below the station I grabbed the *World* and the *New York Times,* then looked around for the *Staats-Zietung* but couldn't find it. When I asked, the man drew it out from under the counter as if it were pornography. "Had some soldiers up here the other day harassing me about selling a German paper while we're at war with the Kaiser," he said, giving me a look that seemed to ask why I wasn't in uniform myself. I paid him and took the papers, my heart murmur and color blindness none of his business.

The smell of malt was thick in the air as I entered the brewery. After greeting the receptionist I called for the elevator to take me upstairs to the offices. I'd been surprised by the building's opulence when I'd come here a year ago to interview for my job with the Colonel, but by now I was used to the inlaid oak paneling and polished marble floors. In the anteroom to the president's office, two desks faced each other across an expansive Persian carpet. I nodded at Miss

Grunwald before setting the newspapers on my desk and taking off my hat.

"Cutting it rather close, aren't you, Mr. Kramer?"

Before I could answer, the cuckoo in the Black Forest clock on the wall poked out its head and chirped the hour — nine o'clock. "I had some trouble with the train," I said. "How are you today?"

"As well as can be expected, Mr. Kramer." Miss Grunwald was a holdover from the last century and she looked it, too, with her long skirt and pinned-up braids. She'd been wary of me at first, unsure why the Colonel needed a personal secretary when she'd been secretary to the president of the brewery since his father's time. We'd since grown used to each other, but I knew that, as far as she was concerned, I was little more than a millionaire's fashionable accessory. She peered at me through her wire-frame glasses. "You're looking cheerful this morning, Mr. Kramer." I wasn't sure what she meant by that but before I could ask, in walked the Colonel.

Though a man of modest stature, Jacob Ruppert cut an imposing figure. From his starched collars to his polished shoes, he was always impeccably dressed — I'd never seen him in anything less than a tailored three-piece suit no matter the season, though in summer he did swap out his bowler hat for a straw boater. He kept his broad cheeks clean-shaven and the mustache above his thin lips groomed to transparency. His blocky head was out of proportion to his narrow shoulders and tiny feet, but his stern face made you feel he was looking down on you even if he had to crane his stubby neck to meet your eye.

As the Colonel passed Miss Grunwald's desk, he gave her a tip of his hat and wished her good morning. Though he'd been born right here in New York, he spoke with a German accent, the result of his family keeping up the language at home. Turning to me with a curt nod, he said simply, "Kramer."

"Good morning, Colonel." Normally these brief greetings hardly broke his stride, but this morning he paused and scowled at me for a moment. Imagining he somehow knew I'd nearly been late, I regretted again my foolishness on the train.

Once he disappeared into his office, there was no need to instruct us in what came next. After exactly two minutes, Miss Grunwald gathered up the brewery's business and gave a single rap of her knuckles on the door, then waited with her hand on the knob for his muffled call of *komm herein*.

I busied myself with the correspondence piled on my desk, slicing open envelopes and assessing their contents, jotting down notes on a stenographer's pad, though I knew less than nothing about shorthand. Indeed, my only qualifications for the job were my uncle's recommendation and my degree in Germanic languages from Princeton. I had no business training whatsoever. I didn't even like beer.

When Miss Grunwald came out of the Colonel's office, she held the door ajar for me. "He's ready for you now, Mr. Kramer."

With some trepidation, I gathered up my notes and went into his office. Gilt-framed oil paintings hung from the oak-paneled walls and dust motes danced in the light streaming in through spotless windows. Behind a broad walnut desk, the Colonel, hatless, sat centered between the telephone and a Chinese vase fitted as a lamp. He gestured me closer. "Go ahead, Kramer."

I flipped a page on my notepad. "The members of the Brewers' Association are getting nervous, now that Massachusetts has ratified. They're asking for an emergency meeting to plan strategy in case the amendment becomes law."

"Prohibition will never pass as long as women don't have the vote. It's just those frontier states trying to tell the rest of the country how to live." I almost interrupted to remind him that Virginia and Delaware had ratified before Montana and Texas, but I held my tongue. "Anyway, intoxicating liquor isn't the same as beer. Beer is food. You can raise babies on it. Put them off until the annual assembly. What's next?"

"Miller Huggins sent a note asking to see you this morning."

"Am I free?"

"You don't have anything until that man from the orphanage at noon."

He tilted back in his chair. "What's that about, a donation?"

"No, real estate." I checked my notes. "Felix Stern. He wants to sell the property and thought it might interest you."

"What did they do, run out of orphans?"

I smiled at his joke. "I'm not sure, but the property's two entire blocks. It's in Harlem, between Broadway and Amsterdam. They already have the cross street closed. He says it's five acres."

"Five acres?" The Colonel got a distant look in his eye as I imagined him visualizing a map of Manhattan. "My engineers would prefer ten, but that seems impossible to come by in the city. What else?"

At twelve thirty he had lunch in the

private dining room with his brother, George, who ran the daily operations at the brewery, followed by their usual game of pool in the billiards room. In the afternoon he had meetings with his real estate lawyer and his public relations man. "After three o'clock your calendar is clear until your dinner at Delmonico's with Mr. Astor." I flipped a page on my pad. "Oh, and Ethel Barrymore's starring in a new comedy at the Empire Theatre, the reviews have been very good. I had tickets set aside for you at the box office in case you cared to attend on Saturday."

He nodded. I sensed his satisfaction at my efficiency, the way I'd come to know his routines and habits. "Anything else?"

"That's all, sir."

I turned to go, but he cleared his throat. "That bow tie, Kramer."

"Is something wrong, Colonel?"

"Rather festive for the office, don't you think?"

I put my hand to my neck. "Isn't it brown?"

"I forget, you're color-blind, aren't you? No, Kramer, it's not brown. It's red, bright red."

I felt the blood drain from my face. It really was of no consequence, but I tended to panic anytime my worlds collided, even in as innocent a way as this. "I must have picked it out by mistake."

"Of course you did. Come here." He rose from his desk and went over to a closet where he kept a change of clothes in case he needed to go directly from the office to an evening affair. He offered me a bow tie that was unmistakably black. "Take that one off."

"Certainly, sir." I undid the knot and pulled the offensive tie from around my collar. I reached for the black one, thinking I'd go put it on in the washroom, but instead he stepped close and looped it around my neck. He began to tie it for me, our faces inches apart. I could smell the peppermint on his breath.

"That's better." He tugged the knot into place and stepped back. "I can't have people mistaking my personal secretary for a window dresser, can I, Kramer?"

I had assumed he objected to the tie because it was too colorful for a place of business. I hadn't expected him to understand its other meaning as the calling card of a pansy. "Of course not, sir."

He stuffed the red silk into my pocket. "Let me know when Huggins arrives."

"Yes, sir."

I gathered up my notes while the Colonel went back to his desk and dialed the telephone. As I closed the door behind me, I heard him say, "Hello, Teresa?"

CHAPTER 3

Exhaustion caught up to me as I got home from the Olde Playhouse. When Clarence saw me staggering up the walk, he ran out to take my arm. Grateful, I allowed the weight of my elbow to sink into his steady hand. He steered me into the lobby, sweeping a newspaper off his stool and sitting me down. "What were you thinking, Helen? You know you shouldn't be out on your own."

"That's what you say, but see? I made it home all by myself. I am tired, though."

"You're lucky to be alive, girl." He turned my wrist over to measure the pulse of my blue veins, his brown fingers warm against my pale skin. I looked at his face, so different from mine yet more familiar to me than my own brother's. Rex had only been five years old when our mother moved us to Manhattan, so hard on the heels of our father's death I was in a daze all that summer before the start of sixth grade. It was

Clarence who'd introduced me to the city, teaching me how a single nickel dropped into a turnstile of the El could buy us an endless flying carpet ride above the streets of New York. I remembered standing in the vestibule between the train cars, our hands gripping the swaying chains, while he tutored me in the geography of the city.

"We almost lost you, Helen. That's not something to play around with." His breath, as he spoke, was scented with clove.

"You worry too much, Clarence. I'm a grown woman, not one of your little sisters. Anyway, now you know how I feel about you enlisting with that Negro regiment. You'll be risking your life, and for what? What have the Germans ever done to you?"

"You're not going to change the subject by bringing that up again. We're talking about you, Helen. Where did you go?"

I reclaimed my wrist and dropped my eyes. "To the Olde Playhouse."

"Not to see that director, I hope." Clarence had been up late studying in the lobby one night when Harrison dropped me off. What kind of man, he'd asked, would leave a woman at the curb in the middle of the night? Though I'd defended Harrison at the time, I was inclined now to agree with Clarence's assessment of his character.

"No, not to see him. But I did see him, and it was fine. I'm fine, Clarence, really I am."

"He better not come around here is all I'm saying. Let's get you up to your mother before she comes looking for you." Taking my arm, he led me to the elevator. He reached in to press the button for my floor, our faces so close I could see hints of green in the brown of his eyes, like moss on tree bark. I resisted an urge to rest my forehead against his rib cage.

My mother yanked open our door as soon as she heard the scrape of my key in the lock. "Thank God, Helen. I've been worried sick."

That morning, I'd felt brave sneaking out of the apartment. Now, I felt guilty for the wrinkles that marred her mouth. Growing up, she'd been the prettiest of all the mothers, her blond hair curling sweetly around her slender neck, her eyes like gemstones in her delicate face. She was still beautiful, though the years since my father's death had taken their toll. I remembered how, when I was a girl, people who saw us together often said I must have gotten my looks from my dad. I knew it wasn't meant as a compliment, but I took it as one. As far as I was concerned, my father was the best man in the world.

I tried to sound casual, but she could see how worn out I was. "I'm sorry, Mom. It was such a nice day, I just wanted to go for a walk." I dodged her questions about where'd I'd been by saying I needed to lie down. Before I went into my bedroom, though, I remembered to tell her the butcher had telephoned.

"The butcher?"

"I think that's who it was. He sounded German. Anyway, he asked for you."

"German? Oh, Helen, that must have been Jacob Ruppert."

"Ruppert?" I shuddered to say his name. "Why would he be calling?"

"He calls me every year. Don't you know what day it is?"

I looked across the living room at the calendar on the wall. My sense of time had been disrupted by the months of illness — my own birthday in March had come and gone unremarked — but seeing the numbered square on the month of May, I was ashamed of myself for not noticing sooner. "I can't believe I forgot."

She came over and brushed the hair back from my forehead. "I can hardly expect you to remember the anniversary of your father's death, not after everything you've been through."

I hugged her close. "I'm sorry just the same." Leaning back, I asked, "But why does Ruppert call? Does he still feel so guilty about Daddy?"

"I hope not. Your father's death was an accident. The coroner was clear about that. Even so, he does feel responsible."

And well he should, I thought, shutting my door. I flopped onto the bed, my shirt-waist twisting around my chest as my thoughts were pulled back to childhood. I supposed it was the texture of nostalgia that made those years seem so idyllic. I smiled to recall the Saturday mornings when I'd evade my mother in the kitchen, skipping across the backyard to my father's garage. I could still picture that big barn door rolled open, its contents displayed like a diorama: walls studded with hooks from which hung loops of wire and chain; shelves weighed down by tubs of grease and cans of oil; a wooden workbench fitted with clamps and strewn with saws and screwdrivers. I'd find my father with a tool belt buckled around his stained overalls, crouching next to a disassembled machine or standing at his workbench fixing a gear. I'd enter and he'd look up, squinting against the sunlight behind me, his kind face bracketed by thick sideburns. Instead of sending me away, he'd gesture with his chin to a hook on the wall. "Better put on a smock," he'd say.

When I was little it had been a novelty that made the neighbors smile, the way Jerry Winthrope's daughter could hand him any tool he asked for. As I got older, though, my mother cringed to see me handling tools with dirt under my nails. She'd expected my interest in the garage to disappear as I grew into a proper girl, but there I was, finishing fifth grade and still eager to fix an engine. No one seemed to care that I was better at mechanics than housework. Everyone said eventually I'd have to learn how to bake biscuits and stitch quilts and knit scarves and every other thing a girl needed to know — but not if I could help it.

That morning, I tied the smock over my dress and joined him at the workbench. Glancing at the gear in his hand, I selected a slender screwdriver with a flat head and a worn wooden handle. He grunted appreciatively as he fit it perfectly into the screw on the shaft. "So, Helen, what do you think of that?" He pointed to a dark corner of the garage. I approached what looked like a complicated bicycle with big white wheels. Between the chrome handlebars and the leather seat was a cylindrical tank emblazoned with the word INDIAN. Dad went over to the window and opened the shutters. Sunlight streamed in, making the gilt letters glow.

"Is it a motorized bicycle?"

"A motorcycle. Built for racing. They say it can go fifty miles an hour. The company loaned it to me so I can learn how to maintain it, but I'll earn a commission if I sell it."

"It's beautiful." I ran my hand across the bright handlebars. "Can't we keep it?"

"Not unless you have three hundred and sixty dollars saved up that I don't know about. But I am thinking of branching out into sales. That's where the real money is nowadays." He put an arm around my shoulders. I looked up at the hollow place at the base of his neck where tufts of hair peeked through his open collar. The tang of bleach cut through the musty smell from under his arm as I inhaled my father's familiar scent.

The sound of an approaching engine drove us apart. The most magnificent automobile I'd ever seen pulled up to the garage. Behind its ornamented brass grille, the body of the car dipped nearly to the ground while its fenders arched up like wings over the huge tires. My father whistled. "That's a brand-new American Underslung Roadster." The engine switched off and black smoke coughed from the tailpipe. "With an oil leak."

The driver slid across the tufted leather seat and stepped out of the car, removing his gloves and driving goggles. Black hair swooped back from a broad forehead above dark eyes set in a stern face. "That's right. My chauffeur can't make heads or tails of it. I said to myself, if Jerry Winthrope can't fix it, no one can." The strange way he talked reminded me of my friend Gretchen's grandpa. He extended his hand, a gold cuff link winking in the white fold of his shirtsleeve. "How have you been, Jerry?"

My father slid his palms down his overalls to wipe away the grease, then took the man's small hand in both of his own. "I've been good, Jake. It's good to see you. How long has it been?"

"It's been a dozen years since my father stopped racing his trotters. I suppose that was the last summer you came down to Linwood. Do you still race?"

"Not horses, no, not since I got into engines. I heard you sold off your stable."

"Belmont was too crooked for me. I don't mind losing a fair race, but I hate to be cheated."

"Admit it, Jake." My dad, laughing, finally let go of the man's hand. "You hate to lose, period, full stop."

"I forget how well you know me, Jerry." He turned to me. "And who do we have here?"

"This is my daughter. Helen, meet Colonel Jacob Ruppert."

I managed a shy hello in response to his rather formal bow. He glanced at my stained smock and dirty hands. "Is this what the new century is coming to, Jerry? We have girl mechanics now?"

I smiled, liking the idea. "I help my daddy whenever I can."

He frowned. "And what does your mother think of that?"

"She thinks girls should keep house, but I want to do other things."

The two men's eyes met and they shared a laugh. "You've got yourself a suffragette here, Jerry. I hope she's not for temperance, too. Say, what's that?" Dad and I trailed after Colonel Ruppert as he stepped toward the back of the garage. "Now there's a beautiful motorcycle."

"It's brand new. Indian started producing a factory model, but it's still fast enough to be a racer."

Remembering what my dad had said

about earning a commission, I spoke up. "It can go fifty miles an hour."

Colonel Ruppert whistled. "Fifty miles an hour is almost as fast as my Roadster."

"I bet it can go even faster than that," Dad said, picking up on my sales pitch. "Do you want to try it out, Jake? If you like it I can sell it to you."

A car horn sounded in the street. "That will be my chauffeur. I had him follow me up from the estate."

I sidled closer. "Are you neighbors with the Vanderbilts and the Astors?"

Colonel Ruppert gave me a searching look. "Linwood is not exactly in Hyde Park, but we do visit. So, Jerry, can you fix my Roadster?"

"It's probably a gasket or a bad seal. I expect I'll have it done for you tomorrow afternoon."

"I'll come back then. How fast did you say that motorcycle can go?"

"I've heard of it getting up to sixty."

"If that's true I might just want it. There's nothing like going fast, is there, Helen?" I shook my head, though I couldn't begin to imagine what the world would look like whipping by at such speed. "Until tomorrow, then, Jerry." Colonel Ruppert got into the back of a black Packard, complete with a hard roof and glass windows, and motored down the street.

Dad combed his fingers through my hair. "Jake seemed pretty taken with the motorcycle, didn't he, Helen? I'd make a fortune if those millionaires from the estates started buying from me. I might have to turn you into a girl mechanic after all."

I shuddered now to remember how proud I'd felt that day for having spoken up about the motorcycle. If only I'd kept my mouth shut, my father might still be alive. We might all still be living upstate in our little house. I might have even become a mechanic — but no, that was taking my 'what ifs' too far, I thought, turning over in bed and punching my pillow. Still, I blamed myself for bragging to Ruppert about the Indian's speed. When he came back the next day, he challenged my dad to a race. If the Indian could beat his Roadster he'd buy it on the spot, he said, displaying the cash to prove it. The very last time I saw my father, he was kick-starting the engine and fitting driving goggles over his eyes.

It had been years since I allowed myself to think about what happened next. I'd been in the living room, watching my little brother and darning socks, a hated task my mother insisted I accomplish. I'd finished one sock and was starting on another when a fist began to bang on the front door. Rex looked up from his building blocks spread across the braided rug. Still holding the darning egg, I opened the door. Colonel Ruppert was standing there, his canvas duster smeared with mud and blood. I squinted up at his dirty face, eyes outlined like a raccoon's from the driving goggles that hung, forgotten, around his neck. Fear rose up in me, freezing my lungs so that I could hardly breathe.

He scanned the room with shocked eyes. Seeing it was only us children, he put his hands on my shoulders and turned me away from him. With a nudge, he pushed me forward. "Go get your mother, Helen, then take your brother outside."

She was out back taking in the laundry from the line, a pouch of clothespins at her waist. Too frightened to speak, I beckoned her wordlessly. Not knowing what was the matter, she picked up the laundry basket before following me into the house. Colonel Ruppert still stood in the doorway, the afternoon sun rendering him a shadow.

"Teresa, I'm so sorry."

The choke in his voice told my mother all she needed to know. She dropped the basket, clean clothes unfolding themselves as they fell. I took Rex by the hand and dragged him outside. We huddled on the back porch, the sound of our mother's cries reaching us through an open window. Across the lawn, the doors of Daddy's garage stood open, as if expecting his return.

The coroner declared it an accident. The tree that stopped my dad at full speed was no one's fault, he said, but I knew that wasn't true. Ruppert could have purchased that motorcycle just by opening his wallet. He didn't have to force my father into risking his life. It disturbed me to discover he'd been telephoning my mother every year, his voice an unwelcome intrusion on the anniversary of my dad's death. I'd last seen the man at my father's funeral. It still pained me to remember how he'd walked beside the casket as a pallbearer. People said it showed respect, but all I could feel was the unfairness of my father's broken body prone in a box while Colonel Ruppert stood upright and unharmed.

He'd come to the house afterward, mingling awkwardly with our friends and neighbors from around the town. Most of my classmates had a parent who worked at one of the grand Rhinecliff estates as a carpenter or stonemason, gardener or laundress, maid or cook. The Vanderbilt mansion alone seemed to employ half the town, stories of its opulence passed among us like fairy tales. Having Ruppert in our living room was as unsettling as having a storybook character jump off the page. I glared at him as he took my mother aside to offer his condolences, knowing no apology could ever make up for what he'd taken from me. When my mother gestured in my direction and Ruppert turned to stare, I worried I might have muttered my thoughts aloud.

A few evenings later, Ruppert sent his private lawyer to help my mother prepare the insurance claim. She was grateful for the man's assistance, but I didn't like to see my father's life reduced to a series of signatures. I'd been nurturing the childish hope that we'd maintain his garage as a sort of shrine until I was old enough to become a mechanic myself, but my mother quashed that dream by putting it all up for sale. It made me sick to my stomach to see my father's tools haggled over by strangers. By the time my mother announced we'd be moving to Manhattan — more opportunities, she said, and fewer memories — I was numb to the news. Before I knew it, the house had been sold, our belongings were boxed, and I was saying good-bye to my friends of a lifetime. It all happened a decade ago, but I could still conjure the grief I felt as we pulled out of Rhinecliff station, everything I'd ever known receding with the mournful sound of the train's whistle.

CHAPTER 4

The Colonel was still holed up with Miller Huggins, the Yankees' new manager, when Miss Grunwald answered the telephone. "I'll let him know, thank you." She hung up and called across to me. "Mr. Kramer, you made an appointment for a Mr. Stern? He went to the baseball team's office on 42nd Street by mistake, but he's on his way over now."

We both looked at the clock and I knew she was thinking the same thing I was: by the time Felix Stern arrived, the Colonel would be at lunch with his brother. When Miller Huggins finally shuffled out of the office, as shabby and hunched over as ever, the Colonel called me in. He asked what happened with that orphanage fellow. When I told him, he scowled. "Everyone knows I take all my meetings here at the brewery."

"It was my fault, sir. I wasn't clear with Mr. Stern when I made the appointment.

He's on his way."

"Well, I won't have time now. George is waiting for me. And you'll need to reschedule my afternoon appointments, too. Huggins has convinced me to come to the ballpark to see a Boston player he wants me to buy."

"I'll have Mr. Stern come back next week, unless you'd rather wait until you can reach Mr. Huston?"

"I don't care a jot about reaching him." They put on a good show for the press, but I knew how much it annoyed the Colonel to share ownership of the Yankees with his gregarious partner. "As far as I'm concerned, Kramer, the best thing about this war is that it got Tillinghast Huston out of the country. The more time he spends playing soldier in France the better, as long as his money's still here in New York."

"So I'll reschedule Mr. Stern for next week, then?"

The Colonel drummed his fingers on the arm of his chair. "Five acres, you said? Listen, Kramer, why don't you meet with him."

"Me?" Though the Colonel often delegated, he'd never entrusted me with that kind of responsibility before.

"Why not? Take the man to lunch, hear

him out, let me know what he's proposing. You understand these things well enough by now to give me a report."

"I appreciate your confidence in me, sir." I touched the black bow tie around my neck, silently acknowledging his forbearance. "Should I take him to the brewery cafeteria?"

"No, I don't want every truck driver and brewmaster overhearing my business." He looked to me as if awaiting a suggestion.

"Don't we have a company account at that German restaurant on 91st Street?"

"Good thinking, Kramer. Take him there. Order the schnitzel. Jews love veal." The Colonel put his hand on my shoulder as we walked out of the office. "I'll be curious to know what this fellow has to say. Why don't you finish work a bit early and meet me at the ballpark to fill me in?"

"If you want me to, of course I will. I'm sure I can find my way to the Polo Grounds."

"You haven't been there?" I shook my head. He stopped and faced me. "Don't tell me you've never seen my boys play, Kramer."

"I haven't had the chance to take in a game." The truth was, it seemed to me like a waste of a Saturday to spend hours in crowded stands watching distant men run in circles.

"You'll come and sit with me in the owner's box. Here." He extracted one of his business cards from an inside pocket. "Just show them this at the gate."

"Thank you, Colonel."

"You don't have a boater, do you?"

"No, only a bowler."

He reached for the business card he'd just given me, took the pen from my hand, and jotted something on the back. "You'll need one come summer. Here's my haberdasher. Have him put one on my account."

I tucked the card into my shirt pocket next to the ballet tickets. "Thank you, sir, that's generous of you."

"You'll enjoy baseball, Kramer. I didn't expect to like it so much when I bought the team, but it's turned out to be more fun than owning a stable. The games last a lot longer than a horse race."

"Yes, sir." I returned to my desk without further comment, afraid of what he might do if I admitted to never having been to the track at Belmont.

When the receptionist called to say that Mr. Stern had arrived, I rode the elevator down to meet him. I found Felix Stern dabbing his brow with a handkerchief as he paced, hat in hand. There was a shadow of a beard on his narrow face and his suit hung on him loosely, as if he had raided his father's closet. He was younger than I expected, though, and better-looking. "Mr. Stern? I'm Albert Kramer, Colonel Ruppert's personal secretary."

He put away the handkerchief to shake my hand. His fingers were so long their tips brushed the inside of my wrist. "Hello, Mr. Kramer. Did you hear I went to the Yankees' office by mistake? Once they told me, I got here quick as I could."

"I apologize. I should have made that clear."

"So when can I see Colonel Ruppert?"

"I'm afraid he's at lunch now and unavailable for the rest of the day."

Felix Stern's face fell. He slapped his forehead with what looked like real force. "I'm so stupid."

I'd heard that Jews were an emotional race, but his sudden shift in mood alarmed me. "Please, don't say that. It confuses many of his business associates. He asked me to meet with you instead, if that's acceptable."

He looked at me, his eyes fringed with lashes so black I thought for a second he was using mascara. The idea made me realize I'd never met a Jewish pansy; my friend Paul always joked they were as rare as virgin brides. "Thanks, Mr. Kramer. I'd appreciate the opportunity to explain the situation to you. Our trustees meet on Sunday afternoons, and I was hoping to have something to report."

"Then it's settled. How about we discuss it over lunch?"

He agreed and I led the way down the block to the German restaurant. When war had been declared, the owners of the Kaiserhof had covered their portrait of Wilhelm with an American flag and renamed their restaurant the Edelweiss Café, but nothing else about the place had changed. Walking in, we were enveloped by the smoky smell of sausage and cigars. The lighting was dim and the booths had backs so tall each table seemed tucked into its own little room. I bought some cigarettes from the coat check girl. Opening the pack, I held one out to Felix, but he declined. "My mother says they're filthy. Sorry, I don't mind if you do, of course."

I put them in my pocket. "I'll smoke one later."

When the waiter came for our order, I asked for the schnitzel and salad with a glass of Riesling. I would have preferred a chopped steak but I was following the Colonel's suggestion, thinking Felix would copy my order.

"Just coffee for me," he said.

"You're not eating? But the veal here is excellent."

The waiter hesitated until Felix assured him coffee was all he wanted. "I couldn't deprive you of your lunch hour, Mr. Kramer, but I hardly eat on Fridays."

"Is that because of your religion?" Growing up, I hadn't learned much about Jews. They didn't live in my family's part of Pittsburgh, they weren't allowed at the boarding school my uncle sent me to, and if there were any at Princeton I'd never spotted one. But in New York City every third person you bumped into was Jewish, and I was catching on. I knew their Sabbath was Saturday but that it started on Friday. For all I knew, it began with lunch instead of supper.

Felix laughed. It was good to see his face relax. "In a way. My mother likes to stuff me to bursting at Shabbat dinner. I have to starve myself all day so I don't disappoint her."

The waiter returned with my wine and his coffee. "So, tell me about this property of yours."

"Okay." He leaned across the table, his intensity of purpose palpable. "Everyone in the city knows that since Colonel Ruppert acquired the Yankees he's been on the hunt for a ballpark of his own. He can't keep leasing from the Giants forever, can he? I've been up to the Polo Grounds. The property we have to offer is better situated and more accessible. We've owned it free and clear since the 1880s with no liens or entanglements. It's five acres with no cross street."

"I did mention that to the Colonel this morning. He said his engineers preferred ten."

"Good luck finding ten acres in the city. No, there's no better site for a ballpark in Manhattan than the Orphaned Hebrews Home."

My plate arrived, the breading on the veal still sizzling. "What about the neighborhood?"

"When the Home was built it was practically countryside, but now there's all kinds of people. Jews have moved up from the Lower East Side and Negroes are coming down from Sugar Hill, but the streets are pretty quiet. The Harlem nightclubs are all the way over on Seventh Avenue. For a sporting venue, it's an ideal location."

I remembered the Colonel joking they'd

run out of orphans. "You're closing the orphanage, then?"

"No, not at all. We've got over a thousand children under our care. We're looking to rebuild out in the countryside. We have an entire plan drawn up for cottage homes, gardens, and playgrounds. We've already purchased land in Westchester and we're about to start a fund-raising campaign. As soon as we build there and relocate the children, the Manhattan property could be the Colonel's. If we had a contract, or even an option, it would give us the certainty to move ahead with construction."

I took a bite of the schnitzel, the veal buttery on my tongue. "And how exactly are you connected with the orphanage?"

"My father's a trustee, but I took over his seat when he became too ill to attend meetings. Now I'm leading the campaign for relocation."

"So, you haven't even begun to build? What's your time line for this?" The Colonel didn't care to deal with complications, and I knew he liked to move fast. I'd just started working for him when he bought the office building on 42nd Street where Felix had mistakenly gone. Because the owners had managed it badly and fallen behind on their taxes, the Colonel was able to swoop in and take title for a fraction of its worth. He'd invested in the necessary improvements and installed new tenants, including the Yankees' front office. He had the building turning a profit within a year. This business with fund-raisers and options didn't sound like his style at all.

"The time line depends on how soon we get things started. Look, why don't you come see the orphanage for yourself, before you present my proposal to Colonel Ruppert? Then you'll be completely informed."

For a man with such a thin face, his lips were surprisingly full and supple. I held his gaze for a long moment, but the look he gave me in return was so guileless I couldn't tell if he understood my meaning. "Perhaps that would be a good idea," I said. "Colonel Ruppert's very busy right now."

"I imagine Prohibition isn't a pleasant prospect for a brewer."

"It's ridiculous, amending the Constitution over alcohol," I said, raising my glass. "It's one thing for my mother in Pennsylvania to advocate temperance, but I can't see how it would ever work in this city. Anyway, I doubt enough states will ratify the amendment. New York will never vote for it, that's for sure."

The waiter came by to warm up his coffee

and clear my plate. "How long have you been living in the city?" Felix asked, lifting the cup to his mouth.

"Just over a year, but I used to come up from Princeton while I was in college. I started working for the Colonel right after I graduated. You're born and bred I assume?"

"My people came over from Bavaria in the 1840s, same as Ruppert's family. We all considered ourselves Germans then, but over here we got sorted out by religion. His people are Catholic, aren't they?" I nodded. "How about you?"

"My mother's Episcopalian, but I don't practice anything myself."

"So, you'll come?" Felix seemed to be holding his breath. There was something attractive about his desperation.

"To see this orphanage of yours? I will."

He exhaled as a smile creased the corners of his eyes. "How about Saturday?"

"As in, tomorrow?"

"Like I said, the trustees meet on Sunday and I'd like to tell them I've made some kind of progress. In the afternoon, though. I go to synagogue with my parents in the morning."

I agreed, supposing it would be all right with the Colonel. I'd ask him about it at the ballpark and cancel if he disapproved. The

71

waiter saw we were finished and set down the check. Felix reached for it and I took the opportunity to place my hand on top of his. "Let me get it. I'll charge it to the Colonel. You're representing a charity, after all, and he's running a business."

Out on the sidewalk we shook hands and went our separate ways. Though I was fairly certain Felix Stern's interest in me was merely professional, I found myself stepping more lightly at the prospect of seeing him again. I busied myself rescheduling the Colonel's other appointments and responding to the afternoon mail. When the cuckoo on the wall chirped four o'clock, I bid Miss Grunwald a good weekend and headed out for the Polo Grounds.

CHAPTER 5

I didn't realize I'd fallen asleep until my mother woke me. "I made you some coffee," she said, setting the cup on the nightstand. I rolled onto my shoulder, eyes bleary. "Here, it'll revive you. I let you rest as long as I could, but you have to get ready now."

I took a tentative sip. It was hot. "Ready for what?"

"We're going to the Polo Grounds as soon as Rex gets home from school. Jake's sending over his limousine. He invited us to sit with him in the owner's box at the Yankees game this afternoon."

I spit my mouthful of coffee back into the cup. "This morning you were mad at me for walking around the block. Now you want to drag me out to a baseball game?"

She patted my arm. "I told you, we're going in the limousine, you'll only need to walk as far as your seat. I suppose the owner's box must be close to the field, don't you think? And it's such a nice day, you said so yourself."

"But, Mom, I don't understand. When did all this happen?"

"I called him back while you were resting."

"No, I mean, going to the baseball game. You said he calls you once a year on the day Daddy died. How did that turn into an afternoon at the ballpark?"

"Well, it was you." She hadn't looked this happy since we decorated the Christmas tree. "It made an impression on him, talking to you this morning. I may have said something about you being ready to get out more. The next thing I knew, it was all arranged."

I tried again to swallow some coffee, hoping it would drive the cobwebs from my brain. "I don't see why I have to come along. Colonel Ruppert's just about the last man on earth I'd want to see today. Besides, Rex is the one who's crazy about baseball." My brother had been devouring the sports pages ever since he learned to read; he was fifteen now and claimed to know more about the game than Damon Runyon. "You two go ahead if you want. I'm not up for it."

Her tone became serious. "Listen to me, Helen. This is a chance we can't afford to pass up."

"A chance at what, Mom?" I noticed now that she'd changed into a brocade skirt and matching jacket. Her waist was corseted, and she'd draped her prized possession, a stole of mink pelts, around her shoulders. "What are you so dressed up for?"

She stroked one of the minks. "It's the best thing I have." I rolled my eyes at her choice of evening clothes for a ballgame. "You don't know these people like I do, Helen. Everything they own is of the highest quality. Besides, I'm not thinking of myself. It's you and Rex who still have a future. Now, get yourself up and dressed. You're coming with us."

I had no idea what attending a ballgame had to do with my future, but I didn't have the strength for an argument. My skirt was a crumpled mess on the floor so I changed into a yellow linen dress I'd purchased back in the fall. The style suited my boyish figure, hanging in a flattering line from my shoulders to my calves. I shook my head at the irony of dressing up to meet the man who'd ruined our family. Ruppert probably thought he was being generous with this invitation, but what were a handful of

75

baseball tickets compared to my father's life?

The apartment door slammed. Rex's voice echoed down the hallway. "Mom, there's a limousine outside. Clarence said the driver's asking for us."

Down in the lobby, a uniformed man stood hat in hand. "Mrs. Winthrope? I'm Schultz, Colonel Ruppert's chauffeur. Please, come this way." He indicated a black Packard parked at the curb. Clarence gave me a quizzical look as I followed them out, but all I could do was shrug.

Rex was nearly as excited about the car as he was about the ballgame. He watched with fascination as the driver shifted through the gears. "Mr. Schultz, do you know who the Yankees are playing today?"

"Boston, I believe."

Rex's eyes looked like they were going to pop out of his head. "You mean we're gonna see Babe Ruth?" By the time we arrived at the ballpark, Rex had filled me in on every detail of Babe's biography, from the priest at the Catholic orphanage who taught him how to play, to his statistics as a pitcher and his batting average for the Red Sox. "I hope we get to see him hit a home run," Rex said as we climbed out of the limousine.

"Remember, young man, he's playing against Colonel Ruppert's team," Schultz said. "You wouldn't want the Yankees to lose, now would you? Here, Mrs. Winthrope, just show this card at the gate."

We walked around the Polo Grounds, its high walls plastered with advertisements, to reach the entrance. My mother enjoyed presenting Colonel Ruppert's business card to the ticket taker, I could tell. After asking a vendor on the concourse for directions, we emerged from a dark tunnel into the open embrace of the ballpark. The way the tiered stands curved around that wedge of green field made me feel as if I were inside a giant layer cake with a slice cut out. Though late in the afternoon, the sun was still high from the new daylight saving scheme, leaving the spectators shaded but flooding the field with light. The outfield gave way to views of the swing bridge over the Harlem River and the lumberyards of the Bronx beyond.

An usher led us to the owner's box, a section of empty seats surrounded by a simple railing. I wasn't impressed — I'd been picturing the box seats in a theater — and my mother was disappointed, too. "Are you sure this is Colonel Ruppert's box?"

The usher shrugged. "He doesn't own the ballpark, but it's the Colonel's box when the Yanks are playing."

"Where is he, then?"

"Perhaps he just meant this to be his present, Mom," I said, relieved at not having to see the man.

"Game's already started." Rex threw off his school jacket and leaned against the rail. "Look, Mom, we're right over first base." He shaded his eyes with his hand as he examined the scoreboard. It was the bottom of the inning and Boston was on the field. "There he is, Helen, past third base, look." I stood beside my brother — When had we become the same height? I wondered — and followed his pointed finger to a thick-chested player with a squashed-looking face and a mop of black hair.

"Is that Babe Ruth? He doesn't look all that special."

"Oh, why don't you just sit down, Helen, if you don't know what you're talking about?"

I laughed for the first time in what felt like forever and took a seat beside my mother, who was tugging off her gloves. "I'm sure he asked us to join *him* for the game, Helen. I didn't misunderstand." Hoping to distract her, I bought a bag of peanuts from a passing vendor, but she wasn't interested. "I thought he wanted to meet you."

The Yankees had just taken the field for the top of the next inning when I sensed the presence of someone lurking behind us. I turned to see a distinguished gentleman standing just outside the box, staring at me. I lifted my chin to meet his gaze and a smile broke across his stern face. He extended his arm, a gold cuff link catching the light. "You must be Helen."

I readied myself for a surge of resentment that never came. In person, Jacob Ruppert wasn't the sinister figure I'd remembered him to be. I offered my hand, which he covered with both of his own. Before I could say anything, my mother spoke up. "Jake, hello."

He gave her a slight bow. "Hello, Teresa."

She was about to stand up when he leaned over to kiss her cheek, resulting in an awkward collision. Flustered, she offered him the seat beside me, as if she were the hostess of a dinner party instead of his guest at the ballpark. When he asked me if I was enjoying the game, my mother cut in before I could answer. "We're enjoying it immensely, Jake, aren't we, Helen?"

"Yes, I guess we are."

"I'm glad to see you looking so well." His accent was less pronounced in person than on the telephone. He was smaller than I remembered, too, though of course I'd only been a child then.

"Thank you, Colonel Ruppert." I didn't know what else to say. We sat in silence for a long moment.

"May I have a peanut?" he finally asked.

"Of course." I held out the bag, into which he dipped his manicured fingers.

Apparently he wasn't sure what to make of me, either. Finally he came up with, "You were just a little girl when I saw you last."

I thought it was a tactless thing to say, as I was sure the last time we'd seen each other was at my father's funeral. But no — now I remembered another meeting, some months after we'd moved to the city, when he'd come to our apartment bearing gifts. "Was it at Christmas? You kissed my cheek. I remember because your mustache scratched."

"That's right." A smile wrinkled his eyes. "Do you recall what present I gave you?"

"No, I can't say that I do." Though my answer was curt, I was quickly losing my animosity toward the man. Indeed, I felt strangely comfortable beside him. Perhaps it was the way he smelled. He had the clean scent of a man who bathed daily and always wore a freshly laundered shirt. Bleach and starch and shoe polish, with a hint of peppermint. "Wait, I do remember. Was it a bag of candy canes?"

Ruppert slapped his knee with delight. "What a sharp girl you are, yes. There was something else, too, a porcelain doll from Germany, but I could see from your face when you unwrapped it that you were too old for dolls."

"Oh yes, I'm sure I still have it somewhere." Actually, the last time I'd come across the doll I was cleaning out my closet and couldn't remember how it had gotten there. I'd offered it to Clarence for his sisters but he'd refused, saying their mother wouldn't want them playing nanny to a white baby. Miffed, I'd tossed it into a donation bin at church. I supposed some little orphan was cradling it now.

"Look, Helen, he's coming up to bat." Rex turned around and seemed surprised to find Colonel Ruppert sitting there.

"You must be Rex. Do you like baseball?"

"Like it? I know everything about it." Rex squinted at him suspiciously. "You do know who Babe Ruth is, don't you?"

"I certainly do. He's the reason I'm here today myself."

We all turned our attention to the field. The pitcher lifted his knee, reached back with his arm, and hurled the ball. Ruth twitched but didn't swing. "Low and outside," Rex said. "Mogridge isn't gonna walk him, is he, Colonel?"

"Oh, I don't have anything to do with those decisions, Rex. Miller Huggins is the manager, I just write the checks." And cash them, I thought, looking at the thousands of spectators in the stands. Though I had no idea what Ruppert paid to lease the Polo Grounds from the Giants, I'd noticed the ticket prices when we came through the turnstile. Doing a quick calculation in my head, it seemed to me the Yankees must be turning him a tidy profit.

Babe fouled the next pitch. He spat and kicked at home plate then lifted the bat. A hush fell over the crowd as the pitcher wound up and threw a fastball. Rex explained afterward that he probably meant to crowd Babe off the plate, but the pitch went a little wide and Babe's bat caught it. His entire body followed the swing until I thought he might trip over his own feet. But he didn't trip. He was running to first base, thin calves churning away, when the roar of the fans told him the ball had traveled clear out of the park.

Rex jumped up and down as Babe jogged the bases. He turned around, eyes shining. "A home run, did you see that?"

My mother winced. "Rex, please, you keep forgetting whose guest we are."

"Don't apologize, Teresa. The boy has got every right to be excited. You think he's a great player, don't you, Rex?"

"The best. Can you imagine if he played for the Yankees?"

After watching the next inning, in which Babe didn't get another chance to bat, Ruppert stood up. "If you'll excuse me, I have to go talk with Huggins. I'm expecting my personal secretary to join me. Keep an eye out for him, won't you? His name's Kramer."

Once we were alone in the box, our mother tugged on Rex's sleeve. "You shouldn't cheer for the other team when you're sitting with the owner."

"Well, he should've bought a better team than the Yankees if he wanted to win."

"I don't think Colonel Ruppert minded, Mom," I said. "Here, have a peanut."

With a defeated sigh, she stuck her hand in the bag and drew out a fistful of nuts. By the time another inning had passed, her lap was littered with shells.

I hadn't realized what a lifelong companion I'd made of my anger toward Ruppert. Watching the game, I felt strangely bereft. I hardly noticed a pressure on my shoulder so slight that I lifted my hand without thinking to brush it away. It was a shock to feel fingers instead of some scrap of paper or a hapless ladybug.

"I'm sorry to startle you, but I'm here to meet Colonel Ruppert. Isn't this his box?"

A handsome young man stood uncertainly in the aisle, hat in hand, a black bow tie clashing with his fashionable tan suit. I blinked, as if my eyes were camera lenses with which I could capture the moment in stereoscope. The crowd behind him blurred as he came into sharp focus. His eyes were expressive and his mouth sensitive, his jawline refined and his cheeks smooth-shaven. It was uncanny how certain I felt that I was seeing the face of a long-lost friend. There you are, I thought. There you are.

I held out my hand. He took it gently. It crossed my mind that it would take two of him bundled together to equal Harrison's weight. "You must be Mr. Kramer. I'm Helen."

CHAPTER 6

Helen greeted me as if we were already old friends, shaking my hand warmly and putting me immediately at ease. She wasn't pretty, exactly, but her face was so open and her smile so genuine that I liked her right away. The woman beside her stood up, and Helen introduced her mother. There was a boy, too, who didn't bother to turn around.

"Have a seat, Mr. Kramer," Mrs. Winthrope said. "Jake asked us to look out for you."

"Jake?" I'd only ever heard his brother call him by his Christian name. "Oh, you mean the Colonel. He's not here, then?"

"He went down to the dugout, but he said he'd be back soon." Helen held out a paper bag of peanuts. I took a handful just to give myself something to do. Not having any idea who these people were, and not knowing when the Colonel would return, I settled into a seat and cracked one open. I looked around at the thousands of men in the stands who apparently had nothing better to do on a Friday afternoon. No wonder the legislators in Albany were so set against allowing games on Sunday, I thought. They'd empty out the churches.

"Look, Mom, he's coming up to bat again." The boy pointed to home plate.

"Who's that?" I asked.

"Don't you people know anything? That's Babe Ruth."

"You'll have to excuse Rex," Helen said, putting her hand on my arm. "When it comes to baseball, my brother is a fanatic."

The New York crowd, eager to see Babe Ruth hit, cheered as he tapped home plate with his bat. Readying himself for the pitch, he set his spindly legs wide apart and lifted his elbows high. He made a solid hit deep into the outfield and hustled to first base, advancing the player ahead of him to second before the ball found its way to the short-stop's mitt.

"It's a wonder such small feet can propel such a bulky man," I remarked.

Helen laughed. "I was just thinking the same thing."

"What inning is it, anyway?"

Rex gestured impatiently at the scoreboard. "Top of the sixth. Here, give me those."

Helen handed him the bag of peanuts, then turned to me. "You're not a fan?"

"I'm not really the sporting type, but the Colonel insisted." The next batter popped a fly that was handily caught, retiring the side. As the Yankees jogged to the dugout and the Red Sox took the field, I asked Rex if he wouldn't mind educating me about the game. Relishing his role as expert, he began commentating for my benefit. The time between pitches allowed for narration and I began to understand the lazy loveliness of the game, its languid pauses giving rise to sudden bursts of action. I appreciated that the boy, steeped in the sports pages, saw so much more than was apparent to me. "Thanks, Rex," I said. "It seems baseball's not as pointless as I thought."

"Pointless?" Rex glared at me, incredulous. "Where are you from, anyway?"

"He's from Pittsburgh." The voice came from just behind the box. We turned our heads as one to see the Colonel standing in the aisle. "And for what it's costing me, it better not be pointless, Kramer." I was embarrassed that he'd overheard my remark, but he seemed more amused than offended. He came into the box and addressed himself to Rex. "And how's your favorite player doing?"

"He got a base hit his last at bat, but he didn't score the run."

"That's good news for my team, isn't it?" The Yankees were heading into the dugout after the top of the seventh inning, but the Red Sox, who were up by two runs, seemed in no hurry to take their places on the field. The Colonel extracted a one-dollar note from his billfold and handed it to Rex. "Why don't you go get yourself a hot dog during the stretch? And you can keep the change." The boy's face lit up as he dashed off toward the concourse.

"Thank you again, Jake," Mrs. Winthrope said. "Rex is having such a good time. We all are, isn't that right, Helen?"

"Yes, I am," she said, seeming surprised.

The Colonel took the seat beside me. With a nod at the newspapermen assembled along the railing below us, he said softly, *"Wo bist du so lange geblieben?"*

He didn't usually speak German in public, especially with the war on, but the sporting press were notorious snoops. I responded in kind. *"I apologize for causing you to wait, the trains here were slow to arrive."* My German, learned in the classroom and from the pages of books, was always more formal than the

88

Colonel's.

"What do you think of Ruth?" It sounded like "root" in his accented English. Switching to German, he said, *"Huggins says he'll be worth whatever I have to pay to bring him to New York."*

"I didn't see much, but Rex greatly admires him."

"That's what troubles me, Kramer. Ruth's not an admirable man. From what I hear, he's hardly more than a greedy child. But by Gad he can hit. Frazee will hold me over a barrel before he'll let Ruth go, but Huggins promises me a pennant if I can get him."

Rex returned, mustard dripping from his hot dog as he leaned over the rail. The Colonel looked wistfully out at the field as the game recommenced. The teams held each other scoreless through the eighth. In the bottom of the ninth, Boston tagged the last runner at base, winning the game. The Colonel winced, the loss physically painful to him. I began to understand his keen interest in acquiring a talented, if troublesome, player.

The teams cleared the field and spectators started leaving the stands. A group of uniformed soldiers jumped down from the bleachers and jogged onto the diamond. Huggins emerged from the dugout to chase them away. They protested that they just wanted to hit a few balls before they shipped off to France.

Someone in the stands shouted, "Let them hit!" The cry was taken up by those fans still lingering in their seats. A few of the newspapermen turned around and set their cameras back up. One of them said, "Let 'em play, Colonel, it'll make a great picture."

Huggins looked up at the Colonel, who was as keen as anyone for good publicity. He nodded. "Just don't waste any new balls on them."

The soldiers on the field — there were half a dozen of them — took up loose positions around the bases. Huggins carried a bucket of old balls from the dugout and handed it off to one of the soldiers, who brought it to the mound. The soldier behind home plate picked up a discarded bat and gave it a practice swing. They weren't trying to get up a game (even I could see that), they just wanted a chance to make a run around the bases.

"Kramer, tell me, how did it go with that fellow from the orphanage?"

"I had lunch with him, as you suggested. There are some complications to his proposal, but I think you'll be interested in what he has to say." I knew better than to utter the word *ballpark* so near the press. "He's invited me to tour the orphanage tomorrow, if you approve, of course."

"What orphanage is that?" Helen interjected.

"The Orphaned Hebrews Home."

"Oh, we saw their marching band in a parade one time. Do you remember, Mom?"

"It was after President Wilson's last election, I believe," Mrs. Winthrope said.

"That's right. They were such darlings in their little uniforms. Why are you going there?"

I wasn't sure what to say. The Colonel stepped in. "They're after a donation. Kramer's going to see if they run a sound operation."

"Wünschen Sie dann dass ich gehe?" I whispered.

"Yes, I want you to go. Take a good look around and let me know if you think it's worth pursuing."

Out on the field, a strapping soldier stepped up to the plate. His shoulders seemed twice as wide as his waist, his limbs stretching the fabric of his uniform tight. He raised the bat, planted his foot, and waited.

"Watch out for King Arthur," the soldier on the mound yelled, winding up to pitch.

The rest of them stepped back off the infield. We all turned to watch him hit. The motion started in his hip and traveled to his knee, which swung out even before his arms moved. The ball met the bat with a clean crack and flew far into the outfield. One of the soldiers ran after it only to pick it up off the grass and trot it back in. The batter ceremonially rounded the bases in an easy lope.

Rex turned around, eyes shining. "Did you see that? He's almost as good as the Babe."

The Colonel took notice. "Let's see what he can really do, hey, Rex? Run down and tell Huggins to send out one of our pitchers."

The photographers got Rex's picture while Huggins disappeared into the clubhouse. Slim Love, already in street clothes, followed Huggins out, his gaunt face looking none too pleased. "Throw him a fastball," I heard Huggins say. While Love trotted out to the mound, Huggins called the soldier back to home plate. "Try it again, son. The Colonel wants to see what you've got."

The other soldiers let out a hoot. "Show 'em, King!"

"You ready, soldier?" Love yelled.

The plate was in deep shade by now, but King's fair hair seemed to generate its own light. He set his shoulders and walked his grip lower on the bat. "Ready."

The pitcher wound up and sent the ball fast and straight over the plate. The crack of the bat echoed back from inside the dugout. The ball sailed up into the bleachers. The soldiers on the field whooped and rushed the plate before King could even think of running the bases.

"Let's have him up," the Colonel said, waving at Huggins. Led by Rex, King came up to the owner's box. "Just wanted to wish you good luck, son." They shook, King's big hand engulfing the Colonel's dainty one, while a cameraman's bulb flashed.

"Thanks for letting us on the field, sir."

The Colonel took out one of his business cards and handed it to him. "You be safe over there. Give us a call when you get back. I'd like to see you try out for the team."

King beamed as if the war had just been won. "Thank you so much, Colonel Ruppert, I'll do that."

"Why do they call you King Arthur?" Rex asked.

"Well, Arthur's my last name. I guess my mother liked the idea of having a King in the family."

"I bet you'll kill a lot of Germans, King."

"Rex, don't talk like that. I hope you come home safely," Helen said to King. "You and all your friends."

"Thank you, miss." He turned the Colonel's business card over and held it out to her. "Won't you give me your address, so I can say I have a pretty girl back home to write to?"

I expected Helen to blush and giggle, but she didn't. "If you'd like, of course I will." I offered her my pen.

The Colonel leaned over to me and said in German, *"Why can't Huggins find me a fine boy like that for my team?"*

"He certainly is a handsome one." The words slipped out before I could stop myself.

"Write yours down, too." King winked at me. "I'll send you a postcard from France."

I jotted down the address of my rooming house on Washington Square even though a postcard of some Parisian chorus girl was the last thing I wanted. "Good luck over there."

"Thank you all again." He gave a salute then climbed back down to join his comrades on the field.

We filed out of the owner's box, around the ballpark, and down to the Speedway

94

where the cars were parked. The Colonel's driver was waiting beside the limousine, but when he opened the door it was Rex who got in, followed by Mrs. Winthrope. Helen held out her hand to me. "It was nice to meet you, Mr. Kramer."

"Albert, please. You too, Helen."

I expected the Colonel to join them, but he didn't. As the Packard pulled away, his new National Roadster was revealed parked beside it. I hadn't realized he'd driven himself. "What time is my dinner with Astor?" he asked. "Eight o'clock? I'll hardly have time for my bath."

It was only six. I wondered how intricate his preparations for a night out must be that two hours wouldn't suffice. The Colonel buttoned a canvas duster over his clothes, adjusted his driving goggles, and cranked the engine. I could feel the thrum of those twelve cylinders in my chest. "Until Monday, then, Kramer." He settled himself behind the wheel and put the car in gear, tires kicking up dirt as he zoomed away from the Polo Grounds.

I retraced my steps around the ballpark and joined the hundreds of fans jostling to climb that twisting stairway up Coogan's Bluff, my thighs burning as I reached the top. The train downtown was jammed and the journey seemed interminable. Perspiring and rumpled, I envied the Colonel who was, I imagined, at that very moment, stepping fresh from his bath.

CHAPTER 7

By the time we got home from the Polo Grounds, all I wanted was a long soak in a hot tub. I shut myself up in the bathroom while my mother made supper and Rex ran off to regale his friends with tales of Babe Ruth's home run. I lowered myself into the steaming water, the heat pinking my skin. Closing my eyes, I let my aching limbs float and my mind wander.

I hadn't realized the extent to which my illness had confined me to a world of women. Other than Rex, I hadn't had a complete conversation with anyone except my mother or the nurse in months. It was invigorating to see how the men I'd encountered that day moved through the world with such purpose: Harrison directing his play, Richard Martin managing the theater, Clarence preparing for his deployment, Colonel Ruppert overseeing his baseball team. Even his secretary had work to do and missions to accomplish. He was the opposite of Harrison in so many ways, I thought. Instead of wanting to be in charge of everything around him, he seemed content to observe. I liked how he'd been happy to let Rex lecture him about baseball rather than pretend he knew all about it. With Harrison, I always felt I was acting a part, whether or not I was on his stage. Next to Albert I was simply myself.

When the bathwater cooled, I pulled the rubber stopper to drain it down a bit, then added more hot. Sliding the bar of soap along my arms and legs, I lamented how the muscles beneath my skin had gone soft from disuse. I planned a regime of increasingly longer walks to build up the strength I'd need if I had any hopes of getting back on the stage. Recovering from my surgery, surviving the pneumonia — for the past few months, that had been my career. Despite my current exhaustion, I was eager for my life to be about something bigger than the four walls of my bedroom.

With slick hands I soaped my breasts, concentric circles of white and brown and pink. The nipples hardened at my touch, sparking the memory of how greedily Harrison had once gobbled them. He'd been glad to see me today, I could tell. Though I knew he'd never abandon his philosophy of free love and turn suddenly faithful, I couldn't help feeling drawn to his energy and flattered by his attention. But Richard Martin was right, I reminded myself as I put down the soap. I was better off without him.

Beneath the water, I pressed my hand against the puckered line of my appendectomy scar. It stretched from the tip of my index finger past my wrist. Though the ache of my missing organ had finally vanished, remembering its persistent pain made me realize I hadn't menstruated since being released from the hospital. I might have had my period while I was there — the memory of those weeks was so muddled by morphine I wouldn't have known. I'd been bleeding when my appendix burst, of course, a week of bleeding that was tapering off when the fever shot up and I collapsed. I supposed the pneumonia must have disrupted my cycle, anemia robbing my blood of iron. It would probably start back up soon. The doctor who'd taken care of my trouble had assured me I'd be good as new in no time. I sometimes wondered if the one event had precipitated the other, but my understanding of anatomy, rudimentary as it was, assured me there was no connection between my appendix and my womb.

When Colonel Ruppert telephoned that morning, he'd asked about my appendix. If he really did call only once a year, as my mother said, how had he found out about my illness? I wondered what I would have done if I'd known who I was talking to at the time. I recalled to my mind's eye the image of Colonel Ruppert as he stood in the doorway of our house, his duster smeared with my father's blood. I'd always considered him practically a murderer, but now I remembered the look of shock and sadness on his face. In all these years, I'd never spared a charitable thought for the man, but having sat beside him at the ballpark, having seen his smile and smelled his scent, it occurred to me that my father's death must have been terrible for him, as well.

Tired as I was, my mind wouldn't stop racing. I submerged my head and let my thoughts drain away. I stayed in that muffled world, only my nostrils above the surface, until my skin was as plump and puckered as something salvaged from the river. Curls of steam trailed after me as I emerged from the bathroom, my robe tied around my waist and a towel on my head. My mother called from the kitchen for me to come have something to eat. Taking a seat at the table, I was surprised to find my appetite strong for the ham salad sandwich and glass of milk she placed before me.

"I'm so glad to see you eat like this, Helen. Didn't I tell you an enema would do you good?" I didn't share her belief in the curative powers of enemas and had forgotten she'd even suggested it. I took a bite of my sandwich to avoid answering. "So listen to this, Helen. I telephoned Jake at home, to thank him for this afternoon, and guess what?" She paused dramatically. "He's invited you to go along with his secretary tomorrow to visit the orphanage."

I had to swallow before I could respond. "Why would he do that?"

"It was something you said, about how adorable the orphans were. He thought you'd be interested, so he offered to arrange it. He'll call in the morning to say what time."

I washed the ham salad down with a swig of milk. "But I can't tomorrow."

"Why not?"

I knew the can of worms I was about to open, but there seemed no way around it. "I promised Richard Martin I'd help him at the Olde Playhouse."

She looked puzzled. "When did you do that?"

"This morning. I went there on my walk."

"You went to the Playhouse?" My mother stood and tossed her napkin on the table. "I don't understand you, Helen. How could you ever want to see that man again?"

"Who, Richard?"

She placed a fist on her hip. "Joseph Harrison. Don't pretend you didn't go looking for him, though for the life of me I don't know why you would, after what he did to you."

I pulled her back into her chair. "Don't worry, Mom. I guess he did break my heart, but I've gotten over it."

"I'm not talking about your heart, Helen. The man nearly killed you. If only you'd come to me instead of taking matters into your own hands."

My gut understood her words before my brain could figure out their meaning. I broke into a cold sweat as nausea riled my stomach. "What do you mean, into my own hands?"

"You know what I mean, Helen." She lowered her voice to a whisper. "You shouldn't have let him bully you into an abortion. We could have made him marry you."

I wanted to tell her he didn't bully me, that I'd never even told him. Instead, I blurted out the more pressing question. "How did you know?"

"I had to hear it from the surgeon at the hospital. He held your X-ray up to the window so I could see it with my own eyes."

My mind conjured the image of a tiny baby floating across the milky radiograph as if on a cloud. But it couldn't have been. It was gone by then. "What did you see?"

She shivered. "The fishhook in your womb. You could have bled to death, Helen. How could you let someone do that to you?"

The memory of that dark hotel room came back to me in a rush. Instinctively, I wrapped my arms around my abdomen. "I don't know what he did. He used ether. It was all over by the time I woke up. The wardrobe mistress gave me his name. She said I could trust him, that he was a real doctor."

"A butcher is what he was. The surgeon wanted to report you both to the police. He said the evidence couldn't have been any clearer."

I tasted bile as I pictured the fishhook I'd unknowingly carried inside me all those days. "Is that what made my appendix burst?"

"What are you talking about?" My mother stared at me, her face shifting from anger to pity. "We discussed this, Helen, at the hospital. Don't tell me you don't remember?"

"I don't remember much of anything about the hospital. They had me on morphine the whole time. It was all dreams, I thought, just crazy dreams."

"Oh, Helen." She reached into my lap and took both of my hands. "You looked right at me and said you understood."

"Well, I didn't. I don't. Explain it to me now." Tears welled up in her eyes and began rolling down her cheeks, terrifying me. "What is it, Mom, just tell me. Am I in trouble with the police?"

"No, not that. The surgeon said he wouldn't call the police, that he'd change the surgical report, if I paid what he was asking."

New York City was famously corrupt, but this was a new low. "He blackmailed you?"

"He wanted a thousand dollars. It was all my savings, Helen, everything I had."

I felt sick. I'd made a decision I'd thought would affect only myself, yet I'd managed to bankrupt my mother in the process. "Mom, I'm so sorry. I'll find a way to pay you back, I promise."

"You're alive, Helen. That's all the compensation I need."

Her kindness only deepened my guilt, but I was still confused. "So you paid him, and then the doctor took out that fishhook when he removed my appendix, is that what you're telling me?"

"What I'm telling you, Helen, is there was nothing wrong with your appendix. It never burst. He didn't remove it."

It was like seeing Houdini wriggle free of a straitjacket — unbelievable, despite the evidence before your eyes. "Then how did I get my scar?"

"He said by the time he opened you up, the infection was so severe he had no choice but to take it out." She let go of my hands to blot her wet face with a napkin. "A hysterectomy, he called it. He said you would have died if he didn't. You nearly died because he did."

The wet hair on the back of my neck felt like ice. "I never had appendicitis?"

"No, Helen, it was the infection that ran up your fever. I explained this to you. I'm so sorry, I had no idea you didn't remember." She took a breath and leveled her gaze at me, making sure there would be no further misunderstanding. "I'm not exactly sure what the operation entailed, but the surgeon told me that you'll never be able to have a child."

I turned my head and vomited chunks of masticated bread and ham salad onto the kitchen floor. Just then the door to the apartment slammed open as Rex came running in asking what was for supper. I stumbled out of the kitchen and took refuge in my bedroom. Covered in sweat and shaking, I opened my window and gulped in the cool evening air. Another wave of nausea swept over me and I crawled into bed, burrowing under the blanket, knees pulled up to my chest. My mother knocked on the door, wanting to come in, but I didn't deserve her comfort. Through my sobs I told her to go away.

I'd carried Harrison's child less than three months. It had never even quickened. That those brief weeks should constitute my life's allotment of motherhood was too tragic for me to contemplate. The pit of regret that fed my tears seemed bottomless. Eventually, though, it emptied out, giving way to moans at the back of my raw throat. I hadn't cried this hard since my father died. How ashamed of me he would have been, I thought. I tried to find some solace in the fact that he'd never know what a stupid girl I'd turned out to be.

The appendicitis story sounded so ridiculous to me now that I wondered how I'd never questioned it before. But it was the story everyone in the neighborhood knew, repeating it back to me as I walked the block leaning on my nurse's arm. Had the nurse known the truth? Surely the scar wouldn't have fooled her — though maybe it had. I remembered her remarking on the surgeon's sloppy work as she rubbed me down with alcohol.

It was all too much for my mind to contend with. A crashing headache followed my crying fit. I crept from under my blanket to search the nightstand for an aspirin tablet. I would have sworn the glass of water I kept at my bedside was empty, but there it sat, cool and full. I fell back on my pillow, the bitter taste of aspirin on my tongue.

CHAPTER 8

It was nearly an hour after I left the Polo Grounds before I finally got off the train at Christopher Street. I decided to stop by the Life Cafeteria for dinner. Looking in through those big windows for anyone I knew, I spotted Paul sitting alone. It was unusual to see him by himself. Admirers were attracted to his beauty like bees to cherry blossoms, and though he wore his clothes loose, there was no camouflaging his magnificent dancer's body. We used to tease him that he could be the next model for the Arrow Shirt Man if Leyendecker ever got tired of Charles Beach. The wonderful thing about Paul, though, was that he didn't take his good looks seriously. They were an accident of birth, he said, for which he deserved no credit.

"Oh, thank God, a friendly face. I was absolutely dying of boredom." Paul kicked out the chair opposite him and I dropped into it. "You look wretched."

I took off my hat and yawned. "It's been a long day."

"And after last night, too. We were pretty lit up."

"I can hardly remember, it seems like a century ago. What're you doing here all on your own?"

"Killing some time before I have to make an appearance." His ballet company was hosting a reception for its wealthy benefactors, he explained, and the dancers were expected to attend. "Which I wouldn't mind if our director didn't insist we arrive coupled, like animals entering the Ark." He took a sip of his coffee, which looked as if it had gone cold. "I've been paired with Geneviève again. If I escape without a mauling it'll be a miracle."

I asked if he wanted anything but he said he was fine. What he was, I suspected, was broke. We'd shared rooms for a couple of months when I'd first moved to the city, but I was the one who'd ended up paying the rent. I hadn't minded, though. Supporting Paul felt like being a patron of the arts. I went to load my tray with two coffees, meat loaf and peas, potatoes with gravy, and pie. When I came back to the table, I handed one of the coffees to Paul. "Here, I brought you a hot cup."

"You're a prince, Albert. Ha!" It was his favorite joke. "I swear I don't know how you can eat like that."

"Here, have some."

"God, no." Paul lit a cigarette and drank his coffee. "We're opening Sunday night and I can't afford to put on an ounce. Did I tell you the leotards are flesh tone? We look positively naked under the stage lights. It's going to be scandalous."

"I can't wait." I ate while he shared some backstage gossip. When I said I was too full to finish the meat loaf or start on the pie, he gave in to his hunger and took what was left. I hated how he starved himself. The thought reminded me of Felix Stern. I pictured him at his mother's house for their Sabbath dinner, his stomach growling while she waved her hands over the candles like a vaudeville *yiddishe mama.*

"Are you listening to me?" Paul said.

"What? Yes, sure, the choreographer and the set designer in the wardrobe room, I heard you. Are you going to Antonio's to see Jack's show tonight?"

"Of course I am, and so are you, Albert. You know how nervous he is about headlining. We promised to lend moral support, remember?"

"I'll be there." Antonio's was a step up from Polly's, where Jack used to perform. "I hope he's not planning to sing that new Gladys Bentley song in public, he'll get himself arrested. What time?"

"He's on at ten."

"Good," I said. "I need to rest if we're going to be out all night again."

"And get dolled up while you're at it." Paul pointed to my neck. "Change that tie, at least, it's positively funereal."

I'd forgotten all about it. "It's not mine. Colonel Ruppert put it on me today. I wore a red one by accident."

"Naughty boy, you. And he made you change it?"

"He said he didn't want anyone mistaking his personal secretary for a window dresser."

"Really? What does he know about window dressers?" Paul leaned forward and clasped my hand. "Don't tell me he's one of us? Oh, it all makes sense now. He isn't married, is he? Doesn't he live with his mother? And aren't you always telling me how particular he is about his clothes?"

"Stop it, he's a man of the world is all." I drained my cooling cup of coffee. "I have to be more careful, though."

Out on Sheridan Square we parted ways, promising to meet up at Antonio's in a few

111

hours. Walking home, I wondered if what Paul said could be true. The Colonel was famous for saying he liked women — as long as they were married to some other man. I'd always figured it was his appetite for autonomy, rather than an aversion to the female sex, that led him to avoid the institution of marriage. I supposed it was possible he might be partial to pansies, but he'd never given me so much as a sidelong look, let alone a lingering glance. I reviewed in my mind that business with the bow tie, searching for a clue I might have missed.

As I turned the corner I noticed a uniformed figure camped out on the stoop of my building. With deployments to Europe in full swing, there were servicemen wandering all over the city. This one had probably stumbled on my stoop, too drunk to get up again. I hoped he wouldn't cause any trouble. I started climbing the steps. His fair hair caught the streetlight. It was the soldier from the ballpark. I stopped in my tracks. "King?"

"Don't look so surprised. After all, you gave me your address. Lend me a hand, will you? I've been on these steps so long my foot fell asleep." He extended his arm and I hauled him to his feet. "Say, can I use your bathroom?"

There was a public toilet at the entrance to the subway station in the square, but I figured I might as well do my part for the war effort by being hospitable. "Sure, come on up."

He followed me inside, past my landlady (whose cardinal rule of the house was that no women were allowed), and up the stairs. My room stretched across the front of the house, its three windows each eight feet tall. At one end stood the bed and a nightstand adjacent to a dresser. Against the other wall was a clothespress that held my entire wardrobe of four suits and half a dozen shirts. By the window was a desk that I had set up as a bar. In the middle of the room, two threadbare armchairs and a low table sat on an old rug. I closed the drapes, the heavy fabric covering only the lower half of the windows. Above, the casements glowed from the streetlight outside. King looked around, approvingly. "I like this."

"Bathroom's at the end of the hall."

"Mind if I wash up while I'm at it?"

I traded him the jacket of his uniform for a towel and a square of soap, hanging up his jacket and mine on the hat rack by the door. While he was gone, I took off the Colonel's tie, detached my collar, and poured two glasses of whiskey and water.

They were the same series of actions I might have taken after bringing home a stranger. I smiled to think how innocent it would all seem to King, who'd probably lost track of his buddies and was simply looking for a place to relax before shipping out in the morning.

He came back barefoot, carrying his boots. "Sorry, but my feet were killing me. We only got these issued a couple of days ago and there was no time to break them in." He turned his ankle to show me the angry blister on his heel. "That's not going to be any fun in the trenches."

I winced, handing him a glass. "Here. Should I run out for ice?"

"Don't bother. This is great, thanks."

I visited the bathroom myself and returned to find him by the desk.

"You have your own telephone?"

"The Colonel had it installed when I told him there wasn't one in the house yet." I went to the dresser and got out a thin pair of cotton socks. "Why don't you take these? Wear them under your wool ones. It might help."

"Thanks. Kramer, is it?"

"Albert. And you're Arthur?"

"Just call me King."

We sat opposite each other in the armchairs. Though his eyes held mine, they were devoid of the knowing gaze I searched for. He lifted his feet over the low table and asked if I minded if he put them up. I said no, of course not. A flap of skin waved from his heel. It was such a little injury, but it got me thinking of all he was about to risk. I didn't want him to look at me the way that man at the newsstand had, wondering what I'd done to dodge the draft.

"I have a heart murmur," I blurted out.

"Lucky you. Think I could borrow it?"

A current of seriousness ran under his joke that betrayed how scared he was, and rightly so. Only a fool wouldn't be afraid to go to war. To lighten the mood, I said, "What, the socks aren't enough, you want my heart now, too?"

He laughed. "Too bad you don't have a spare." He held up his glass. "Cheers."

We each drank a little too fast. When I asked if he'd ever been to New York before, he said he'd never been farther than Milwaukee until his division went down to Camp MacArthur in Texas for training. I lit a cigarette and gave it to him, then lit one for myself. He settled back in the chair, resting the glass on his thigh. "We wanted to make the most of our shore leave in the city, but I'll tell you, wandering all over Manhattan has worn me out. It must be nice to have a cozy place like this to come home to." He yawned and rolled his shoulders. "Makes me want to curl right up for the night."

Though I assumed he didn't mean it that way, I added a touch of flirting to my response to test the waters. "You'd never be comfortable in that chair until morning. We'd have to share the bed." A quiver of panic crossed his face as he glanced back at me. Afraid I'd gone too far, I added, "Too bad I have to go out later, though. My friends are expecting me." I couldn't very well invite him to Antonio's, and I felt I'd done my patriotic duty getting him off the streets for a while. If all he was looking for was a place to flop for the night, he could go get a room at the YMCA.

He drained his glass. "How about one more for the road?"

"Sure, one more."

"Listen," he said, after I'd handed him a fresh drink. "Can I tell you something?"

If he weren't so handsome I might have become impatient, but there were worse things than looking at King while he spun some tale. "Go ahead, I've got some time yet."

"Okay. So, the night before they put us all

on the train for New York, this doctor came in to the mess hall to give us a lecture on the evils of prostitution, right? He had these pictures on a strip of film, not a motion picture, just stills, but they were horrible, huge on the wall like that. Syphilitics without noses, shriveled dicks covered in scabs and sores. Those pictures had us cringing, I can tell you. He told us, whatever you do, be careful of the women in New York."

I wondered now if that's what he was after — a recommendation for where he could find a clean girl. Remembering his wink as he held out the Colonel's business card for my address, I supposed to a farm boy like King any New Yorker seemed a man of the world. In fact, I could point him in the right direction. Everyone in the Village knew where the Raines Law hotels were, though I couldn't guarantee the women he'd find there would be clean.

King helped himself to another cigarette. He took a deep drag then leaned forward to tap it into the glass ashtray on the table. "Now, most of the guys I was training with had never so much as kissed a girl, and they'd been talking big about how they wanted to be real men before they went to war, you know? So on the train, our sergeant, who'd been to New York plenty of times, started telling us about pansies. He said they were men who were like women on the inside, and you could do whatever you wanted to them, the same as you'd do with a woman, even some things women wouldn't do, and it was safe, because they weren't women, you know? And this one friend of mine — he grew up on the next farm over to my grandparents' place — he just couldn't understand how a man could use another man for sex, so the sergeant started explaining it, you know, in detail. He said most pansies didn't even want to be paid for it. They just did it because they liked it."

Now I understood what King expected as he lounged on my stoop. But what had tipped him off? I wasn't dolled up when he met me. The red bow tie was hidden in my pocket. I cringed to think it showed on my face. It was one thing to catch the eye of a man on the street and decide, over drinks or a show, what we wanted from each other. Handsome as King was, I resented his assumption that a wink was all it took to get me into bed. As he sat there in his uniform, broad chest rising with quick inhalations, thick leg bouncing up and down, I recalled stories of pansies who'd been savaged by the rough men they'd brought home. To be safe, I put on a scowl and lowered my voice. "Why are you telling me this?"

He blushed and stared at his hands. I noticed they were shaking. "Because you said I was handsome."

When did I say that? Oh yes, to the Colonel at the ballpark. How had he understood? *"Sprichst du Deutsch?"*

He shrugged. *"Jeder in Milwaukee spricht Deutsch."*

I hadn't known everyone in Milwaukee spoke German. "And that made you think I was a pansy, because I said you were handsome?"

"No, you don't understand." He looked at me, the blue of his eyes leaping out from the black and white palette of my vision. "It's because I realized, when the sergeant was talking, that's what I am."

I laughed as the whole uncomfortable situation finally made sense. He wasn't looking for a place to flop, or even someone to fuck. He just wanted someone to put a name to his desires. I remembered what it had meant to me, when I started coming up to New York from Princeton, to find myself among my own kind. It was funny, though, how confused he was about how it all worked. "You're no pansy, King, take it from me." I didn't mean to dismiss his confession, but one look at him was enough to see he was a normal man.

"No, really. Listen." He crossed his legs nervously. "I always knew there was something different about me, but no one could ever tell me what it was. I thought maybe I could talk to you."

I looked more closely at his trembling lip, his shapely brows, his hand resting limply on his crossed knee. I thought of Jack, how in his street clothes he looked like a quarryman. It was only after he got dolled up for his show and started flapping his hands and singing in falsetto that anyone could see he was a pansy through and through. I supposed it could be the same for King. I reached over and placed my hand on his leg. "It's okay, I'm the same way, you can talk to me."

He sighed with relief. "I was hoping so, but I couldn't tell. You just seemed so nice."

"How old are you, anyway?"

"Twenty-one. Why, how old are you?"

"Twenty-three." So close in age, yet such a gulf in experience. I'd never been the older, wiser one. I got up, taking his glass. "Let's have another drink."

We talked about ourselves for a while then. He told me about spending summers on his grandparents' farm, helping his *opa* plow the fields and his *oma* milk the cows. He told a story about having to tie up his dog so it wouldn't follow him down the road when he left for training camp, how he could hear it howling from a mile away. We talked about the war, too, I suppose, though I'm not sure either of us was paying much attention to the words. His limbs relaxed as his nerves melted away. I decided there were worse things than relinquishing my bed to a soldier for the night. It wouldn't be the first time I'd slept in one of those chairs.

"Up for another one?" I asked. "I've been mixing them weak."

"Sure." I took his empty glass and went over to the desk. King came up behind me, his chin bumping my shoulder. "I'm so glad we met. For so long, I thought I was the only one."

"You're not, believe me." I turned around. "I'm meeting my friends at Antonio's, why don't you come out with me? You'll see how many of us there are."

"Can't we just stay here?" He placed his hands on my chest.

I think I stopped breathing. "What are you doing?"

"I want to know what it's like, before I ship out. I thought you could show me."

"I don't think that's such a good idea." Everyone knew two pansies couldn't be lovers. Paul and I had tried it once when we were both soused, but it had fizzled, each of us waiting for the other to make the decisive move. I couldn't imagine even attempting it with Jack.

"At least let me kiss you." King circled his hands around me, his thumbs pressing into my ribs as his fingertips met behind my back. He could have broken me with that grip. That's when it hit me: King was no pansy. It was only his age, his inexperience, that made him think he was like me. As soon as he understood what it was all about, he'd realize he was as normal as any man who preferred a pansy to a girl.

"One kiss." I didn't know why I was being so coy.

He smashed his mouth into my teeth and poked me with his tongue until I turned away. "I'm sorry. I've never done that before."

"I can tell. Here, let me show you." I put my hands on his face and brought our mouths together. This kiss went on until his knees sagged and a groan rose in his throat. I knew then we wouldn't be going out that night.

I pushed him back so I could unbutton

my shirt. He took his off, too, and the pants of his uniform, while I stepped out of my trousers and pulled off my socks and garters. I unbuttoned his wool union suit from neck to groin until it fell to his ankles. Naked, he looked like a picture out of *Physical Culture* magazine. I took his hand and led him across the room to the bed. As we lowered ourselves to the mattress, he said, "I don't know what to do."

"That's okay, I do."

I started at his earlobe and slowly, slowly moved down his body. Every touch of teeth and tongue was a revelation to him. By the time I arrived at his swollen sex, I knew he wouldn't last long. I took him in my mouth all at once. He climaxed quickly and I sucked him dry until he was soft. I figured he'd soon be ready for more so I lingered there, but King had other ideas. He reached under my armpits and pulled me up alongside him.

"Now it's my turn," he whispered, tugging at my cotton shorts. I reached for the tin of Vaseline I kept tucked under the mattress, but to my surprise he didn't turn me over. Instead, he began to repeat my performance, doing everything to me I'd just done to him. I knew it was his inexperience that made him believe he owed me this. I should have stopped him, but I'd never been reciprocated before. I allowed myself to imagine that he was bringing me out, that this was my first sex experience. By the time I climaxed, I almost believed it.

I opened my eyes to see King's concerned face hovering over me. "Did I hurt you?" he asked.

"No, why do you say that?" He wiped tears from my cheeks. I hadn't realized I was crying. "It's nothing, I'm fine."

"Good." He kissed me, then his stomach growled and we both laughed. "Did I forget to tell you I was starving?"

"I'll go see what we can do about that." I pulled on some clothes and snuck down to the landlady's kitchen to swipe a loaf of bread and a heel of cheese. We made a picnic with a couple of wrinkled apples I had in my room. Afterward we lounged in bed, drinking and smoking, the glass ashtray balanced on his abdomen. He yawned.

"What time do you have to be back?"

"We start boarding at six. If I'm not on the pier by five I'll do the crossing in the brig."

"Do you want to get some sleep?"

"I've got the whole Atlantic to sleep." He set the ashtray on the floor and put his arms around me. "You made this so nice for me.

No matter what happens in France, I'll be able to picture us in this room." He stroked my neck with the back of his hand. "How about you, what was your first time like?"

I shook my head. "I don't want to ruin your night."

"Why, what happened?"

For ten years I'd never spoken of it, but I'd dropped my defenses with King, and before I could shore them up the words came spilling out. It was because of my heart that I wasn't allowed to participate in sports at boarding school. Still, I had to be out with all the other boys, so while they scrimmaged or tackled I walked the track, circle after circle. Sometimes they ran by me, a posse of footfalls approaching from behind, their heavy breathing getting louder and louder then fading as they passed, trailed by the smell of their sweat. That day, one of the boys kept running after the others had gone inside. He came up alongside me just as we drew even with the old equipment shed. I hardly knew what lifted me off my feet as he swept his arm around my waist and carried me into the shed. I was thirteen but small, my growth set back by the year I'd spent recovering from rheumatic fever. He said he'd been watching the way I swished around the track. He said I was a pansy. He grabbed me by the hair and pushed me to my knees. He said this was what pansies did, and if I ever told anyone, every boy at school would be lined up for it. I struggled to understand his words as I choked and gagged, tears and snot smeared across my face. If I kept quiet, he said, it would only ever be him. He was a senior, but it was only March. He didn't graduate until June.

The whole time I was talking, King kept his arms circled around me. I didn't know what he must have made of my story. Perhaps he was thinking it was a good thing no one in Milwaukee had figured out what was different about him.

"If I'd been there, I'd have killed him for you." For the first time since we met, King sounded like a soldier.

"Don't be silly. You would have only been eleven years old."

"I shot my first deer when I was eleven."

A fist clenched in my chest. *"Mein Ritter in glänzender Rüstung."*

"If I'm your knight in shining armor, what does that make you?"

"Ihre Jungfrau in Nöten?"

"If you were a damsel," he said, reaching for me, "I'm the one who'd be distressed."

Eventually we slept — at least, I did. I

never heard King leave. The next thing I knew I was shocked awake by a shrill persistent ringing. I thought the house was on fire. I stumbled naked across my room to the telephone, barely taking in my empty bed, his missing boots.

"Kramer, listen." The Colonel's voice was like a nail hammered into my brain. "I'm sending Schultz to drive you to that orphanage this afternoon. And I want you to take Helen Winthrope with you."

CHAPTER 9

All night long, terrible thoughts crashed through my mind, tossing me in my sheets like a boat caught in a storm. I imagined myself etherized on a hotel bed, that so-called doctor kneeling between my spread legs, a fishhook in his dirty hand. I pictured myself on the operating table, the surgeon deciding for himself what my future would be. Who knows if it was even true, what he told my mother? Perhaps the infection wasn't fatal. Perhaps he'd simply decided, as he wielded a knife over my unconscious body, that a girl like me didn't deserve to breed. It was nearly dawn before my exhausted mind calmed enough for sleep to drop anchor.

My mother appeared around noon with breakfast. I felt like an invalid all over again as I sat up in bed and accepted the tray she placed on my lap. The smell of coffee started my thoughts right back to churning.

Harrison had wanted me to have a complete experience of life, but what woman's life was complete without the experience of a child? Even the most successful Bachelor Girls eventually gave up their jobs for the chance at motherhood. I'd thought I'd have plenty of time to make my mark as an actress before exchanging my freedom for the bonds of matrimony. Yet here I was, not even a wife and already barren.

My mother opened the curtain. Sunlight flooded the room. I sipped some coffee, the bitter liquid warming my mouth and prompting a growl from my empty stomach. "Go ahead and eat, Helen. I made the farina the way you like it, with cinnamon and raisins."

I swallowed a few spoonfuls, the familiar taste a comfort. She sat beside me on the bed. "You can't punish yourself, Helen. What's done is done."

"Please, let's not talk about it."

She placed a gentle hand on my cheek. "We won't ever talk about it again, if that's what you want." She kept me company in silence until I'd finished the farina and drained the coffee. "Feeling better?"

Compared to what, I thought? "I suppose so."

"Good, because I just spoke with Jake.

Mr. Kramer is coming in the limousine to pick you up on his way to the orphanage."

"No, Mom. You can't expect me to do that. Not now, not today."

"I'm afraid so, Helen. It's more important than ever. You know I have no savings left, and if it weren't for Jake, the hospital bill would have bankrupted us."

"Why, what did he have to do with it?"

"He paid it. Thank God the report said appendicitis. His people are Catholic, you know. It was his suggestion to hire the nurse when you developed pneumonia. He paid for that, too."

I was astonished. In the course of a single day, I'd gone from blaming Colonel Ruppert for my father's death to finding out I owed him my very life. I supposed a hospital bill and a nurse's salary were a drop in the bucket for a millionaire, but still he must have thought me ungrateful, as I sat beside him at the ballpark, not to have given him my thanks. "I guess he feels awfully guilty about Daddy to spend so much on me."

"I told you, Jake takes his responsibilities seriously. And now he's gone to the trouble of arranging this visit to the orphanage for you. I'm sorry, Helen, but we're in no position to look a gift horse in the mouth."

I threw back the blanket with a groan.

Compliance, it seemed, was the only currency with which to repay Colonel Ruppert. "Okay, I'll get ready."

"And do something about your hair. You know what happens when you sleep on it wet."

I washed my face and brushed my hair, but as a form of protest I put on the same yellow linen I'd worn to the ballpark without making the effort to iron it out. When she saw what I was wearing, my mother told me to take it off. Then the bell rang and she couldn't decide which would be worse — me appearing in a wrinkled dress, or keeping Mr. Kramer waiting. In her moment of indecision, I grabbed my jacket and hat. Riding down in the elevator, I wondered how many more invitations from Colonel Ruppert I would be forced to accept before the scales between us were balanced.

Seeing Albert Kramer in the lobby lifted a bit of the weight from my heart. It wasn't just that he looked so handsome, hair combed back from his elegant forehead and hat dangling from his slender hand. It was something else that cut through my sadness. A feeling, when I saw him, of being a little less alone in the world.

Albert was deep in conversation with Clarence, who seemed to be giving a speech on Negro rights. He was becoming more and more political the closer he got to shipping out — which could happen any day now. His commander had deferred his deployment until he completed his degree so that he'd be eligible for promotion if the War Department could ever be persuaded to commission black officers. Though Clarence complained about being left stateside while the 369th were seeing action at the Bois-d'Hauze, his mother, I knew, was grateful for the reprieve. For years Mrs. Weldon had taken in the tenants' laundry, every cent she earned from washing our clothes dedicated to Clarence's education so she could sit, proud in a new hat, to see her son receive a college diploma. He'd make a good teacher when he got back from the war, I thought, watching him lecture Albert.

"You see, Mr. Kramer, it isn't that I have anything against the Germans, but I agree with Dr. Du Bois that participating in the fight to defend democracy abroad will strengthen our case for justice here at home."

Albert nodded thoughtfully. "I saw that Silent Protest Parade last summer. It made a deep impression on me."

He was about to continue his harangue when I spoke up. "Hello, Albert. I see you've met my friend Clarence Weldon. I hope he hasn't talked your ear off."

"No, not at all. We've been having a most enlightening discussion." He extended his hand. "Good luck to you in France."

"Thanks. Here, why don't you take this." Clarence grabbed the latest issue of *The Crisis* off his stool. "It'll broaden your perspective. If you only read the *New York Times* you'd hardly know about the massacre in East St. Louis, let alone the Fort Sam Houston hangings."

Albert thumbed through the pages of the magazine Clarence had thrust into his hands. "Thank you, Mr. Weldon, I'm sure it will. Are you ready, Helen? Schultz is waiting."

Clarence held open the door, his manner softening as we came abreast. "It isn't too much for you, Helen, going out two days in a row?"

It is, I wanted to say. Remembering the pressure of his fingers on my wrist as he measured my pulse, I wondered if he'd be so sympathetic if he knew it was my own stupidity that had nearly cost me my life. "I'm fine, Clarence. Please don't worry."

As Albert escorted me to the limousine, he asked if I'd been ill. Unwilling to elaborate, I simply said yes. Once we were settled in the back of the Packard, Albert fanned himself with his hat. I noticed the pallor of his skin and the dark circles beneath his eyes. "Aren't you well yourself this morning, Albert?"

"Just a headache. Not enough sleep and too much whiskey." He gave me a weak smile. "I don't usually work on Saturdays."

"As far as I'm concerned, we could do this another time, or not at all. It wasn't my idea to tag along, you know. Colonel Ruppert arranged it, and my mother convinced me I couldn't say no."

Albert snugged his hat back on his head. "The Colonel is a hard man to refuse." We sat in awkward silence as Schultz drove up Amsterdam Avenue, Albert nursing his headache, me distracted by my thoughts. Finally, he said, "I hope you'll enjoy visiting the orphanage at least."

I didn't expect to enjoy much of anything that day. There was a question, though, that had been niggling at my brain. "Why is the Orphaned Hebrews Home coming to Colonel Ruppert for a donation? I thought Jews took care of themselves."

He blinked slowly, as if roused from some reverie. "I guess because they're German, too." The Packard made a sharp turn. I slid across the leather of the limousine's rear seat, my hip bone pressing into Albert's thigh.

"Sorry, Mr. Kramer," Schultz said, bringing the Packard to an abrupt stop. "There's your orphanage."

Stepping onto the sidewalk, we craned our necks to look up at the turrets and spires of the building, its decorative ironwork bristling from the roof. The clock tower soared above our heads, and the wide windows across the front of the building were too numerous to count. "I can hardly believe that's a home for children," I said.

"Over a thousand of them. That's what Mr. Stern told me."

"It must be like living in a castle."

"Orphans only live in castles in fairy tales." I was surprised at Albert's harsh tone. "I'm sorry, Helen, but my father died when I was very young and my mother and I have been the poor relations ever since."

His eyes met mine, and I felt a spark of sympathy arc between us. "I lost my father, too, Albert. I know it's no fairy tale." When he said he was sorry to hear it, I had to look away to stop myself from crying. "Come on, let's get this over with."

Linking arms in solidarity, we mounted the steps and entered a spacious foyer in which a broad marble staircase doubled back on itself for three stories or more. Peering up, I couldn't tell how far it climbed. I withdrew my arm from Albert's, worried we might look to the children like prospective parents. It would be cruel, I thought, to get their hopes up.

A man came toward us, hand outstretched. His dark eyes and elegant nose were attractive enough, but there was something haphazard about his appearance, what with his ill-fitting suit and crooked tie. I noticed, as the sleeve of his jacket pulled up, a gold watch from a fine maker with a badly scratched face and battered band. The dramaturge in me wondered what it signified about his character: a reckless nature, or simply a careless one?

"Thank you for coming, Mr. Kramer." He turned to me and took my hand rather stiffly. "Mrs. Kramer, welcome."

"Oh no, I'm not his —"

"— she isn't my," Albert interrupted, then continued. "I'm sorry, I've made a mess of the introductions. Miss Helen Winthrope, this is Mr. Felix Stern, a trustee of the orphanage."

"Pleasure to meet you, Miss Winthrope," he said, his hand relaxing.

"Miss Winthrope is acquainted with Colonel Ruppert. She was curious to visit the orphanage."

Making the best of the situation, I said, "I hear it's the finest in the city."

"In the nation," he replied. "At least, it was. When it was built, there wasn't an institution in the country to match it."

"Helen, do you mind if I have a word with Mr. Stern for a moment? Just a bit of business before we begin our tour."

They stepped away and spoke quietly together, Albert explaining my presence, I assumed, though I doubted he understood it any better than I did. Just then a bell rang, loud as a fire alarm. I jumped out of my skin.

"You'll get used to it," Mr. Stern said as he and Albert returned. "I hardly hear it anymore." The sound was still ringing in my ears when hundreds of children began streaming down the staircase. They didn't exactly walk in step, but it was eerie the way they moved without speaking or shoving, no bursts of laughter or calling out of names. The three of us held our places in the center of the foyer as the children flowed around us and down the corridor.

"Let me show you around." Mr. Stern gestured up the stairs. "We can start with the infirmary on the third floor and work our way down."

"I'm mostly interested in seeing the grounds," Albert said. I thought it strange, since Colonel Ruppert was considering donating to the orphanage, that his secretary wouldn't want to get a full tour, but I supposed Albert's headache made him want to cut it short.

Mr. Stern seemed disappointed. "At least let me show you the synagogue before we go outside." He took us to an auditorium that was easily as large as the Olde Playhouse. They used the space not just for religious services, he said, but also to put on pageants and plays. I wondered who directed these theatricals. The thought brought me back to my conversation with Harrison. If I had known, as I sat beside him yesterday, the true consequences of our affair, I never could have withstood his gaze so coolly. Maybe I should have gone to him when I realized I was in trouble, but my mother was delusional to think he would have married me. Neither would he have wanted to imperil the success of his play by pulling me off the stage for the duration of a pregnancy. The decision, I'm sure, would have been the same, the accidental product of our coupling expelled from my womb. Harrison, though, with all his experience, might have placed me in a steadier pair of hands.

"Are you coming, Helen?" Mr. Stern was leading us out of the synagogue and down a wide corridor. Along the way, we passed a library and a music room and a club room, where a group of teenagers around Rex's age was laying out a magazine. From there we descended to the basement level, windows high in the walls letting in a slanted light. The floors in the dining hall were being washed, so Mr. Stern took us instead through an industrial kitchen. On a table next to an enormous oven, enough loaves of rye bread were stacked to feed an army.

"Exactly how many children are living here?" I asked.

"Last week's count was one thousand two hundred and seven, if I remember correctly."

"Don't any of them get adopted?" Asking the question brought home to me that adoption was now the only way I'd ever be a mother.

"Most of them aren't available for adoption, though there are a few." Mr. Stern paused to scrutinize me. "Even if you were Jewish, though, Miss Winthrope, unmarried women aren't allowed to adopt."

Finally, we emerged from the building

onto a barren expanse of gravel the size of a city block. On it, hundreds of children were running, skipping, hopping, tossing and catching, jumping and shouting. Compared to their strange silence indoors, the cacophony was overwhelming. Albert excused himself to go walk around the property. Mr. Stern and I watched him negotiate his way through the mob of children and out a gate in the stone wall. I would have apologized for Albert's rudeness by explaining about his headache, but it wasn't my place to offer excuses for a man I barely knew. As if reading my thoughts, Mr. Stern asked, "Have you known Mr. Kramer long?"

"We only met yesterday." I gave a summary of our afternoon at the ballpark, to which he listened with polite interest while his gaze swept over the heads of the children like a lighthouse beacon. He was looking, I supposed, for Albert's return, but I spotted him first. "There he comes, see?" Albert reentered through a gate on the opposite side of the yard, having apparently gone around the block. He raised his hand to wave, and both of us lifted our arms.

Suddenly, a strange call went out among the children. At the sound, each child froze in place. It was frightening how their little limbs stopped moving all at once, as if a sorcerer had cast a spell over the lot of them. One child — a little boy who couldn't have been more than five years old — hadn't managed to stop the momentum of his last jump and was caught out as the children around him turned to stone. An older boy stepped up to him and, to my astonishment, slapped him across the face. Without thinking, I started across the gravel toward them as the older one raised his hand for another slap. Albert had seen it, too. He ran over and grabbed the boy's wrist while it was still in the air. I knelt in front of the little one, who stood trembling, cheek ablaze and eyes dripping tears. He looked at me with quivering expectation, as if his fairy godmother had magically appeared. I asked him his name. In the silence of the statue children, his whisper was clearly audible.

"Are you okay, Victor?" It was a stupid question for me to ask. Of course he wasn't okay. I wondered what family tragedy had landed him here. Despite being surrounded by so many children, he seemed completely alone. I imagined scooping him up and carrying him home, his arms tight around my neck.

But I couldn't take Victor home, and clearly the boy was wilting in the glare of our attention. It was time to go. Glancing up at Albert, I noticed that his hand was still clamped around the older boy's wrist. I stood and lifted his fingers one by one. As the boy yanked his arm away, I saw a cluster of bruises bright as crushed berries on his skin.

A bell rang, breaking the spell and bringing the children back to life. Mr. Stern, putting a hand on each of our shoulders, steered us toward the building. "You shouldn't have bothered, Miss Winthrope. It's how the monitors maintain discipline. I know it seems harsh, but they do keep order."

"What will happen to him?" I asked, meaning what punishment awaited the boy who'd done the slapping.

"Oh, he'll be fine. He must be new. They learn soon enough." I realized he was referring to the one who'd been slapped. I caught Albert's eye and saw he shared my distress.

On our way out, Mr. Stern picked up two loaves of rye bread to offer us as souvenirs. Their baker was such a genius, he said, that the trustees took home loaves every Sunday. At the main entrance, our tour concluded, Mr. Stern asked, "So, what did you think of the Orphaned Hebrews Home?"

I thought it was an inhuman factory for the manufacture of obedient children, but I knew the alternatives for orphans in the city were even more bleak. I remembered reading about the charities that sent street children out west on trains to live with farm families. It seemed better than being raised in an institution, but I supposed there weren't many Jewish farmers.

"The elevation is fairly steep, but the location is ideal," Albert said. He, too, must not have wanted to reveal his true thoughts about the orphanage. "I'm sure Colonel Ruppert will be impressed."

"It is impressive what we do here, but even so, institutions like ours are falling out of favor. Too big, too impersonal, is what they say nowadays. That's why we need to relocate." He turned to Albert, pointedly excluding me. "I was wondering if you'd let me take you out to Westchester to show you the land. Tomorrow, in the morning? I need to be back for our trustees meeting in the afternoon. I know you want Colonel Ruppert to have the entire picture."

Albert looked at him for a long moment. I assumed he was thinking of a polite way to turn the man down — he'd already worked one day of the weekend — but instead he said, "I might as well see how far along you

143

are with your building plans."

They agreed to meet at nine o'clock in Grand Central Station. Outside, Albert and I found Schultz instructing a group of neighborhood boys on the inner workings of the Packard. He shooed them away as we approached. I looked back to watch the castle recede as we drove away. "Wasn't it terrible to see that little boy slapped? I wished I could have rescued him, poor thing."

Albert looked as though he might begin to cry. "I hate to see a child bullied. Boys can be so cruel."

"You don't have to tell me about the cruelty of boys." I thought of Harrison and all he had cost me. Free love, it seemed, was only free for the man. It was the woman who was left to pay the price.

"We have that in common, then." Albert pulled his knee up on the seat to face me. "You might have saved me from breaking that boy's wrist."

I shifted in my seat, too. "I guess you don't know your own strength."

"I doubt that, but it was a good thing you came with me today."

I offered him a weak smile. "At least it was more eventful than spending another day in bed." He listened sympathetically as

I told him about my battle with pneumonia.

"I know how you feel, Helen. I had rheumatic fever as a child. It weakened my heart, but even after I recovered my mother would hardly let me outside. If my uncle hadn't sent me to boarding school, I might still be in that shuttered mansion with my widowed mother and grandmother."

"But that sounds like a Dickens novel," I teased.

"Funny you should say that. When I read *Bleak House,* it reminded me of home."

We were surprised by the cessation of motion as the limousine pulled up to the curb in front of my building. Reluctant as I was to leave him, there seemed nothing left to say. I picked up my loaf of rye bread, sad to think I might never have occasion to see Colonel Ruppert's secretary again.

Unexpectedly, Albert caught my arm. "Listen, Helen, I have an extra ticket to the ballet tomorrow night. A friend of mine is one of the dancers. I wonder, would you like to go with me?"

CHAPTER 10

It was impulsive of me to offer Helen the ticket that, only yesterday, I'd been scheming to give that man on the train, but my night with King had drawn my emotions close to the surface, making me receptive to the sympathetic vibration I felt between myself and Helen. Perhaps we half-orphans shared a sixth sense that enabled us to recognize one another as comrades in an uncertain world.

Schultz pulled the limousine away from Helen's apartment building and headed downtown. Though her residence was decidedly middle-class, I imagined her family and mine lived on much the same level. Despite my mother's girlhood memories of regattas on Lake Conemaugh with the Fisks and the Carnegies, we'd been existing on a meager income since the Panic of 1893 brought my father's fortunes crashing down as suddenly as the floodwaters into Johnstown. Bankrupt and depressed, he capsized his sailboat in Lake Erie when I was just a baby. (Years later, my uncle told me what it had cost to get his suicide reported as a boating accident.) My widowed mother had taken on the role of Grandmother's companion in exchange for a fashionable address she could no longer afford.

Schultz rolled down his window to argue with a traffic cop who was holding us up. Glancing around, I saw we'd advanced no farther than Times Square. I closed my eyes, settling in for a lengthy drive.

When was the last time I'd asked a girl out? I wondered. Back in Pittsburgh, that summer before going down to Princeton. Someone was hosting a dance and they needed young men for the cotillion, my mother said. Normally I would have resisted her efforts to push me into society, but it was so gloomy at Grandmother's that I jumped at the chance to get out for the night. I was outfitted in an old tuxedo of my father's that had been cleaned and altered for the occasion. "Thank goodness these things never go out of style," my mother said as she poked a white rose through the buttonhole. I set off on foot for a grand mansion at the top of the hill that dominated our neighborhood. The hostess, a steel heiress, had been sent to Europe as a teenager to marry an aristocrat. Returning a baroness, she'd made a career of impressing Pittsburgh society with her purchased nobility. Uniformed footmen were arrayed around the drive to escort the young ladies from their carriages. Young men arrived in automobiles, their engines annoying the horses. Though my mother had assured me I'd know everyone, I found that my years away at boarding school had turned me into a ghost among my peers, who all seemed to have spent the past decade playing together on some team or other. I felt easier around the girls, who were smart and spirited and desperate for a partner. Before long my name had been penciled in on a dozen dance cards (it was a very old-fashioned affair) and I enjoyed myself immensely. When the music stopped and we all went in for supper, I escorted a lively young woman who turned out to be the baroness's daughter. She was a wonderful conversationalist and not at all snobbish; we talked so much we both forgot to eat. After supper, she suggested a walk. We wandered through the empty streets of Shadyside, glowing porch lights dotting the velvet darkness. It was midnight by the time we strolled back up her drive, emptying now of cars and carriages. When she turned her face up, I kissed her cheek. "Aren't you a proper gentleman," she said. I invited her to picnic with me the next afternoon and she happily accepted. I walked home delighted at the prospect, as was my mother when I told her over breakfast. Privately, I dared to believe that horrible boy at boarding school might have been wrong about me. Perhaps I still had a chance at a normal life. At least I'd have the summer to find out, and this lovely girl to help me do it.

Then a note arrived from the baroness's daughter, saying she wasn't feeling well and was sorry she wouldn't be able to picnic with me after all. "I hope she recovers soon, I quite like her," I told my mother. "She won't get well, because she isn't ill," my mother said, her voice thick with disappointment. "She found out you have no money and she's decided not to waste her time on you." I said she must be mistaken, the girl wasn't like that at all, but she just shook her head and patted my cheek with a sad hand. "Believe me, I know these people. I was one of them, remember?" I went down to Princeton wondering if things might have turned out differently for me — if I might have turned out differently — if I'd been worthy of that girl. College was certainly no place to change my ways. I was pegged for a pansy while I was still a freshman. When an upperclassman introduced me to Greenwich Village, I fit in so well that I wrote myself off as a lost cause. It hadn't occurred to me in years to question if the act of being a normal man I performed at work could carry over into my private life as well.

"Here you are, Mr. Kramer." Schultz's voice seemed to come from a long way off. I roused myself to exit the limousine. "Don't forget your bread."

I encountered Mrs. Santalucia mopping the hallway and offered her the loaf of rye, saying I owed it to her. "So you're the thief who was in my kitchen last night." She dried her hands and took it, appreciating its size and weight. "Thank you, Mr. Kramer, this'll more than make up for the one you took."

Was it only last night King had been waiting on my stoop? The hours we'd spent together seemed cut from a different cloth than the fabric of my day-to-day existence. For a moment my daydreams in the limousine and my memories from last night collided. I imagined King leading me around a dance floor, dashing in his uniform. He was the kind of man a baroness's daughter would marry even without a fortune. Except King didn't want a damsel, did he? He'd wanted me. The thought weakened my knees in a way no woman ever had. I supposed I was a lost cause after all.

"Oh, your friend stopped by. He left you a note." Mrs. Santalucia handed me a slip of paper. For a ridiculous second I imagined it was from King — though how could it have been, unless he'd jumped ship? I read the scribbled words, from Paul, scolding me for missing Jack's debut and insisting I come to Antonio's that night.

I went up to my room in need of a nap. I noticed, on my dresser, a brass button stamped with an eagle. King must have torn it from his uniform and left it there for me to remember him by. Silly boy. I dropped the button into a drawer and shut it tight. Getting into bed, I fell back on my pillow, inhaling an unfamiliar scent. Even before I could put King's name to the smell, it gave me a pang in my chest like those nights at boarding school when I had lain despondent in my bed, wishing my mother would come to whisk me home. But how could I be homesick for a man I'd known for only a few hours? It didn't make sense. Still, I clutched the sheets to my face and breathed him in.

Those angled streets around Bedford and

Commerce were so confusing I ended up wandering the cobblestones until Antonio's appeared, a brightly lit window on the garden floor of a nondescript town house, its name painted discreetly on the glass. The front door was propped open, laughter and smoke and piano music carried out on streaks of warm light.

Once I pushed through the people clotting the entry, I saw the place was only half full. Later it would be shoulder to shoulder — Antonio's was featured on those maps of the Village for tourists who wanted to go slumming — but it was still early. Along one side of the narrow room were snug booths with wood benches. On the other side was a monstrous bar decorated with carved gargoyles, the counter in front of it barely wide enough to prop an elbow. I squeezed through the space between the counter and the booths to reach Toni (only strangers called the proprietor Antonio), who was in conversation with Edith at the far end of the bar.

"Hello Toni, Edith." I shook Toni's hand and kissed Edith on the cheek. They were a lovely couple, Edith always stylish from her bobbed hair to her satin shoes, Toni invariably wearing a striped vest and pleated trousers, sleeves rolled up and short hair slicked back. I doubted if any of the tourists who wandered in realized they were both women.

"Where were you last night, Albert?" Toni asked. "Paul was looking for you."

"I was detained by a soldier." My face grew warm as I said it. Edith laughed, and Toni cuffed me on the arm. I caught sight of myself in the beveled mirror behind the bar but couldn't tell if my cheeks were mottled from blushing or the rouge I'd dusted on at home. I'd touched my lashes with mascara, too, and toweled the pomade out of my hair so it hung loose over my forehead. I pointed my pinkies to the ceiling as I adjusted the red bow tie around my neck. Though it still looked brown to me, I'd stitched a thread into it so I wouldn't make that mistake again.

"Aren't you a proper pansy." I turned at the sound of Paul's voice (he never had to doll himself up to attract attention; his beauty was its own billboard) and saw Jack was with him. "What happened to you last night? We were in tears." Jack leaned over his shoulder, mouth turned down and fists to his eyes like a mime weeping.

Toni smiled. "He says he was detained by a soldier."

"Well, well, Prince Albert. We better have

a drink so you can tell us all about it. Gin and lemonade?"

"I'll bring them over," Edith said as Toni went to mix the drinks. Past the bar, the room opened up to accommodate a smattering of small tables covered in checked cloth. Paul and Jack led the way and we dropped onto wobbly bentwood chairs.

"How was ballet rehearsal?" I asked Paul.

"A disaster, but that only means opening night will be perfect. Don't try to change the subject. What's this about a soldier?"

Edith deposited our drinks. "I've still got your tab from last night, Paul."

"Don't you worry, Edith." He winked, and she smiled (no one, it seemed, was immune to Paul's charms). "I'll pay for everything before the night is over."

"Did you strike it rich?" Jack asked as she walked away. He hadn't dolled himself up yet, and with his barrel chest and meaty biceps he looked like a lumberjack who'd accidentally wandered into a pansy bar. Though his gestures were fluid and his voice naturally melodious, he saved the swishing and lisping for his act. With his friends, Jack didn't need these affectations for us to recognize his feminine nature.

"I'll explain later," Paul said, "but first,

our little prince here has a soldier to tell us about."

So I told them about King, from the ballpark to the stoop to my bed — but only what we'd done there, not what we'd said. Usually it was Paul or Jack who regaled us with scandalous tales of their liaisons. I'd never had them so captivated by one of my adventures. When the gorgeous young waiter came to refill our glasses, we ordered dinner (Antonio's wasn't known for its kitchen, but they could throw together a plate of lasagna) then watched as he walked away. "Where does Toni find them," I wondered.

"I think he imports them from Italy along with the wine," Jack said, turning to Paul. "You're up next, sweetie. Tell us how you struck it rich."

"I met someone." It was Paul's admirers who typically got a sheepish look when he paid them the compliment of his attention, but now it was Paul, grinning like a school-girl.

"Here, last night, during my show? How did I miss it?"

"No, earlier, at that reception for the ballet company. I caught the eye of one of our benefactors." The name Paul whispered was so famous he made us promise never to utter it aloud. "I was talking to his wife — she was positively dripping with diamonds — when I saw him staring at me. You know the look. I peeled Geneviève off my arm and we met up in the men's room. Nothing much happened, we just exchanged a few words, but I mentioned I'd be at Antonio's tonight and he said he'd meet me here."

Jack and I looked at each other, eyebrows raised. "You'd better be careful," he said. "That's some very blue blood to be dragging down to a dump like this."

"I've never heard his name mentioned in our world," I said. "Have you?"

"No, I haven't," Jack said, "and I thought I knew everyone."

Paul gave us an impish smile. "Maybe I'm his first." It was entirely possible. If anyone could expand a married man's horizons, it was Paul.

Our plates arrived. "Now, tell me what I missed last night," I said. "How was the show?" Across the back wall of the restaurant, between the upright piano and the kitchen door, a tiny stage was raised a few inches above the floor.

Jack didn't wear a dress for his act (that would have been illegal), but by making up his face and tossing a feather boa across his shoulders, he stepped so far from the narrow rut of normal masculinity that his alter ego required a new name. His transformation into Jacqueline came not from his clothes but from the extravagance of his gestures, the inflection of his voice, the bawdy jokes with which he parried any insult. His singing was almost beside the point. The audience hardly noticed he could hold a note to break your heart.

"She was wonderful," Paul said. Jack bowed his head. "She absolutely slayed the crowd. There were some rowdies, but Jacqueline put them in their place."

Antonio's began to get crowded. We capped off our dinner with another round. By the time Jack had to go upstairs to Edith and Toni's apartment to get ready, my head was spinning. "You're staying for the show, aren't you?" he asked me.

"I wish I could, darling, I really do, but I have a business meeting in the morning. If I don't get some sleep I'll be dead on my feet."

"Who does business on Sunday morning? It's uncivilized."

"It's with a Jewish fellow. I guess they don't care about Sundays."

"Is he handsome at least?" Jack winked at Paul, then poked me in the ribs. "He must be if you're willing to ditch us so early."

"It wouldn't matter if he were," Paul said.

"Everyone knows Jews don't go for pansies."

"Stop it, both of you." I exchanged kisses with Jack. "I'll make it up to you, I promise."

"Say, you are coming to my opening night tomorrow, aren't you?" Paul asked me. "You've still got those tickets? You can bring this soldier boy of yours."

"He shipped out this morning, remember? Actually, I invited a girl."

Paul tilted his chair back and looked at me, amused. "Now, that you'll have to explain." I started telling him about Helen when he kicked me under the table. "Look, there he is."

I'd forgotten about his mysterious benefactor. I turned and saw a rather ordinary man in exquisite clothes. He stood at the bar, a drink in one hand and his hat in the other, gazing at Paul. You could have powered a streetcar on the electricity in the look that passed between them.

"Don't worry about the bill, I'll settle up with Toni." Paul weaved his way through the tables until he reached the bar. His benefactor set down his drink and placed a hand on Paul's lovely cheek as they conferred, heads together. With a flash of diamond cuff links, he produced a wallet and motioned to Toni. From the glimpse I got at the notes he handed over, the amount was more than sufficient to cover our table as well as Paul's outstanding tab. I stretched my neck to watch them leave.

I got up myself then and realized I shouldn't have had that last drink. I needed the waiter to steer me to the door, where the cool air revived me a bit. I wobbled home through the dark streets of Greenwich Village, placing one foot carefully in front of the other. My legs managed to find my house with no help from my muddled brain. After some fumbling with the keys, I hauled myself upstairs. It was worse lying down. The ceiling above my bed whirled like a carousel and I knew there was no cure but to sleep it off. Setting my alarm clock, I cursed myself for agreeing to meet Felix Stern so early on a Sunday.

CHAPTER 11

"It's a shame the stores are closed on Sunday." My mother surveyed the sad contents of my closet. "You could've gotten a new dress for the ballet."

The dozen hangers offered a depressing display. Everything looked out-of-date, from the skirts and shirtwaists I'd worn since high school to the dresses I'd thrown on to go to acting class. Truth be told, I'd gotten so used to cadging dresses from the wardrobe mistress at the Olde Playhouse that the only thing I'd purchased in ages was the yellow linen, but I'd worn that twice in two days now. Thinking back to my dates with Harrison, I realized that never once had I been dressed in my own clothes. No wonder I owned nothing suitable for a night out with Albert Kramer. I took my prettiest shirtwaist from the closet, with embroidery down the front and a lace collar. "I'll just iron this."

"No, Helen, that won't do. Doesn't Mr. Rabinowitz keep the back door of his tailor shop open on Sundays? I saw a beautiful blue dress in his window yesterday, as nice as anything you could get at Gimbels."

I objected to spending money on myself when I owed her so much, but she reminded me of my promise to begin paying her back after I started working again. "Besides, you can't wear rags to go out with the secretary of a millionaire."

I didn't think much of Ruppert's millions found their way into Albert's pockets, but I took her point. If there was one thing I'd learned in drama school, it was the importance of dressing the part.

An hour later, as I turned this way and that to catch my reflection in the mirror on the back of my closet door, I had to admit my mother had been right. The dress, a modern silhouette of periwinkle crepe de chine trimmed in velvet, looked like something Gordon Conway might have drawn. "I could be on the stage in this."

My mother frowned. "You know you're not strong enough for that yet."

"Well, I've got to do something, and acting is all I know." I thought of Richard's offer to work at the Olde Playhouse and regretted standing him up the day before —

that business with Albert and the orphanage had driven it right out of my mind. I decided I'd stop by and apologize after the ballet.

Leaning over the bathroom sink to apply my mascara, I had the same flicker of anticipation I'd felt before my dates with Harrison — a flicker that was quickly extinguished by a cold cramp in my gut as my optimism was swamped by another round of recrimination. I was no better than the women in the asylum out on Wards Island, I thought, sterilized for being judged insane. Except I wasn't crazy, just stupid. It made me wonder what those women had done to deserve their fate. Perhaps they'd been no worse than I was: headstrong and gullible, pregnant and unmarried, willing to break the law to save themselves. Plenty of mothers would have kicked their daughters to the curb for less. I shuddered to think what might have become of me under different circumstances.

I gave my reflection a hard stare. Enough, I told myself. So you can't have children. Neither can lots of women, they just don't know it until they try. Besides, there were thousands of Bachelor Girls all over New York enjoying their careers and their freedom, and plenty of men like Harrison who didn't care about marriage. I wondered if Albert Kramer might be one of those men. He worked for one of the most famous bachelors in the city. Rex, who'd been reading up on the Yankees, had shown me an article in which Ruppert was quoted as saying a man only needed a wife if he didn't have a butler, a cook, or a laundress — and he had all three. Perhaps the Colonel preferred his personal secretary to be similarly unencumbered. Even if he disapproved of marriage, though, he couldn't very well demand chastity from his employees. Sex with Albert would be nothing like it had been with Harrison, I mused, if for no other reason than he was half Harrison's weight. "Stop it," I said aloud. "You're being ridiculous."

"Are you talking to me, Helen?" my mother called from the living room.

"No, Mom, I'm not."

The buzzer rang just as I was pinning on my hat, causing me to poke my finger. Sucking away the drop of blood, I hurried to the elevator. Clarence wasn't in the lobby to open the door, so Albert was stuck outside. He greeted me with a friendly handshake when I came out. "You look nice, Helen. I like that dress." He was smartly attired, too, in a double-breasted jacket and wide-cut trousers, but I wasn't sure how to compliment a man on his outfit. "The theater's just on the other side of Times Square. We could catch a streetcar if you're not up for the walk."

"No, a walk will do me good," I said. We made a fashionable couple, I thought, as we strolled up the block, streetlights and lit windows easing the evening darkness. I stumbled among the hectic crowds on Broadway and Albert offered me his arm. I accepted, grateful for the steadiness he provided. We found we shared a talent for observation and began pointing out to each other little sights along the way: a lady's ridiculous hat, a traffic cop with theatrical gestures, a dachshund wearing a jeweled collar. When the conversation flagged, I asked about his visit to the orphanage's new location that morning.

"It was miserable. I woke up with another hangover. I hope you won't think I'm a lush, Helen, but I don't usually work on the weekend and my friends were expecting me." He went on to tell me about his trip to Westchester, where he'd been disappointed to find nothing more than an overgrown field.

"But Mr. Stern made it sound as if they were ready to break ground."

Albert pulled me aside to let a business-man stride by. "Hardly. I stood there while he described it to me, as if painting a picture with words were the same thing as having an architect's prospectus. When I told him I had trouble envisioning it, he said he should have shown me the plans first. He apolo-gized for dragging me out there for noth-ing, but I'm glad I went."

"Why's that?" Though we were stopped at a crosswalk, he let me keep hold of his arm.

"So I can tell the Colonel their relocation plans are more pipe dream than reality."

"He should know the facts before he com-mits to a donation."

"A donation? Oh, yes. I did agree to meet Mr. Stern one more time, to see the plans, but I imagine that will be the end of it."

We arrived at the theater before I realized how far we'd walked. The doors were open and people were being seated, but there was enough time before the curtain that I could excuse myself to visit the ladies' room without inconveniencing him. Touching up my hair in front of the mirror, I wondered when I'd ever felt so comfortable with a man.

I'd expected the ballet to be lush and romantic, but the music was quite modern and the dancers more athletic than ethereal.

I was shocked when they first leaped onto the stage until I realized their beige tights blended with their skin. Albert leaned over to whisper that his friend Paul was the dancer at center stage, impressively lifting a ballerina over his head. After the finale, Albert brought me backstage where we found his friend in a communal dressing room shared by all the male dancers. A quick peek revealed the men sweaty and undressed. I covered my eyes and stepped back into the hallway as Paul, wrapped in a dressing gown, came out to greet us.

"I thought Albert had invented you." Instead of taking my hand, Paul kissed both of my cheeks like a Frenchman. Up close his good looks were stunning, even with the greasy stage makeup smeared across his face. "So this is the princess to our prince."

I turned to Albert, confused. "It's a joke. He calls me Prince Albert, like the tobacco. You were magnificent, Paul, really."

"Yes, it was wonderful." I liked knowing that Albert had already mentioned me to his friend.

"So what are you kids up to next?"

We looked at each other and shrugged. "I guess we'll stop off for a drink, if you'd like, Helen. How about you? Are you going out afterward?"

166

"The dancers are all going out together, but I'm sure I'll end up at Antonio's eventually." Paul glanced at me and raised an eyebrow.

"I don't plan on monopolizing his night, if that's what you're wondering."

"Then I guess I'll see you later on?" Paul directed his question at Albert.

"No promises. I've had a hell of a weekend."

"I'm glad you came, both of you." He kissed my cheeks again and then repeated the gesture with Albert. I thought it was very European.

We made our way through the bedlam backstage to emerge onto the street. "There is someplace I'd like to go, Albert, if you wouldn't mind." I told him how I'd missed my meeting with Richard Martin because of our visit to the orphanage.

"Lead on." I took him up a few short streets and down two long blocks to the Olde Playhouse, where a handful of people were lingering under the marquee. Richard spotted us entering the lobby and came out from behind the ticket window.

"Helen Winthrope, it's like a miracle the way you appear. Come here, I need to speak with you." I barely had time to introduce Albert before Richard hustled us into his cramped office. He dropped into the only chair, leaving me and Albert shoulder to shoulder in the doorway. "I was hoping to ease you into this, but I'm in a crisis, Helen. I don't know what to do." His glasses swung from the chain around his neck as he leaned forward to put his head in his hands.

Alarmed, I knelt in front of him. "Richard, what is it?"

Haltingly, he explained he'd been suffering from a nervous disposition for years. He'd ignored his symptoms, always too busy to take time for his health, but that morning he was so overwhelmed with palpitations he'd gone to the hospital. The doctor had put it bluntly: if he didn't immediately arrange for a convalescence, free from the stress of the Playhouse, his heart would certainly give out. "I have a friend who's invited me to stay with him in Montauk. The doctor said the recuperative powers of the ocean were just what I needed." Now that the current show had ended its run, he explained, Harrison would be moving to evening rehearsals, leaving the theater dark for a fortnight until the new play opened. "If you could step in for me during the day, Helen, just for a couple of weeks while I rest, I'm sure I'd be good as new by opening night. Perhaps you could bring some

168

order to this chaos, while you're here."

I looked around the office. Posters from past performances were peeling from the walls, haphazard heaps of paper obscured the surface of the desk, and the floor was piled with teetering stacks of ledgers that seemed to go back decades. I couldn't imagine how I'd begin to sort out the mess, but I wasn't about to pass up a chance to get back to the world of the theater. "I'll step in, Richard, don't worry."

He lifted his head. "Would you really, Helen? I'm not asking too much of you, am I?"

"I'm not strong enough for the stage yet, but it looks like I'd be spending most of my time sitting right here, wouldn't I? It's not exactly strenuous."

"To be honest, I've been letting things go for a while now. Perhaps it isn't as bad as it seems?" I could hear the lie in his voice and assumed the state of the Playhouse was even worse than Richard was willing to admit.

"I'll get you a taxi if you'd like, Mr. Martin," Albert said. I looked up at him with gratitude.

Confessing his predicament had apparently sapped Richard of his last reserves of strength. He leaned heavily on the desk as he stood and stuffed a few things into a satchel that had been tucked below his chair. "I can't express my appreciation, Helen. Here are the keys to the office and the lobby. The custodian will lock the stage doors. The rest of it" — he waved a hand around the office — "you'll get the hang of in no time." I waited with him under the marquee, the lights exaggerating the sallow tone of his skin. "You may have saved my life, Helen. I'm sure a couple of weeks by the ocean will do me wonders." He bid me a weak good-bye before getting into the taxi Albert had hailed.

I looked at the keys Richard had pressed into my hand. "What have I gotten myself into?"

"Come on." Albert led me back into the Playhouse. "I'll help you close up."

We wandered through the theater, checking stalls in the restrooms and switching off lights. It was half an hour until the last of the patrons had finally cleared the lobby and we locked the doors. Under the dark marquee, I thanked Albert again for his assistance. "I wish you could help me sort that mess in Richard's office."

"You're better off without me, Helen. I really wouldn't know what I was doing."

"But you must have taken some business courses?"

"Nothing so practical as that, I'm afraid."

I offered to get myself home — he'd already spent more time with me than he'd been planning to — but he refused to hear of it. Together we traversed Times Square, my hand contentedly clutching Albert's arm. I'd known I was lonely, but until that moment, I hadn't realized how much room there was in my life for a friend.

Chapter 12

How strange it was to walk through Times Square with a woman on my arm. I noticed the lingering looks as pansies eyed men on the crowded sidewalk, their parade of passion an invisible undercurrent among the bustling Broadway crowds, but with Helen's little hand tucked into my elbow I was excluded from their glances. I felt like one of those foreign agents the papers kept warning us about as the queer world revealed its secrets all around me.

It had been like that at the ballet. Instead of furtively meeting a stranger and hoping no one discerned our true intentions, I'd walked into the lobby with Helen beside me and my chin held high. So what if people assumed we were on a date? Their eyes swept over us unperturbed, our appearance neatly fitting their pattern of what a couple should be. I couldn't help but envy the normal men who walked so nonchalantly through the city. How easy life was for them.

Easy, but narrow. After leaving Helen at her door, I crossed Times Square on my own, testing the difference. The sidewalks were as packed as when Houdini, in a straitjacket, had dangled himself over 42nd Street from a crane. Pushing through the crowd, I gave a rather rough man a very long look. Checking back over my shoulder, I was gratified to find him gazing after me. Our eyes met, and there it was: that spark of desire lighting me up from the inside out. If I hadn't been planning to meet up with Paul at Antonio's, I might have stopped to let him catch up with me. For now, though, the recognition had been enough to remind me of my true tribe.

As it happened, by the time I got down to Washington Square, I'd decided a night of abstinence would do me good — exactly what the prohibitionists had in mind, though what a dull existence they wanted to force us into. Up in my room, I poured myself a whiskey just to spite them but went to bed without finishing it. I sought King's lingering scent, but my nostrils were met with the sharp tang of bleach. I remembered, then, that the landlady always laundered the linens on Sunday. Did his bunk on the ship even have sheets? I wondered. I fell asleep imagining King stretched out on a blanket tossed over webbed hemp.

Monday morning, I got to the brewery early for a change. As I prepared my notes about the orphanage and sorted through the Colonel's mail and messages, I jotted a reminder to myself to call Helen to ask how she was managing at the Playhouse. Miss Grunwald arrived, then the Colonel, punctual to a fault. For the first time since I'd become his personal secretary, he said he wanted to see me right away and that Miss Grunwald should come in with the brewery business after we had spoken. She took the demotion hard, I could see, and I felt a little sorry for her. Supposing the Colonel was simply anxious to hear what I'd learned about the orphanage, I quickly gathered up my notes.

"Sit down, Kramer." The Colonel unbuttoned his jacket and hung up his hat. "How did you like the game on Friday? I don't go often enough myself. I can't stand seeing the Yankees lose. If Huggins could manage to put together a winning team, I'd spend more afternoons at the ballpark. The key is acquiring Ruth. I want you to see what you can dig up on the Red Sox's owner, Harry Frazee, but keep it quiet. I don't want word getting out to the press."

"But don't you know him well enough already?"

"I need to know what I don't know. Start with his file at the clipping agency, you know the one we use."

I did. "I'm not sure their clippings will include articles from the Boston papers."

"Then go on up there for a day, but don't let on you work for me. I want to hear what you find out by the end of this week. I'll hire a Pinkerton detective if I have to, but I've got to find something Frazee wants more than Ruth if I'm going to get him away from Boston." As I took notes, he lifted the lid of a jar carved from onyx and extracted a peppermint, which he popped in his mouth. "Now, Kramer, tell me about this orphanage. If I'm going to be sitting in the owner's box, I want to own the stands I'm in as well as the team. How's the land?"

"The property is perfectly situated, as Mr. Stern said, and they are eager to sell. However, it seems to me there are some significant impediments."

"There always are." The Colonel settled into his chair, the vest of his suit snug across his stomach. "When my father started Ruppert Realty, all it took to build in Manhattan was a fat bribe in the right hands at Tammany Hall. Now there are commissions for safety, review boards for preservation — they even tried to set a height restriction over Carnegie Hill to protect the old mansions. My mother thought it was a fine idea, but I opposed it because you should never set limits on the future. Now there's a fourteen-story apartment right across 93rd Street. Mother is dismayed, but I told her, you can't fight progress."

"No, sir, I suppose you can't."

"So, what impediments?"

I checked the list I'd made. "First of all, the orphanage is massive. I can't imagine how many cranes and wrecking balls it would take to demolish the place, or how the rubble would get hauled away or where it would go. About a quarter of the property has been deeply excavated for the basement, that's where the dining room and the kitchens are. The oven alone must weigh over a ton. It may be five acres, but it's not as if they're offering you an empty lot."

"Well, the city's not going to let me take over a park. Demolition is a necessity if I'm to build in Manhattan. Go on."

"Secondly, as far as I can tell they've made no real progress with their new location. I went out to Westchester with Mr. Stern yesterday morning to see for myself. It's nothing but an empty field."

"You went to see it? That was enterprising of you. Do they have plans at least?"

"Mr. Stern says they do, but I haven't seen them yet. The plans aren't supposed to leave the orphanage, but he agreed to bring them home with him on Thursday evening if I wanted to have a look."

"Do you mind?"

"Of course not, if you'd like me to."

He tugged on his cuffs. "What else?"

"I'm not sure they have the money to actually accomplish what Mr. Stern described to me. He said they were planning a major fund-raising event for the fall, but I suspect he'll need an agreement or an option on the property to encourage the donors to open their wallets, whereas you would probably want to know they had the funds to rebuild before you agreed to anything."

The Colonel grunted. "You're not painting a pretty picture for me, Kramer. Any other problems you want to mention?"

"There is one more thing." I looked at my notes. "Mr. Stern says they own the whole five acres, but there's a public school on the Broadway side of the property. The orphanage children attend, but so do the kids in the neighborhood. I'm not sure who you have to bribe to close a school."

"You leave that to me, Kramer. So, there are problems, there always are. You walked the grounds?"

"I did." I set aside my notes and spoke to him directly. "If it could be done, it would be a magnificent location. The Broadway Line subway stops immediately behind it and the Amsterdam Avenue streetcar runs in front. You'd be able to see clear out to the Hudson from the upper stands, depending on how a ballpark was situated on the site."

"Not a ballpark, Kramer. A stadium. That's what I want for my team. That's what this city deserves, and I'm going to give it to them, one way or another." The Colonel looked around restlessly. "Go ask Miss Grunwald to call for some coffee, will you?"

She was up and out of her chair before I could explain the Colonel wasn't ready for her yet. "Will that be coffee for two, Mr. Kramer?" Just to annoy her, I said yes.

Back in his office, I was about to run through the Colonel's other messages when he asked, "What did Helen think of it?"

"Of the orphanage?" It had upset her, I knew, especially seeing that child being slapped, but remembering that the Colonel had arranged it to please her, I said only that she thought it was impressive. "Of course, she assumed I was looking into it on your behalf for a donation. I took Mr. Stern aside at the beginning of our tour so he wouldn't mention the idea of a ballpark — I mean, a stadium — in front of her."

"Good thinking." He lifted the lid of the onyx jar but set it back down without taking another peppermint, recalling, I supposed, the coffee he'd just ordered. "What did you think of her?"

"Of Helen? She's very nice, I enjoyed her company." I paused, uncertain of his reaction, then continued. "We went to the ballet together last night."

He seemed to scowl at me, but perhaps he was simply taken aback. "You asked her out?"

"Was that inappropriate? It wasn't a date, I just had an extra ticket. Would you rather I not see her again?"

His features relaxed. "No, of course not. She's a grown woman, isn't she? And an independent one, too, ever since she was a girl." His expression became somber and his eyes actually moistened. For a moment, I thought he'd start to weep. "Jerry Winthrope died in my very arms. I'll never forget that day as long as I live." He pinched the bridge of his nose to stop a tear. "I've taken an interest in the family ever since.

Helen was hospitalized a few months ago, did she tell you? Burst appendix." Again his eyes moistened. "That's what killed my dear sister Cornelia. As if her eloping with Nahan Franko wasn't heartbreak enough for my parents. At least we got her body back."

"Excuse me?" This was a story I'd never heard before, but the Colonel dropped the subject and spoke again of Helen.

"I wanted to see how she was doing. That's why I invited them to the game. Rex is a firecracker, isn't he? What an expert on baseball. I might see if we can't find a place for him in the Yankees' organization when he graduates high school. Think he'd like that?"

"Rex Winthrope would be thrilled, especially if you manage to get Ruth for the Yankees."

A knock on the door preceded Miss Grunwald's entrance carrying a tray laden with a coffeepot, milk pitcher, sugar bowl, and cups. It seemed precariously balanced and I got up to take it from her. "I can still bring Colonel Ruppert his coffee, thank you very much." She managed to set the tray on the desk without anything toppling over.

"Thank you, Miss Grunwald," he said. "I'll be with you soon."

After she closed the door he sighed. "She's

not the most efficient secretary anymore, but Mother won't let me fire her, even with a sizable severance." It was the first intimation I'd had that Miss Grunwald was not as indispensable as she believed herself to be. "I respect her years of service, but I don't like keeping things around once they're no longer of use. Did I ever tell you the story of how I sold my entire stable of racing horses in a single auction?"

The Colonel was in a voluble mood that morning. I put down my pencil and helped myself to a cup of coffee while he regaled me with the well-known tale. Once he finished, I reviewed our other business and was gathering up my notes when he asked, "Did Helen care for the game?"

I shifted in my seat. "She enjoyed the afternoon at the ballpark, but her interest is in the theater." I related to the Colonel the story of stopping by the Olde Playhouse after the ballet and how Helen had agreed to cover for its manager.

"My father used to own an opera house," he said, waxing nostalgic. "How I loved going there as a boy. I used to play hide-and-go-seek with my brothers and sisters behind the curtains of our box. You said this theater is in financial difficulties?"

"Mr. Martin, the manager, said they were

on the brink of disaster. He may have been being dramatic, but the office was in serious disarray."

"Where exactly is it located?" I jotted down the address on a slip of paper and handed it to him as I stood. He read it and snorted. "No wonder it's failing. It's on the wrong side of Tenth Avenue."

Maybe he did carry a map of Manhattan in his head. "Shall I send in Miss Grunwald now?"

"I suppose." I started toward the door but he waved me back. "One more thing, Kramer. I want you to have the head of Ruppert Realty come see me before I go to lunch."

"Yes, sir." I imagined he wanted to review what I'd told him about the orphanage property. My hand was on the door when he called me back again.

"Kramer, do you have your own expense account yet?"

"No, Miss Grunwald has been reimbursing me."

"That's going to get cumbersome if you start traveling on my behalf. Go to the accounting department and get yourself set up. I'll call down to authorize it."

"Which accountant should I see, sir?" The Colonel's enterprises operated as separate entities: the brewery, the realty company, and the baseball team each kept their own accounts.

He thought for a moment. "Might as well make it all of them. There's no telling what I'll want you to do for me from now on."

I returned to my desk, surprised and pleased by the sudden elevation of my responsibilities. The Colonel's trust was a hard-won commodity. Once given, only a betrayal could occasion its withdrawal. The cuckoo sang out the ten o'clock hour. I picked up the telephone and asked the operator to put me through to the Olde Playhouse, but there was no answer. Apparently, Helen hadn't arrived yet. Theater people, I thought, as I made myself a note to call her again later that afternoon.

CHAPTER 13

I was struggling to unlock the door of the Olde Playhouse when I heard the distant ring of the telephone echo across the lobby. I shouldered my way in and hurried toward the office, my shoes sliding on the marble floor, but I was too late to catch the call. I thought it might have been Richard — but no, I noticed now the telegram that had been slipped under the door. He'd sent it from Pennsylvania Station earlier that morning, its block letters conveying a blunt message that the Playhouse's banker would be coming by that afternoon. I set the yellow telegram atop a pile of papers on the desk and looked around the office. Richard had asked me to bring order to the chaos and this I set out to do, draping my jacket over the back of his chair and pinning my hair behind my ears.

But there was barely room in the small space for me to turn around, let alone sort through the drawers haphazardly jammed full of bills and letters and receipts. From the shelves, reviews clipped from newspapers fluttered down like autumn leaves, while the waste bin so overflowed with notes in Richard's cryptic scrawl that I couldn't tell where the mess stopped and the trash began. A plume of dust sent me into a sneezing fit that drove me out of the office. I couldn't accomplish anything in that tiny, filthy space, so I started carrying papers out to the lobby and stacking them on the upholstered benches, glad there'd be no shows for the next two weeks. My plan was to create piles of like items, then order each stack by date or name or production before returning the papers to their designated place in the office. But there were no designated places, I soon realized. The time card holder by the door was stuffed with postcards from touring actors and actresses. The broken-down letter boxes were crammed with old copies of *Playbill.* Hard candies shed of their cellophane wrappers were stuck in the ink wells, a conductor's baton was shoved into the pencil sharpener, and the corkboard on the wall was so riddled with holes there wasn't any cork left in which to stick a pin.

Overwhelmed, I took refuge in the ladies'

room where I splashed water on my face and combed dust from my hair. If Richard had been there to train me, perhaps he could have explained his arcane methods and eccentric procedures. Together we might have arrived at a sensible organizational scheme, but I dared not interrupt his convalescence. In his absence, I had no choice but to start over from scratch. The challenge of imposing my own order invigorated me. Refreshed and determined, I carried the remaining papers out of the office by the armful. I dragged the broken letter boxes and useless corkboard to the curb, removed the baton from the sharpener, and put a point on an old pencil. Before asking the custodian to give the denuded office a thorough cleaning, I called down to the lunch counter on the corner to have their delivery boy bring me a sandwich and a thermos of coffee.

The lobby benches were covered by now with papers, so when my lunch arrived I took it onstage where a table and chair were part of the set. As I made a list of things I'd need from the stationery store, it struck me that my mind hadn't been this occupied since the last time I'd memorized a script. As an actress, though, I'd spoken words someone else had written, dressed in clothes someone else had chosen, moved around the stage according to someone else's direction. Now I was making my own decisions with no one telling me what to do. I never thought there'd be a role for me in the theater other than on the stage, but as I stepped more confidently into Richard's shoes, I decided the part of manager was one I might like to continue playing.

Until that very day, acting was the only occupation I'd considered. My mother had disapproved at first, but she'd come around after seeing me as Portia in our high school's production of *The Merchant of Venice*. The auditorium of parents had given me an ovation after the courtroom scene when, disguised as a man and speaking of mercy, I outwitted the greedy Shylock. Ever since junior high, my drama teachers had been impressed by my ability to disappear into a role so completely that I no longer seemed to exist. Though it appeared effortless, it was a skill I'd been practicing ever since my family's arrival in the city, my grief and confusion hidden behind the mask of a confident student. In high school, I'd avoided the secretarial classes many of my friends had chosen — friends who were now swelling the ranks of New York's Bachelor Girls, working in shops or offices, living in their own apartments, coming and going as they pleased. As much as I'd longed for financial independence, my heart had been set on drama school. Though the expense meant living at home to economize, I'd been willing to delay my freedom for the chance, one day, to have a career on the stage. I'd nearly gotten there, too. Last year, as the lead in Harrison's play, I was earning enough to put a deposit on an apartment that allowed single women. My plan was to spend one last Christmas at home before moving out on my own. But then I discovered I was pregnant, and my troubles had started.

I gave my head a vigorous shake. I didn't want to think about all that right now. I stretched my arms and mouth in an acting exercise meant to dispel stage fright, then returned to the lobby, where I began the tedious task of putting the bills and receipts in order by date. It seemed Richard hadn't been lying when he said the Olde Playhouse was on the brink of disaster. I found a notice for back taxes due to the city, but it was so old I assumed it must have been paid. Though he was behind on the bills related to the theater itself, Richard continued to incur new expenses on behalf of the productions, spending more to stage each play than he earned in ticket sales. I supposed this was the conflict of being both the owner of the theater and the producer of the shows. During rehearsals, whenever Harrison had an inspiration that involved a costly change in set design — or costumes, or lighting, or any one of a number of things — he'd gone storming into Richard's office to launch into a Shakespearean rant worthy of Edwin Forrest about the absolute necessity of whatever it was he wanted. Richard had always given in, and I'd been impressed at Harrison's powers of persuasion. Now, I wondered what I would do if Harrison were to approach me with one of his extravagant requests. I hoped it wouldn't come to that. I doubted I'd have the spine to turn him down.

The banker finally arrived, the tips of his nervous fingers stained yellow from nicotine. He handed me a statement and instructed me to reconcile it with the ledger as soon as possible, then presented papers for my signature, explaining that I'd need him to countersign any checks over fifty dollars. "I don't envy you, Miss Winthrope. I understand Mr. Martin had a rather eccentric method of bookkeeping."

"I'm not sure Richard had any method at all," I said, signing where he told me to.

After he left, I dutifully attempted to reconcile the Playhouse's ledger, but there were pages missing from the checkbook. I hoped Richard had lifted them from the binder and simply misplaced them. If he'd written them out, I'd have no idea how much they were for until they were presented for payment. Unsure how to proceed, I put the ledger aside and called a nearby stationery store to place an order for a large corkboard, a filing cabinet, clean ink wells, fresh pencils, and boxes of paper clips and pins and labels. When they were delivered later that day, I felt very professional writing out a check for the purchases and taking possession of the receipt.

I decided my day's work was done when the custodian showed me the desiccated mouse he'd discovered under Richard's desk. I'd just put on my hat and jacket when the phone rang. I hesitated before answering it — rehearsals would begin soon and I didn't want to run into Harrison — but was pleased to hear Albert's voice humming in my ear.

"I've been curious all day to know how you were managing, Helen. Was the office in as much disarray as it looked?"

"Even more than I imagined." I sat down in Richard's chair and spun it back and forth as we spoke. Albert was such a sympathetic listener that I found myself pouring out all the details of my day. He didn't interrupt to instruct me in what I ought to do. Instead, he encouraged me to trust my own decisions. I was flattered by his faith in me, but when I asked for his advice regarding the ledger and the missing checks, I was disappointed he had none to give.

"It looks like I'll be going up to Boston on business this week," he said, wrapping up the conversation. "I'll telephone again when I get back. Good luck, Helen."

Glancing at the clock, I was surprised at how long our call had lasted. I hung up just as the first cast members began to arrive for that evening's rehearsal. Grabbing my jacket, I locked up the office and made a hurried escape.

CHAPTER 14

Helen spoke so enthusiastically about the job she was undertaking that I stayed on the line with her even after I should have left for the day. I thought back to when I'd initially come to work for the Colonel. Neither of us had a clear idea of what a personal secretary did, and it took some time to define my position. I envied Helen her chance to decide things on her own and encouraged her to trust herself, knowing that whatever system she came up with couldn't be worse than the mess Richard Martin had left behind.

Going home, my pockets were weighed down with cash advances from three different expense accounts. The money made me nervous. In my room, I hid it between the pages of a book and made a note to purchase a lockbox. Tuesday morning, instead of heading up to the brewery, I spent the day at the clipping agency on Madison

Avenue. They had a file on Harry Frazee so thick it was held together with rubber bands, but most of the articles concerned his theatrical ventures: shows he produced, theaters he owned, actresses with whom he was rumored to be keeping company. But the New York papers didn't have much to offer about Frazee's history with the Red Sox, so I decided to take the Merchants Limited up to Boston that very evening. After stopping at my room to stuff a few clothes into a battered satchel and fill my wallet with the Colonel's money, I hurried up to Grand Central to catch the train.

I wasn't used to playing the part of pampered businessman. I wondered, as I cut into a thick steak in the dining car, if this was how my father had traveled, back before he lost his fortune. To me it was a novelty made possible by an expense account, but to him it must have seemed a birthright. I felt out of place walking into the Lenox Hotel, where the crisp notes I counted out for a single night's stay would have covered a week's rent in the Village. A bellhop carried my satchel with as much deference as if it were monogrammed luggage. A chambermaid filled my tub with steaming water while a valet took my suit to be pressed and my shoes to be polished. Alone at last, I soaked until my fingers were as wrinkled as raisins, relishing the luxury of having a bathroom to myself.

I spent Wednesday at the clipping agency on Beacon Street. I'd been rehearsing a story to explain my interest in the owner of the Red Sox, but the clerk at the agency never asked — for a fee she handed over whatever file I requested. I sat at a table in the cramped reading room alongside actors scanning their own reviews, investors researching companies whose stocks they were buying, and journalists searching for background on their subjects. I wasn't sure what the Colonel needed to know, so I wrote down everything that caught my eye. I'd brought two full Parker pens, not wanting to have to mess with refilling the ink. By the time I was done taking notes on Harry Frazee, both pens were empty and my last few scribbles were in smudgy pencil. Hastily gathering my notes, I got to South Station just in time to board the five o'clock Merchants back to New York.

I'd skipped lunch so as not to waste my time in Boston. My stomach growled as I settled into an upholstered seat in the parlor car, waiting for the porter to announce dinner. A rather elegant man across the car kept glancing my way. I pulled out a cigarette then patted my pockets, pretending not to have any matches. He appeared instantly at my side. I stood as he flicked his lighter, the tang of flint and petrol in my nostrils. "Would you care to join us?" he asked, gesturing to another man, equally refined. I followed him to the corner of the car, where the three of us leaned together as best we could in those bulky seats. They were on their way to New York for some meetings, they said. After ascertaining that I was a resident, the second man asked, with studied casualness, "Do you know of any gay places to spend an evening? We haven't been to the city in years and we're not sure where a man might enjoy himself."

Most Manhattanites would have suggested a burlesque theater in Hell's Kitchen or a racy supper club in Harlem, in which case the conversation would have ended politely, no harm done and none the wiser. Instead I said, "There's a nightclub called Polly's in the Village that's quite entertaining, unless you were thinking closer to Times Square?"

They looked at each other, then at me, and we all smiled, our recognition complete. "I can't believe Polly's is still in business," the one who'd lit my cigarette said. "It was shabby five years ago, and what a sad parade of performers! There was one, though, who was quite good. What was her name?"

"It wouldn't have been Jacqueline, would it?" I asked. They both agreed and were delighted when I told them Jack was my friend and that he'd moved his act to Antonio's. When the porter announced the first seating for dinner, I explained that I'd missed lunch, and they agreed to go in with me. We enjoyed a pleasant meal together, though at such an early hour they ate lightly. I didn't like to mention the Colonel's name (he'd made me paranoid about the press sniffing out his pursuit of Babe Ruth), so I simply said I was a secretary sent up to Boston on business. They didn't press. Respecting one another's secrets was the glue that held our world together.

We couldn't speak freely with the waiters hovering over us, so when they meant to refer to each other, they invoked their imaginary wives (left at home, presumably, with batches of mythical children). In this way, I learned they'd been together for twenty years. One worked as a draughtsman and the other wrote for the *Atlantic Monthly*. I wasn't sure what to make of them. With their refined manners and hearty hand-shakes neither seemed like a pansy, but as we relaxed over dinner the writer's gestures did become looser, his hands swishing a bit

196

as he talked. I decided he must play the woman's part, though he was no more like the dolled-up pansies who populated places like Antonio's than his friend was like the rough men our rouged faces were meant to attract.

We went back to the parlor car where we passed the hours smoking and talking about the war. I supposed King's ship must be nearing the coast of France. I didn't like to think of him in harm's way so I changed the subject by mentioning an article in the paper about the Turkish invasion of Armenia. That got us on the topic of Constantinople and Byzantium and Alexander the Great. For a while I actually forgot, as our conversation covered the events of the wider world we all shared, about the difference that segregated the three of us into our own secret circle.

My companions and I parted in Grand Central Station with tentative plans to meet over the weekend. Lining up with the other businessmen at the taxi stand, I reached into my pocket for the last of the Colonel's cash. The cab whisked me down to Greenwich Village where I was asleep in my own bed before midnight.

When the Colonel arrived at the brewery Thursday morning I was at my desk, sorting through my scribbled notes. He gestured for me to follow him into his office, eager to hear the results of my research on Harry Frazee. Miss Grunwald's remark about supposing we'd be wanting coffee was meant to be cutting, but the Colonel simply said that would be appreciated.

I summed things up as succinctly as I could. Whereas the Colonel had always been a competitive sportsman (he'd once sailed a yacht fitted with metal runners over the frozen Hudson in a race against one of Vanderbilt's locomotives along the bank), Harry Frazee was an entertainer. To Frazee, the entire baseball enterprise was more about filling seats than winning games. He considered Fenway Park equivalent to an outdoor music hall, viewed the players as performers rather than athletes, and saw Babe Ruth as a prima donna who thought the entire production revolved around him.

After a brief interruption as Miss Grunwald precariously delivered our coffee, I concluded, "Of course, it's because of Babe Ruth that the Red Sox are a winning team, and winning teams fill ballparks, but there's a great deal of speculation in the Boston press that he's becoming more trouble, and costing more money, than Frazee thinks he's worth."

"He'll cause me just as much trouble if I can get him, if not more," the Colonel said. "New York is a bigger stage for an ego like Ruth's to play on. But that's the difference between me and Frazee. Any trouble Ruth brings with him will be worth it if he can turn my boys into champions. I'd love to put the Giants in their place, and the Dodgers, too. Frazee lacks the vision, Kramer. If we can put a winning team in a modern stadium in this city, the Yankees will outsell every other enterprise in the league. They won't be able to touch us." He smiled as an idea occurred to him. "Can you imagine if we were allowed to sell beer at the games? Why, I'd have myself a monopoly."

"I suppose it will be a matter of finding the point at which what Frazee can get for Babe Ruth outweighs what he'll lose by letting him go."

"You've given me plenty to think about, Kramer." We reviewed his schedule for the day, then he asked, "What do you hear from Helen?"

"I spoke with her on Monday. It seems the Playhouse was even more disorganized than she realized. I was thinking of stopping by after work to see the progress she's made."

"You'll have to leave early, then. Don't you have an appointment with that orphanage fellow tonight?"

"That's right." It amused us both that the Colonel was keeping my schedule for a change. "Mr. Stern promised to show me the plans for the new property."

"Let's hope they're further along than you thought." He took a peppermint from the onyx jar and popped it into his mouth, then stood and walked me out, his hand on my shoulder. "You've done good work this week, Kramer. Take tomorrow off, why don't you. I'll be out of the office in the morning on some real estate business, then I'm taking Mother up to Rhinecliff for the weekend. I'll see you back here on Monday."

"Yes, sir, thank you."

He told Miss Grunwald he was ready for her. She followed him back into his office, turning to shoot me an evil glance. The old order had been overturned, I realized. Whatever grudging acceptance Miss Grunwald had developed for me would be replaced now with antipathy. I gave it no mind. It was the Colonel's esteem I coveted, not hers. I settled myself behind my desk, still glowing from his brusque praise.

CHAPTER 15

I stood in the center of Richard Martin's office and slowly turned a complete circle, admiring the results of my work over the past three days. The mahogany desktop was polished, the white marble floor was a revelation, and even the Edison bulb burned brighter, now that its glass globe had been washed. I'd relocated the time card rack backstage and relegated the collection of *Playbills* to a high shelf. The posters that had once obscured the walls were neatly rolled, tied with twine, and consigned to a storage closet. I'd sorted the bills and receipts into labeled folders in the filing cabinet and boxed the faded clippings and out-of-date paperwork for Richard to some-day sift through. The new corkboard dis-played an orderly array of postcards and production notes, each pin a silver dot. The only items on the desktop now were a cup of pencils with points sharp as knitting needles, the telephone, and the ledger, which I still hadn't figured out.

I imagined Richard's amazement on his return from Montauk. As if rehearsing in the absence of a scene partner, I gave him a tour of the office, narrating aloud as I pulled open drawers with fluid gestures. Then the telephone rang, startling me back to reality. I was dismayed to hear the banker's nervous voice on the other end of the line warning me that our account balance had sunk alarmingly low after a series of checks had been presented for payment that morning. Realizing those must be the missing checks, I dutifully wrote down the information the banker related to me, then entered the check numbers and amounts into the ledger. Running my finger down the column of sums, I was ashamed to realize that the check I'd written to the stationery store would practically empty the account once it cleared. I told myself I'd had no way of knowing. It was Richard's faulty bookkeeping that had gotten the Olde Playhouse so close to insolvency, not a filing cabinet and a corkboard. Still, the pride with which I'd imagined presenting my accomplishments dissipated.

"There's nothing I can do about it now," I said to no one. Besides, I reminded myself, once Harrison's new play opened next week, sales were sure to replenish our coffers. I went out and settled myself on the stool behind the ticket window and tried to slide open the drawer below the counter. It stuck. I gave it a hard tug, releasing an explosion of stubs that I scrambled after on my hands and knees. I tried to sort them out, but Richard's system for keeping track of which seats were sold for which performance baffled me completely. If it had been up to me, ticket sales would be organized in an entirely different way. But it wasn't, so I spent the next few hours bundling old stubs and preparing new tickets for the upcoming production.

The quiet of the afternoon was interrupted by a messenger delivering a frantic note from Harrison. He was insisting that I come up with the money for a long list of demands, most of them intended to enhance Jessica's role. She must not be carrying the part on her own, I thought, if Harrison wanted to include a dog in the show. Not only was he asking for an animal with stage experience accompanied by a trainer, he also wanted an elaborate bouquet of fresh flowers (replaced daily), an extra stagehand (they already had two), and a new change of costume for Jessica (whose character, he claimed, would never wear the same dress to dinner as during the day). I sent the messenger away without a reply so I could take my time composing a letter explaining that the finances of the Olde Playhouse were too precarious for me to spend the money.

Writing to Harrison, however, put me in a confessional mood. It's such an intimate act, writing a letter, the soft tip of graphite looping across the surface of the paper as secrets and feelings are shaped into words. I found myself composing a very different letter in which I revealed to Harrison the ordeal he had put me through. When my vision blurred, I was careful not to let my tears fall upon the foolscap. Pent-up sentences spilled for three pages until I finally rested my cramped hand.

Blotting my eyes and stretching my fingers, I glanced over the letter, knowing I'd never give it to him. Harrison believed in freedom, in passion unencumbered by convention. He would see my words as an accusation meant to trap him into some obligation. I'd read enough novels in which the woman schemes to catch the man; I was unwilling to play my part in a plot that invariably ended in misery. Better to carry my secret with dignity, I decided, than to let its revelation reduce me to melodrama. I tore the paper into strips, crushed the strips into a tight ball, and tossed the ball into the wastebasket. Then I thought of the custodian. I retrieved the ball of paper and shoved it into the pocket of my skirt where it pressed against my thigh. With a deep breath, I took a fresh sheet of foolscap and started again, explaining plainly to Harrison why the Olde Playhouse could not afford to meet his demands. I had just finished when I heard someone calling for me across the lobby.

"Helen, are you here?"

Though I'd spoken to Albert only a handful of times, already my ear was attuned to the timbre of his voice. I emerged with an outstretched hand, but as we met he drew me close for a kiss on the cheek, the European manners of his dancer friend apparently now a ritual between us. His lips, as they touched my skin, were wonderfully soft.

He stepped back and searched my face. "Are you feeling well, Helen?"

"Yes, of course." I brought my hands to my cheeks, realizing how blotched they must be from crying. "The dust gets in my eyes sometimes is all. How was your business trip?"

"Uneventful, just some research. The hotel was nice, though. Anyway, I've been wondering how you were managing, so I decided to come see for myself."

"Let me show you." Leading him to the office, I enjoyed acting out the scene I had rehearsed on my own to such an appreciative audience.

"It's miraculous, Helen. I can't believe what you've accomplished. I wouldn't have known where to begin, this place was such a disaster. The room itself seems twice as large."

"It is, actually. There were so many things piled on the floor I could hardly move. Now look." I sat down and, with a push of my heels, rolled the chair across the office, my arms outstretched. Albert laughed along with me, sharing my delight.

"Helen Winthrope!" Harrison's booming voice echoed across the lobby. I jumped out of the moving chair, losing my balance. I would have fallen if Albert hadn't caught me. I was still in his arms when Harrison's shadow preceded his appearance in the doorway. He was in a dangerous mood, I could tell. His hair, which needed cutting, was raked back from his forehead in a greasy mane, his smell as he waved his arms was pungent, and the black smudges under his eyes were so pronounced I suspected him of dramatizing his appearance with makeup.

"Joseph Harrison, this is Albert Kramer." I hoped the introduction would put Harrison on better behavior, but he dismissed Albert with an impatient nod then focused on me.

"Helen, I will not be snubbed by a substitute manager with no experience in production. It's all well and good you helping out while Richard is recuperating, but you have no right to ignore me. He made you a signatory on the Playhouse accounts for exactly this reason. None of my requests are more than fifty dollars taken separately. You could write the checks immediately." I had no time to ask how he knew so much about our finances before he waved a sheaf of notes in my face. "Here are the invoices from the dog trainer, the florist, the dressmaker, and, oh yes, this one is for an electrician. I want Jessica to be able to switch on the light beside her bed, not just simulate it with a spot, but the stage isn't wired properly. And I need you to hire an extra stagehand. In rehearsals, the hands we've got are too slow changing from the garden scene to the bedroom scene and back again."

My fingers worried the ball of paper in my pocket as I felt how easily the force of his personality could bring me again to tears. To resist him, I summoned the strength of Shakespeare's Portia. It was in this role that I faced him as dispassionately as I had once argued to spare a man's life. "I'm afraid it's impossible, Harrison. I can't spend money we don't have."

He waved his arm around the office. "You've had no trouble spending freely at the stationery store, I see. Richard always made the production the priority, not redecorating the office. Besides, I've already placed the orders. The Playhouse is obliged to pay."

I took a step back and bumped into Albert. I wanted to look at him to gauge his reaction, but I didn't dare take my eyes away from Harrison. "You placed the orders, not me. There's just not enough money. Unless you plan to pay them from your own pocket, you've got no choice but to cancel them. Now, the stagehands tell me if they add wheels to the bed they can move it more quickly. I'll have the flowers replaced every Friday for the run of the play, but not for every performance. And while a fine lady might dress for dinner, if Jessica changes her costume the audience might get confused and think it's another day, not the same evening."

"So you're a dramaturge now, too?"

"Perhaps you need one."

Harrison looked as if he'd forgotten his lines. His forehead wrinkled in thought. "Helen." He placed his hand heavily on my upper arm. "It's admirable what you're doing, truly it is. Allowing Richard this time to recuperate is a great service to us all. But I think you misunderstand your role. By taking his place, you should be guided by what he would have done. You know he always supported my artistic vision. He chose me to direct because he believes in my work. I know I'm not the easiest person to deal with." His hand slid up to my shoulder as he tightened his grip. "But it's only because I'm so passionate about my work, Helen."

It was embarrassing to be manhandled like this in front of Albert. I considered acquiescing to Harrison's demands just to bring the scene to a close, but then I felt Albert's palm on the small of my back, a light touch that reminded me I wasn't alone. In his gentle way, Albert gave me the strength I needed to shrug Harrison's hand off my shoulder. "I'm sorry, but it's impossible. What good would it do you, or the Playhouse, to pass off bad checks?"

"But, Helen, we open in a week. If we don't start rehearsing with the dog tonight there won't be time to bring it into the show."

"No dog, then. Perhaps your society lady prefers cats? I can get one of those off the street for free."

"Helen, be serious." He ran his hands through his hair. "Okay, no dog. But Jessica can't get into character without the evening dress."

"You cast her, Harrison. If she can't carry the part without it, you'll have to buy the dress yourself." Or look in your closet, I thought, certain some woman must have once left a perfectly good dress behind.

He sighed. I could see he was realizing he wouldn't get his way and was becoming bored by our conversation. "Will you stay for rehearsals tonight at least?"

"Perhaps." I turned to face Albert, his hand sliding around my waist. "Would you like to watch the rehearsal with me?"

"I'm sorry, Helen, I can't tonight. I have that meeting with Mr. Stern from the orphanage."

"Are you going to see the elusive plans at last?"

"Exactly." Albert addressed his next remark more to Harrison than to me. "I'm free Friday night. I could watch the rehearsal with you then."

"Good." I turned back at Harrison. "Tomorrow night, okay?"

I'd never seen him so deflated. "Thanks, Helen. There are a few moments I just can't seem to get right." He looked at me as if finally seeing me clearly. "I'd appreciate your thoughts. You always had such good instincts."

I couldn't help being flattered by his compliment. "Of course. Tomorrow night, then. You'd better get cleaned up before the cast arrives."

Harrison looked around as if getting his bearings. Without so much as a good-bye, he headed for the dressing rooms.

"So that's the famous Joseph Harrison," Albert said. "I've heard he was temperamental. You're a brave woman to stand up to him like that. I don't expect many do."

"No, they don't. I should know." I was afraid for a moment I'd said too much, but Albert didn't seem to notice.

"Next time you need a dog, I'll ask the Colonel to lend you one of his Saint Bernards."

I laughed at the notion. "I doubt that's what Harrison had in mind for a society lady's pet. Thanks for saying you'll come tomorrow, Albert. Are you sure you don't have other plans?"

"Maybe later on, but I couldn't very well let you face him alone." He checked his wristwatch. "I better get going or I'll be late for Mr. Stern."

"Give me a second, I'll walk out with you." I got my pocketbook and locked the office behind me. At the corner, I turned up my cheek for Albert's kiss as we parted ways. I watched him walk toward Ninth Avenue to catch the El while I stayed to wait for the streetcar, the shape of his back already dear to me.

CHAPTER 16

Helen's argument with Joseph Harrison kept me at the Playhouse longer than I intended, but I couldn't very well leave her alone with the man. When I placed my hand on her back, I felt not only the strength of her spine but also the tremor of her nerves. It didn't come naturally to her, it seemed, that show of strength, but I admired how well she pulled it off.

Hustling uptown from the Playhouse, I was sorry I'd let my attraction to Felix Stern sway me into agreeing to see the plans for the new orphanage. When we'd gone up to Westchester to visit the land where they intended to build it, Felix had draped his arm over my shoulder, and for a thrilling moment I thought he was making a pass. Instead, he'd waved his other hand like a conjurer. "Can't you picture it, Mr. Kramer? All those children growing up in the fresh air, away from the city. I've dedicated myself to giving them that future." I told him I couldn't see anything without drawings. That's when he said he'd bring them home to show me. I could have turned him down, but the Colonel was trusting me to evaluate the orphanage's proposal and I wanted to be thorough. Unless they were much further along than the undeveloped land suggested, though, I doubted if, after tonight, I'd ever see Felix Stern again.

I arrived at his address, an imposing brownstone on the Upper West Side a block off Central Park. I thought at first it must be his family's residence, but climbing the stoop I saw a neat row of five bells, each beside a tidy name card, and realized the brownstone had been converted into apartments. I rang and waited for the door catch to click, but Felix, who'd been lurking in the vestibule, swung it open.

"Mr. Kramer, there you are. I was worried you'd forgotten all about me. Please come in." The brownstone was a beautiful home, the hallway richly trimmed in chestnut with glowing sconces along the papered walls. French doors opened into a large parlor that served as a common lounge for the tenants. A couple of men were relaxing on an old-fashioned settee, jackets open and drinks in hand, while a third was seated at an upright Steinway, playing a pretty tune. They waved at us and I hoped we'd join them, but Felix pulled me away. As he led me up a handsome staircase with a carved newel post and a plush runner, he explained there were two apartments on the second floor, two on the third, and one in the attic — all men.

"That's my landlady's rule as well. My rooming house isn't nearly as nice as this, though."

"Where's that?" he asked.

"On Washington Square Park."

"It's too Bohemian down there for me." Felix ushered me into his apartment. I found myself standing on a Persian carpet in a generous room with a pair of tall windows that shimmered in the sunset. A chandelier dangled from the high ceiling, and a gilt-framed mirror was mounted above the marble mantel. I remembered how impressed King had been at my shabby little lodging. What would he have said about this? I wondered. I turned my head to hide the blush that warmed my cheeks at the thought of him. Through a half-opened door I caught a glimpse of white tile.

"You have your own bathroom?"

"Don't you?"

"No, I share one with the other rooms on

my floor."

"We each have our own, and there's even a kitchenette." He showed me an alcove overlooking the garden that had been outfitted with a sink and an icebox and a gas ring.

"I wouldn't know how to cook for myself," I said.

"Neither do I, unless warming up chop suey counts as cooking. I had to buy an electric percolator just to make coffee. I thought you might be hungry after work, though, so I brought some things in." On a side table in the living room was a platter from the delicatessen: bread, smoked fish, pickles, and a dish of something that looked like liverwurst with hard-boiled eggs mixed into it. I asked him what it was. "Chopped chicken liver. Do you know it? It might be an acquired taste." He handed me a plate. "Please, help yourself. I have a bottle of Knickerbocker in the icebox for you."

"Thanks, but I don't care for beer. Silly, isn't it? The Colonel hasn't seemed to notice yet. Do you have any wine?"

He smacked his palm to his forehead, hard enough to leave a fleeting mark. "I should have thought of wine. Give me a minute."

I told him it didn't matter, but he dashed out of the apartment. I chose a few pickles and some bread to go along with the

216

chopped liver and sat on a Victorian sofa upholstered in velvet. The furnishings must have come with the place, I thought, balancing the plate on my knee.

Felix reappeared, panting, his fist wrapped around the neck of an open bottle of white wine, a gift from one of his neighbors. He found a glass and brought it to me, brimming. I sipped from the rim to keep it from spilling over. His eagerness to please would have been endearing if this were a date, but I figured he was just trying to impress me as Colonel Ruppert's secretary. I swallowed the wine, which was pleasantly sweet, and nodded toward an easel set up across the room. "Are those the plans you were telling me about?"

"Yes, they are. It was stupid of me to drag you out to Westchester before you knew what we were planning. Let me show you." There was a drape over the drawings and Felix fiddled with it nervously, like a child who has demanded that all the adults in a room pay attention to him and then gets shy under their collective scrutiny.

"Go ahead," I prodded. With a theatrical flourish, he revealed the first drawing. It was a watercolor showing the empty field I had seen but now dotted with cottages, all identical and shaded by imaginary trees that would need decades to reach the height of the artist's imagination. Felix explained that groups of children would live in the cottages, each staffed with a counselor and equipped with its own kitchen.

"It's a very nice rendering." I smeared a slice of pumpernickel with chopped liver. It was tasty, especially with a bite of pickle.

He showed the next drawing, another watercolor of the property but from a different angle, depicting a playground and a garden and even a baseball diamond. After he talked about the possibilities for outdoor exercise the new land would afford, I nodded and he showed a third drawing. Again a watercolor, though now closer to one of the cottages, showing children helping to hang laundry and shake out dusty rugs.

"Our aftercare program has been finding that the children who come out of the Home have a difficult time adjusting to life on a smaller scale. You remember the size of our kitchen, and those ovens? It wouldn't be safe to let children in there. But the result is they grow up never having prepared a meal or washed their own clothes. As a boy, I loved sitting at the kitchen table while my mother baked. On Friday mornings, I'd help her braid the challah bread." Felix looked wistfully at the rendering, as if he were watching the children go about their day. "There's so much they miss, growing up without a family. In the cottages, they'll have the chance to learn all these things."

"They're very nicely drawn, Mr. Stern. I'm able to picture it now, your vision for the property. You can show me the elevations next."

He looked at me blankly. "But these are all the plans we have."

Though Felix's devotion to the project was touching — I felt it myself, as he spoke — my suspicions about the property were now confirmed. Even if the trustees raised the money and began to build, years would pass while the Colonel waited for a thousand children to be resettled into cottages that existed now merely as paint on paper. It was a shame. In many ways, the Orphaned Hebrews Home was the perfect location for a stadium for the Yankees, but I'd have to tell the Colonel the situation was impossible.

I set aside the plate, brushing crumbs from my hands as I stood. "Mr. Stern, I'm afraid an artist's rendering is not the same as an engineering plan or an architectural elevation. These may be good for fundraising, but you must know you can't develop a site or estimate construction costs

219

based on a pretty picture. Thank you so much for the supper."

I held out my hand, but he refused to take it. "You can't leave yet," he stammered. "I can give you more details. I have notes."

"It wouldn't make any difference, I'm afraid. Based on what I've seen, your offer of the property is entirely premature." I'd spoken gently, but I might as well have slapped him, the way Felix's face darkened. Suddenly his arm jutted out and he knocked the easel over. I jumped back. "Watch out, you'll ruin the drawings."

But the easel was the least of it. For a moment he stood there, trembling like a fever victim. Then he strode to the wall and slammed his forehead against the plaster. This was more than a burst of emotion. Felix seemed motivated by an inner torment that went beyond the passions of his race. Though I couldn't imagine the Colonel doing business with such a man, I felt responsible for his distress and didn't want to leave him like that. My heart was in my throat as I went over to him. I put one hand on his shoulder. The other I placed on the back of his neck, which was hot as an empty kettle left on a lit gas ring. It burned my hand to touch it. "Stop that now. Come away from the wall."

I led him to the sofa where he sat, head back and eyes closed. I saw then the lump that was swelling on his forehead. "Stay there." I went to the kitchenette and picked at the block of ice until I had a pile of chips. Wrapping them in a dish towel, I knelt beside the sofa, pressing the makeshift ice pack to his brow. "Please don't be upset, Mr. Stern. Your proposal does have some strong merits, and the Colonel is very interested in your property. You're just too early in the planning stages for him to commit to anything. Maybe next year, after you've raised the money and started excavating the new site, we could meet again."

"I can't wait another year."

I shifted the ice pack to his neck to cool his blood. "A deal of this scale takes time. A year isn't so long in the scheme of things."

"Not for that." He reached up and covered my hand with his. His dark eyes opened and stared into mine. A second passed — I heard my wristwatch tick — then another, and another. Still he held my gaze. It really was extraordinary, how long his lashes were. He didn't have to say anything for me to know what had shifted between us, but he said it anyway. "I can't wait a year to see you again."

The lump on his forehead was beginning

to bruise. I leaned over and blew on it. "You could have told me, Felix. You didn't have to hurt yourself."

"But what if I was wrong about you? I'd have ruined our chances with Colonel Ruppert." He swallowed, his Adam's apple sliding up the tube of his throat. "I was afraid you'd be disgusted."

So that's how it was with Felix Stern; no wonder I hadn't cottoned on to his restrained attentions. "Why would you think that?"

"Because it's disgusting, isn't it, what we are?"

It was true most people thought of us that way, if they thought of us at all. It's how I'd felt about myself, too, after what that boy at boarding school made me do. But it was meeting other men like us, I told Felix, that made me see we were born this way. He agreed that yes, nature makes her mistakes: dwarfs and midgets, pinheaded children, women with beards, men without legs. When you go to see them at Coney Island, you don't blame the freaks for being the way they were, he said, but still you wanted to look away. But it wasn't like that with us, I argued. Sure, there were some pansies so feminine there was no hiding it, even some who could pass themselves off as women.

For most of us, though, the imbalance was internal. Inversion, the doctors called it. It was only because society reviled us, persecuted us, sent us to prison, that we learned to be ashamed of an abnormality over which we had no control.

"You should come down to Greenwich Village with me sometime and meet my friends. Paul is such a beauty, it's as much a part of him as his talent as a dancer. And Jack — he does a wonderful act as Jacqueline — he says he wouldn't give it up even if he could."

Felix shuddered. "Those painted pansies turn my stomach. You don't do anything like that, do you, Albert?"

His question made me think of the Colonel replacing my red bow tie. Maybe he had known what it said about me. If so, he didn't seem to care — as long as it didn't show. "I only do it a little, when I go out. It's not as if I pluck my eyebrows."

We conversed through the night, his leg draped over mine as we reclined on the sofa, shoes kicked off and collars unbuttoned. He told me he'd applied to Princeton, too, but said they'd reached their quota of Jews for that year. He'd ended up living at home and attending Columbia. That got us talking about our families. For me, the distance

223

between Pittsburgh and New York was a necessary buffer between the life I lived and the one my mother imagined for me. Felix, on the other hand, spent every weekend with his family: Sabbath dinner at his mother's table, Friday nights sleeping in his childhood bed, Saturday mornings walking to the synagogue. After services, his mother would introduce him to yet another young woman, baffled that her handsome son had not yet married and given her the grand-children she craved. He said the pressure after college had become too much and he'd suffered a nervous breakdown. When he recovered, he finally moved out on his own.

"The composer who lives upstairs is a friend of mine. He's queer, too. We all are, here. The landlady has no idea." It wasn't raucous and celebratory like Antonio's, but I could see that the brownstone did for Felix what the Village did for me — gave him a place to be himself.

When I said I'd heard of men like us mar-rying anyway, just to have a home and children, Felix swore he'd never do that to a woman. "And what if this thing is heredi-tary? It would be a sin to pass it along to a child. No, Albert, men like us aren't meant to breed."

It didn't make sense, what he was saying.

After all, we all were born to normal parents. The very nature of our abnormality prevented most of us from having children of our own, and yet we persisted. I reminded him that Dr. Havelock Ellis had proven conclusively that men like us could be found in every society, all through history. "When you think of Alexander the Great, Leonardo da Vinci, Michelangelo, Walt Whitman — well, you could almost be proud to be part of it."

Felix's mouth turned down as if he'd tasted poison. "I try to accept it, Albert, I do, but it's nothing to be proud of." For a Jew, he explained, a man didn't take pride in his own accomplishments, but in his contributions to their people. Unmarried and childless, a disappointment to his parents, he'd dedicated himself to improving life for the orphans.

We stayed awake until the sky turned pink and the trains started to run again. The Colonel had given me the day off, but Felix was expected at work that morning. "I'll be okay," he assured me as we stood by his door. "I often don't sleep." He buttoned my collar and straightened my jacket, holding on to the lapels, the weight of his clenched hands tilting me forward until our noses touched. From there it was only a little tilt

225

of my chin until our lips met. For all his talk of sin and shame, his kiss was deep and unrestrained. As frightened as I'd been by his excessive display of emotion, I found myself drawn to the promise of his passion.

The alarm clock rang, breaking our kiss. He ran into the bedroom to switch it off before it woke his neighbor. "Can I come see you, Albert, on Saturday? After sunset, once the Sabbath has ended." I gave him my address and said I'd be waiting. As I rode the train downtown, I thought how strange it was to think of a new day beginning with the sinking rather than the rising of the sun.

CHAPTER 17

I came down Friday morning to find Clarence perched on his stool in the lobby, head bent over a book. He blinked at me to refocus his vision. "You're pushing yourself too hard, Helen, I can see it in your face."

I knew I should have powdered my cheeks. "I didn't sleep well is all. What about you, studying in this light? You'll strain your eyes."

He closed the book and set it aside. "That hardly matters anymore. Today's my last exam. You're coming to the party, aren't you?"

Mr. and Mrs. Weldon had invited all the tenants to celebrate in the courtyard of our building tomorrow evening after the graduation ceremony. "I wouldn't miss it, you know that. I might invite Mr. Kramer, if you don't mind. You liked him, didn't you?"

"Albert Kramer?" Clarence frowned. "He seems nice enough. Better for you than that director, anyway. But I was hoping we'd have a minute to say our own good-byes."

I leaned against the wall and rested my foot on the rail of his stool. "So you've got your orders, then?" For the safety of the troops, the War Department kept the sailings such a secret that we New Yorkers never got the chance to see our soldiers off.

Clarence nodded. "You can't tell a soul, but there's a troop ship scheduled for dawn on Sunday. Colonel Hayward got me a berth." He curled his lip, showing the edge of his teeth. "I'm qualified now to be an officer, but it looks like I'll have to work my way across the ocean disguised as one of the galley crew." My baffled look prompted an impatient explanation. "The 369th crossed all together, but on this transport I'd be the only black man in a uniform. The ship's captain doesn't want any trouble."

"What kind of trouble?" I was thinking of his lectures on rights for Negroes. Surely he wouldn't drag a soap box on deck and start hectoring the soldiers? But no, I'd gotten it wrong.

"A bit of khaki cloth's no protection from a thousand white soldiers, Helen, and if there's one thing there's plenty of on a ship it's rope."

"Oh, Clarence." My sudden burst of tears

228

surprised us both. "Don't say such things."

He gave me his handkerchief. "Never mind, Helen. I'll be fine, I promise. Don't act like this in front of my mother, okay?"

"I won't." I returned the damp handkerchief. "You know we'll all be thinking of you every single day until you get home."

"Promise me you won't overwork yourself."

"We'll promise each other, how's that?" When we were kids, we used to spit and shake hands to formalize an agreement. For old time's sake, I blew some spittle into my palm. He did the same, keeping hold of my hand for a long while.

As I made my way to the Olde Playhouse, I tried to imagine how it would feel to be the only member of my race among a thousand black faces. There had been plenty of times I'd found myself the sole woman in masculine company — it sometimes seemed as if the sidewalks of New York were populated exclusively by men. But I'd never been in a classroom or an audience or a Sunday service where I was the only white person in sight. There were neighborhoods in Manhattan where such an experience could easily be had, but even before my illness my world was largely confined to the blocks between my apartment and the theater district. I hadn't been north of Central Park since Clarence and I had explored the city as kids — but then he'd been by my side, so I wouldn't have felt alone no matter what neighborhood we ventured into.

Arriving at the Olde Playhouse, it occurred to me how few colored people attended our performances. Did Richard Martin have a policy against them, I wondered, or did they simply have no interest in drama? But that couldn't be it, I thought. Ira Aldridge had been famous for playing every great dramatic role from Hamlet to Lear. Last summer, when Richard had staged Othello, I'd thought of the Moor's stage makeup as part of his costume, but now I imagined Clarence's reaction to seeing a white actor strut across the stage in blackface. It would be as dispiriting as it must have been for the women in the audience when all of Shakespeare's heroines had been portrayed by boys in frocks. But that had ended centuries ago, I reminded myself, while blackfaced performers could still be seen in every vaudeville act in the city.

I was writing advertising copy for the upcoming play when an insistent knock on the office door interrupted me. Assuming it was Harrison back with some new demand, I took a breath to compose myself before opening it. I was met not with Harrison's rank odor but with the clean smell of bleached cotton and peppermint. Jacob Ruppert stood there, bowler hat in hand. "I've been looking for you, Helen."

"Colonel Ruppert, come in." I stepped aside, baffled by his presence. It was a moment before I remembered my manners and offered him my seat.

"Kramer said the office was a disaster when you took over, yet you've accomplished all this in just a few days." His large head swiveled on his short neck. "Impressive. So tell me, Helen, do you like this job? You wouldn't rather be acting?"

I leaned back, my hands braced on the desk behind me. "I'd still love to act again someday, but I'm not ready yet. My personality hasn't quite caught up with my physical recovery, if that makes sense." I wasn't sure it did. I didn't even know what I meant, exactly.

"It does, yes. Acting is more than speaking lines. To properly occupy the stage requires a strong presence. You remember watching Ruth hit the other day? It wasn't just his arms that swung the bat, it was his whole personality. I used to see the same thing with my horses. The winning ones, they had an aura about them. They understood their worth. Out on the track, they shimmered." Ruppert's eyes settled on my face. "Do I understand you?"

I nodded, mesmerized. "Perfectly. I couldn't have explained it better myself."

"Well then," he said, getting up from the chair. I, too, stood up straight. "Why don't you give me a tour of this place, as long as I'm here?" He held out his elbow, as if offering to escort me to dinner. I saw no alternative but to take it, though doing so meant we had to edge our way awkwardly through the door.

"Well, this is the lobby." I had to laugh at the obviousness of my statement. Ruppert, too, smiled. "Let me take you backstage and show you how it all works."

"Did you know my father once owned an opera house?" Ruppert kept up a running commentary as I took him onto the stage, into the wings, and through the twisting hallways that led to dressing rooms, props, and costumes. Finally, I opened the loading dock door. The flood of sunlight caused us both to blink.

"It's a larger building than it seems, but it doesn't take full advantage of its site." He indicated the narrow service alley that ran alongside the building and out to the street.

"I didn't know this was part of the property."

Ruppert tilted his head up, assessing the height of the structure. "There are no upper floors for offices, either."

I realized what he was getting at. Theatergoers rarely noticed the additional floors above the blinking marquee, but many of the newer venues were built to generate income from rentals. "No, the Olde Playhouse is such an antique. That's what I love about it, really. It's so small, even from the back row you can hear every sigh and whisper. It's wonderful for Shakespeare. Richard — Mr. Martin, I mean — brings in a traveling company every summer. The tourists love it." Back inside, stagehands were putting the finishing touches on the new set ahead of that evening's rehearsal, while electricians adjusted lights up in the rigging. I noticed the carpenter attaching wheels to the bed and smiled to myself.

"How are ticket sales?" Ruppert asked, following me into the office.

"There are none yet. I'm still trying to get a handle on how they're organized, but I guess I'll muddle through until Richard comes back from Montauk."

"That's what I'm here to talk to you about. Sit down, Helen." He closed the door, shutting us into the small space. Ruppert, standing, placed his hat on the desk. "Richard Martin is not coming back."

"What do you mean, not coming back?" I knew Richard's health was precarious, but I couldn't understand how Ruppert would have gotten word of it if he'd taken a turn for the worse.

"Kramer told me the Playhouse was on the brink of disaster, so I had Ruppert Realty look into the situation. Did you know you've fallen behind on the taxes? One more missed payment and the city would have started procedures to seize the property."

I felt my face grow hot. "I had no idea. I saw the notice, but I assumed Richard took care of the taxes before he left."

"I'm sure you've done your best, Helen, but this place has been mismanaged for years. Your banker explained how precarious the accounts are. I had one of my bookkeepers go over the records. There seems to be potential for profit from ticket sales, but then the balance drains away during every production." I didn't have any background in business, but it did seem strange that the banker who handled the Playhouse's account would divulge so much information to Ruppert. "Tell me honestly, Helen. Do you think you could make a go of it here?

Your mother said you were enjoying the work."

"But I only stepped in until Richard — is he really not coming back?"

"No, he's not. I bought him out. I sent a representative from Ruppert Realty to Montauk to make him an offer. He signed the papers yesterday."

I was speechless. My mind flipped through questions like cards in the drawer of a library catalog. I finally chose one to pull out first. "So, do I work for you now, Colonel Ruppert?"

"That's what I'm offering, Helen. Would you like to manage the Playhouse and see if you can turn it around? I'll provide you with a salary, and assign one of my bookkeepers to assist you."

I tried to speak, but no words formed on my lips. His offer seemed too good to be true, like a trick or a trap. Then I remembered that porcelain doll he'd given me the Christmas after my father died. I hadn't realized its value when I thoughtlessly gave it away, but I'd recently seen its twin in an advertisement from Schwarz's Toy Bazaar. It was a Kestner doll; even on sale, it cost ten whole dollars.

Impatient for my answer, he spoke up. "If that isn't what you see yourself doing, don't feel obligated. I can easily sell the property to a developer for much more than I paid."

I placed my hand on his arm. "Wait, you're saying if I don't take over management of the Playhouse, you'll close it down?"

"A developer is more likely to knock it down, but yes, unless you want to take it over. I don't expect it to generate a profit even under the best management, but if you can prevent me from taking a loss, I'm offering to employ you."

I looked around the office I had so carefully organized. Would I be betraying Richard to accept? But no, he'd taken Ruppert's offer without so much as a telephone call to me. I had nothing to regret. The theater had always been what I wanted, and managing the Olde Playhouse would be a more important role than any I could hope to be cast in. It seemed my mother had been right to insist I go to that baseball game. But no, it was Albert who'd mentioned the Olde Playhouse to Ruppert. A week ago, I'd been an unemployed invalid. Now, thanks to Albert Kramer, I was being given the opportunity to manage a theater.

"I appreciate the offer, Colonel Ruppert, I do." Why was I hesitating? He'd already invested so much in me, what with the hospital bill and the nurse's salary. But that was just kindness. This was business. "I'm surprised you have that much faith in me."

"I expect you can do whatever you set your mind to, Helen. Weren't you a mechanic already when you were only a girl?"

"I can't believe you remember my daddy calling me his girl mechanic." I held out my hand. "I accept, Colonel Ruppert. Thank you so much for the chance."

He grasped my hand in both of his own. "All I expect is that you won't lose me money. I'll have Kramer act as liaison, since you two get along so well."

"We do. In fact, Albert's coming to the rehearsal tonight. I'll tell him all about it."

"Very good." We walked outside together. He turned to me under the marquee. "Helen, what do you know about Harry Frazee?"

"The producer? Oh, well, everyone on Broadway knows him."

"But what do you know of him personally?"

"Not much." I remembered something Rex had said, about Frazee being the owner of the Red Sox, and realized what Ruppert's motivation must be. "Is this about that player, Babe Ruth?"

"You've always been a sharp one, Helen.

Anything you can find out about Frazee could be helpful to me. Keep your ear to the ground and let me know if you hear anything." He sniffed the evening air. "Weather seems good, don't you think? I'm taking Mother up to Rhinecliff this afternoon to spend the weekend."

A pang of longing made me sigh. "I wonder what it would be like to see the town again."

"You've never been back?"

"My mother prefers to leave the past behind. I've never even visited my father's grave." I felt a sudden surge of guilt about doing business with Colonel Ruppert — after all, it had been my father's eagerness to attract the millionaire's money that led him to risk his life on that motorcycle.

"Your father was a fine man, Helen. You must miss him very much."

"I have so few memories of him anymore. I think you might have known him better than I did."

"I knew Jerry for many years. Before he got into engines, he built sulkies. Do you know what they are?" I had to shake my head no. "They're the carts we use in harness racing. We'd bring Jerry down to Linwood when we needed an extra driver on the practice track. He was such an eager

238

young man back then. Handsome, too. Before long, he was challenging me to races. That's how they met, your parents. When your mother was a maid at Linwood, she'd come stand at the rail to watch us circle the track."

"I never knew that," I said, grateful for this picture of my parents I now had in my mind. I supposed I had nothing to feel guilty about after all. Trotter against trotter, motorcycle against Roadster — the competition between Ruppert and my father dated back to before I was born.

"Jerry Winthrope was my friend, but you were his daughter, Helen. You knew the best of him." He cleared his throat. "I almost forgot. Richard Martin told my man you hadn't been paid yet." He reached into his pocket, withdrew his billfold, and handed me a fifty-dollar Federal Reserve note. I wondered if he always carried that much cash or if he'd brought it for this very purpose. "Consider this a signing bonus. I'll instruct the bookkeeper that you're to earn twenty-five dollars a week, plus expenses."

I took the note from his hand, entranced by that image on the back of a woman rising like a goddess from the waters of the Panama Canal. As a bonus it was generous, but the salary he proposed was less than I'd been making as an actress — when I was working, that is. This would be a steady salary, but I'd have to keep living at home if I ever hoped to pay my mother back. "Thank you, Colonel Ruppert, for everything."

"Let's not be so formal, Helen. Why don't you call me Jake? Your mother does."

"In that case —" I held out my hand, which he again took in both of his own. "Thank you, Jake."

Schultz, having spotted us standing under the marquee, came motoring up from his parking place.

"Kramer will handle the details. Good luck to you, dear."

I watched the limousine disappear down the block, disoriented by the sudden change in my fortunes. For a while I wandered through the Olde Playhouse, getting used to the idea that I was now in charge. In which case, I thought, I would reorganize the ticketing system according to my own plan. But first I had to get the advertising copy to the newspaper. I added the telephone number of the Playhouse to the ad, an innovation I'd been thinking of suggesting to Richard, so people could call ahead to reserve their tickets.

Albert would be so happy for me when I told him about my new position. I'd been thinking an invitation to Clarence's graduation party would make a good excuse to see him again, except from here on out, I wouldn't need excuses. We'd see each other often, now that Colonel Ruppert — Jake, I reminded myself to think of him — had designated Albert to be my liaison. I liked the taste of the word on my tongue. I repeated it throughout the afternoon as I counted down the hours until the rehearsal.

CHAPTER 18

"I'm so sorry I'm late, Helen. Have I missed any of the rehearsal?" I snatched off my hat and kissed her cheek.

"Not yet, no, but I was starting to worry."

"Did you ever have one of those days where you just couldn't get a grip on the clock? The hours seem to be creeping by and then, all of a sudden, there's no time to spare." It was close enough to the truth, which was that, after staying up all night with Felix, I'd slept right through the afternoon. I woke up that evening confused even as to what day it was until I looked at the clock and jumped out of bed.

Helen placed her hand on my chest. "Calm down, Albert, it's fine." She was hoping we'd have a chance to talk first, she said, but just then one of the stagehands came to tell us the rehearsal was about to start. "Let's go in, Albert. We'll talk afterward."

The seats in the Olde Playhouse were as

uncomfortable as they were cramped. The play was very serious with lots of long speeches and my thoughts often wandered back to Felix as the actors and actresses intoned their lines. After spending the Sabbath in the bosom of his family, would he have the courage to come see me as he'd promised? Though we shared the same affliction, he was tormented by it in a way none of my friends seemed to be. I worried Helen would notice my inattention, but her eyes were fixed on the stage, especially whenever Joseph Harrison strode on from the wings to bellow a direction. At one point, he took Jessica Kingston by the arm in the middle of a soliloquy and dragged her closer to the audience, instructing her to try it again from there.

"And don't stand full front, give it a left quarter turn." He jumped down from the stage (for a big man he was surprisingly agile) and dropped into the seat beside Helen. "Tell me if you think this staging works," he said, stretching his arm behind her shoulders.

After witnessing their argument yesterday, I expected Helen to pull away. Instead, she seemed to relax back into his embrace. It made sense, I supposed. Joseph Harrison did exude a brutish charm. I felt it myself as his fingers accidentally brushed the fabric of my jacket. Still, I resented his sense of entitlement. Why should he assume I was there as Helen's friend instead of as her date?

The play seemed to last forever. Bored, my thoughts turned to food. Except for an apple I'd grabbed from the bowl in my room and a pretzel I'd gotten from a vendor in Washington Square, I hadn't eaten since the middle of last night. The memory of chopped liver on pumpernickel flooded my mouth with saliva.

When the rehearsal finally ended, Jessica Kingston addressed her director from the stage. "Aren't you coming, Harrison?" He told her to go ahead without him, that he'd catch up later. I watched Jessica stomp off into the wings, her hands balled into frustrated fists, and realized Harrison must be sleeping with her.

Turning in his seat (no small task for a man of his size), he thanked Helen for sitting through the rehearsal with him. "I was glad to, Harrison. It's going to be a wonderful success, I'm sure of it."

"One can only hope." He dropped a hand on her knee. "It should have been you up there, Helen."

Whether out of pride or protectiveness I

wasn't sure, but I stood and pulled Helen to her feet. "I telephoned ahead for a table at the restaurant." I made a show of looking at my watch. "We better get going or they'll give it to someone else."

"Oh, well then, let me get my pocketbook."

"But you can't leave," Harrison said, as if Helen and I were actors on his stage to be placed where he directed. "You saw how Jessica floundered through that soliloquy. I want to know what you think she should do."

"I'm sure you'll figure it out, Harrison." Helen started up the aisle beside me, then turned back. "The speech lasts too long for her to be onstage alone. You were right to think she needs a little dog that she can hold in her arms and act like she's talking to it."

"Then you'll pay for the trainer?"

Helen shook her head. "There's really no money. But listen. The core of her character is her inability to distinguish truth from fiction, right? That's why she believes the gardener instead of her own husband. What if her dog died years ago, but she had it stuffed and keeps it on her bed? That way, when she addresses herself to it the audience will have to wonder if she believes the poor thing is still alive."

Harrison grabbed her hand and brought it to his mouth in an exaggerated gesture. "That's brilliant. I'll have to add a line to the script, but yes, I think that's even better than a live animal. Thank you, Helen."

"You can thank me by making sure this play of yours turns a profit." She took my arm. "Let's go, Albert."

Once we were outside, I confessed that I didn't really have a reservation.

"But you are starving, aren't you?" Helen said. "I heard your stomach complaining through the entire rehearsal. Come on, I know a place." She led me to an Italian restaurant on Eighth Avenue. On the way, she asked if I'd go with her to Clarence Weldon's graduation party the next evening. I turned her down, saying a college friend from out of town was staying with me Saturday night. I hoped there was some truth to my lie and that Felix Stern really would show up at my door.

At the restaurant, the maître d' assumed we were a couple and led us to a quiet table in a dark corner. "I hope I did the right thing, Helen, rescuing you from Joseph Harrison."

"Is that what you were doing? I can take care of myself, Albert, but I'm glad you suggested dinner. We have business to discuss."

"What business?" A violinist sidled up to us and started sawing away at a Chopin nocturne. We listened politely for a minute before I gave him a quarter and waved him off. That's when Helen surprised me with her news about the Colonel's purchase of the Olde Playhouse and his offer to make her the manager. I'd had no idea that was in the works. "Congratulations, Helen. I'm happy for you."

"I hope you don't mind, but Jake wants you to help me with the business end of things. He said you'd be my liaison." A waiter brought out a plate of antipasto and filled our glasses with Chianti. I ordered a lamb chop with buttered beets, eagerly anticipating a meal superior to anything I could get at Antonio's.

"I suppose the Colonel will tell me all about it on Monday." Tamping down a sense of betrayal at having been kept in the dark, I lifted my glass and offered a toast. "To your new career, Helen."

"A career girl?" Paul said when I caught up with him at Antonio's later that night for Jack's show. "You better watch yourself with her, Prince Albert."

"But won't that make us perfect for each other? From what I read in the paper,

247

women like her aren't looking to catch a husband. They just want a man to take them out for dinner. Anyway, I like Helen. Why shouldn't we be friends?"

"Don't you know that saying? *The Bachelor Girl life is one sweet song, providing it doesn't last too long.* Believe me, women all want to get married sooner or later." He pointed at Edith whispering to Toni. "See, even the lesbians want to marry each other."

It was nearing midnight and the place was packed. If my Boston friends from the train came by, I never saw them. A group of uptown swells on a slumming trip through the Village had taken over half the tables. The more they drank the louder they got until I was afraid they'd drown Jack out. I shouldn't have worried. In character as Jacqueline, he came strutting down from that little stage and shushed the loudest of the group without losing a word of the song. When the guy's friends laughed at him for being shamed by a pansy, he jumped up from his seat and threw an unsteady punch. Jack reached out and caught the guy's fist in his lumberjack hand and forced him back into his chair. "That'll teach you to insult a lady, sonny boy," he said, dropping his voice down to a masculine register before spinning around, squealing like a girl, and sashaying back to the piano. The place broke into such wild applause even the guy who'd been belligerent got up and took a bow.

"By the way, Albert," Paul said, "let me give you my new address." I assumed he'd gotten behind on his rent and been kicked out of his measly garret. Anticipating another address just as dodgy, I raised my eyebrows when he slid a card across the table on which he'd scrawled a house number on Waverly Place. Turned out, his benefactor had arranged the move. "He can't stand coming up to my shabby room, and he doesn't like the idea of running into neighbors in the stairwell, so he bought this place — just wrote out a check and signed the deed. It's a narrow old town house, but he's having it fixed up with steam heat and he's put me in charge of furnishing it. It's still a wreck, but we're inviting Jack and some people up for drinks tomorrow to celebrate. You'll come, won't you? But don't bring that girl."

If I brought anyone, it would be Felix. I imagined he was asleep by now in the narrow bed of his childhood, the smell of roasted chicken and candle wax lingering in his hair from his family's Sabbath dinner. Paul would have welcomed him, of course, but after what Felix had said about pansies,

I didn't think it was the kind of party he'd want to attend. I made an excuse about having work to do and left it up in the air.

Sleeping all day had transformed me into a nocturnal animal. After Antonio's closed, I wandered down to Corlears Hook Park to watch the Saturday morning sun come up over the Navy Yard across the river. Seeing the troop ships at anchor turned my thoughts to King. It had been a week since he'd shipped out. They must have disembarked in France by now, those stiff boots of his tearing up his blistered heel as he marched toward the front. A pang of worry pierced my ribs and made it hard to breathe.

I decided it was time to go home when a drunken sailor tried to lure me into the bushes. Crawling into bed, I pictured Felix seated with the men at the synagogue, a skullcap pinned to his hair. As I punched my pillow, I wondered if he'd pray (as I once did) for God to cure him of our shared affliction. I'd given up asking for divine favors back in boarding school, but perhaps Felix still believed such grace was possible. To be a husband, to father children: our strange desires did not divorce us from these common longings.

I slept fitfully through the day. That evening, I met up with some friends at the

Life Cafeteria for a meal that was both supper and breakfast. When the sun went down and the streetlamps came on and still there was no knock on my door, I shut my curtains and figured Felix's prayers had been answered.

Then the landlady called up to say I had a visitor. There he was, Felix Stern, standing tall and nervous in the hallway. He came in. I shut the door. I took his hat and jacket and hung them on the rack. We were awkward for a moment, mumbling words of no consequence. Then he stepped forward and put his mouth on mine. I unfastened his collar, unbuttoned his shirt, unbuckled his belt, untied his shoes. As we fell into bed, it soon became apparent that the excessive passion I'd witnessed at his apartment carried over into his lovemaking. I sent up my own little prayer, thanking God for leaving the field uncontested.

Around midnight we locked ourselves in the common bathroom and filled the tub. I poured water over his hair to rinse out the soap. The lump on his forehead had gone down since Thursday night, but I imagined his mother fussing over it. I felt a pang of jealousy as I pictured her lips on his skin. "So, every week you disappear for an entire day?"

"Every week, yes, but look at it this way, Albert. You'll always have Friday nights to spend as you please. That's the advantage of being with a Jew."

Being with. Those were the words he used. It was a bold assumption after such a short time, but one I welcomed. It made the coming summer shimmer for me, the notion that Felix and I would be with each other, even on the nights we spent apart.

CHAPTER 19

Though the heat of July had lifted, Manhattan had a way of making even the most tolerable of August afternoons uncomfortable. I fanned myself with a *Playbill* while I paced the lobby of the Olde Playhouse, listening to the click and grind of the adding machine from the office. Finally, the sound ceased. I leaned through the doorway. "Don't keep me in suspense, Miss Johnson. What's the verdict?"

"Do you want the good news, or the bad news?" the bookkeeper said, removing her horn-rimmed glasses. Though a young woman, Bernice Johnson favored old-fashioned outfits, from high-collared shirtwaists that covered her neck to long skirts that hid all but the toes of her shoes. As if to add to the effect, she wore her black hair in a bun from which a few tightly curled strands escaped at the nape of her neck. She reminded me of when ingénues play matronly roles — the costume, the posture, even the voice could all be right for the part, but still the pretty face undermined the act.

I pushed aside the ledger so I could sit on the desk, my feet swinging. "Let's get the bad news over with."

"You were hoping to replace the seats before the opening of the next production, but I'm afraid there's not enough surplus in the account to complete the project."

"Oh no." We were set to open the fall season with an original drama about a returning soldier confronting infidelity on the home front. Harrison's play had run through June, followed by the Shakespeare troupe Richard had scheduled for July and August, so booking this new production had been my first big decision as manager. I'd had a difficult time convincing the playwright, who'd hoped his Broadway debut would be closer to Times Square, to stage it at the Olde Playhouse. It was my promise of improvements — replacing the seats and the spotlights, installing new rigging for the backdrops — that had clinched the deal. When I heard of a theater downtown that was closing, I'd negotiated a good price for their seats which, though well used, were decades newer than ours. But I still needed to have them installed, and here was Miss

Johnson telling me we didn't have enough to pay the workers. I was sure the new play would bring us acclaim, but I worried my artistic ambitions as producer had compromised my financial obligations as theater manager. I pinched the bridge of my nose, understanding now the pressures Richard Martin had been under. "You said there was good news?"

"I did. As of today, the Olde Playhouse is officially in the black."

"Thank goodness for the summer Shakespeare season; it always saves us." The troupe, which had come in from Peoria, was so impressed to be in New York they never complained about the shabbiness of the house. I'd told their director to stage only comedies, fearing that seeing Henry storm Agincourt would make the audience worry about our boys in France.

"You were right, Miss Winthrope. *A Midsummer Night's Dream* is sold out for the final performances this weekend. After all the expenses, you've realized a modest profit."

"But not enough to finish the improvements I promised. What am I going to do, Miss Johnson?"

She looked at me, amused by the question. "Why not ask Colonel Ruppert for the money? After all, it would be an investment in his own property."

I wasn't sure how much more I could ask of Jake. I hadn't even seen him since he'd come to the Playhouse back in May to tell me he'd bought out Richard Martin. Everything went through Albert. "I'll ask Mr. Kramer what he thinks. Is there anything else?"

"No, that's all." She covered the adding machine and picked up her pocketbook. Miss Johnson's olive skin, along with her old-fashioned style, made me think she must be Italian. Perhaps her people had changed their name from Giovanni.

I walked out with her. "Have a nice Labor Day weekend, Miss Johnson."

"Same to you, Miss Winthrope, you and your young man."

"You mean Mr. Kramer? I wouldn't say he's my young man, exactly."

She frowned playfully, as at a child telling a silly falsehood. "If he's not your young man, then what is he?"

That's a good question, I thought. Albert and I had been seeing each other every Friday night for months now, but I still didn't know to what extent our weekly dinners were dates as opposed to business meetings. We always ended up discussing the management of the Playhouse or his work as Jake's secretary instead of more personal topics. I knew I should have talked less about myself and asked more about his ambitions and goals, but there was no one else who listened so attentively to the challenges I was facing at work. I did look forward to that moment at the end of every Friday night when, in the lobby of my apartment building, Albert placed his lips sweetly on my cheek. It was such a contrast to Harrison's boorishness that I wasn't sure what to make of it until I read Miss Rowland's advice column in the paper: *Kissing a girl,* she told young men, *without first telling her that you love her, is as small and mean as letting a salesman take you for a free ride in an automobile when you have no intention of buying it.* Albert was neither small nor mean, but he was no more ready to make a declaration of love than I was ready to receive one. It made no difference what label we attached to our relationship, I decided. He was my young man in all the ways that mattered to me.

Whatever our dates meant, though, I still needed to get ready for tonight's. I went backstage to find the wardrobe mistress. Racks of hanging costumes muffled my voice as I called for her. "Mrs. Harshman, are you in here?"

She emerged with a pincushion on her wrist and a measuring tape around her neck. I often wondered what mixing of the races had produced her freckled complexion, a bright bronze that lent a hint of red to her braided hair. Her talent and competence certainly gave the lie to those eugenicists who ranted against mongrelization. "Hello, Miss Winthrope. I was just about to leave for the day. I mended that rip in Oberon's trousers and reattached the tail to the donkey costume. I'll pack everything away after closing night. We're not likely to need Elizabethan gowns again until next summer, are we?"

"Maybe next summer the Shakespeare troupe will bring their own costumes."

"Oh, they did, Miss Winthrope, but a sadder assortment of shabby scraps you've never seen. You wouldn't have wanted them on your stage in those rags. That's why Mr. Martin always insisted we maintain our own wardrobe."

"It's lucky for me that we do. Do you have anything I could borrow for tonight?"

Her wrinkles deepened as she smiled. "That dress you ordered from Gimbels for the new play arrived this morning. I haven't even had time to sew the Playhouse's label into the seam."

I stepped behind a screen to change into the frock, a sheath of crimson satin that cost more than my weekly salary. Mrs. Harshman fussed with the hem as I admired myself in a mirror. "Sometimes I feel guilty for taking advantage of our wardrobe this way."

"You shouldn't, Miss Winthrope, not as hard as you work to keep us all in jobs. But speaking of guilty, did you hear?" She peeked her head into the hallway to be sure no one was listening. "That doctor whose name I gave you? He's been arrested."

A cramp clutched at my gut. "Will we be in trouble, do you think?"

"Oh, he's never heard of me, and you used a false name, didn't you? Then we can breathe easy."

Back when I realized the trouble I was in, I'd gone to Mrs. Harshman. As dresser to all the actresses, I figured she'd know better than anyone when someone's belly was beginning to swell. She'd passed along the name of a doctor who'd fixed things for another girl, apparently without injury. It was my bad luck that his skills had deserted him by the time he got to me. Relieved to know he wouldn't be damaging any other women, I thanked her for the dress and stepped into the hallway.

"Oh, wait a minute." She pinched my sleeve to hold me in place. "Remember when you asked me if I knew anything about Harry Frazee?"

I'd forgotten, actually. The day-to-day demands of being a theater manager had driven Jake's one request from my mind. "Have you heard something?"

Mrs. Harshman pulled me back into the stuffy wardrobe room and lowered her voice to a conspiratorial whisper. Discussing abortionists was one thing; gossip about one of Broadway's most revered producers was quite another. I listened, our heads bent together, as she told a secondhand tale. I thanked her for the intelligence, though I doubted the rumors she'd repeated would do Jake any good.

I found Albert waiting for me on a bench in the lobby, smoking a cigarette and reading the paper. In profile, his features were indistinct: his nose a bit too short to be aquiline, his chin too round to be considered strong. But when he turned toward me, his smile lit up a face in which every feature was perfectly proportioned. He said hello then looked me up and down. "Is that a new dress?"

"It is new, but it's not mine, I'm afraid. If

you promise not to tell, I'll make a confession. I borrowed it from wardrobe. Next time you see this dress it'll be on the stage."

He seemed amused. "Borrowing a dress hardly counts as a sin. Besides, I don't believe in any of that. Are you ready?"

"We can leave as soon as Richard gets here."

"How's he doing? It must be hard for him, demoted to ticket taker after owning the whole theater."

I'd thought so, too, when Richard Martin had come into the Olde Playhouse to offer his services. A month in Montauk had improved his health, he said. Now that he was relieved of the worries of management, all he wanted was to keep his toe in the theatrical world. How could I refuse? With Miss Johnson handling the books and Richard taking tickets, I saw now it took three people to do the job he had been doing by himself all those years. I was saying as much to Albert when Richard came in, his steps a bit tentative but his face cheerful, glasses swinging, as usual, from the chain around his neck.

The maître d' welcomed me and Albert like returning family, the little place on Eighth Avenue where we'd shared our first meal having become our regular spot. Once our antipasto had been served and the violinist had gone to serenade another table, I asked what he thought about the idea of Jake providing the money to pay for the installation of the new seats. He asked how much I'd need. I told him five hundred would cover it.

"That's not so bad, Helen. He just paid twice that for an autographed edition of Bret Harte novels. Seats for an entire theater ought to be worth as much as a set of books."

After our waiter had refilled the wine-glasses and gathered our antipasto plates, I shifted my chair closer to Albert's. "I heard something about Harry Frazee today."

"Really? I've been looking into the man for months. Tell me, what have you got?"

"Mrs. Frazee is suing him for divorce. She's asking for alimony and custody of their son."

Albert looked skeptical. "I haven't heard anything about this. When were the legal papers filed?"

"That's the thing, Albert. They haven't been filed yet, but I heard they were delivered to his office on Broadway a week ago."

"And you believe it?"

I dropped my voice to a whisper. "I heard it from the wardrobe mistress. Her cousin works for Elizabeth Nelson, the actress. Apparently, Frazee's been dating Elizabeth since she was a teenager."

"His philandering isn't exactly news." Albert propped his elbows on the table. "Why would his wife sue him for divorce now?"

"Frazee's notorious, has been for years, but now he's gone and bought Elizabeth a house out in Great Neck. I guess that was the final straw for Mrs. Frazee."

The waiter returned with fettuccini fragrant with basil and tomatoes, grating Parmesan over our plates before backing away. "If she's suing him for alimony she'll want a complete accounting of his finances," Albert said. "He won't like that. The Colonel says wealthy men are either worth more than they let on or only half as rich as they appear."

I twirled the pasta around my fork. "Do you think Jake will be interested?"

"I think he will, Helen. I'll tell him about it on Monday at the Polo Grounds."

Pleased with his reaction to my news, I lifted my wineglass. "Last game of the season, isn't it? Rex said they're ending early this year."

"The war's taken a toll on baseball as much as anything. Seems like half the players are off fighting in France, and half the spectators, too."

The juxtaposition of war and baseball jogged my memory. "Did you ever get a postcard from that soldier we met at the ballpark, what was his name?"

The wine made Albert's face flush. "King Arthur. No, I never did. Did you?"

I shook my head. "I hope he's okay."

"I haven't seen his name listed. What do you hear from Clarence Weldon?"

"He writes his mother that he's fine, but I worry he's lying to protect her." He was protecting me, too, I thought. In the letters he sent me, he wrote little about the fighting. Instead, he described the farms and fields of the French countryside, the taste of cheese cured in a cave, the wine that flowed like water. It was Clarence's father who told me the 369th had been attached to the French army because our own troops refused to fight beside Negro soldiers. "You'd think if there was one thing that would bring free men together, it would be battling a common enemy."

"The black man in America has been fighting for his rights here at home a lot longer than the United States has been fighting the Germans." Albert reminded me of Clarence when he talked like that, and no wonder — turned out he'd taken a subscription to *The Crisis.* The waiter exchanged our wineglasses for tiny cups of espresso as the violinist attempted a Vivaldi sonata. Our conversation turned to the progress of the amendment. Fourteen states had ratified so far and none had refused. Albert told me Jake was having his brewmasters perfect a beer low in alcohol in case Prohibition actually passed.

Out on the sidewalk, Albert checked his wristwatch. "Look how long we lingered over dinner. Do you mind if we skip the movie tonight? I promised to meet up with my friends downtown."

I'd been looking forward to seeing Douglas Fairbanks in *Bound in Morocco,* but what could I say? At least Albert didn't offer a false excuse. As he walked me home, my hand tucked into his elbow, he cleared his throat nervously. "There's something I've been meaning to tell you."

"What's that?" Anxiety sped up my heartbeat. Could he be breaking things off with me? But there was nothing to break off, I reminded myself. I hoped Jake wasn't transferring him to another account. Assigning Albert to be my liaison had been as much of a gift as making me manager of the Playhouse.

"I'm moving tomorrow."

"Moving? What happened, did you break the rules at your rooming house?"

"No, it's just too far away. You remember Felix Stern, from the orphanage?" I thought his business with Mr. Stern had come to a conclusion months ago, but no, Albert said, they'd stayed in touch. An apartment had opened up in his building, a brownstone on the Upper West Side across the park from the brewery. "Here, I wrote down my new telephone number for you."

I turned the card he'd given me over in my hand. "Perhaps I could help you decorate?"

"It comes furnished, but yes, I'll have you up. The tenants are all men, but women are welcome to visit."

"That'll be nice." I liked the idea of spending time at home with Albert. I couldn't very well have him over to my place, not with Rex and my mother there. Though I was chipping away at my debt to her, it would be a while yet before I could afford my own apartment like a true Bachelor Girl. But what then? I didn't have any domestic skills with which to impress him. I remembered Jake's quote about a man not needing a wife if he had a butler, a cook, and a laundress. I couldn't even do those things for myself, let alone for a husband. If anything, I was more likely to need a wife than to become one. The idea amused me until I remembered the most important way in which I'd be useless as a wife. Curiously, Jake hadn't thought to list children as a benefit of matrimony. I guessed he'd never wanted them. But Albert would, someday.

I was so lost in my thoughts I was surprised to look up and find we'd arrived at my building. Albert walked me into the lobby before kissing my cheek good night. "I'll let you know what the Colonel says about the money for the seats."

"Thank you, Albert. Oh, I almost forgot. I meant to invite you to the opening of our new play." The actors wanted to avoid the bad luck of Friday the thirteenth, I explained, so the opening was planned for the fourteenth of September.

He smiled, but there was a twist to his expression I couldn't quite place. "I can't on Saturday, Helen. Friday's our night. How about I come to the dress rehearsal instead?"

CHAPTER 20

I felt bad about turning down Helen's invitation, but my Saturday nights were sacred to Felix — not even a new song in Jack's show or a party at Paul's could tempt me away. It was our best night together, with all of Sunday morning to lounge before he went off to his trustees meeting at the orphanage. But that long commute between the brownstone and the Village stole hours that should have been ours. When the opportunity arose, Felix convinced me that taking an apartment in his building was a chance we couldn't afford to pass up. It was the attic apartment that had been vacated, but Felix had persuaded his neighbor on the second floor to move upstairs so I could have the one adjacent to his. We had found, in the back of Felix's bedroom closet, a door from before the house had been remodeled into rentals. It was sealed shut but we had plans to pry out the nails so we could come and go without ever stepping into the hallway. "As cozy as a married couple," Paul teased when I explained it to him. Beneath his sarcastic tone, I heard envy in his voice. Though his benefactor often stayed late into the night at their town house on Waverly Place, he always went home to his wife before morning.

Paul and Jack insisted on throwing me a going-away party. I told them not to be silly — I'd still be in Manhattan, after all — but they said once I left the Village it would never be the same. After dinner with Helen, I met up with everyone at Antonio's, where Toni stood me for drinks and Edith brought out a cake and Jacqueline serenaded me from the stage. Friday night turned into Saturday morning before Paul and Jack and I stumbled back to my room for a nightcap. They collapsed into the armchairs while I ended up backward in bed, my feet on the pillow. It was nearly noon before we rose reluctantly, hungover and fumbling for cigarettes.

It didn't take much of an effort to pack up my few things. Emptying my dresser drawers, I came across that button from King's uniform. I considered leaving it behind — such a silly little keepsake — but in the end I dropped it into the box that held my cuff links and tie clips, put the box in my trunk, and latched it shut.

A taxi driver helped me wrestle the trunk down Mrs. Santalucia's stairs and into the back of his cab. "Good luck to you, Mr. Kramer," she said, standing ready with a mop to clean out my room for the next tenant. I wondered if it would be as much of a refuge for him as it had been for me. It had seemed a solitary affliction I suffered until Greenwich Village showed me we were multitude. Living there made me part of a family whose kinship depended not on shared blood but on the mutual celebration of our secret selves. Living with Felix, I'd be trading the embrace of an entire community for the tight circle of one man's arms.

The cab started up Broadway. I covered my ears against the chaos through Times Square, my head throbbing with every screech of a streetcar and honk of a horn. When we pulled up to the brownstone, the driver whistled. "Moving up in the world, ain't you, mister?" We carried my trunk upstairs and I overtipped him, enjoying the sensation it gave me to be so free with a dollar.

I spent the afternoon settling in (books on shelves, suits on hangers) then joined the others downstairs for cocktails. There was Felix's friend the composer, who sat at the piano in the parlor whenever inspiration struck. The tenant who'd taken over the attic was a writer who made his living in advertising by day while pecking out poems on his typewriter at night. The longest resident was a Broadway character actor whose silk cravats and affected speech led the landlady to mistake him for a displaced English duke instead of an aging queen. It was he we had to thank for populating the building exclusively with queers, one tenant recommending the next until we inhabited all the apartments. The landlady, clueless, counted herself lucky to be renting to such a talented batch of bachelors.

Though I easily engaged in conversation with my new neighbors, I knew we'd never become as close as I was to my friends in the Village. Here I was welcomed more for Felix's sake than my own. Like him, they were intolerant of pansies and I had to be careful, as I relaxed with a cocktail, to keep my pinky finger from pointing to the sky.

I went upstairs to wait for the late summer sun to set. My apartment was similar to Felix's — same ornate moldings, same Victorian furniture, same elaborate chandelier — except that my windows faced the street instead of the garden. Despite the noise coming in through the open casements, I managed to doze off on the velvet sofa. It was dark when I felt the cold weight of steel against my collarbone. I opened my eyes to see Felix kneeling beside me, his face inches from mine, those lashes of his a mile long. He'd brought me a housewarming present: on my chest rested a hammer with which we'd soon pry open the door that separated us. His lips moved into a warm smile. "Welcome home, Albert." I reached to embrace him, the head of the hammer digging into my skin. I lifted it from my chest and set it on the floor as Felix sat back on his heels to pull off his jacket. Greedy for me after the hours apart, he stole the breath from my lungs with his kisses.

It was a novelty preparing a proper Sunday breakfast in my own apartment. Fortunately, the simple lessons I'd learned from my grandmother's cook came back to me and I managed a decent plate of fried eggs and tomatoes. Felix sat across from me, his dressing gown tied loosely over his pajamas, dipping buttered bread into runny yolks as I poured coffee from my new percolator. It occurred to me I hadn't enjoyed such a domestic moment since childhood. From

boarding school to college to Mrs. Santalucia's house, the rooms in which I slept had
always been separated from the dining halls
or cafeterias where I ate.

I cleared the breakfast dishes so Felix
could spread his note cards across the table.
"Are you still working on your presenta-
tion?" I asked, warming up his coffee.

"Just reviewing the numbers."

I planted a kiss on top of his head. "I'm
sure it will go well."

He caught my hand and held it. "Thanks
to you."

Back in May, I'd been honest with the
Colonel when I reported that the plans for
the new orphanage were premature, but I'd
propped up Felix's case by assuring him the
trustees were serious about selling. The
Colonel still wouldn't sign an option, but
he had hired a surveyor to make a prelimi-
nary report on the Orphaned Hebrews
Home. Though not a detailed plan, the
report gave the Colonel some numbers to
work with, and I'd passed along the figures
to Felix. At their meeting today, he'd be
proposing a capital campaign to fund construction of the new cottage homes. I
pictured him cajoling the trustees to approve his proposal, fueled by his fervor for
the project and backed with facts and

figures I'd provided. If anyone could spur them to open their wallets, it was Felix. Though I still had my doubts about the deal, I knew how much the Colonel wanted a stadium, and how much Felix wanted to give the children in the orphanage a better life. I told myself I was helping each of them achieve their ambitions by bridging the gap between them.

Felix gathered up his note cards into a neat stack. "What will you do with yourself all afternoon?"

"The weather's been so nice, I might go up to the High Bridge after I catch up on my reading. And don't forget we've got that concert tonight." Our resident composer was giving a recital and all the tenants were planning to attend, including the landlady, escorted by the actor.

"Oh, that's right. Well, at least we'll have Labor Day together."

"No, Felix, we won't, remember? The Colonel wants me with him at the Polo Grounds for the last game of the season. It's a doubleheader, so I don't know when I'll be back."

"But I wanted you all to myself for the day."

I knew how easily Felix's optimism could sink into angry frustration when things didn't go his way. I'd learned to think of his swiftly changing moods as the price I paid for his passion. Glancing at the clock, I went over to sit on his lap. "Don't sulk, Felix. You have me now. There's still time." I was gratified to see his expression change. He untied the belt of my dressing gown and slid his hands around my waist. Holding me tight, he gave my neck a love bite. I told him not to leave a mark but he didn't listen. By the time he left to attend his meeting, my neck was as bruised as an overripe fruit. I hoped I had a collar high enough to cover it.

Alone, I stretched out on the sofa with a new issue of *The Crisis*. Clarence Weldon had been right about how differently the news was reported in the black press. If not for my subscription, I never would have heard of that poor woman who was lynched in Georgia, her swinging body riddled with bullets, for no other reason than protesting the lynching of her own innocent husband. Shaking my head at the injustice of it all, I set aside the magazine and picked up the Sunday paper. I pored over the lists of soldiers missing or wounded, sick or dead, their names in tiny type filling entire columns in the *New York Times*. It was a habit I'd started after King shipped out. I'd developed a strange superstition that by looking for his name I could prevent it from appearing. That day proved the rule yet again. Wherever he was, King Arthur of Milwaukee, Wisconsin, wasn't on that list.

I took the subway up to 168th Street and strolled back and forth across the High Bridge, the wind ruffling my hair and cooling my skin. Leaning over the rail, I watched boats and barges disappear under the bridge's tall arches while trains snaked along the riverbanks. I gazed down at the Speedway and the Polo Grounds, both quiet on a Sunday. If the Colonel did build Yankee Stadium at the site of the orphanage, he'd be exchanging a view of the muddy Harlem River for a sweeping vista of the Hudson. Standing at the rail of the bridge, Manhattan spreading itself out before me, I felt myself at the fulcrum of the Colonel's ambitions. Even more than the stadium, though, the key to creating a winning team was acquiring Babe Ruth. I hoped the information Helen had given me at dinner on Friday would be useful. If anyone could figure a way to use Frazee's divorce as leverage to pry Babe Ruth away from Boston, it was the Colonel.

The stands at the Polo Grounds that Labor Day afternoon were as full as I'd seen them in months. If this many spectators had come out during the summer, the owners might have resisted the War Department's demand to end the season early. Instead, they'd welcomed the idea, pocketing the unpaid portion of their players' salaries and colluding not to poach one another's rosters. New York was out of contention for the pennant, so I assumed it was Boston the fans had come to see, Babe Ruth chief among them. I made my way down to the owner's box as the Yankees were rubbing the hump of their hunchbacked batboy for luck before taking to the field.

"There you are, Kramer." The Colonel had invited various dignitaries to sit in his box, including the Tammany candidate for mayor, John Hylan, and Al Smith, who had his sights set on being governor, but he'd saved the seat beside him for me. He gave me a once-over as I took it. "Given up on bow ties, I see."

I straightened my necktie and tugged at my collar, which was digging into the underside of my chin. *"Ich habe etwas über Harry Frazee gehört."* I kept my voice to a whisper, as much to hide the subject of my words as the language in which they were spoken.

"Tell me after the game." His gruff inflection did little to conceal his keen interest in whatever it was I'd heard about Harry Frazee, who was sitting in the visitor's box over third base, a very young woman in a very wide hat beside him. A moment later, however, the Colonel's eyes still on the field, he gave my knee a satisfied pat.

The Yankees evened the score at one apiece in the second inning and there it balanced, precariously, until the top of the sixth when the Red Sox batted in two more runs. The Yankees' pitcher held Babe Ruth to a single but angered the fans by hitting him twice with inside pitches. I hoped the youngsters in the stands couldn't hear Babe's curses. The Colonel was miserable until the Yankees got another run in the bottom of the eighth, putting them just one away from leveling the score. It was a run the Yankees never got.

It may have been his eagerness to hear my news, or his disgust over the loss, that prompted the Colonel to leave before the second game of the doubleheader. A marching band paraded onto the field as I followed him down to the dugout where he shook hands with his dispirited players. He told Slim Love he ought to be more careful pitching to Ruth, then clapped Huggins on the shoulder. "I'll see you in Shreveport in the spring," he told the wretched little man. "You've still got my confidence."

Out on the Speedway we found Schultz asleep in the Packard, a newspaper tented over his face. "Let the man rest," the Colonel said, gesturing me away with a nod of his head. "He's got a lot of driving ahead of him. Tell me what you heard."

"It was Helen who heard it, actually." I offered him a cigarette as we walked among the parked cars. He smoked thoughtfully as I summarized her story about Frazee's divorce.

The Colonel exhaled through pursed lips before responding. "Frazee would be a fool to sell Ruth if they win the World Series, but an alimony suit will put him in a tight spot. He'll be looking for money his wife can't get her hands on." He took off his hat and ran his fingers through his hair. "There are plenty of reasons to avoid marriage, Kramer, but none better than divorce. These men churn through wives, and what does it get them but ink in the papers? You remember the scandal when Jack Astor divorced Vince's mother and married that teenager?" I did. The girl was younger than Astor's own son, and already pregnant, if the rumors were true. The publicity drove the couple out of the country and right onto the deck of *Titanic*. "Such a tragedy. Jack was a friend of my father's, you know. My parents, now, that's what a marriage ought to be." He blew a smoke ring before dropping the cigarette to the ground and stepping on it with the toe of his polished shoe. "And now Frazee has gone and bought his mistress a house on Long Island. Good work, Kramer, bringing me something the papers haven't got a hold of yet."

"Like I said, sir, it was Helen who told me."

"Clever girl, isn't she? How's she doing with that theater of mine?"

I told him she had a play lined up for the new season that was sure to be a critical success. "The only problem she's having, sir, is with the Olde Playhouse itself. Those seats are so broken down, the audiences limp away with aching backs after every performance." I took a breath and forged ahead. "She already bought new seats — well, not new, they're used but in good shape — but she's short the cost of labor to get them installed."

The Colonel caught on that I wasn't just conveying news but making a pitch. "How much?"

"She says five hundred would cover it."

He frowned, and I feared he'd turn Helen

down. For a millionaire, he could be quite cheap — I'd seen him hold up a player's contract over a few hundred dollars. Instead he said, "You see a lot of the girl, don't you?"

I nodded, not sure how to characterize my evenings with Helen. I'd expected to be jealous of Felix's weekly Sabbath disappearance, but the moment he walked out the door each Friday afternoon my thoughts turned to Helen with happy anticipation of the hours I'd soon spend with her.

The Colonel put his hat back on. "Stop home with me, Kramer, and I'll write the check. Come on, let's wake up poor Schultz."

On our way down Seventh Avenue, the Colonel filled me in on his vacation plans, now that the baseball season was over. The new Railroad Administration had forbidden the use of private train cars during the war, but he couldn't accept the idea of making the trip up to Rhinecliff as a common passenger. "I'm having Schultz drive me up."

At the sound of his name, Schultz turned his head to address the Colonel. "I hear the Albany Post Road's paved the entire way now." Just then the Packard bounced over a pothole. "Shall I go through the park, sir? It's such a nice afternoon."

"No, Schultz, just get me home."

Sandwiched between the restrained white edifices of luxurious new apartment buildings, the Ruppert mansion jutted out from its stretch of Fifth Avenue as dark and jagged as a rotten tooth. A Victorian mess of porticos and pointed spires, its architecture and proportions were meant to proclaim its prominence, but its location at 93rd Street was purely practical. Old Jacob Ruppert, the Colonel's father, had only to walk a couple blocks to reach his brewery, source of all that wealth. Perhaps it comforted him, on summer nights when the breeze was right, to smell the malt as he slept.

Mr. Nakamura, the Colonel's butler, was waiting in the open door to take our hats. Entering the mansion was like stepping back in time. The craftsmanship was undeniable but the design was appalling, a mash-up of Gilded Age excess and Bavarian kitsch: leaded windows and heavy drapes, curtained archways and hanging tapestries, fireplaces flanked by carved satyrs. The Colonel invited me to have a beer with him, and I imagined myself in medieval Munich as we sat on wooden benches in the basement *bierstube.* The room was cooler than the beer, which was dark and yeasty. It was all I could do to choke down a pint.

"Another one?" he asked hopefully. When I declined, he looked longingly at the bottom of his empty glass. "Let's take care of that business, then." Compared to the *bierstube,* the Colonel's rooms upstairs were practically modern. The curtains had been removed from the north-facing windows, his shelves of leather-bound books were kept in perfect order, and his collection of antique Chinese vases was displayed in glass-fronted cabinets. Sitting at an incongruously dainty desk, he wrote out a check for five hundred dollars and handed it over as casually as a business card. "Don't deposit it. Give it to her yourself tomorrow after work."

"Yes, sir, I will."

"I'll call you at the office once I've arrived at Linwood. Stay by the telephone, Kramer."

Mr. Nakamura handed me my hat and showed me out of the mansion. "Have a pleasant evening, Mr. Kramer." Though he spoke English beautifully, his Japanese accent lent a musical lilt to my name. I wondered where the Colonel had acquired him.

I practically chained myself to my desk all the next day, not even daring to go out for lunch. Even so, the Colonel's call, when it came, took me by surprise. "Kramer, I want you to come up here tomorrow to see a property with me. Take the nine o'clock train."

"Yes, sir, of course."

"What did Helen say when you gave her the check?"

"I haven't gone to the Playhouse yet, I've been waiting for your call. I'm sure she'll be grateful."

"She grew up in Rhinecliff, did you know that? Her father's buried here." There was a pause on the line so long I wondered if he'd ended the call. "When you see her, ask her to come with you tomorrow. It will do her good to see the place again."

Chapter 21

I slid hangers along the rod in my closet. "Maybe I'll run out and get something new to wear up to Rhinecliff. Gimbels is still running their Labor Day sale."

"Wait a minute, Helen." My mother put her hand on my arm. "Tell me again, why did Jake invite you?"

"I think he just wants Albert to have company on the train tomorrow. I did find out something for him, though, about Harry Frazee."

"You were able to help him? That's good, Helen, good for you. You helped him, and then he invited you to Rhinecliff. You might even get to see Linwood." She took out the crepe de chine dress I'd worn to the ballet back in May and held it up. "You'll wear this."

"Isn't that too fancy for a day trip?"

"Not up at Linwood it isn't."

"Well, I guess you would know. Oh, and

that's not all." I paused for dramatic effect. "Albert talked Jake into giving me the money to install the seats at the Olde Playhouse."

She had a distracted expression, as if she were doing math in her head. "I wonder if you'll meet his mother."

"But Albert's from Pittsburgh."

"I mean Mrs. Ruppert, Jake's mother. His sisters might be there, too, and his nieces."

"I thought his sister died."

"Cornelia did, yes. I was working there then. The family was devastated. I meant Anna and Amanda." She looked at me, as if seeing me clearly for the first time that day. "We'll crimp your hair in the morning. Now, are you hungry? I made a pie."

"In this heat?"

"I hated to turn the oven on, but what else was I going to do with all the peaches? They were starting to bruise."

I followed her into the kitchen. In the sink was a pile of stones from the fruit. "Why are you washing the pits?"

"The War Department collects them to make gas masks." She shook her head as she lifted a slice of pie onto a plate. "Thank God Rex is too young for this terrible business. Poor Mrs. Weldon is beside herself with Clarence overseas. I can't imagine what those boys are going through. Lucky for you Mr. Kramer is unfit for service."

"Lucky for him, don't you mean," I said, the words muffled by the pie in my mouth. Meeting Albert had brought me luck, though. It may have been Jacob Ruppert who bought the Olde Playhouse and offered me a job, but it was Albert who'd set everything in motion, wittingly or not. That very afternoon he'd given me a check for five hundred dollars and an invitation to Rhinecliff. Tomorrow we'd spend the entire day together. I wondered if we'd have to stay overnight. What did they say about that inn at the center of town, that it was the oldest in America? Unless Jake offered us rooms at Linwood, though I doubted a woman whose mother had worked there as a housemaid would be invited to stay as a guest.

I was waiting under the clock at Grand Central Station next morning, worried we might miss the train, when Albert came running across the concourse clutching his straw boater in one hand and a satchel in the other. We hustled down to the platform, the train jolting forward the very moment we climbed aboard the New York Central. Breathing heavily, Albert dropped into his seat.

"You shouldn't run like that," I said, "not with your heart."

"I'm fine. Anyway, it's my fault for being late. I had trouble getting out of bed this morning." When the conductor came around for our tickets, he advised us that the dining car was open for breakfast. Albert said we'd take a table for two right away. "You haven't eaten, Helen, have you?"

Clearing my throat, I tasted the cold peach pie I'd had for breakfast and said I'd join him for coffee. I stood, my pocketbook rolling off my lap and onto the floor. Albert, swaying with the motion of the train, bent to retrieve it. Before he could straighten up, I noticed a bruise on his neck, above his collar and below his ear. I touched it with the tip of my finger. "Did you get a bee sting?"

He adjusted his collar. "Something like that."

Albert ordered the royal mushroom omelet and a pot of coffee, which he shared with me. As we left the city behind, the train seemed to be riding on water as it rolled along its tracks, level with the ferries and yachts plying the Hudson. It all looked new to me, though of course I must have seen it before. But no, I remembered, we'd taken a late train when we moved to Manhattan

288

after burying my father. I'd seen only my own sad reflection in the train's dark windows.

"You're sure you don't want some toast at least, Helen?"

I glanced around the dining car and was surprised to see it bustling with activity. "Maybe I'll try the date nut bread."

Albert divvied up the pages of the paper and we discussed the news of the day as we breakfasted. The Czechoslovaks had been recognized as their own nation, and we guessed at what the new country would be called. The Red Sox had arrived in Chicago and Albert predicted their victory over the Cubs in the World Series. I summarized an article about the slacker patrols that were rounding up draft-age men out for a night on the town. I was frightened for his sake, but Albert told me they weren't likely to look for slackers in the places he frequented. Before I could ask why not, he turned my attention to the casualty lists. We spent some solemn minutes squinting at the hundreds of names compressed into tiny type. It made me sad to imagine Mrs. Weldon searching for her son's name in the paper. It had been a while since I'd gotten a letter from France, but I kept my promise and acted brave whenever she delivered my laundry. "I don't see Clarence's name on my lists, thank goodness. How about yours?"

Albert shook his head. "No Clarence Weldon here. What about King Arthur?"

"He's not listed, either."

"So, both of our soldiers live to fight another day." He folded up the paper and signaled for the check.

Schultz was waiting with the limousine at the Rhinecliff station. The Colonel was busy at Linwood, he said, but he'd been instructed to drive us to the cemetery in town. I was touched that Jake remembered me saying I'd never visited my father's grave. At the entrance, we stopped by the flower cart so I could gather up an armload of chrysanthemums, for which Albert insisted on paying. Schultz stayed by the Packard as we wended our way past the hundred-year-old headstones of the town's Dutch and German founders. We finally located the simple granite marker, the letters of my father's name as crisp as the day they were chiseled, his dates of birth and death telling the story of a life cut short. The grass under our feet reached up to our ankles as we stood before the stone.

"Would you like to be alone, Helen?"

"No, Albert, please stay." I held on to his hand to steady myself as I knelt to place the

290

flowers. "Pretty soon I'll have been alive longer without him than I was with him. It was such a stupid accident, too, that's what's so tragic about it." I looked to him for commiseration, but his expression told me he didn't know what had happened. "Daddy was racing a motorcycle against Jake's Roadster when he hit a tree."

Albert nodded as if finally piecing together a puzzle. "The Colonel told me your father died in his arms."

"Really? I never knew that." I took a deep breath and let it out in a rush. "Oh, let's not be maudlin. Come on, I'll show you where I grew up."

Schultz drove us to the center of town and parked while we strolled around the block, stepping carefully down the uneven slate sidewalk. I stopped in front of a modest house off Market Street with a rambling barn behind it. I'd wondered if I would still recognize the place, but of course I knew it right away. The sense of nostalgia was so strong I was afraid my sadness might overwhelm me if I got too near. My hand slipped into Albert's again and held on tight. "That was my daddy's garage back there. He could fix anything. I helped him whenever he let me. He used to call me his girl mechanic."

"So you had your sights set on a career from childhood?"

"I suppose so. Mechanic, actress, manager — I guess I've had three careers already."

"You've got me beat. All I've ever been is a secretary."

I was lost in thought as we drove out of town, every street corner and storefront pricking at my memory. Childhood was a country from which I'd been forced to emigrate by the disaster of my father's death. I couldn't help but wonder what my life would have been like if we'd stayed. I'd be married by now, I supposed, with a little house and a couple of babies and a husband who worked at one of the estates. It was a pretty scene, but it seemed like a play in which no part was right for me. Instead of keeping house, I managed a theater. Instead of relying on one of the estates for an income, I was going to Linwood as a guest. Instead of a husband who laid bricks or trimmed trees, I was accompanied by a college graduate whose fingers had never been calloused from labor. I hadn't realized I was still holding Albert's hand until I thought about how soft it was.

The Packard swerved, knocking me from my reverie. We were traveling along a twisting road beneath an archway of overhanging trees. I wondered if this could be the road my father had been racing on. No one had ever told me exactly where he'd been killed. But who could I ask now? Not my mother; it would be cruel to stir up her grief. Not Jake, either — it would sound too much like an accusation. Besides, what would be the point? After seeing Daddy's headstone and our old house, I didn't need to stand on the spot where he died.

The road narrowed as we passed a series of iron gates set in stone pillars that discreetly hinted at the elegance of the hidden estates beyond. Schultz pulled through the gate for Linwood, the name of the property welded into the ironwork. The Packard crunched along a gravel drive hemmed by hemlocks for a full minute until a broad lawn opened out before us, revealing a turreted Queen Anne mansion wrapped by a wide porch, its cedar shakes painted bright yellow. Beyond the lawn and below the cliff was the river, as wide and enticing as the first time Henry Hudson's schooner cleaved its deep channel.

"I guess the Colonel isn't ready yet." Schultz switched off the engine and came around to open the door. "You might as well have a walk while we wait."

The lawn looked like an unpopulated

public park. The family must have been gathered at the luncheon table inside, or dispersed to their various summer amusements. It seemed unfair for so much beauty to be set aside for the enjoyment of a single family, none of whom, at the moment, was appreciating it. I imagined how out of place my mother must have felt working at such a grand estate. My childhood had been confined to the town, my father's hands slick with grease and my mother's chapped from dishwater. But Jake had grown up here, barely noticing the people who prepared his food, cleaned his rooms, tended the grounds across which he ran. I wanted to resent him for it, but I didn't have it in me. He couldn't help his birth any more than I could.

"My mother would love it here," Albert said. "She spent her summers at a place like this, on a lake outside Pittsburgh, when she was young."

"Did you, too?"

"The money was all gone by the time I came along. The lake, too, come to think of it." He pointed to a stone bench mottled with lichen overlooking the cliff and suggested we take in the view. The water below was the color of bluestone, its surface smooth save for the frothy wake of a ferry. On the opposite shore, hills draped in mist made way for the waters of Rondout Creek. A passing train blew a baleful whistle, casting a melancholy note over the scene that brought my thoughts back to the cemetery. My father's accident had pried me away from everything I knew, while Jake had retreated to Linwood, a manicured world untouched by tragedy. But that wasn't true, I reminded myself. His father was dead, and his sister Cornelia, too. No life was so charmed as a place like this made it seem.

An enormous Saint Bernard suddenly rounded the bench. It rested its head, heavy as a pony's, on Albert's lap. "Well, hello there. Where's your master?"

"Here I am." We turned to see Jake looking like a well-dressed ringmaster with a straw hat on his head and a Boston terrier in the crook of his arm. "Welcome to Linwood. This little bitch is Princess." He lifted his arm to show off the dog, who licked his chin. "And you've met my champion, Oh Boy." The Saint Bernard went to Ruppert's side. He placed a hand on its shoulder without so much as bending his knees. "I'm on my way to the kennel. Come along?"

Oh Boy appointed himself our guide, leading us past the kitchen gardens until we reached a small barn, a sign above the wide entrance proclaiming it the DUCHESS KEN-

NELS. The excited barking within was answered by the sharp yips of Princess, who squirmed out of Jake's arm and bounded inside. It took a moment for my eyes to adjust to the dim light. Low walls sectioned the barn into generous pens. Oh Boy walked through the open gate of one of the pens and flopped down on a pile of straw, sending a cloud of motes into the air. Princess, meanwhile, was leaping and turning like a circus performer before another pen. "She wants to get to her pups," Jake said to Albert, who lifted the wriggling dog over the gate and set her inside. A litter of puppies bounded up to greet their mother, clambering over one another and batting her with their paws. Though her teats were still distended from nursing, the pups had recently been weaned and Princess kept them at bay with a convincing snarl.

Jake stopped in front of a third pen. "And how are your pups, Bulgari?" A Saint Bernard nearly as big as Oh Boy came up to the gate. Rising on her hind legs, she placed her front paws on Jake's shoulders, wilting him with her weight. Behind her in the straw, puppies the size of full-grown spaniels rolled and played.

I pointed to a tiny pup lurking in the corner of Princess's pen. "What about that one over there?"

"That little pipsqueak?" Jake looked over, his hands buried in Bulgari's jowls. "That one's the runt of the litter. Pick him up if you want to."

I eased through the gate and approached the runt. Kneeling down, I extended my arms, and he scampered up to me. I lifted him to my shoulder as I stood, the pup's flat face snuggled against my neck.

"You've found a friend," Albert said.

"Jake called him a little pipsqueak."

Albert scratched the pup's round belly. "What do you say, Pip? Do you like your belly rubbed?" As if in answer, the pup reached its paws up to my nose.

"Bostons are such smart little dogs, aren't they?" Jake joined us, wiping drool from his fingers with a monogrammed handkerchief. "Each of my nieces has claimed one of Princess's pups, but this one's still not spoken for. You can have him, Helen, if you like."

"Me?" I pulled the pup from my shoulder and held him in front of my face. I had no experience with dogs and was about to decline the offer — an untrained puppy was sure to wreak havoc in our apartment — but Jake had offered me something valuable enough to be given to his own nieces. My mother was sure to appreciate that. "Well, Pip, what do you think, would you like to come live in the city with me?"

The pup yipped in seeming delight and Jake declared the matter settled. He had the zookeeper pack a basket with some kibble, a blanket, a jar of water, and a dish. Pip stretched his tiny mouth in a yawn and promptly fell asleep.

Provisioned by the cook with a picnic of sandwiches and beer, we piled into the Packard, leaving the yellow mansion and the green lawns of Linwood behind. Down the road, I spied an old mill through the trees, its wheel now still. Below the mill, a craggy waterfall spilled into a quiet cove, making a romantic scene. I leaned out the window, my hand securely on Pip's sleeping head. "What a beautiful place."

"That mill was worth a fortune, back when Rhinecliff was first settled," Jake said. "It hasn't been used in decades. I used to go swimming in the cove there when I was a younger man."

"By yourself?" It seemed to me a lonely place.

"Yes, by myself, though sometimes I found another swimmer there."

I placed the sleeping pup in his basket as we drove on. Passing through Hyde Park,

Jake pointed out Astor's place at Ferncliff, followed by the Vanderbilt mansion, its magnificent edifice imposing even from the road. Albert whistled. "That's an impressive estate."

"It was built to impress," Jake said. "I never saw the point of it all myself. I want a home where a man can relax with his friends, not host galas meant to be written up in the social pages. Do you know, Helen, I own office buildings and a brewery and a baseball team, but in all my fifty-one years I've never owned my own house? When I heard about the property we're going to see, I thought it was about time I built something for myself."

"I'm glad we could accompany you," I said, still unsure why Jake needed the two of us to come along.

"I want your opinion, Helen, and I'll need Kramer to handle the details if I decide to buy it."

"You won't be going through Ruppert Realty?" Albert asked.

"No, Kramer, this purchase will be personal." He leaned forward to tap Schultz on the shoulder. "Stop here — that must be the land agent." We were joined by a gregarious man who pointed to yet another iron gate set in stone. "It's here, turn here."

Schultz maneuvered the limousine down a rutted drive that skirted the base of a rocky outcropping to the right, while on the left a shallow creek tumbled haphazardly over boulders. We came to a clearing, more meadow than lawn, in the center of which stood a ramshackle house topped with a widow's walk. Overgrown trees surrounded the clearing, blocking any view of the river. We might as well be in the forest, I thought, as on the banks of the Hudson.

"The house is very historic," the land agent said as we piled out of the limousine. "Mostly Victorian, but parts of it go back to the eighteenth century. Shall we start there?"

"I don't care about the house," Jake said. "That would all come down. I'd rather walk the grounds."

I stayed behind with Pip while Albert, a notepad and pencil in his hands, followed Jake and the land agent as they forged a path through the tall grass. Schultz came over, spread out a blanket, and set down the hamper of sandwiches and beer. "Here you are, Miss Winthrope. Might as well have your picnic while you wait."

I invited him to join me and we spent an amiable half hour eating and playing with Pip, who would wander off the blanket then stop, whimper, and come bounding back, ecstatic each time he found me again. Finally, the pup and the chauffeur both stretched out and fell asleep in the soporific September sun. I looked over at the house. It was woefully out-of-date, but it seemed a shame to simply tear it down. The shutters were pinned back and a few casements were raised, the land agent, I assumed, having aired it out in anticipation of Jake's visit. Going up to the door I found it open and let myself in. The fireplaces were blackened by centuries of soot and the chandeliers held melted candles. I assumed the plumbing, whatever there was of it, would be just as primitive. No wonder Jake intended to replace it all.

Upstairs I explored the bedrooms, thinking of the generations of children who'd been rocked in the broken cradles or ridden the abandoned rocking horses. I climbed up to the third floor, where servants would have slept in unheated rooms under the eaves. Finally, I located a steep stair that led, as I'd hoped, to the widow's walk. Spiderwebs were tangled in my hair by the time I emerged onto the small platform perched at the very top of the roof. The view snatched my breath away. Beyond the tops of the untrimmed trees, the Hudson sparkled wide

301

and blue. Across the river, the crenellated fortifications of West Point clung to the cliff like a rookery.

Below, I spotted the land agent leaning on the hood of the Packard. Schultz had gone into the bushes beyond the lawn to relieve himself. I laughed and looked for Albert. There he was, emerging from the grass with Pip in his hands. The naughty puppy must have wandered off again. As if sensing my attention, Albert looked up. I waved. He picked up Pip's little paw and made him wave back at me. My heart hitched at the sweetness of the gesture.

A thud of footfalls preceded Jake's emergence onto the widow's walk. "It's quite a climb, isn't it?" He joined me at the rail, swatting away the webs stuck to his hat. "I'll have those trees cut down so we can see the river from the lawn."

"You've decided to buy it, then?"

He nodded. "Once I see something I want, there's no point in looking further."

I swept my eyes again over the view. A moment ago, it had been mine to contemplate. Now, it belonged to him. As did we all, I realized, looking down at Albert and Schultz, all of us Jake's employees. It made me feel sorry for him, a man without wife or children, forced to assemble a family from a bunch of purchased parts. "It's a beautiful property, Jake."

"It will be, once I've finished with it. I hope you'll come here often, Helen, you and Kramer. I'll feel more at home with the two of you around."

"I'd like that," I said, thinking my mother would be thrilled to hear it. Perhaps she'd be invited, too, as a guest this time instead of a servant. We stood side by side for a while, listening to the lonely sound of leaves rustling in the breeze. Impulsively, I asked the question that had been weighing on my mind all day. "My father, tell me —" Jake's face went white, but he needn't have worried. It wasn't my intention to burden him with blame. "After the accident, did he suffer?"

Jake's jaw, typically so stern, began to tremble. "No, Helen. It was all over in an instant. I was with him for his dying breath. He never felt a thing, I promise."

I hadn't realized how the unanswered question had burdened me until the weight of it was lifted. Tears of relief slipped down my cheeks. Jake brought my head to his shoulder and patted my hair as if I were a little girl.

A sharp cry split the air, driving us apart. I dragged the heel of my hand across my eyes. "What was that?"

"A golden eagle. They nest along the river." Jake pointed to a great wheeling creature, its outstretched wings riding an invisible current of air. "I think I'll name the estate Eagle's Rest. What do you say to that, Helen?"

I didn't associate birds of prey with the cozy retreat Jake claimed to want, but it wasn't my place to say so. "I'd say that's a fine name, Jake."

The eagle plummeted toward the river-bank, searching for food. A moment later it rose up with a screech, slanting through the sky and disappearing among the treetops, the limp carcass of some hapless creature dangling from its talons.

■ ■ ■ ■

1921

■ ■ ■ ■

CHAPTER 22

"I didn't realize how minuscule it was." Helen looked skeptically at the narrow building on MacDougal Street that housed the Provincetown Playhouse.

"It used to be a stable, if you can believe that," I said, stomping my feet to warm them.

She raised an eyebrow. "They must have been awfully small horses."

I laughed and reached out to fold up her collar against the January cold. My gloved fingers touched the brooch I'd given her for Christmas, the cloisonné dragonfly shimmering richly against the threadbare fabric of her coat. I wasn't sure what she spent her salary on, but it certainly wasn't clothes. Whenever I'd complimented her on a new outfit it turned out to be on loan from the wardrobe mistress. When I'd chosen the brooch at Tiffany's I knew it would outshine anything she could pin it on, but I'd wanted her to have something beautiful and fine for everything she'd done for me.

Back in the winter of 1918, when the influenza was so rampant in New York that my mother forbade me to travel to Pittsburgh for Christmas, Helen had come to my rescue, inviting me to her family's cozy apartment. Felix, who never did understand my sentimental attachment to the holiday, scoffed at the stocking I hung for him from my mantel. But at Helen's, there'd been a tinseled tree tucked into a corner of the living room and a supper of candied ham with sweet potato pie enjoyed around the kitchen table. It was all so delightful that I'd managed to invite myself again the next year, too, and this December it was simply assumed I'd be joining them for Christmas. For the third year in a row I gave Rex a season pass to the Yankees games at the Polo Grounds — in the bleachers, so he'd have his chance at catching a fly ball. I always chose a silk scarf for Mrs. Winthrope, who'd (thankfully) given up wearing her ratty mink stole. For Helen that first Christmas I'd gotten a lovely Parker pen and pencil set in a pearl finish. The next year I'd spent rather more on a ladies' Rolex wristwatch. This Christmas, I couldn't resist the brooch; the salesgirl assured me all the colors of the rainbow could be seen in its iridescent wings. Paul warned me Helen would be expecting a diamond ring next, but I told him she was so consumed with her career she had no time to think about matrimony.

The crowd on the sidewalk surged as the doors to the Provincetown Playhouse opened. Taking Helen's arm, I shoved our way to the front of the line. I hadn't wanted to bring her down to Greenwich Village and I was eager to get off the street before we ran into one of my flamboyant friends. After our weekly dinners, Helen and I usually saw a film at one of the movie palaces around Times Square or sat through whatever was onstage at her theater. But she'd been wanting to see *Beyond the Horizon* for weeks now, even though it'd been sold out since it won Eugene O'Neill the Pulitzer. Then Richard Martin called in a favor and got her a pair of tickets — for a Friday night, no less — and Helen was so excited I simply couldn't refuse.

There were no chairs inside, only wooden benches cold as church pews. Enough of us crammed into the little space, however, that I was soon shrugging off my coat in air made warm from our collective human heat. Helen was pressed up close against me, so engrossed by the play that she didn't notice the beads of sweat popping up along her hairline.

I had to admit, the play really was remarkable. I'd never seen anything so true and so sad. The last scene between the two brothers (or, as I had recast them in my mind, the two friends) was still reverberating in my chest as the cast came out to take their bows. When Andy said he loved Rob better than anybody in the world, for a moment as fleeting as a photographer's flash I saw my kind represented on the stage. What would it look like, I wondered, as I blinked back tears, to see ourselves dramatized realistically and with sympathy? But no, people didn't like to think of us as farmers and sea captains. Color our cheeks with rouge, clot our lashes with mascara, put us in a vaudeville act to lisp and croon and flap our hands: that was the only role in which to cast a pansy. But we weren't so unlike those two actors. When Rob put his hand on Andy's hand and Andy said they'd always been together, just the two of them — well, they looked like me and Felix, or Paul with his benefactor, or any of a dozen pairs of men I knew.

"Are you crying, Albert?" Helen pulled a handkerchief from her pocketbook and offered it to me. "I guess it reminds you of your childhood illness, how sick Rob is at the end."

"Just something in my eye. Never mind, Helen." I pushed away her hand. "Come outside, it's stifling in here." The tiny theater was crammed full as a streetcar at rush hour. It was a relief to emerge onto Mac-Dougal Street, the tears freezing on my cheeks.

"Don't lie to me, Albert. You were affected, I could see it."

I took her elbow as we walked toward Fourth Street, those old cobbles slick with ice. "It was all so unfair, how that stupid girl came between the brothers like that."

"Stupid girl? But, Albert, don't you see, it was the brothers who tore themselves apart. She was just a romantic young thing, caught between them and her mother, too. She never had any choice in the matter. Maybe *she* wanted to go beyond the horizon, did you ever think of that?"

"If you had played her, Helen, I might have understood it that way."

"No, I'm not pretty enough for the part."

"Don't say that. You're the prettiest woman I know." It was true. Sure, her jaw was a little heavy and her mouth a bit thin, but I'd grown so used to her face that I couldn't see her as anything less than beautiful.

"I'm not fishing for a compliment, Albert. In the third act, yes, I was imagining myself speaking those lines, but at the beginning — well, the part needs a beautiful woman for it to make any sense. I mean, why else do those boys think they're so in love with her? It's not as if O'Neill gave her any qualities of attraction other than her looks."

We wandered through Greenwich Village as we spoke, the play having distracted me from my fears. "I still don't see why any man would give up a sea voyage for her, or a farm for that matter."

Helen seemed about to speak but shut her mouth with a huff, saying, "Let's get out of this cold at least. Is that a speakeasy over there?"

I panicked as I looked across the street and saw we'd ended up in front of Antonio's. Indeed, at that very moment the door opened, piano music streaming out a shaft of smoky light.

"It is, but I hear it's very Bohemian. You don't want to go slumming, do you?"

"Why not? I'm not so easily shocked." Helen gripped my arm. "And anyway, I've got you to protect me. Let's see if we can't guess at the password."

But the very idea of taking Helen into Antonio's brought bile into my throat. The length and breadth of Manhattan was usually sufficient to keep my worlds from colliding. I was a pansy down in the Village, the Colonel's personal secretary on the Upper East Side, Helen's young man around Times Square. And I was Felix Stern's lover west of Central Park, behind the closed doors of the brownstone. To walk into Antonio's with a woman on my arm was as unthinkable to me as bringing a man home to meet my mother.

"Let's just look for a cab." For once my sense of direction didn't let me down. A taxi was discharging some passengers onto Hudson Street. I grabbed the handle before they could close the door. I gave the driver Helen's address along with the fare, but I didn't follow her in.

"Aren't you coming, Albert?"

I'd never failed to see her home before, but my emotions were so shaken I didn't think I could sit beside her for fifty blocks without blurting out something that might reveal my secret. Not that it felt false, being with Helen. In all honesty, she'd become my dearest friend. It physically pained me to lie to her, but I couldn't risk the truth. Even if she were sympathetic to my plight, what if word got back to the Colonel? If he didn't want people to mistake his secretary for a window dresser, he certainly wouldn't want a self-proclaimed pansy in the job.

"I was planning to meet up with Paul later on, and, well, it doesn't really make sense to ride all the way uptown and back again. You don't mind, do you?" Of course she did. What woman wouldn't? I leaned in as the taxi's meter starting ticking over. "Don't forget, Helen, the Colonel wants to see you tomorrow afternoon at the Ruppert mansion."

"You're sure you don't know what it's about?"

I shook my head. "I'm just as curious as you are. Telephone me after?" I shut the door and rapped my knuckles against the window, watching until the taxi was well up Hudson before retracing my steps. As I walked, I mussed my hair so that it hung loose over my forehead. On the sidewalk in front of Antonio's, I pulled the brown bow tie from around my collar and replaced it with the red one I had tucked, earlier that evening, into my jacket pocket.

CHAPTER 23

I sat speechless in the back of that taxi as the driver started up Hudson Street. Albert had never treated me so shabbily before, but I was more concerned than angry. His excuse was reasonable enough — why come all the way uptown with me just to turn around again? — but I didn't believe that was his real reason. The play had upset him, I could see that plain as day. I wondered if, like O'Neill's characters, Albert had once given up something he wanted more than anything else in the world. I didn't know. Despite all the time we spent together, there was still a gap between us, narrow enough to be overlooked but wide enough for a secret. Sometimes I wondered if he was spending his Saturday nights with a different girl in another part of the city. But no, Albert was as likely to be two-timing me as he was to be spying for the Bolsheviks. The other tenants in the brownstone had a weekly get-together, he'd explained. He and his neighbor, Felix Stern, always attended. Afterward, they'd go out for dinner, or to a party, or to meet up with friends. All perfectly reasonable, nothing for me to suspect, and yet . . . and yet nothing. I told myself to stop looking for trouble where there was none to be found.

Besides, who was I to press him on his secrets? As dear as he was to me, I lived in dread of the day he'd declare his intentions. Confronted with a proposal of marriage, I'd either have to turn him down or confess why I'd never be able to give him children. I imagined that day would eventually come, but until it did I could keep my secret to myself. In the meantime, what more could I want from a man than his friendship and affection, his interest in my work, his company on Friday nights? Thanks to Harrison, I knew what I was missing with Albert. As far as I remembered, I wasn't missing much. I shook my head. My thoughts had gone around in this same circle a thousand times over the past couple of years, and they always led to the same conclusion: Albert couldn't have been more perfect, or a more perfect gentleman, if I'd ordered him from the Sears catalog.

As late as it was, when the taxi dropped

me off I saw Clarence was still awake. He hadn't spotted me yet and I paused for a moment to watch him, the lobby lit like a stage. He was cleaning the floor, the mop swinging rhythmically across the terrazzo. It was a sad scene for me to see. After the 369th had returned from France to parade so triumphantly up Fifth Avenue, I'd expected Clarence to put his college degree to use and become a teacher. But those first months after the war, his nerves were too raw for New York City. The crowded sidewalks, the fast-moving traffic, the sounds of sirens and car horns all put him on edge. It was all he could do to take up his old position in the lobby, where he gazed through the glass doors to see what was happening on the street, and spoke with people one at a time as they came and went. I often stopped for a talk in the quiet lobby of the sleeping building when I returned late from the theater. On Saturday nights, when Albert was busy, Clarence and I would make it an occasion with a picnic basket prepared by his mother, the taste of garlic and coconut strange on my tongue. I was happy to help him reacclimate to civilian life. After all, Clarence had done much the same for me back when my mother first moved us to Manhattan. My grief over my father's death was so fresh, I might never have left the apartment if it weren't for him. I remembered how he'd knock on my door whenever he saw my mother go out. "Come on, Helen," he'd say, jingling a handful of nickels in his pocket. "Let's ride the El."

It took about a year for Clarence to put the war behind him, but just when I thought he'd start looking to the future his father's headaches had begun. The crippling episodes of pain confined Mr. Weldon to his bedroom, silence and darkness the only cure. Clarence had put off applying for teaching jobs so he could cover his father's duties around the building. I knew he was doing it for his family's sake, but still it made me sad to see janitor's overalls on a college graduate and a mop handle in hands that had been trained to fire a rifle.

Clarence frowned as I walked in alone. "Weren't you out with Albert?"

"He was meeting up with some friends afterward, so he stayed downtown." His disapproval made me defensive. "I can find my way home by myself you know."

"I know, Helen. I just thought better of him is all."

I was about to remind him I wasn't one of his little sisters — who weren't so little anymore, anyway — when I noticed how heavily he was hanging his head. "What's the matter, has something happened?"

"It's my father. He was lying down with one of his headaches today when he had some kind of attack. I brought Dr. Wright from the Harlem Hospital to see him." His eyes welled up.

I took his hand. "My God, what is it?"

"It's brain ischemia, Helen. He's practically paralyzed. There's nothing we can do."

For months, my mother had been suggesting that Mr. Weldon was taking advantage of his son's good nature to laze around in bed. She'd be sorry to have even thought such a thing once I told her the truth. "Oh, Clarence. I know it's late, but may I see him?"

He wiped the tears from his eyes with the back of his hand. "I was hoping you'd say that."

We took the elevator to the basement, where the custodian's apartment shared space with the laundry room and the storage closets and the trash incinerator and the furnace. I hadn't been down here since Clarence and I were children. Back then, his sisters had shared the second bedroom while Clarence slept on the couch. Tiptoeing through the apartment, I saw one of his sisters now had the couch, while the young cousin they'd taken in after his parents died of influenza was curled up between two armchairs pulled together. I remembered Clarence saying his other sister had moved back in with her husband and their baby to save money — they must be in the second bedroom. Where, I wondered, did Clarence sleep?

Mrs. Weldon was at her husband's bedside. The poor man was propped up on pillows, his face distorted into a grotesque mask, half of the mouth pulled down nearly to his chin, the sounds he made little more than grunts. His lungs were so labored I became embarrassed by how easy it was for me to breathe. But his eyes were the worst, I thought, as I took his hand and wished him well. They stared at me full of mute intelligence, the thoughts trapped in a body no longer responsive to his commands.

Mrs. Weldon was grateful for my visit but soon said her husband needed his rest. Clarence walked me down the corridor toward the elevator. Outside one of the storage closets, I saw a doormat and a pair of his shoes. "That's not where you sleep, is it?"

He opened the door and switched on the light. I saw a cot neatly made up with a blanket, a tiny end table piled with books, a stack of milk crates that served as a dresser for his carefully folded clothes. It would have been tragic if it weren't for the many pictures taped to the whitewashed walls. Landscapes mostly, some illustrations of birds and flowers, a smattering of postcards depicting Paris. "My sister's family needed the bedroom after my brother-in-law lost his job. But I'm glad they're here. My mother will need their help now that she has my father to take care of on top of everything else."

"But what about you?"

He switched off the light and shut the door. "I've already contacted the owners of the building. They've agreed to hire me as the new custodian."

"But, Clarence, you're qualified to be a teacher. Surely your parents wouldn't want you to give up your career for their sake?"

He spoke as if I were a pupil slow to understand a lesson. "I wouldn't even have my college degree if it weren't for my mother working her fingers to the bone doing laundry, including yours, Helen. I'd never be able to support my whole family on a teacher's salary. Custodian doesn't pay much, but it comes with an apartment. You may not know much about rents in this city, but they're pretty steep, especially for black folks."

I hadn't known New York cost more if you were black than if you were white. Poor Clarence, I thought. Sure, he was helping his family, but it was a shame for him to waste his education cleaning floors. "Tell your father I'll be thinking of him, won't you?"

"I will. Thanks for seeing him, Helen. I'm sure it meant a lot to him."

"He was always so good to me, when I was a kid. I guess he knew I'd just lost my own dad." Tears suddenly rolled down my cheeks. I stopped them with a handkerchief.

"He's a good father, but strict, too. I'll never forget the licking he gave me after your mother caught us kissing. I still have a stripe from his switch across my backside."

My face grew hot. We'd never spoken of that kiss, not in all the years. I remembered being awkward around him that summer, the taste of soap fresh in my mouth. Then we'd each gone off to different high schools and I figured he'd forgotten all about it. But he hadn't. He even had the scar to prove it. "You never told me you got in trouble too."

Clarence shook his head. Reaching into the elevator, he pressed the button for my floor. "You have no idea, Helen. You better get on home now."

I stopped by the next day with my mother to visit Mr. Weldon — mollified, she'd baked him a pie — but we didn't stay long. I was haunted by the image of his twisted face as I hailed a taxi to take me to the Ruppert mansion, Pip hidden in my coat. It was the stuff of tragedy, I thought, how easily a strong man could be cut down. I forced myself to think instead of the play I'd seen with Albert last night. That ridiculous theater didn't do it justice. I knew O'Neill was suspicious of commercializing his work on Broadway, but really, a play that refreshing and honest deserved to be moved uptown. If only I could convince him to bring *Beyond the Horizon* to the Olde Playhouse, we might be able to finally turn a reliable profit.

I figured that must be what Jake wanted to talk to me about. All Jake had asked, when he made me manager, was that I not lose him any money. Technically I hadn't, not in the long run. I'd eventually made up for the loss we took when that first play I'd chosen was so viciously panned in the press. Night after night, most of the comfortable seats Jake had paid for went unoccupied and

I'd kicked myself for guaranteeing the playwright a three-month run. As it turned out, though, the play's bad reviews probably saved my life. With influenza sweeping through the city that fall and winter, any crowded place posed a risk. Albert had agreed, saying it was lucky the baseball season had ended early that year, too. It seemed a cruel coda to the war that our returning soldiers should have brought home an epidemic along with their victory.

Yes, that must be it, I thought. Jake had already thanked me for the information I'd given him about Harry Frazee. The divorce papers had eventually been filed and the court proceedings were spectacularly messy. Selling Babe Ruth had added one hundred thousand dollars to Frazee's balance sheet for the judge to consider when setting alimony, but Albert explained it was the side deal that really clinched Babe's sale. The mortgage Ruppert Realty had offered against Fenway Park put over three hundred thousand in Frazee's pockets, none of it in assets his wife could claim but more than enough to mount a new Broadway show, starring, of course, his Long Island mistress. When the Yankees had announced their acquisition of Babe Ruth last January, it had been thrilling to know I'd played a small part in it. Albert and I had both been in the owner's box at the Polo Grounds on the first of May to watch Babe bat against his old team. When he clobbered a home run in the sixth, Jake had caught my eye and smiled.

At 93rd Street, I gave Pip a short walk in Central Park. Jake had suggested I bring him along so Princess could see her pup again. Fully grown, Pip was still a runt at just a dozen pounds. Even in the neat little vest my mother knitted for him, he trembled in the January cold. Crossing Fifth Avenue, I carried Pip up the steps to the Ruppert mansion. After ringing the bell, I traced the carved stone columns of the portico with my gloved finger. It was a shame, I thought, that a wrecking ball would soon reduce the mansion to rubble. Jake and his siblings had agreed to redevelop the property, now that their mother was dead. Jake himself was moving into a large apartment directly across the street, his address of over fifty years changing by less than sixty feet. Whatever the reason for his summons, I was glad for this chance to offer my sympathies in person. I'd wanted to attend Mrs. Ruppert's funeral but my mother said I shouldn't, as I was neither family nor Catholic. I'd settled for sending flowers and a card, though I was sure my modest bouquet was lost among the profusion of arrangements.

Mr. Nakamura invited me in with a bow. Before I first met him in person, I'd pictured Sessue Hayakawa in the role of Japanese butler. But Osamu Nakamura, short and bespectacled, was no movie star. "Colonel Ruppert is in the library, Miss Winthrope. Please follow me."

The mansion was in that disarray which precedes moving, with furniture shoved out of place and doorways blocked by packing crates full of straw. I set Pip down on the floor, his nails clicking on oak planks from which the carpets had been rolled away. In the parlor, carved wooden satyrs lay prone on the floor like sleeping children, the mantel from which they had been pried left splintered and raw. The yards-long table in the dining room was stacked with dishes exhumed from china closets and sideboards. I imagined negotiations among the family members over which sister would inherit the monogrammed silverware, which niece the crystal punch bowl, which granddaughter the set of Limoges porcelain.

I found Jake sitting behind a surprisingly delicate desk. Princess, a good ten pounds heavier than my Pip, came dashing up to meet us. The dogs circled each other, barks and growls giving way to lingering sniffs. Jake came forward, eager as I was to witness this reunion of mother and son, but if they recognized each other, they gave no sign we humans could read. Princess turned and strutted back to her wicker bed beneath Jake's desk. Pip stretched and scratched at my legs, wanting to be picked up.

"I thought they'd be more emotional, seeing each other again after so long." I stroked Pip's flat little face. "How is Princess when she visits with your nieces? Does she recognize her other children?"

"Children only applies to people, Helen, but yes, she is usually excited to see her pups. She may have forgotten Pip here."

I kissed the top of Pip's baseball-size head and put him down. Calm now, he explored the room, giving his mother a wide berth.

"So much for that." Jake took my hand. "Thank you for coming on a Saturday, Helen. I'm rather overwhelmed here, as you can see." He waved his arm at the bookcases, which were filled to bursting with leather-bound volumes. In the center of the room, a rustic table had been fashioned from planks on sawhorses. On it, an assembly line of sorts had been created: stacked books at one end, followed by a roll of newsprint, then books wrapped neatly as birthday presents, each carefully labeled and ready to be placed in a crate at the far end of the table. "Everything is going to the American Art Association for sale. They'll be back on Monday to finish the job."

I picked up a book of poems by Robert Burns. It was beautiful, the lettering on its embossed leather cover picked out in gold and a hand-colored illustration on the dou-blure. I tried to turn to a poem I remembered from school but was stymied. The pages were all uncut, the printed words visible only by peeking between the tented pages. I realized these volumes were never intended to be read, only collected and displayed, the words mattering less than the handmade paper on which they were printed or the crushed crimson morocco in which they were bound. "I'm surprised you're selling your collection. Albert said you loved your books."

"I do. Such well-crafted things they are, and all in pristine condition. But with Prohibition strangling my brewery, it took all the cash I had on hand to acquire Ruth, and there's still his salary to contend with."

I scanned one shelf, counting the books, then multiplied that by the number of shelves. There were hundreds of titles, many of them in volumes of a dozen or more. I remembered Albert telling me the Bret Harte alone had cost a thousand dollars. I knew they couldn't all be so valuable, but I estimated the collection to be worth around fifty thousand. I supposed some newly minted millionaire might buy up the entire library to fill the empty shelves of one of those gaudy Hamptons estates. I tried to imagine such a thing. In our own living room, we had one bookcase stuffed haphazardly with novels and histories, some magazines and cookbooks, an illustrated encyclopedia and a well-worn dictionary.

I turned my attention back to the man before me. Though he was at home on a weekend, Jake was as elegantly attired as I'd ever seen him, from his gleaming white collar to his polished cap-toed shoes. Albert told me Mr. Nakamura's duties included laying out Jake's clothes every day, as if he were a theatrical production of one. I glanced down at my own outfit. My boots were stained from the slush on the sidewalks, and my blue dress — the same one I'd worn that day to Rhinecliff, still the nicest thing in my closet — was beginning to fray at the cuffs. "I'm glad you invited me, Jake. Ever since your mother passed away,

I've been wanting to give you my condolences."

"Thank you, Helen. It was to be expected, at her age, but still her death has been a terrible blow." He lifted his hand, as if to touch my cheek, but turned the gesture into a tug on his tie. "I regret now I never introduced you."

Mr. Nakamura appeared with a tray of coffee and cakes, which he placed on the small desk. To make conversation as we ate, I asked Jake about his plans for the evening.

"I'm meeting Vincent Astor and his wife for dinner," he said. "I expect we'll drop in on the Hamilton Lodge Ball afterward."

"Is that the queer masquerade, at the Rockland Palace? I've always meant to see one of those." It wasn't something I would have expected him to be interested in, but then again New York society did enjoy its diversions.

"It's always entertaining, and Mrs. Astor enjoys it. What I'm really looking forward to, though, is the Westminster Kennel Club show. It's this coming week at Madison Square Garden. The dogs are down from the country for it." I looked around, wondering where a Saint Bernard might be hiding. "Oh, they're not here! We keep a kennel in the old horse stable at the brewery." He leaned back in his chair and entertained me with the story of how he acquired the breeding stock for his line of Saint Bernards by importing a stud and two bitches from England back in 1892. "They cost me twenty thousand dollars in today's money, but in return I've been rewarded with many championships. You should come with me to the show, you'd enjoy it. Oh Boy always takes a prize, and I expect a ribbon for Bulgari this year, too."

It explained a lot to know that he'd paid as much for three prize-winning dogs as he was spending on Babe's record-breaking salary. Jake's library was magnificent, but I could see why a man who valued winning would cash it in for the chance at the World Series.

Jake cleared his throat and set down his coffee. "Helen, listen. I asked you here to talk about something. I've had an offer from Martin Beck."

It took me a moment to place the name. "The vaudeville producer?"

"That's the one. He approached Ruppert Realty this week about the Olde Playhouse. I guess he doesn't mind being on the wrong side of Tenth Avenue because he wants to buy it."

It took me a moment to understand. "Are

331

you saying that Martin Beck wants to take over the Olde Playhouse?"

"Actually, he wants to raze it to the ground and build a new theater on the land."

I sat back, stunned. It had taken every ounce of my energy and ingenuity over the past couple of years just to keep the Olde Playhouse from bleeding red ink. I hadn't cost Jake anything, but I hadn't added any value to his portfolio, either. No matter how well I managed it, the Playhouse would never be a money maker. I couldn't blame him for wanting to sell it, but I hated to lose my job. Who else would hire a young woman to manage a theater, even a small one, even with my experience? I'd been off the stage for too long to land myself a well-paying part on short notice. Perhaps, with Jake's recommendation, I'd be able to stay on for a while and manage the new theater. "Will you put in a good word for me, with Mr. Beck?"

"Not so fast, Helen. It isn't a done deal. Now, explain to me why the Olde Playhouse never makes any money."

I took a deep breath and laid it all out for him. The problem was that the theater itself and the plays produced in it were at odds, financially. The Playhouse wanted its taxes paid, its plumbing repaired, its roof patched, its seats replaced. The productions wanted actors and publicity and costumes and sets. It was a constant case of robbing Peter to pay Paul. No matter how carefully Bernice Johnson, our bookkeeper, balanced the sums, we never seemed to come out on the winning side.

Jake summoned Mr. Nakamura and asked for some schnapps. He sat in silent contemplation until a carafe of clear liquor appeared on a silver tray with two tiny fluted glasses. Jake filled the glasses and handed one to me. *"Prost."* I sipped at mine, the fumes heady in my nose, while he tossed his back in one quick shot. "The problem, Helen, is that you are trying to run two businesses at once. If the theater itself were its own company, with a manager whose only job was keeping it in good repair, then a producer could pay a fixed amount for the use of the Playhouse and focus on the plays themselves. The question is, which would you rather be?"

"I'm sorry, which what would I rather?"

"Manager or producer. Which would you rather be, Helen? Unless you're ready to step aside from this career of yours and find a husband. Just don't steal my secretary." He wagged a finger. "Kramer is invaluable to me. I wouldn't want him distracted by a wife and children."

I struggled to follow the rapidly shifting topics of our conversation. "Wait, so, you're not going to sell the Olde Playhouse to Mr. Beck?"

"Not if you don't want me to. Now that I know he wants the land, I can always go back to him if I change my mind."

Like a card player analyzing the hand she'd been dealt, I reviewed the options Jake had spread before me. The conventional path was marriage, but Albert, it seemed, was off the table — even without Jake's disapproval, neither of us was ready to take that step. Manager would be the safer choice: a steady salary and no temperamental directors to deal with. I did my shot of schnapps and set the empty glass decisively back on the silver tray. "Producer."

He smiled. "Well then. I'll have Kramer set up the new company."

"But, who will manage the theater?"

The hall clock chimed the hour. Jake stood up and so did I. The dogs at our feet stretched and yawned. "You'll make that decision, Helen."

Mr. Nakamura appeared with my coat over his arm. "I'll walk her out, Osamu," Jake said. "You can go start my bath."

Under the portico, Jake held Pip while I buttoned up my coat. Handing me the dog, he reached out to turn up my collar. "You should have a new coat if you're to accompany me to Westminster. For the women, it's as much a fashion show as a dog show."

I smoothed the placket, embarrassed. "I was waiting for the spring sales to get a new one."

Noticing my threadbare coat must have reminded him of my salary, which he'd never raised. He removed his billfold and gave me five dollars for my taxi fare. As I rode home through the winter's early darkness, my mind whirled as I considered the future. I'd been strict with my income and my mother's savings were finally replenished, but that meant I had nothing set aside for myself. I'd been looking forward to moving out and setting myself up as a Bachelor Girl in a little apartment with a chafing dish and a telephone. But now that I'd be starting over as a producer, I didn't think I could afford it. I wasn't sure how this new company would work, but I imagined I'd be forgoing a salary for a share in the profits. If there were any profits. As manager, I could have happily cashed a regular, if meager, paycheck. As someone's wife, I wouldn't have had to worry about earning a salary at all. Instead, I'd chosen the riskiest option. There'd be no one to blame if I failed. But if I didn't? A smile stretched across my face as I imagined getting all the credit for my own success.

CHAPTER 24

"It's just a bow tie, it's not as if I'm rouging your cheeks. Now stand still, Felix." I knotted the silk tie around his collar. "There."

He turned to his reflection in the bathroom mirror. "I feel so conspicuous."

I looked over his shoulder, wondering what he was seeing. I supposed red must stand out to his vision the way blue did to mine, a bright color that cut through the ordinary. "Believe me, darling, a red bow tie will be the least conspicuous thing at the Hamilton Lodge Ball."

He faced me and smiled. "I have to admit, you do look delicious."

"I do, don't I?" My tinted lips and the mascara on my lashes made me look a bit like Rudolph Valentino. "Like I said, just a touch of makeup. The cabdriver won't even notice, I promise." I gave him a kiss. "Are you ready?"

"As ready as I'll ever be."

Despite my reassurances, he was nervous. To Felix, being queer was a private affliction best kept behind closed doors. The few times I'd cajoled him into coming out with me to Antonio's or a party at Paul's house, he became so uncomfortable we ended up leaving early. I'd certainly never talked him into attending the annual Hamilton Lodge Ball before. Back in 1919, the influenza was his excuse to keep us both home, and last year he'd simply refused. But this past November he'd invited me to the fund-raising gala he'd organized for the orphanage relocation fund. I knew he wanted me there as Ruppert's personal secretary, my presence meant to convey to the trustees an exaggerated sense of the Colonel's commitment to purchasing their Manhattan property. I agreed to accompany him, but only if he promised he'd come with me in January to the "Queer Masquerade," as the newspapers called it.

When word of our plans got around among the tenants in the brownstone, the composer and the old actor decided to come along, too. We shared a taxi up to 155th Street where people were queued around the block to get into the Rockland Palace. We got in line behind a pair of Negro pansies in sequined gowns who told us they saved up all year to make the trip from Virginia for the chance, on this one night, to masquerade as themselves. All around us, short-haired women in suits flirted with men wearing dresses, playfully subverting the difference between our sexes. I noticed that spectators destined for boxes in the gallery went in a separate entrance, richer and whiter than those of us on line for floor tickets. Felix, eager to get off the street, relaxed as we neared the door, the scene awaiting us still beyond his imagination.

Inside, the vast hall throbbed with music and laughter. The sweat of six thousand bodies steamed the air, ice sculptures dripping and potted palms drooping in the heat. Bunting decorated the gallery, and streamers dangled from the ceiling like tentacles. Dancers filled the floor to overflowing, foxtrotting to a lively orchestra. Most couples were of the same race, but there was plenty of mixing, with every shade of skin represented from arms dark as night to limbs pale as moonshine. Champagne glasses were piled into precarious pyramids beside crystal bowls of punch spiked with whiskey. We drank without fear, reassured by the waiters that the fee paid to the police for keeping the peace included turning a blind eye to Prohibition for the night.

We soon lost track of our neighbors, the composer wandering off to watch the musicians and the actor disappearing in the dazzling crush. Emboldened by the crowd, Felix asked me to dance. I remembered a moment during that fund-raising gala when the orphanage band had been playing a waltz. Our elbows touched and our eyes met and our bodies vibrated in time to the music. It was as close as we could come, among the trustees and their wives, to sharing a dance. Now, in the Rockland Palace, Felix took me in his arms and moved me around the floor. People were so densely packed that we soon stopped attempting a two-step and simply swayed, my head on his shoulder, his hand snug on my waist. A tuxedoed lesbian, hair short as a soldier's, glided by with a pretty girl in her arms. For a quick waltz we switched partners until, laughing, we sorted ourselves out again. It wasn't just the alcohol in the punch that propelled our gaiety. In this place, on this night, pansies and bulldaggers who spent their days dodging insult and injury could openly cling to their sweethearts in safety, while those of us who lived our lives hiding in plain sight felt free to be seen for our true selves. It generated a certain hysteria, this mass unmasking multiplied a thousand-fold.

A tap on my shoulder was followed by a voice in my ear. "Aren't you two the love birds tonight." It was a miracle Paul had found us in that crowd. Even among all the finery of sequins and feathers, his unvarnished beauty was devastating. I didn't blame Felix when the kiss he placed on Paul's cheek wandered perilously close to his mouth. His benefactor had taken a box in the gallery, Paul said, and the three of us fought our way through the throng and up the stairs. We emerged among the socialites and swells who'd come to the Rockland Palace to gawk at the curiosities below. Let them be amused, or scandalized, or superior, I thought. At least they were witness to the reality of our existence.

Paul's benefactor had brought bottles of champagne, and we toasted one another as the first of the contests was announced. The crowd cheered and whistled while parades of men and women in all sorts of costumes (geishas, Turks, Amazons) cakewalked across the stage. Some seemed not to be costumed at all until you realized that demure lady was really a boy, or that uniformed officer a woman. Some seemed to have stepped out of the pages of an illustrated history text in their royal robes, while others transcended humanity altogether to become spectacular birds or mythical creatures. When Jack appeared I almost didn't recognize him, so complete was his transformation. He didn't win a prize (there was a surfeit of Marie Antoinettes that year), but he was so well known and loved that the applause as he traversed the stage was deafening. Even Felix clapped wildly, caught up in the euphoria of the night.

"Who's that across the way, darling, can you see?" Paul asked.

His benefactor raised a pair of opera glasses and trained them at the gallery opposite our own. "That's Vince Astor. I'm surprised to see him here. Everyone knows he can't stand pansies." He passed the opera glasses to Paul. "The woman is Astor's wife. It must have been her idea to come tonight. Rumor has it she's a lesbian. I don't know the short man with the big head."

"Oh my." Paul lowered the opera glasses. "Isn't that your boss, Albert?"

I followed the direction of Paul's pointed finger. My heart dropped inside my rib cage like an elevator with a cut cable as I recognized the Colonel. Before I could make sense of what I was seeing, Felix hissed in my ear. "Is that Colonel Ruppert with Vincent Astor?"

"Yes it is." I turned to Felix. "Don't worry, though. If he sees us, we'll say we're spectators, like he is."

"Why do you think he's just a spectator?" Paul draped his arm across my shoulders and handed me the opera glasses. "I mean, look at him."

Framed in the circle of the convex lenses, the Colonel's grinning face leaped across the distance between the galleries. Seeing him in this setting made me reassess his eccentricities. Not many men that rich managed to remain bachelors their whole lives, not with eligible socialites scheming after their bank accounts. I hardly ever saw him lately without his Boston terrier bitch on his lap, his voice rising to a girlish pitch as he spoke to the dog. His clothes were entirely masculine (his tailor still tapered his trousers despite the new fashion), yet he often lamented that only women were expected to dress well. I thought of my neighbor, the aging actor who our landlady referred to as a confirmed bachelor. It wasn't unusual for men not to marry — bachelors filled the city's boardinghouses and lunch counters, plenty of pansies camouflaged among their ranks — but it made me wonder what kind of bachelor the Colonel was.

And then there was his bow tie. It wasn't black, I could see that much, but I couldn't tell if it was red. I turned to hand Felix the opera glasses so he could take a look, but he was stumbling out of the box, his foul mood wafting off him like a scent. I asked Paul what happened. He shrugged and said he had no idea. I glanced along the gallery to see Felix disappearing down the stairs. "I'd better go."

"But you have to wait for Jack to join us," Paul protested.

"I can't. Give Jacqueline my love, tell her she was spectacular."

For a few panicked minutes I lost track of Felix as I shoved my way through the crowd. I caught up with him out on the sidewalk. Panting, I grabbed his elbow and spun him around. "What's the matter?"

He raised his arm for a taxi. "You saw them, Albert. Ruppert and Astor. Don't you know what that means?"

The meaning of it was exactly what I wanted to talk about. I was about to ask Felix if he'd noticed the color of the Colonel's bow tie when a cab pulled up and Felix shoved me in. "Go over to Amsterdam," he told the driver, who protested about the traffic we'd run into. "Just do it, then head downtown."

"I don't think the Colonel saw you, Felix, if that's what you're upset about."

"I don't care about him seeing me. It's who I saw him with. You never told me Ruppert and Astor were friends."

"They're all friends — the Rupperts, the Astors, the Vanderbilts. Well, the men are, at least. They're all in the same yacht club. I don't know about the women. But what's any of that got to do with you?"

He didn't answer. We stewed in silence until Felix called out, "Pull over here, driver, and wait for us." We were in front of the Orphaned Hebrews Home. It was a hulking thing in the middle of the night. As Felix paced in front of the locked gate, I imagined the somnolent exhalations of those hundreds of children in their prison of a castle. He stopped suddenly and smacked his hand, hard, against his forehead. "I've been so stupid!"

I pinned his arm at his side. "What's the matter?"

Felix yanked his arm back, waving it at the dark building. "Don't you understand? Vincent Astor inherited everything after his father went down on *Titanic*. I'm sure he has a parcel of land somewhere in this city big enough for a stadium. Ruppert's been playing me for a fool, as if there weren't a thousand little lives at stake."

The conclusion Felix jumped to seemed outrageous to me. "Those two socialize all the time, it doesn't mean a thing."

My words had no effect on him. He grabbed my lapels, the streetlamp casting his face in sinister shadow. "You keep telling me to be patient, but you know what I think? I think Ruppert's been stringing me along all this time. Maybe you have, too."

I put my hand on his cheek. "Look at me, Felix. You know that isn't true."

He covered my hand with his, shaking his head as tears distorted his eyes. "You don't know what it does to me, Albert. Every Shabbat I spend with my family, my mother weeps becaouse I haven't married yet, and my father says it's my obligation to have Jewish children." He raked his fingers through his hair. "I can't do it, Albert, you know I can't. My work for the orphanage, all the promises I've made — it's all I have to make up for being what I am." He began to beat his closed fist against his breastbone. "Ruppert's got to build his stadium here. He's got to."

I managed to get him back into the taxi and bring him home. I assured him, as we argued through the night, there was no impending deal with Astor, that as far as I knew the orphanage property was still the only viable location for a new stadium. I reminded him of the substantial investment the Colonel had recently made in having Osborn Engineering come out from Ohio to complete a comprehensive plan for the site. It was just the way he did business, I said. There'd be nothing in writing until the entire deal had been negotiated. For now, the Colonel was too distracted by his mother's death, the sale of the mansion, Babe Ruth's salary demands, the upcoming dog show — I reeled off all the reasons why he hadn't made his interest in the orphanage official. "Once the dust settles," I told him, "the Colonel will be in a better position to make a deal."

Felix, however, wasn't convinced. "I'll bring him to the table, even if it means forcing his hand!" Those were the last words he uttered before storming through our secret door and slamming it shut behind him.

I was too exhausted to go after him. When he got himself into one of his moods, sometimes the best thing was to let him cool off on his own. Still, our argument cycled through my brain for another hour, slowly winding down as the streetcars started up outside. I took the telephone off its hook before crawling into bed where, in the thin light of the winter dawn, oblivion finally overtook me.

CHAPTER 25

I pressed Albert's bell for two full seconds, but still the door catch didn't click. I was so eager to tell him about my new career as a producer that I'd called last night, despite it being Saturday, but of course he was out. Then this morning when he didn't answer, I thought he might have gone for breakfast or a walk. But now it was noon and I was getting worried. Every week there was a story in the paper about some poor drunk found frozen in a dark corner of the city. A sick feeling soured my stomach as I imagined Albert cold and alone in an alleyway. Just as I wondered whether I should start calling the hospitals, I heard his voice from above my head.

"For God's sake, who is it?"

Relieved, I stepped back off the stoop and looked up. Albert was leaning out his open window, hair tangled from sleep and dressing gown open at the neck.

"I didn't mean to wake you, Albert. I called first, but there was no answer."

"I had the telephone off the hook." He disappeared for a moment, then leaned out again. "Here. Don't try to catch them, you'll hurt your hand."

He tossed a set of keys out the window. They landed on the sidewalk at my feet, brass clattering on the concrete. Inside the brownstone, the notes of a softly played piano followed me up the stairs, my steps muffled by the plush runner. It made me jealous of the men who got to live here. So many landlords refused to rent to single women that most Bachelor Girls were forced to huddle together in cheap boardinghouses. Oh, if a woman was rich enough she could have whatever she wanted, but a working girl's only other choices were tiny single rooms or pricey apartments swarming with roommates. I still planned to move out on my own eventually, but an elegant house like this, with private bathrooms and kitchenettes for every tenant, was a luxury I could only dream of.

Upstairs, I let myself into Albert's apartment, pocketing the keys while I unbuttoned my coat. I called out his name, but there was no answer. Where had he disappeared to? I turned around from hanging my coat on the rack and there he was, as if by magic. He'd gone to check on his neighbor, he said, though how he'd managed to sneak past me from the hallway I couldn't imagine. "Is Mr. Stern ill?"

"No, we just had a late night. But anyway, Felix wasn't there. He must be at the orphanage already. The trustees have their meeting on Sundays."

"I know they do, that's why we went on a Saturday."

"Oh, that's right, we did go there together. My brain's not awake yet. Let me make us some breakfast."

I kept Albert company in the kitchenette while he ground coffee beans and plugged in the percolator. He put a pan on the gas ring and melted butter in it, then poured in eggs scrambled with milk and onions. I sliced some bread and toasted it while he slid the eggs onto plates and poured the coffee. We sat at the little table by his front window, watching the comings and goings of the street. I supposed if I'd ever spent the whole night with Harrison, we might have sat like this the morning after, though I'm sure he'd have expected me to cook the eggs. As we ate, I told Albert about my meeting with Jake and his offer to make me a theatrical producer.

"I didn't know women did that sort of thing."

I kicked him under the table. "How can you say that when Mary Pickford produces all her own movies? Anyway, why shouldn't I try my hand at producing? Even Harrison says I have good instincts for the theater. I guess you'll still be my liaison, Albert." I got up to refill our coffees. "Jake said he'd have you set up the production company."

Jake's ears must have been burning because at just that moment the telephone rang. Albert answered it, the conversation apparent from his replies. "Yes, sir. Yes, she was just telling me about it. She's here now, sir. Can we come to the mansion this afternoon?" Albert looked at me, his eyebrows raised. I nodded. "Certainly, we'll be there. Within the hour, sir." He hung up the receiver. "Are you up for another audience with the Colonel, Helen?"

"I am, yes. Are you?"

Albert glanced down at himself, still in his robe and pajamas. "I better go take a shower." The sound of splashing from the bathroom put thoughts in my head of Albert's body, slender and pale beneath the steaming water. To distract myself, I went into the kitchenette to wash up the breakfast dishes and rinse out the percolator. "Don't look," Albert called, though I did catch a glimpse of him wrapped in a towel before he could shut his bedroom door.

I settled myself on the couch, the winter sun washing the living room in light. Picking up an issue of *The Crisis,* I fanned through the pages, stopping at the story of a lynching. It was the most terrible thing I'd ever read, the poor man tortured with iron rods heated in a fire before being burned alive. I tossed the magazine back onto the table, then scanned the contents of several other issues. Every month, it seemed, they published an article like this, which meant every month there was a scene like this to report. And all this in the country Clarence had fought to defend.

"Ready?" Albert stood before me, smartly dressed with his hair combed back and his necktie knotted. When we went downstairs, he introduced me to the composer, who was at the piano in the parlor. A very young man leaned over his shoulder, turning the pages while he played. They must have assumed I'd spent the night with Albert because they stared at me with a mixture of amusement and disbelief that made me blush.

Though it was cold out, the day was bright and I suggested we walk across Central Park. Arm in arm, we looped around the reservoir, emerging onto Fifth Avenue through Woodman's Gate. Jake himself opened the door to the Ruppert mansion when we rang, though no one would ever mistake him for a butler in his tailored gabardine suit. Grumbling that Sunday was Mr. Nakamura's day off, he ushered us in but didn't offer to take our coats, which Albert and I ended up tossing over the newel post. Princess, whining, circled my ankles. I bent down to pet the dog, who was happier to see me than she had been her own pup.

"Come into the parlor, I have a fire going."

Princess followed as we picked our way past packing crates and rolled-up carpets. In the parlor, the satyrs were propped up against the wall now, wrapped in blankets like overgrown babies in papooses. "Where are they going?"

Jake handed us little glasses of schnapps. "They're being sent up to Eagle's Rest. I had the architect incorporate them into the design. His firm just delivered the plans, let me show you." Jake brushed aside stray pieces of straw and twine from a tabletop and rolled out the architectural drawings. "I wanted the zoo completed first so I could stock the animals. See, here is the duck pond, and the dog kennel, and the chicken house. The peacocks can wander the grounds, but the monkeys and the parrots will need to be caged."

"Monkeys and parrots?"

"Kramer told you I'm sponsoring an expedition to South America, didn't he? They've promised to send me some specimens. So," he said, pulling aside that drawing to expose the next, "with the zoo finished, come spring we begin work on the house." The ramshackle Victorian with its widow's walk had been demolished to make way for an entirely new structure. The illustration showed a stately Tudor faced in limestone, with pitched roofs and mullioned windows but lacking the pretension of half-timbers or carved corbels.

"It's very restrained," Albert said.

"If I wanted to show off, I would have stayed up near Hyde Park. What I want at Eagle's Rest is a place where I can relax with my friends." Jake handed Albert a cigarette. "You don't mind if we smoke, do you, Helen?"

I said no, of course not, noticing that it never occurred to him to offer me one. "You'll be able to have as many friends as you like, Jake, with fifteen bedrooms."

"Naturally, I'll have to host some parties and receptions. Anyway, half of the rooms are for my staff. The caretaker and the zookeeper are married men, so they'll have their own cottages, and Schultz has rooms over the garage, but see here." The third-floor plans outlined a series of bedrooms placed under the pitches of the roof, with shared bathrooms off the hallway and a back staircase that could take someone from the attic to the basement without ever being seen by the guests. "There are rooms for my cook and my laundress and my house-keeper. This one is for Osamu." Jake then pointed to a rectangle that offered no view of the river. "I was thinking of this one for you, Kramer, so you can always see who's coming up the drive. I'll have a telephone installed, and a desk where you can work."

I saw, across the hall from Albert, a comparable room with a window facing the Hudson. I pictured waking up to sunlight glinting off the water, imagined how the river breezes would flush out the heat sure to build up under the eaves. I hoped that room would be mine, when Jake invited me to stay.

"That looks perfect, sir," Albert said. "What about yours?"

He revealed the next page of plans. A wide staircase led up to a generous second-floor hallway, off of which were several guest rooms, each with its own bathroom. At the end of the hall was Jake's suite. The bedroom featured a wide bay window overlooking the lawn, while windows on the adjacent wall opened onto the river. A dressing room bigger than my mother's kitchen led to a private bath.

"I'm having an electric bell installed that will ring in Osamu's room upstairs, and one that rings for the cook. I'll have one put in your room, too, Kramer, in case I need you." He made a note on the drawing. He then indicated the guest room adjacent to his suite, a space larger than many Manhattan apartments. "I was thinking of this for you, Helen."

"For me?" I wasn't sure why I merited a better room than Albert did.

"I hate to eat breakfast on my own," Jake said, as if that explained anything. He looked up at me, his eyes shining. "I used to share breakfast with my mother every morning before I went to the office."

I couldn't imagine living with my mother into my fifties — it was irritating enough to still be at home in my twenties. But Jake and his mother had been the only family members left in the mansion after his father died and his siblings established homes of their own. I supposed no matter how mature he seemed to me, with his mother Jake had been able to remember himself as a boy.

"There's more than enough space in your suite for a breakfast table," Albert pointed out. "Are you having a dumbwaiter installed?"

"The kitchens are under the opposite wing of the house, so the architect tells me a dumbwaiter is not practical. Osamu can bring up a tray." He contemplated the drawings with a frown. "I plan to host the Yankees, and members of the Brewers' Association, too. It would be a help to have you there, Helen, to entertain the wives. I'd hate to expose you to gossip, though, coming into my room in the morning." He placed the tip of his pencil on the wall that separated his suite from the guest room beside it and drew in a doorway. "I'll have the architect put in a pocket door."

"I'll be happy to keep you company for breakfast, Jake." It was sweet of him to be so protective of my reputation, though I doubted the two of us eating together would cause a scandal. And, of course, Albert could always come through Jake's room to visit me. It would be our own cozy world, like the play within the play in *A Midsummer Night's Dream*, the pocket door a chink in the wall for us to blink through.

Jake rolled up the plans for Eagle's Rest. "Now, let's talk about this production company Helen is to run."

We three pulled up chairs close to the fireplace and addressed the first order of business: a name. I was afraid Jake would think my suggestion of Pipsqueak Productions too frivolous, but, with Princess on his lap, he heartily approved. Next was the question of officers for the company. Jake proposed Albert as president so we'd have a male figurehead, though I'd be doing all the actual work as vice president. For a moment I was offended, but really, what did it matter to me whose name was listed first on the incorporation papers? We all knew it would be my company to run, and I was glad that Albert and I would be working together.

"You'll need a third officer as treasurer," Jake said.

"What about Richard Martin?" Albert suggested.

I'd been thinking of Bernice Johnson, the bookkeeper, but Jake responded before I could speak up. "A name with such a long history in the theater would give her credibility. Good idea, Kramer. Just make sure he doesn't have any authority over the money. Now, tell me, Helen, how do you propose to finance this company of yours?"

I'd put a lot of thought into it, of course, and I pitched my idea. Once all the assets of the Olde Playhouse had been divided between the theater and the production company, I expected there would be plenty of extra costumes and props that I could sell to raise some money, which we could use to fund the first production. I was already planning to approach O'Neill with an offer to bring *Beyond the Horizon* uptown.

"I doubt if selling some dresses and swords will yield enough capital to mount a production," Jake said. "Instead of liquidating your assets, it would be better if you used them as collateral against a loan. Would twenty thousand give you enough to get started?"

I hadn't allowed myself to dream so big. "Do you really think a bank would lend me that much?"

"Not a bank, Helen. Me. I'll make you the loan." Jake nodded at Albert, who pulled a pad of paper from his pocket and began taking notes. "I'll defer repayment for the first year, then we'll begin monthly installments on a graduated scale at a modest rate of return. And you can prepay without penalty if you have a hit show."

Though it was a fraction of what he'd

spent to acquire Babe Ruth, it was much more than I expected. Still, I'd have to be frugal if I hoped to tempt a renowned playwright like O'Neill. If my salary was to be contingent on profits, it would be a long time before I made any money for myself. It looked like I'd be following Jake's example and having breakfast with my mother well into my thirties. "Thank you, Jake. That's a generous offer."

"Very good. Kramer will take care of the rest of it."

"Is there anything else, sir?" Albert asked. "Any impending business with Mr. Astor, for instance?"

Jake gave Albert a long look which I found inscrutable. I wondered if there was some other topic they'd be discussing if I weren't there. "No, nothing else. Just leave the loan papers on my desk when they're ready for my signature. I'll be at Madison Square Garden most of the week for the dog show. How about you, Helen, would you like to go?"

The play that was currently at the Olde Playhouse was in the middle of its run and selling well. There was nothing Richard Martin couldn't manage on his own for the week. "Thank you, Jake, I'd like that. I'll make sure to go to Gimbels tomorrow for a new coat."

"You're doing me a favor, Helen, accompanying me. You shouldn't have to spend your own money on clothes. Kramer, set her up with an account at Macy's."

Another woman might have been suspicious of such an offer from a millionaire, but I knew Jake only wanted me to look smart enough to join him for the dog show. It wasn't as if he expected me to swan around on his arm in evening clothes. Besides, now that he was backing my production company, the way I presented myself would be a reflection on him as well. When I thought about it that way, buying my clothes was practically a business expense.

Jake's cook came in to ask if he still wanted an early supper. We took that as our cue to wrap up our business and say our good-byes. We rode back across the park in a taxi, the short winter day already coming to a close. Dropping me off at home, Albert kissed my cheek and promised to have that account set up for me tomorrow. "Have fun shopping," he said, then gave the driver his own address.

I wished he could go with me to Macy's, but I figured he was too busy a man to waste his time on women's clothes. Turning to go inside, I was glad to spy Clarence in the lobby. I was anxious to hear about his father's health, and excited to tell him about my new venture. I hoped it wouldn't make him jealous by comparison. Though it was no fault of mine, I felt guilty that I was being given the chance to live my dream while his was being stolen from him.

But he wasn't alone. He was speaking with a woman perched on his stool, her booted foot swinging beneath the hem of a long skirt. They were so caught up in conversation he didn't notice me standing at the door and I had to let myself in. It was only when I dug in my pocket for my key that I realized I still had Albert's set as well. They must have been spares because he hadn't missed them.

Clarence turned when he heard the door shut behind me. The woman did, too. I was surprised to find I recognized her. "Miss Johnson?"

"Miss Winthrope, finally." She hopped down and smoothed her skirt. "I'm sorry to intrude on you at home, but I've been wrestling with my conscience all weekend and I finally decided I had to come tell you." She glanced at Clarence, who gave her a nod. "A proposal came across my desk at Ruppert Realty on Friday, about the Olde

Playhouse."

"An offer from Martin Beck? I know, Jake told me. But it isn't going to happen. He's going to turn the offer down."

"I'm so relieved to hear that, Miss Winthrope."

Clarence smiled at her. "You see, Bernice? You weren't doing anything wrong telling her."

Bernice? We'd been working together for over two years and I still didn't call her by her Christian name. "I'm sorry, are you two acquainted?"

"No, but I've been waiting a while. I might have given up, but Clarence kept me so engaged in conversation I never realized how the time was flying by."

"I appreciate your concern, Miss Johnson," I said, baffled as to why she and Clarence were so relaxed around each other. "In fact, I meant to contact you myself, but as long as you're here." I glanced at Clarence, thinking he might take the hint so we could talk business, but he seemed reluctant to leave her side. "The Olde Playhouse isn't being sold, but we are reorganizing the company. I'm going to focus on producing the shows, which means I need to hire someone full-time to replace me as manager. I immediately thought of you. Do you think I could woo you away from Ruppert Realty?"

The idea pleased her, I could see, though it was Clarence she looked at when she said yes, she could be wooed. "Of course, I'll need to know the particulars of my duties and the salary before I make a decision."

"I'm so glad you'll consider it, Miss Johnson. I need to speak with Mr. Kramer about how it's all going to work. Do you have a telephone number where I can reach you?"

"My parents recently had one installed, yes." She took a calling card from her pocketbook and handed it to me. The address was on Minetta Lane, near the Italian section of Greenwich Village they used to call Little Africa. "I'll look forward to hearing from you, Miss Winthrope." To my surprise, she handed one to Clarence as well. "Perhaps I'll hear from you, too."

"You can count on it." He smiled as he plucked the card from her fingers and held open the door. I watched him watch her walk away, astonished at his brazen gaze. "Bernice sure is an impressive woman, isn't she, Helen?" He tucked her card into his pocket. "You must see it, too, for you to offer her a job like that."

"She's an excellent bookkeeper. But,

Clarence, don't you think you should be more careful?"

"Why, is there some reason I shouldn't call her? She isn't engaged, is she?"

"No, not that I know of." I cringed, remembering that lynching story in *The Crisis*. "I suppose you were in France so long maybe you've forgotten what it's like here for men who flirt with women like her."

"You mean bookkeepers?"

He was being ridiculously dense. "New York's not Mississippi, but even so, Clarence, I'd hate to see you get hurt."

He stared at me, confused, until his eyebrows shot up and he broke into a guffaw. "You think she's white, don't you?"

Now I was the one who stared back, baffled. "Isn't she Italian?"

"She lets them think so at work, but no, Bernice is colored. Like me."

I thought of the tight curls at the nape of Miss Johnson's neck. Should I have known from that tiny hint? But her skin was only a shade darker than mine. Olive, I'd call it. Maybe tan. Not brown. Certainly not black. "How could you tell?"

"I didn't see it right away myself, her complexion's so bright. But once we got to talking, I knew." Deliberately, Clarence took my wrist and turned up my hand, pressing his thumb into the center of my palm. "For most of us our color is right there on the surface, but for some it's more in the blood than on the skin." He let go of my hand, the blood rushing back into the white circle he'd formed with the pressure of his thumb. "You won't change your mind about offering her that job now, will you?"

"Of course not." As soon as I said the words I realized I had, in fact, been about to change my mind, but only because I feared Jake would disapprove. I just wouldn't tell him, I decided. Once Bernice Johnson proved herself as manager, no one would care about her race. "I'm just surprised I didn't know, is all."

"There's plenty of us who pass right out of the black world and into the white without anyone the wiser. Didn't you read that Charles Chesnutt novel I gave you?"

"*The House Behind the Cedars?* I guess I've been too busy." Actually, I'd forgotten all about it; I was eager, now, to crack its spine.

Clarence pulled open the elevator door. I stepped inside. I looked at him, his face so familiar I sometimes forgot to notice its color, and wondered what white ancestor put that fleck of green in his brown eyes. "Would you pass, if you could?"

"I don't believe a man should have to pass himself off as something he's not just to get ahead in this world, Helen."

I agreed with him on principle, but it wasn't getting ahead in the world I was thinking of. Riding up to my floor, I stared at my hand. Though the difference between my skin and Miss Johnson's was slight, it was enough that she and Clarence could kiss without being punished for it.

CHAPTER 26

When I picked Helen up for our date Friday night, she was wearing a straight skirt and loose jacket over a button-down shirt with a little necktie. I made her turn around under the lights of the marquee. "You look very smart. Is that a new outfit from Macy's?"

She checked her reflection in the glass doors of the Olde Playhouse. "I thought I was just getting a coat, but the salesgirl said she'd been authorized to make me over head to toe. It's the new look for women, but except for the skirt I feel like I'm wearing my brother's clothes."

"No one would mistake you for Rex, believe me." We automatically walked toward the Italian restaurant where we so often ate on Friday nights. After taking some time to taste our wine and listen to the violin, I asked her to tell me what happened at the dog show that week.

"I hardly know how to explain it. Once

you get all the Saint Bernards together in a ring, I can't tell them apart. Bulgari took reserve, whatever that means, but Oh Boy flat out lost to a dog with no pedigree whatsoever. It seemed terribly unfair, given what Jake spent to establish his kennel." She took a last bite of her antipasto before the waiter exchanged it for the pasta course. "Oh Boy did snarl at the judge, but that shouldn't have been held against him. Madison Square Garden was so crowded it's a wonder the dogs behaved themselves at all."

"I read the results in the paper. I didn't have the heart to ask the Colonel about it."

"I'd avoid the subject if I were you. A reporter asked him how it felt to lose and he was so annoyed he said he was going to trade in his Saint Bernards for beagles."

I laughed. "He'd never give up Oh Boy and Bulgari, even if he stopped showing them. He loves those dogs too much. And I don't think he cares at all for beagles."

Our talk turned to the establishment of Pipsqueak Productions. I'd met with the lawyers that week to set up the company, and opened a bank account where I'd deposited the Colonel's loan. "I'll have everything ready for you to sign on Monday, Helen, if you can get Richard Martin to meet us at the lawyer's office. Have you found someone to replace you as manager?"

Helen told me she'd offered the job to the bookkeeper from Ruppert Realty who'd been handling the accounts for the Olde Playhouse. "She's smart as can be, and she understands the workings of the theater. Can I quote her the same salary I was making?"

"Go ahead. It'll be an improvement on her wages at the realty company, I'm sure."

I asked which movie she wanted to see after dinner. *Prisoners of Love* was playing at the Capitol Theatre and Helen had read a good review of the picture. "Not only that, but Betty Compson produced it herself."

"*Prisoners of Love* it is, then," I said, signaling the maître d' for the check.

The next evening, I sat by the front window of my apartment looking down at the snowy street, watching for Felix to come home. He usually returned from the Sabbath weighed down by his parents' expectations, but on this Saturday he moved through the circles of streetlight with a delightful swagger, chin high and gloved hands swinging freely. At our stoop he looked up and saw me, my forehead pressed against the glass. Blinking back snowflakes, he blew me a kiss. I committed the image to memory, like a figure captured in a snow globe, before rushing off to heat up our supper.

I was setting two bowls on the table when Felix walked in through our secret door, his cheeks still red from the cold. He grabbed my lapels and pulled me in for a kiss.

"What are you so happy about?"

"Just glad to see you."

I forgot about the chowder I had warming on the gas ring until we heard a sizzle in the kitchenette. We ran in to find the pot boiling over. "See what a mess you made of everything, Felix."

He teased me for being so dramatic, and he was right, the chowder was only singed. All through the meal, a smile tugged at the corner of his mouth. There was something he wasn't telling me. When I brought out the coffee and cake, I demanded to know what was up.

"Do you think Helen can take care of herself next Friday? Because my mother invited you to join us for Shabbat."

"Really?" I knew where his parents lived — we often walked down that block and he'd pointed it out — but I'd never been inside the house. "Why, what's happened?"

"I want you to know them, my father especially. We're going to be doing a lot of business together once Colonel Ruppert

signs the option on the orphanage property."
I was glad to hear he'd given up his conspiracy theory about Ruppert and Astor. All week, I'd been reassuring him there was no deal in the offing. Still, I was afraid he was getting ahead of himself again and told him so. "Don't worry, Albert. I'm optimistic we'll have some good news before the trustees meeting tomorrow. Look, it's still early. Why don't we go out to a show?"

"What, right now?"

Felix shrugged. "Why not? You've been wanting to see *Shuffle Along,* haven't you?" He wasn't usually so impulsive, and I jumped at the chance. On 63rd Street, we enriched an unscrupulous scalper five whole dollars to get ourselves two seats, but as the show commenced it seemed worth every penny. *Shuffle Along* was even better than the reviews had promised. The enthusiasm of the performers was contagious, the dancing so concussive it shook the stage. I wondered what Paul would think of the stomp and kick of the tap routines, so different from the lifts and spins of the ballet. The story was a pretty thin thread on which to string the song and dance numbers, but the audience didn't seem to care. It was a mixed crowd — in our row, Felix and I were in the minority — and as we came back from intermission, I wondered what would happen if our secret difference were as recognizable as our race. Would it make it that much easier for people to target us with their disgust? Or would our hidden legions made manifest force society to make a place for us in their shops and schools, at the tables of their restaurants and dining rooms, on the pews of their churches and synagogues? I tried to talk these thoughts over with Felix when we got home, but he stopped my mouth with kisses and I gladly gave up speaking. The cold opinions of the world outside seemed not to matter in the shared warmth of our bed.

Which was where I hoped we'd stay all that Sunday morning, drawing out the hours until Felix left for his trustees meeting. But there he was, in the first light of the winter morning, nudging me awake with a cup of coffee. I sat up against the pillow and took the cup he handed to me. "Why are you dressed already?"

"I went out for the paper." The *New York Times* for January 30, 1921, was so fresh off the press I could smell the ink. "Do you want to read it?"

He knew I usually took my time with the Sunday papers, saving them up to fill the afternoon hours he spent at the orphanage.

"Let me have my coffee first."

"Just the front page." He unfolded it with trembling hands, as if presenting me with a rare gift. I glanced over the rim of my cup and scanned the headlines, wondering what in the world had happened. The words were blurry at first and I squinted, hoping I was mistaken. But no, there it was, in letters half-an-inch high:

YANKEES PICK SITE FOR NEW BALLPARK
DECIDE TO PURCHASE PROPERTY OF
ORPHANED HEBREWS HOME GREAT STADIUM
PLANNED FOR HARLEM PLOT

Glancing down the column, sentences popped out at me. A deal had been reached. Plans had been drawn up. The Colonel had until the end of the week to exercise his option.

My stomach turned inside out. "My God, Felix, what have you done?"

"I told you I'd force his hand." He tossed the paper on the floor, spilling my coffee across the blanket. "Ruppert's got no other place to build, you said so yourself. Now that it's in print, he'll have to make it official, or look like a fool in front of the whole city."

I threw back the wet blanket and shoved

him aside as I knelt to pick up the paper. The article went into detail about the engineering plans, the cost estimates, even the seating capacity of the proposed stadium. All the information I'd given Felix to help him make his case to the trustees was right there on the front page. "He'll know it came from me. I'll be fired, Felix. As soon as the Colonel sees the paper, he'll know I betrayed his trust."

His expression shifted as he began to register the enormity of his miscalculation. "I'm sorry, Albert, maybe I hadn't thought it all the way through. But it's just a job, you can get another one. For the children, it's a chance for a whole new life. Their future is more important than either of us."

His obsession with those children was maddening. "If you think the Colonel will ever do business with the orphanage now, you're delusional."

The color drained from his cheeks as his lip started to tremble. "You're wrong, Albert. You're only worried about yourself. Ruppert won't miss out on the chance to build in Manhattan."

I was gathering the words to tell Felix that trust and privacy were the Colonel's watchwords, that he'd never consummate a deal with anyone who would expose him in the press this way, when the shrill ring of the telephone startled us both. I scrambled to my feet. Felix grabbed my arms, stopping me. "Albert, wait, I didn't mean —"

"Get out of my way, damn it." My instinct to answer the Colonel's call was stronger than my dread at hearing the words he was certain to hurl at me. I imagined him on the other end of the line, the *New York Times* quivering in his angry hands.

"Half you seen zee paper?" His fury so exaggerated his accent, my brain assumed he was speaking German. I answered in kind.

"Ja, ich habe es gesehen." The words were out of my mouth before I switched back to English. "I'm so sorry, sir, I —"

"Get over here, Kramer. Immediately." The line went dead. I fumbled the receiver twice before hanging it back on its cradle. I looked around for Felix, but he was nowhere to be seen. Then I heard footsteps clomping down the stairs and a door slam. I ran to the front window and watched him stumble down the stoop, toppling precariously as he missed a step. Instinctively, I stretched out my hand to steady him, my fingers pressed against the glass.

My guts were a knot of nerves as I got dressed, grabbed my coat, and hailed a cab.

At the corner of Fifth Avenue and 93rd Street I stalled for time, staring at the ruin of the Ruppert mansion. Only last Sunday, we'd had dinner in front of the fire in the parlor. Now it was shrouded in scaffolding, windows knocked out and the chimney dismantled. At this rate, the developer would be able to start construction in the spring on a new apartment building identical to the one across the street, which is where I now dragged my reluctant feet, like a criminal giving himself up to the police.

I was shocked when the Colonel opened the door in a wool dressing gown knotted over his silk pajamas, hair uncombed and slippers on his feet. In the five years I'd known the man, I'd never seen him in a state of undress. "Where's Mr. Nakamura?"

He scowled. "I offered him three days off next week if he'd stay with me today. I only moved a few days ago. I don't know where anything is yet. But nothing can pry that man away from his precious Sundays, though it's a mystery to me where he goes or what he does."

The Colonel's new apartment was restrained, stylish, and modern — everything the Ruppert mansion had never been. I followed him through a series of elegant rooms in which furniture was haphazardly placed and packing boxes were stacked along the walls. In the library, no curtains had yet been hung and morning sunlight lit up the windows. We headed toward a mismatched pair of chairs, my shoes clacking across the parquet floor.

"I'll need a carpet in here. What do you think, Kramer, nine by twelve?"

Confused, I glanced around the room, estimating its size. "Yes, that would fit."

"I saw in the paper Bamberger's has imported some nice Persian Saruks. Why don't you and Helen go pick one out for me?"

Was he sending me to buy a carpet as my final task before being fired? "If that's what you want, sir."

"What I want is a retraction." Out of habit, I took out my notepad and pencil. "It had to be the Jews who gave all this to the papers. It is you who's been keeping your neighbor informed of our progress on the stadium, am I right?"

My courage failed me and I equivocated. "Mr. Stern and I may have discussed —" Only after he interrupted me did I wonder when I'd ever told him Felix and I lived in the same brownstone.

"They have their meeting this afternoon. Get yourself on the agenda. Demand a full retraction. I want complete denial, no half measures, and I want to see it in Monday's paper."

The cook, pressed into service as butler for the day, appeared with pastries and coffee. She looked around, uncertain, until I got up and dragged over an unopened box on which she placed the tray. I poured, his with sugar but no milk, mine the opposite. The Colonel accepted the cup I held out to him, stirring the sugar cube with a tiny silver spoon. "You know I hate to see my business made public, Kramer."

Here we go, I thought. I wondered if I should resign or wait for him to let me go. Either way, the Colonel would never give me a letter of reference. I'd be ruined as a secretary. What other millionaire would want a man he couldn't trust to handle his personal affairs? I put down my coffee with a trembling hand. "Sir, I —" But he wasn't done speaking.

"Vince Astor telephoned this morning. 'What the hell is this about an option on some orphanage,' he said. 'I thought we had a deal.' I told him we would have a deal if we could come to terms. Otherwise, I said, I'd go ahead and build my stadium in Harlem." The Colonel laughed. "I should let my business leak to the press more often,

Kramer. Astor has agreed to my price." He pointed a finger at me. "Not a word to anyone until the ink is dry, but we should have an announcement by the end of this week."

"You're buying land from Astor?" I couldn't believe it. Felix had been right all along.

"In the Bronx, right across the river from the Polo Grounds." His mouth stretched into a delighted smile. "Wait until the Giants see what we have planned. This country has never had a stadium to match it. It will be New York's own Coliseum. Tillinghast Huston and I agreed to let Osborn Engineering think they were designing it for that orphanage parcel in case the press got wind of it, but all we have to do is reorient the plan to situate it on the new site."

I felt strangely like a cheated lover. "I had no idea, sir."

"I didn't want you knowing too much, living next door to one of their trustees. As long as you believed we were serious about that orphanage, the less likely the Jews were to entertain other offers. I like to have something in my back pocket, just in case. Now, though, I wouldn't buy from them if they paid me."

I was stunned to realize he'd used me as a

diversion. And why would he assume I'd pass information along to Felix? Perhaps he suspected all along that we were more than neighbors. I thought back again to when I wore the red bow tie to work. But if that was all it took for the Colonel to know the truth about me, what did that say about him? "I saw you last week with Mr. Astor, at the Hamilton Lodge Ball."

The Colonel sat back in his chair. "I know you did, Kramer. You were smart to steer clear of us. I figured you could guess what I was up to. I didn't even tell Huston how close we were to a deal until he saw the paper today and called me, ranting and raving." As if on cue, the telephone on his desk began to ring. "Go on now, Kramer, get me that retraction. And be at the brewery early tomorrow. We have a busy week ahead of us."

The doorman had ushered me out of the building before I fully understood what just transpired. The way the Colonel did business often took me by surprise — he'd draw things out until suddenly there it was, the deal struck, signed, and notarized. But this? I'd thought I was integral to his stadium plans, yet he'd kept me in the dark. Perhaps, though, in revealing to me how he'd manipulated my relationship with Felix, he'd tipped his own hand. Who but another pansy would have suspected I was Felix's lover? And yet, he'd admitted nothing about himself. If we were part of the same world, why not acknowledge it?

As confounded as I was by the Colonel, it was a profound relief to know I hadn't betrayed him. Even so, the deal Felix had been working toward was ruined. The orphanage would never raise the money now to build those charming cottages out in Westchester. The children would remain confined to their castle in the city. I pictured Felix crippled with regret. Desperate to console him, I hailed a taxi, urging the cabbie to drive faster across the park.

But Felix hadn't come back to the brownstone. I telephoned his parents' house, but he wasn't there, either. I called the main office at the orphanage, locating him at last, but he wouldn't come to the telephone. All I could do was ask to be put on the agenda, my action item the Colonel's demand for a retraction.

So it was that I found myself pacing the wide hallway of the Orphaned Hebrews Home that afternoon, waiting for the trustees to call me into their meeting. When Felix had trotted me out at that fund-raising gala, he represented my presence as tantamount to the Colonel's signature on an option. Now, I'd have to call him a liar in front of everyone.

A secretary brought me in, then took her place in the corner, a stenographer's pad balanced on her knee. I noticed a pyramid of rye breads stacked on a side table, the huge loaves scenting the air with caraway seed. Looking around, I recognized some of the men from the gala, including Felix's father, who didn't usually attend these meetings. Felix must have called him in to reinforce his position, despite the embarrassing tremor that shook his father's hands. And there was Felix, at the far end of the long table. His eyes were cast down, as if reading his own palms. What future did he see there, I wondered?

I was introduced. I did not sit. As simply as I could, I explained that Colonel Jacob Ruppert, though he had long been interested in the possibility of erecting a stadium on this property, had never suggested a deal nor signed an option. Though it was true he'd hired Osborn Engineering to develop a plan for the stadium, he'd never specified it was to be situated on this site. When the engineers confirmed the story to the papers, they were simply mistaken. "I can understand how Mr. Stern might have taken the

Colonel's interest to mean more than it did. No one is at fault, but now that the misunderstanding has been made public, Colonel Ruppert insists on a public retraction."

"And what about the children?" A dozen heads turned toward the sound of Felix's voice, cracked with emotion. "What are we supposed to tell them? That some millionaire got his pride hurt, and that's why they'll never live in the fresh air and sunshine?"

I opened my mouth to reply, but Felix's father spared me from speaking. "That's enough, son." He raised a trembling hand and placed it on the table, capitalizing on his infirmity to shame Felix into silence. "You tried your best, we all know that. But this is business now. We'll face a libel suit if we don't retract the story. We'll contact the *New York Times* this afternoon, Mr. Kramer. You'll see your retraction in tomorrow's paper."

Felix twisted around in his chair and hung his head. I wanted to leap across that table and take him in my arms. Instead, I looked away and thanked the gathered men for their time. The secretary showed me out. I found my own way to the entrance, promising myself that as soon as Felix and I were alone together, I'd find the words I needed to make this right.

But he never came home. For hours I watched for him out the window, but no matter how hard I stared he didn't appear. I picked up the telephone to call his parents but was afraid he'd simply refuse to speak to me. Instead, I did the unthinkable and went to their house. A crack of light appeared in a window as curtains were drawn back in response to my ring. I waited so long I was about to ring again when Felix's father answered the door. Instead of inviting me in, he stood beside me in the cold vestibule, having put on a coat for this very purpose.

"I'm sorry, Mr. Kramer, it's thoughtful of you to inquire, but I'm afraid my son is not up for a visitor right now."

I tried to keep the emotion out of my voice as I pled my case. "But I have to talk to him about the meeting today. I'm so sorry about everything."

"You shouldn't blame yourself, Mr. Kramer. Felix has done this before."

Done what, I wondered — broken a man's heart?

"Convinced himself of things that weren't true." Mr. Stern thrust his hands deep into his pockets. "If I may speak with you in confidence, Mr. Kramer? Sometimes my son becomes fixated on a person, or an idea, that he can't let go of. When he's finally confronted with the truth, as you did today, it can precipitate a crisis."

I remembered what Felix had told me about suffering a breakdown after college. "A crisis, what does that mean?"

"The last time, he needed a long rest in the country before he was himself again. This time we're taking him to Vienna. There's a doctor there who specializes in cases like his."

I felt as if I'd been plunged into an icy river, my heart stopped by the cold shock. "You're taking him to Vienna?"

"We've booked passage on the *Zeeland.* It departs Tuesday. His mother and I are going with him to make it look like a vacation. He has enough clothes here for the journey, but perhaps you could do us the favor of packing up his apartment? We'll send someone to pick up his things."

I thought of that trick Houdini did, chained in a locked box and dropped from a bridge into the frozen Hudson. "Can't I see him, at least, to say good-bye? There's so much to explain."

Mr. Stern cleared his throat. "Our doctor has insisted he be kept sedated until we're at sea. He was rather wild after the meeting this afternoon. I shouldn't be telling you this, but you've been such a good friend to him."

How Houdini struggled underwater with the chains and locks. "You can tell me anything, I'm sure Felix wouldn't mind."

"I don't know if you've noticed, but he has a tendency to hurt himself when he's distressed. We thought he'd overcome it these past few years. You've been a good influence on him, Mr. Kramer. But this afternoon he seemed in danger of doing himself irreparable harm."

Houdini had almost died down there, lungs on fire and vision fading to black, until the ghost of his mother appeared, guiding him to a hole in the ice. "Please, Mr. Stern, let me see him. I'm sure I could help —"

He withdrew a trembling hand from his pocket and reached for the door. With a concentrated effort, he closed his fingers around the knob and pulled it open, giving me no choice but to step outside. "I'll let him know you came by once we're safely at sea."

I staggered blindly up Central Park West, my mind as numb as my hands and feet. I imagined Felix slumped in a chair, eyes glassy from laudanum, those long hands of his limp in his lap. I was drowning in guilt for abandoning him, but what more could I have done? His parents didn't know what we were to each other. If they did, they'd have sent him away years ago.

I turned down my street. There, on my stoop, haloed in lamplight, stood Helen. Without a word, she opened her arms to me. I grabbed hold of her, gasping.

CHAPTER 27

I'd known that morning, when my brother had shown me the article in the Sunday paper, that something was terribly wrong. Albert had never said anything about a deal for the orphanage property, and Jake would never announce something so momentous as a new stadium in such an undisciplined way. I'd come to the brownstone after a day of telephone calls had gone unanswered. I'd been ringing Albert's bell to no avail. I was about to let myself in when I turned and saw him lurching blindly up the street. I thought he was drunk until I saw the tragic mask of his face.

Whatever calamity had befallen him, I knew it was of a greater magnitude than some workplace mishap. He didn't need to speak for me to understand his desperation. He collapsed into my open arms, knocking me back against the brownstone's front door. Somehow I managed to fit a key into the lock. We stumbled into the vestibule, where the composer and his young friend saw us struggling. Together we got Albert up the stairs and into his apartment. The composer told his friend to go find Felix, but now was no time for neighbors. "Never mind that. I'll take care of him," I said, shutting them out in the hallway.

I managed to get us out of our coats. They fell to the floor, crumpled lumps of wool. I maneuvered Albert to the couch where we dropped, me supine, he clutching at me as if I were a lifebuoy on a storm-tossed sea. "What's happened, Albert? Are you hurt? Should I call for an ambulance?"

"No." His mouth was pressed against my neck. The movement of his lips as he formed the word felt like a kiss.

I massaged the back of his head with my fingers. "I knew something was wrong, as soon as I saw that headline this morning."

"Oh God, Helen, it's all gone to hell." He burrowed deeper into me, the weight of his body full on mine. My urge to comfort him was overwhelming. I put my hand beneath his chin and raised his face. Bending my neck, I brought my mouth to his. At first, he seemed not to notice that our lips touched. Then his mouth opened so wide I feared he'd choke me with his thrust tongue.

He broke away suddenly, leaving my jaw agape. His voice cracked. "If only I could be with you, Helen."

This was it, the declaration of his intentions. Why it was so tortured I didn't know, but I understood that only the fabric of our clothes held us back from a complete union of body and soul. If I hesitated a minute longer, it would be too late. I'd never again find the courage to tell him the truth.

"Before you make me any promises, I need to tell you something. I can't get pregnant. I did, once, with Harrison, but I had — I tried to fix it, and it all went wrong. I could never give you children, Albert. I've been so afraid to tell you. I didn't think you could love me, knowing I was damaged goods."

He focused his surprised eyes on me, as if he hadn't noticed until that moment I was even there. "I could never love you any less." He stroked my face. "My darling Helen. We can be damaged together."

It wasn't an answer I'd ever imagined. "How are you damaged, Albert?"

"Haven't you guessed by now?"

I struggled to sit up, my skirt tangled in his legs. "Guessed what? Is it something to do with your heart?"

Tears fell from his eyes like water over the

edge of a cliff. "Maybe it is in my heart. I don't know where it is, or how to change it. It's who I am, I don't know why."

"You've got to believe I'd love you no matter what was wrong with you, Albert. Unless it's me you can't love?"

He took my hands in both of his own. "It's nothing to do with you, Helen. You're the finest woman I've ever known. I can't be with you because I'm an invert. Do you know what that means? Have you read Havelock Ellis?"

"The eugenicist?" I was unable to fathom what he was getting at. Was he worried about passing on his weak heart? But I'd just told him I couldn't have children. Whatever damage he carried, no child would inherit it through me.

"That, too." He let his head fall against the back of the couch as if the weight of it threatened to snap his skull from his spine. "He studies the psychology of sex. He devoted an entire volume to the congenital abnormality of sexual inversion."

"Inversion?"

Drained now of emotion, he spoke like an automaton. "I'm a pansy, Helen. Don't you know what that is?"

A pansy, sure, I'd heard the word. I was an actress, wasn't I? That's what people called the actors who wore makeup even when they weren't onstage, or the costume designers who were always accompanied by a young apprentice. They were pansies, fairies, queers. But Albert was none of these things. "Why would you say that, Albert? You aren't like that at all."

"I may not seem like it to you, but you have to believe me, Helen. I can never love you the way a man like Harrison could love you."

"But he never even pretended to love me, Albert. All he wanted from me was sex."

"That's exactly what I could never give you."

Was that the damage he was so afraid to confess? But I couldn't care less about a few minutes of slippery grunting. Albert might as well have told me we couldn't be together because he'd been injured in the war, a piece of shrapnel in the groin that prevented him from completing the act of intercourse. What woman who truly loved a man would jilt him for a wound he never asked for? Not me.

I placed my cheek against his cheek and spoke softly into his ear. "I don't care what you are, Albert. You know I love you. How we are with each other, that's all I want. And to hold you, like this, whenever you

394

need me to. The rest of it doesn't matter to me."

We kissed then, softly, my lips a balm to his pain. "I don't deserve you, Helen."

"Don't say that, darling." He didn't seem to understand that loving him required no sacrifice. I didn't care about what he couldn't give me, just as he didn't want what I couldn't give him. There was more to life than children and sex. So much more. And we could have it, together.

I held him close, knowing he was the prize I was lucky to win. "Let's just love each other, Albert, exactly as we are."

■ ■ ■ ■

1923

■ ■ ■ ■

CHAPTER 28

"The set looks amazing, darling." Albert put his arm across my shoulders and pulled me in for a quick kiss. "I'm so proud of what you've accomplished."

"Let's wait until the reviews come in to count my accomplishments." I hooked my thumb in his belt loop. "It does look good, though, doesn't it?"

"It's not just good, Helen. It's remarkable."

He was right, the set was remarkable. The entire stage was taken up with a cutaway of a train car, the inside lit up like a diorama. On one side of the coupling was the stateroom, where the sick girl would lie prostrate, as if on an altar. On the other side of the coupling was the parlor car, where men would be seated in plush seats, the doctor flanked by his two acquaintances. There was space between the seats for the girl's father to confront the doctor with arrogance and hatred in act one, begrudging necessity in act two, and genuine gratitude at the end of act three. I felt certain the play would be a critical success — maybe even a hit — but I didn't want to jinx it by saying so out loud.

Albert had promised to be my date for the invited dress tonight as well as the opening tomorrow. "You're sure you don't mind sitting through it twice?"

"Of course not. I was with you when you first got the idea for this play, wasn't I? Nothing could keep me from seeing it performed. It's too bad Rex is going to miss it, though."

My brother wasn't all that interested in my career, but if he'd been in town I supposed he'd have attended. As assistant to the Yankees' traveling secretary, Rex had gone down to Louisiana ahead of the players to organize their accommodations for spring training. It had been his dream come true when he got hired by the Yankees right after high school. Rex thought it was because he knew so much about baseball, but I suspected Albert had pulled some strings to get him the job, another one of his many favors to me.

Albert tightened his arm around me. I leaned into him, expecting another kiss, but he was only checking his wristwatch.

"Lunch hour's over, I'm afraid. I've got to go. The Colonel's doing another walk-through of the stadium this afternoon and he wants me along to take notes."

"He must be thrilled to be getting so close to completion."

"He's thrilled, but the engineers aren't. Every time the Colonel walks through, he issues more change orders. If Yankee Stadium isn't ready for opening day, it'll be his own fault. See you tonight, Helen."

I watched Albert disappear into the lobby, then turned back to the stage where the electricians were testing the lights ahead of our final rehearsal. My mind went back to last summer in Albert's apartment when inspiration had struck. It had become our habit to spend Sundays together and I'd come to the brownstone that morning with a box of rolls fresh from the bakery and Pip on his leash, letting myself in with the set of keys that had become my own. Albert, still in his pajamas, brewed coffee and fried some eggs, Pip dancing on his hind legs for a taste. After breakfast we settled ourselves on the couch, prepared to let the day slide deliciously by. Later on, we'd go for a walk or to a museum, but for now we listened to the phonograph as we lazily sifted through the newspapers.

"I can't read another word about Russian Bolsheviks or Italian socialists," I said, tossing the pages of the paper to the floor. "What else is happening in the world?"

"Did you see this article about the race riots in Macon?" He pointed it out to me and I ran my eyes down the column, shaking my head when I reached the sentences about innocent Negro boys being beaten and shot.

"At least the police are doing their job for once and rescuing people from the mob." I handed the page back to Albert. "Isn't there something nice to think about?"

He passed me the advertisements for the upcoming August sales. "We should go shopping tomorrow, Helen. Look, there's an Alaska seal coat with a skunk collar and cuffs on sale for three hundred dollars. That would look wonderful on you. I'll ask the Colonel about it when he gets back from the Yacht Club regatta."

"You don't think it's too much, asking him to buy me a fur?"

"I'll remind him how much cheaper they are out of season. Don't fret, Helen. He's got Babe Ruth under contract for fifty-two thousand dollars a year. I'm sure he can spare a couple hundred on a coat."

"He does like me to dress up for the dog

show." I went over to the phonograph, swapping a record by Bessie Smith for a new orchestration of the Charleston. On my way back to the couch, I picked up an old issue of *The Crisis* and leafed through its pages. I skipped the gruesome accounts of lynchings, looking instead for poetry and fiction. I found myself engrossed in a short story about a black doctor traveling by train to meet his fiancée. During the journey, a white girl on the train falls ill and he is prevailed upon to treat her. But when her parents express their prejudice against his race, he withholds his lifesaving ministrations until they publicly apologize. The story was written with such verve, the scenes rendered so theatrically, it was as if a play were being staged in my mind. My heart was beating fast as I came to the dramatic conclusion. "Albert, have you read this story?"

If he had he didn't remember it, so I read it to him aloud, standing up to act out the parts. By the time I got to the triumphant final lines, Albert, too, was on his feet. I felt a hot flush in my cheeks as I looked at him. "This would make an extraordinary play, don't you think?"

"Absolutely, Helen. It's as dramatic as anything O'Neill has staged. Do you think he'd be interested?"

"Don't talk to me about O'Neill." I still resented him for refusing my offer to bring *Beyond the Horizon* to the Olde Playhouse. "Anyway, he doesn't do adaptations. I'm thinking of producing it myself."

Though I hadn't had a hit yet, I'd managed to build Pipsqueak Productions into a modest success. I'd continued putting on a summer Shakespeare series with an out-of-town troupe, and I'd backed a number of comedies that had filled enough seats to offset the costs of staging them. I plowed nearly every cent I made back into the company, taking just enough for my daily expenses. Only my account at Macy's kept me from walking around Manhattan in rags. I often envied Bernice Johnson her steady salary as manager, a job she performed to perfection. She'd turned the Olde Playhouse into a self-sustaining operation, finding savings in every nook and cranny. It made my job so much easier. Once I'd budgeted a fixed payment for the theater, I was free to spend the rest on the productions. Our bank account at the moment was fairly flush, but was it enough to commission an original play?

I paced Albert's living room, thinking out loud. I'd have to negotiate the rights from the story's author and hire a playwright. Then I'd need to get the actors under contract and the set built — I could see in my mind's eye the cutaway train car and knew it would be expensive. Not to mention finding a director willing to take on a modern play about the race question with an integrated cast.

"What about Joseph Harrison?" Albert said. "He's got the right passion for a project of this sort. If it's not too painful for you to work with him, that is."

Albert had never alluded to my affair with Harrison before. Any other boyfriend would have been too jealous to suggest I work with a former lover. But that was the beauty of my relationship with Albert. Our love was too pure for possessiveness and jealousy. "I'm sure I can handle Harrison. If I could get him on board, we might have as big a sensation as O'Neill had last year with *The Emperor Jones.*" I grabbed his hands. "Can you imagine if I could persuade Charles Gilpin to play the doctor?"

"I'm sure you could do anything you set your mind to, Helen," Albert said, placing a series of sweet kisses across my knuckles.

And I had done it, all of it, just as I'd imagined. But putting on this play had completely drained our accounts. If it flopped, Pipsqueak Productions wouldn't survive the loss, and the weight of its failure would fall squarely on my shoulders. But if it succeeded? We'd beat O'Neill at his own game, and I'd show that a woman could produce plays as well as movies.

Onstage, the electricians cycled through the spots. One side of the train car disappeared into darkness as the focus shifted from stateroom to parlor. Then both sides of the train vanished as the spot shifted to downstage center, where the various characters would come forward to enact scenes from their past, scenes that revealed the source of the doctor's wounded pride and the seeds of the father's irrational prejudice. During the doctor's scenes, the electricians switched to a different gel in order to bring out the features in his dark face. They'd never lit a black man before, one of them told me, and it took them a while to settle on the right filter.

"It's magnificent." Harrison came up behind me and settled a heavy hand on my shoulder. "You always had a good eye for sets."

"I only made a rough sketch," I protested, giving the set designer her due for executing such a complicated vision.

"O'Neill can keep his jungles and drumbeats." Harrison pulled me closer. "Without Gilpin, *The Emperor Jones* would have been a farce. Wait until the critics see what he does with this role."

I broke away and turned to face him. "Wait until they see what you've done with it, Harrison. You found the playwright, you had the vision. It's more yours now than it ever was mine." It was true. Harrison had understood the tightrope we were walking with this play. Though it had an integrated cast, for the production to be a success we'd need white theatergoers to fill the seats. With that in mind, Harrison had worked with the playwright to shift the emphasis of the original story. In the play, the white father was now the protagonist, the audience meant to sympathize with his struggle to accept the assistance of the black doctor. The doctor's refusal to treat the girl after being snubbed turned him into the antagonist, and though Gilpin was being paid more — after his Drama League accolade and star turn in London, he had the leverage to drive a hard bargain — the actor playing the father got lead billing.

"Without the producer, nothing gets off the page and onto the stage, we both know that, Helen." Harrison trained his gaze on me. "Audiences only think about the actors, and critics focus on the director, but you're the one who's taken the real risk."

"So have you, Harrison."

"Forgoing my salary for a percentage of the profits is the best decision I ever made. I'm sure this play will be the making of us both." Harrison looked away from me and toward the stage. It felt like stepping out of a hot spotlight.

"Who did you invite to the dress rehearsal?" I asked.

"No one, Helen. This play has been my only mistress." He let his words hang dramatically for a moment, but I knew his celibacy could be chalked up to the casting: the ingénue playing the dying girl was too young even for Harrison, the actress playing her mother was too old, and the doctor's fiancée, though beautiful, was black. "Albert's coming, isn't he?"

"Of course, and my mother, too. Bernice Johnson is bringing her fiancé, Clarence Weldon." It stuck in my throat to call Clarence her fiancé instead of my friend. We were still friends, of course, but not like before. I was with Albert now, and he was with Bernice. We didn't have time for long talks in the lobby anymore, not with me so busy and him working a second job. Bouncer at the Sugar Cane Club was no more suited to his education than custodian, but his military training qualified him, and it paid well, which was all that mattered, he told me, now that he and Bernice were saving for their wedding.

"What I can't figure out, Helen," Harrison said, assuming a familiarity I resented, "is why you and Albert aren't engaged yet. He doesn't strike me as a free thinker."

"Not as free as you, Harrison. Go on now, and break a leg tonight."

"Thanks." He jumped onto the stage, his agility still a surprise, and disappeared into the wings.

"Where is he, Mom?" I asked, as if my mother could intuit Albert's whereabouts. When the lights had gone down and he hadn't arrived yet, I figured he was just running late. But now it was the intermission and he still hadn't appeared. "You don't think something's happened, do you?" Every day in the paper there were stories about people being hit by streetcars, or dropping into open manholes, or being crushed by falling debris. Just yesterday, chaos broke out when the city was plunged into midday darkness by coal dust permeating the fog. Albert had sworn he'd be here for the dress rehearsal. Nothing short of injury, I thought, could explain his absence.

"Jake must have needed him for something. Try not to worry, Helen. Oh, did I show you the telegram Rex sent from New Orleans?" My mother extracted a yellow piece of paper from her pocketbook. I glanced at the blocky letters wishing me luck with the play and said it was nice of him to remember. "Watch the rehearsal now, Helen. God knows you worked hard enough to put on this play. I'll bet you anything Albert will get here before the curtain falls."

But it did, and he hadn't. As the cast came onstage to take a bow, I wished I could skip the socializing and go in search of him, but everyone involved in the production had invited guests to the dress rehearsal. As the producer, I was obliged to meet them all: the wives of carpenters and electricians, the costume designer's mother, the set designer's husband, the friends and family of every actor and actress. Bernice introduced me to her parents, who I'd been curious to meet. Her mother was obviously colored, but her father was so light-skinned he could have been mistaken for Cuban. If Bernice had decided to pass as white to the point of marriage, like the woman in that novel Clarence had given me, she could have easily had children who would never have known there was a trace of Africa in their blood. Choosing Clarence, though, guaranteed her children would be seen as black. I'd wondered, when Bernice told me she'd accepted his proposal, if that was a compromise on her part or part of the attraction.

"The play is splendid, Helen," Bernice said. "Don't you think it's splendid, Clarence?"

"I do. It took a lot of courage for you to stage it, Helen." He held out his hand. I was tempted to spit into my palm before taking it. "Congratulations, the rehearsal went perfectly."

"Too perfectly." Harrison's deep voice vibrated in my ear. Clarence and Bernice started talking to my mother as he tugged me aside. "It's a bad omen for opening night, Helen."

Impatiently I said, "I could call in a favor and have you kneecapped."

For a moment he looked at me with complete sincerity, as if weighing the benefits of my suggestion. Then he broke into a laugh and threw his arm over my shoulders. "If it comes to that, I'll sacrifice myself for the good of the play. Come backstage, we've got a bucket full of ice and a gallon of gin. If we're lucky, some stagehand will fall down drunk and crack his skull."

"You all go ahead. I'm not staying."

"You can't leave, Helen. I need to talk to you." He pulled me out of the aisle, our knees knocking together as we dropped into seats in the middle of a row. "I've been thinking about the scene when the doctor examines the girl. From the back of the house I couldn't see a thing. The way her father holds up her dressing gown, it's like a screen. Gilpin might as well have been checking his watch as palpating her stomach. I'm going to move the father upstage and let the gown fall open so the audience can see the doctor is simply doing his best to diagnose her."

"She'll be up there in nothing but her nightgown."

"The girl's covered head to toe in satin, there's nothing indecent about it."

I tried to imagine how it would look staged as Harrison described it, but I was too distracted. "You're the director, it's up to you. I've got to go."

I found my mother in the lobby and told her I was going to Albert's and to call me there if she heard anything. At the brownstone, I mounted the stoop and let myself in without bothering to ring his bell. I hoped his landlady was sound asleep — she was used to me visiting during the day, but she complained if she caught me staying too late. The lights were off in his apartment but the curtains were open, the streetlamp casting a ghostly glow over the empty living room. His wallet and keys, which he always set on the small table by the door, were gone, but his coat and hat hung on the rack despite the snow flurrying outside. He must have rushed out in response to some emergency. Perhaps his mother had called with news that his grandmother had finally died. But no, he'd have found a way to let me know if he was taking a train to Pittsburgh. Maybe there'd been some crisis at the stadium, or perhaps Albert had been sent to bail Babe Ruth out of jail again. Whatever had happened, I decided to wait there for his return.

I put up a pot of coffee, listening to the wheeze and sigh of the percolator as I sleuthed through Albert's things. I stuck my hands in his coat pockets: matches, cigarettes, a capped pen. I opened drawers: city directory, subway tokens, a hammer. I lifted the lid of a box on the mantel: cuff links, tie clips, a brass button stamped with an eagle. None of it gave me a clue as to his whereabouts. If he'd been injured or killed, the police would never know to notify me. I wasn't his wife. I wasn't even his fiancée, as Harrison had reminded me. Cradling my coffee on the couch, I realized it wasn't enough for Albert and I to love each other. We needed, somehow, to be bound together.

I remembered reading that book Albert had mentioned, about sexual inverts. Dr. Havelock Ellis claimed the condition was an "inborn perversion of the sexual instinct, rendering the individual organically abnormal." But among the many case studies of men whose only desire was for others of their own sex, there were some accounts of inverts who had married women, their paternal instincts providing the motivation to engage their wives in intercourse. Perhaps the prospect of children would have motivated Albert, too, but I didn't have that incentive to offer. I'd skipped to the end of the book, looking for words of hope regarding some cure. My blood ran cold at the discussion of castration which, Dr. Ellis concluded, was as useless a treatment as large doses of alcohol, the manipulations of prostitutes, prolonged hypnosis, or even psychoanalysis. In the end, I'd put the book aside. Albert was no more damaged than I was. I loved him as he was, and he loved me in every way he could, and that was all that mattered.

The telephone rang. I lunged for it, certain it would be his voice I'd hear as I lifted the earpiece. "Has there been any word, Helen?"

"No, Mom, nothing." She offered to call Jake, but I told her she'd just wake up Mr. Nakamura. "If Jake heard of anything happening to Albert he'd let us know. You might as well go to bed, Mom. I'm going to stay here."

I poured another cup of coffee, kicked off my shoes, switched off the light, and curled up on the couch. I thought back to Harrison's question. Why shouldn't Albert and I be engaged? I was in no hurry to give up being a Bachelor Girl, and I knew Jake preferred his secretary to be a bachelor, too. But Albert wouldn't be a secretary forever. One day we could make a home of our own, buy rugs and furniture for ourselves rather than purchasing them on Jake's behalf. I remembered Mr. Stern saying an orphanage wouldn't give a baby to a single woman, but if Albert and I were married, we could adopt the way Babe Ruth and his wife had adopted their daughter, Dorothy. They'd tried to keep the adoption a secret, but the press, which followed Babe like hounds after a fox, had finally sniffed the story out. It must have been hard on Mrs. Ruth to admit so publicly to being barren, but adopting a child was a noble thing to do, everyone said so.

The hours crept by. Outside, streetlights punctured the deep black of early morning. I used Albert's bathroom, drying my face with his towel. The pillows on his bed were dented with the impression of his head and I stretched myself out on his sheets, pulling up the blanket. Perhaps we could share a bed, I thought, nuzzling his pillow for the scent of his hair. What difference did his condition make in the end? That he couldn't complete the act of sex, that's all. How many nights did most married couples sleep peacefully side by side? Albert had arms. He could hold me. He had a heart behind his ribs. I could rest my head on his chest and listen to it beating.

CHAPTER 29

I was already running late for Helen's rehearsal when the telephone rang. Figuring she was calling to ask where I was, I decided it would be faster to simply knot my necktie and head out the door than stop to talk with her. The Colonel had kept me at the stadium until dark, critiquing every detail, as if we weren't already scrambling to finish on time after a winter of challenges on the construction site. The railway strike put the delivery of steel a month behind schedule, freezing temperatures slowed the pouring of concrete, and a slew of change orders delayed progress and pushed costs well over the million-dollar mark. There were so many disputes with the contractors the whole project was put into arbitration, and the Colonel's constant interference didn't help matters. In October he'd insisted on relocating the club rooms and offices from the first to the third base side of the field over the strenuous objections of White Construction, Osborn Engineering, and Tillinghast Huston. On our walk-through today, when he'd discovered that the window sashes in the club room were blocked, he insisted the radiators be removed and replaced by shorter ones, even though that meant getting the pipe fitters back on-site. Then, as we were leaving, he decided he wanted the offices repainted, as the color on the walls was not to his liking. I had to wonder if he did these things deliberately to aggravate Huston, who was so fed up with the stadium project he'd finally taken up the Colonel's offer to buy out his ownership stake before opening day.

The telephone just wouldn't stop ringing. Sometimes I wished Helen could just leave me in peace. I'd told her I'd be there for the rehearsal and she had to know I was doing my best. In my haste, my fingers caught in the knot of my tie and pulled it out again. Frustrated, I yanked the thing from around my neck, stuffed it in my pocket, and answered the call.

"Albert, finally, thank God. It's been ringing for hours." Paul's voice had an edge to it that put me on alert. I imagined him in jail, needing to get bailed out — but no, that wasn't it. "Something's happened to

Jack. He was at Antonio's trying out a new number when he just, I don't know, collapsed. Toni called me. I got here fast as I could, but he's asking for you, Albert."

"You're still at Antonio's? Haven't you called a doctor?"

"He doesn't want a doctor, Albert. He wants you."

I was concerned, of course I was, but I didn't know what I could do for Jack. "I've got to go to the theater, it's the dress rehearsal for Helen's play. Why don't you take him home? I'll come down after and visit."

"For Christ's sake, Albert, you're at that woman's beck and call every hour of the day. Can't she make it through one night on her own?" I opened my mouth to object, but there was some truth to Paul's words and they stung. "You know Jack doesn't have any family but us. You wouldn't let him die alone, would you?"

"My God, Paul, no, of course not. Tell him to hang on. I'll be there as fast as I can."

"You'd better hurry, Albert. I'm not sure how much longer he's going to last."

"Okay, okay, I'm on my way." I rushed out with my coat left hanging on the rack and my jacket flapping open. I flagged the first taxi I saw and jumped in, offering the driver double his fare to get me downtown as fast as he could. Running my hand nervously through my hair, I realized I'd left my hat at home. We'd picked up Broadway before it occurred to me I should have telephoned the Olde Playhouse to let Helen know I might not make it. But it was only the rehearsal, after all. It wasn't as if I were missing opening night. She'd understand, I was sure. Though they'd never met, she knew Jack was my oldest friend in the city. The thought of him on the floor at Antonio's, clutching his heart and gasping out my name, brought me to tears. I supposed he must be dolled up for his act, embarrassed to be taken to the hospital in rouge and mascara, but that shouldn't matter if his life was at stake. I'd call an ambulance as soon as I got there, even if Jack objected. I could phone Helen from the hospital, once I knew Jack was out of danger.

The taxi got caught up in traffic around Washington Square, coming to a standstill at the Arch. "Never mind," I told the driver, "I'll get out here." I dashed across the park, oblivious to the cold. I didn't come down to the Village as often as I used to, and I hoped this wouldn't be one of those nights where I lost my way. But no, there it was, Antonio's, just ahead. I slowed a bit to steady my heart. Out of habit, I shook my hair loose before going inside.

Paul was waiting for me at the door. "Prepare yourself, Albert, it's going to be quite a shock."

I'd imagined the place cleared out for Jack's sake, but it was crowded as ever on a Friday night. I raised myself on tiptoes to look for him through the crowd, hoping they'd at least brought him upstairs. Then I heard a trill from the piano as a voice rose up in song. It was Jack, performing from the stage. But how could he have recovered in the time it took me to get downtown? "You said he was dying. Was it a false alarm?"

"Oh, don't worry about Jack, he's fine. Forgive me, darling, but I couldn't think how else to get you here."

It took me a moment to realize Paul had played me for a fool. Picturing Helen at the theater, anxious about my absence, I grabbed him by the arm. "What the hell is going on?"

A pair of large hands closed over my eyes as a man came up behind me. "Guess who?"

I would have thought it was Jack if I hadn't heard his voice coming from the stage. Was it Toni? But no, despite his short hair and trousers, Toni's hands were small

421

as a woman's. "I don't have time for this nonsense tonight, Paul."

"Be a sport, Albert. Try to guess."

I reached up, searching the hands with my fingertips. No rings or cuff links, so not Paul's benefactor (who, at any rate, was not nearly as tall). The jacket sleeves were wool, the fabric stiff and thick. I felt the buttons sewn to the cuffs, traced out the pattern stamped into the brass. An eagle, wings outspread — but that couldn't be. "I give up."

"Hast du deinen Ritter in glänzender Rüstung vergessen?"

My heart forgot to beat while my brain translated the words. No, even after all these years, I hadn't forgotten my knight in shining armor. "King?"

He stepped back and came round to face me. My obligations for the evening were forgotten as I filled my eyes with the sight of King Arthur, still in uniform, his chest now decorated with ribbons. What dim light there was in the smoky air caught in his hair and shone.

"I told you he'd remember, didn't I?" Paul said. "As soon as I clapped eyes on King here, I knew he must be the one." He squeezed my hand. "We didn't mean to frighten you, Albert, but Jack and I wanted it to be a surprise. Wasn't it worth it?"

"It wasn't my idea, Albert. I only just found out what Paul here told you." King's voice had a strange lilt to it that reminded me, weirdly, of the Colonel's accent. Had he always talked this way? But we'd only spoken that one time, while the war was still on and he was about to fight in it. Hearing his voice made the years between that night and this disappear like a dove in the folds of a magician's cape.

Edith put a trio of setups on the bar. Paul mixed us all drinks from a flask as he explained how King had come into Antonio's that evening, asking for me. He and Jack, remembering my long-ago story about being detained by a soldier, had hatched their plan.

"No hard feelings, I hope." King extended his hand. I remembered how it had engulfed the Colonel's after that baseball game at the Polo Grounds. "It's good to see you again."

"I'll leave you to it, then," Paul said.

"You're going?" I felt ridiculously nervous all of a sudden.

"I've got a performance tonight, and Geneviève can't very well lift herself, can she?" Before walking away, Paul whispered in my ear, "You're welcome, sweet prince."

I turned to King, intending to say something smart and gay. Instead I blurted out, "How did you know to look for me here?"

The blue of his eyes knocked me back against the bar as he lifted his glass. "A knight can always find his damsel in distress."

How had he known I was in distress? I hadn't known it myself until that very second. If I'd been asked that morning, I'd have said all was well with my life. For two years, Helen had been my boon companion, healing and sheltering my fragile heart. With her by my side, I'd gotten over Felix and steered clear of new entanglements. There were entire weeks when I forgot about the difference that set me apart from normal men. I felt it now, though, under the spotlight of King's gaze. It was like being recognized at a masquerade by someone who knows you so well no disguise can fool them.

We slid into a booth near the door where it was quiet enough to hear each other speak. King had gone by my old place on Washington Square, he explained, but not seeing my name next to a doorbell, he recalled me saying something about meeting up with friends at Antonio's.

"I can't believe you still remembered where I used to live."

He extracted a well-worn rectangle of paper from his pocket and held it out to me. I recognized it as one of the Colonel's business cards. On the back was my old address, and Helen's, too. Helen. The dress rehearsal must be half over by now. I should have excused myself, made a call, let her know not to expect me. But I was unable to tear myself away, even for a minute.

"I've kept that card close to my chest all these years." King plucked it from my fingers and put it away.

"Even in the trenches?"

"I didn't see too many of them, I'm ashamed to say." We finished our drinks as he filled me in on his war years. He'd been tapped as a translator soon after landing in France and spent the conflict far from the front lines. Then, after the armistice, he worked for the Americans negotiating the peace treaty with Germany. By the time that got settled in 1921, he'd grown fond of Berlin. King gave a glance around Antonio's that suggested he saw it as a dingy little dive. "You can't imagine what life is like for us there. We've got our own restaurants and bars and coffee shops. We can buy our magazines out in the open at the newsstand. Men like Jack and women like Toni can walk down the street in the middle of the day with no fear of arrest. There's even a scientific institute advocating for our legal rights."

I couldn't quite grasp what King was describing. It had seemed to me no place could be more accommodating of queers than New York City, but even so we had to be careful how we dressed and where we gathered. I remembered Jack teaching me never to go out with my identification on me, so I could give a false name to the police if necessary. The thought brought my hand to my jacket pocket, where my wallet was tucked, my name — and the Colonel's — on a dozen pieces of paper.

"So you can imagine," King was saying, "when I had a chance to stay on in Berlin attached to the diplomatic corps, I took it."

I had a moment of jealousy, picturing some handsome young German on King's arm as they strolled together through the Tiergarten. "Why did you leave, then, if life was so good?"

"My *opa* died." King finished his drink and signaled to Edith for another round. He'd missed the funeral, of course, being so far away, but he'd returned to Milwaukee to help his *oma* bring in one last harvest before selling off the farm. "She wanted me to take it over, but there was no way I could settle for being a Wisconsin dairy farmer, not after Berlin."

Edith replaced our empty glasses with a fresh round of setups. King sipped the seltzer and grimaced. "I keep forgetting about Prohibition."

I waved over a waiter and gave him five dollars. Two minutes later he returned from a quick trip out to the alley with a full flask of whiskey. I topped off our drinks. *"Prost."*

"Prost. Everyone in Europe thinks America is crazy for outlawing alcohol."

"Most Americans do, too. Are you making a career of the army, then?"

He looked down at his uniform. "You mean this? No, I was discharged months ago. I only wore it today for luck. You see, I never got the notion out of my mind of trying out for the team."

It took me a second to put together his wearing of a uniform and the idea of a team. I remembered then those pictures that ran in the paper of soldiers on the field at the Polo Grounds, how pleased the Colonel had been at the publicity. "You want to play for the Yankees?"

He shrugged. "I want to try, at least." We both knew how unlikely it was that he'd win a spot on the roster. Even so, he said he'd gone to the team office that day and presented the Colonel's card. I imagined the receptionist was as dazzled by King's blue eyes as she was by his story. She'd placed a call to Miller Huggins down in New Orleans, who happened to remember that day in 1918 when a talented soldier hit one out of the park. "He said to put me on the train with Waite Hoyt and the others going down for spring training. I may not last long, but at least I'll have a shot. I'm leaving on Sunday."

"But that's the day after tomorrow."

He reached across the table and stroked my cheek. "That's right, two whole days from now. So, Albert, tell me, what's happened to you since I shipped out?"

What was it about King that turned me into an open spigot? I heard myself telling him about Felix — how we'd lived together, how it all ended. I told him about Helen, too, and the way she'd embraced me when I told her I was a pansy. I didn't know how I would have gotten through those dark months after Felix's parents took him away if it hadn't been for Helen. I'd written him, of course, careful not to say too much in case his correspondence was being monitored. It was a year after he'd been whisked off to Europe before I finally got a curt note thanking me for my concern and wishing me well on my future endeavors. It was as if that doctor in Vienna had replaced Felix's heart with a mechanism incapable of feeling. But then again, I supposed that had been the point.

"I've heard about that treatment," King said, refilling our drinks. "I can understand a man wanting children, but what's the use of trying to change who you are? It's the laws that should change, not us. The way I see it, Albert, we can't choose our desires any more than we can choose the color of our skin."

Was that what I'd been trying to do with Helen? I'd gotten so comfortable, moving through life with a woman by my side. Helen and I could dine together as a couple, go dancing at a public hall, kiss hello and good-bye out on the street — all the things I could never do with a man. When I'd first come to New York, it was playing it straight for work that had seemed like an act I put on. But the more my life revolved around Helen, the more being a pansy seemed like a role in which I'd once been cast. Strolling through Central Park with Helen on my arm shielded me from the hungry glances of men until I'd lost the knack for glancing back. In the two years since Felix was taken from me, I'd had only one encounter with a man. He'd stopped me on the street to ask for a light, so confident and persistent I followed him home like a lost dog. I expected no reciprocation and he offered none, and though the hand he held to the back of my head was warm, he didn't use it to help me up from my knees.

I compared that to the countless times I'd kissed Helen's cheek, taken her hand, wrapped my arms around her waist or rested my head in her lap. We loved each other, truly. Yet here was King Arthur, our knees pressed together in that little booth, the whiskey and soda going to my head. I didn't love Helen any less than I had at lunchtime, but it was past midnight now and the part of me that had nothing to do with her had woken from an enchanted slumber.

Jack's act was coming to a close. A more raucous performer would soon take his place. I could hardly hear myself think. "Listen, do you want to get out of here?"

King's smile sped up my heart. "Sure, let's go." He stood up. So did I. I wobbled. King took my elbow to steady me. There was a crash as the kitchen door and the front door both banged open at the same time. The music ceased. A squeal rose from the gathered pansies as uniformed officers barged into the place. I glimpsed Jack duck through the door offstage that led up to Edith and Toni's apartment.

It was a raid. I thought of the cards in my wallet and got weak in the knees. It would be the end of my career if the Colonel were to see my name in the paper. Not for drinking alcohol — New York's courtrooms were a revolving door when it came to those charges. But Antonio's hadn't been targeted for the flasks of bootleg liquor now knocked to the floor. The Committee of Fourteen was more intent on policing perverts than upholding Prohibition. I'd be arrested for indecency, and those charges were likely to stick. I trained my panicked eyes on King. He seemed to read my expression. *"Vergib mir,"* he said. Forgive him for what, I wondered? Then he curled his hand into a fist and smashed it into the side of my face.

My vision went black, the darkness broken by an explosion of stars in colors I'd never before seen. A police whistle pierced my ear. I felt a shove in the gut as my feet left the ground. Everything turned upside down as King tossed me over his shoulder like a wounded comrade. He carried me right up to the sergeant in charge and spun some story about having been sent to bring a missing soldier back to the base. "Believe me," I heard him say, "this pansy'll get worse from our commander than he'll ever get from a judge." That, and a ten-dollar note in the sergeant's hand, got us ushered out of Antonio's while the rest of the patrons were herded into a police truck.

The next thing I knew I was in the back of a taxi, King holding a bloody handkerchief to my face. Cold air from the open window cleared my head. "You saved me."

"Hush now, Albert. Just give the driver your address."

I used my injury as an excuse to rest my head on King's shoulder as we drove uptown. We stumbled out at the brownstone, his arm around me the only reason I didn't sink to the sidewalk. Miraculously my keys were still in my pocket — how they hadn't fallen to the ground along the way I couldn't fathom. He led me up to my apartment, our footsteps muffled by the runner on the stairs.

I switched on the light in my living room. He gave my blasted eye a critical look. "We better put some ice on that. Stay here, I'll get it." He found the kitchenette and I heard the ice pick at work. I went over to the mantel, opened the lid on my box of curiosities, and picked out the button. He returned and held the ice against the side of my face.

I winced at the pressure.

"It's just a black eye, *liebling.* Don't be a baby."

"Look." I held the button out in my open palm. "I kept it all this time."

"I got a demerit for losing that button." He gave a rueful smile. "I was so young that night. You were so kind to me."

"You were the one who was kind." Carefully, I brought my mouth to his. It was a patient kiss, our closed lips lingering over their renewed acquaintance before his tongue tested for more. I put my arms around his broad back. Opening my jaw jolted me with pain, but it didn't matter. Inside my chest, a key fit into a lock and turned.

CHAPTER 30

What a relief it was to hear the sound of Albert's voice coming from the living room! All that worry, and for what? He was alive and well. He'd explain what happened, I would forgive him, and we'd go on as before. Well, not exactly as before. I had in my mind, now, a new vision of our future. A home of our own, someday. A child, perhaps, saved from some orphanage. A ring on my finger and a shared bed.

Albert's bed. Remembering where I was, I pulled the blanket over my head. To fall asleep on his couch was one thing, to crawl into his bed was another. Embarrassed, I slid out from under the blanket, wanting to at least be on my feet when he found me.

Wait — it was Albert's voice I heard, but he wasn't alone. Had he been out with his friends while I worried myself sick? From the darkness of the bedroom I saw the silhouette of a man cross the living room. I couldn't see his face, but from his size and the way he moved I knew it wasn't Paul. I crouched behind the door, peering through the gap between the frame and the hinges.

My brain didn't understand, at first, what my eyes were seeing. I'd never beheld two men kissing, not on the street or on a motion picture screen or in the pages of a magazine. I searched my memory for a template against which to measure what I witnessed. Into my mind popped an illustration from our encyclopedia of male gourami fish fighting with their open mouths. But that didn't explain the curve in Albert's spine as he leaned into the man's embrace, or the exposed stretch of neck as he invited the man's kiss. I heard a sigh, smelled the scent of sweat as their jackets fell to the floor.

I backed away, stumbled into the bathroom, slammed shut the door. I bent over the sink, the tap fully turned to mask the sounds emerging from my throat. When Albert told me he was a pansy, I'd thought it meant he was incapable of sexual passion. I'd believed the affection he showed me was all he had to give. I saw now how wrong I'd been.

His voice came through the bathroom door. "Helen, is that you?"

My hands shook as I splashed cold water on my face. "Albert, you're back. I fell asleep waiting. Give me a minute?"

When I came out, I saw what my narrow angle from behind the bedroom door had hidden: the bruised side of his face, the swollen lid stretched tight, a red cloud of blood in the white of his eye. "My God, Albert, what happened?"

"I got caught up in a police raid at a speakeasy."

"You were out drinking? I thought you'd been run over by a streetcar."

"I'm so sorry, Helen. I should have called. I was on my way to the theater, honestly, it's just —"

"Never mind. You're okay, that's all that matters. I need to get home." I pushed past him into the living room and stopped short, as if taken completely by surprise to find someone else there. Harrison would have critiqued me for overacting. "Oh, hello."

The man stepped forward. "I don't suppose you remember me."

I stared at those blue eyes, that blond hair. Five years ago, at the Polo Grounds. Soldiers on the field after the game. One of them came up to the owner's box. I gave him my address. So did Albert, but neither of us received a postcard. Later, we looked for that soldier's name on the lists in the newspaper. King Arthur, Albert Kramer — even their initials were interchangeable.

"King, of course I remember." I indicated his uniform. "But the war's over."

"I stayed on in Germany." He looked at Albert. "Perhaps I should leave."

"No. Please, stay."

The urgency in Albert's voice withered me. "Yes, stay. I'm going home."

"I'll call you a taxi." Albert roused the dispatcher from sleep while King and I stood in awkward silence. "He'll have a cab here in just a minute. Come on, Helen, I'll walk you out." He took my coat down from the rack. I wondered how they hadn't noticed it before, or my shoes kicked under the couch, which I bent to retrieve. It was as if I were invisible to them.

In the vestibule, Albert caught my hand. "I'm so sorry to have worried you, Helen. Paul called to say our friend Jack was sick so I rushed out, but it was only a trick they played to surprise me that King was there."

I couldn't put it together. Albert's friends hadn't been at the Polo Grounds that day. "How did Paul know who King was?"

"I told them about him. I saw him later on, after the ballgame." The blush in Albert's cheek competed with the bruise of

437

his blackened eye. "He stayed with me that night. He had my address, remember?"

For five years, I had treasured the memory of the day Albert and I met, a gilt-framed picture in the album of my life. The thought had even crossed my mind that if we married it should be on that same date so we'd have only one anniversary. But that's not the memory Albert carried from that day at all. He remembered it for meeting this soldier.

"I was going to call you, but then there was the police raid —"

I couldn't help touching a tender finger to his blasted eye. "The police did that to you?"

"No, King did. Don't blame him, though. He did it to get me away from the police. It would have been a disaster if I'd been arrested. You know how the Colonel hates publicity."

I did know. How often had Jake complained about Babe Ruth's bad behavior? Drinking, speeding, womanizing. Not even a Pinkerton detective with a camera could shame the man into moderating his behavior. "I have to go, Albert. I'm sorry you missed the rehearsal, but I'll see you at the opening tomorrow —" I looked at my watch, saw it was almost morning. "Tonight,

I mean."

"No, wait." He took my hands and brought them to his mouth. He touched his lips to my knuckles, a once-cherished gesture. I pulled back my hands, knowing now what paltry crumbs he tossed me with those kisses. "King's leaving Sunday for New Orleans. He's going down to try out for the Yankees." I looked at him blankly. "He's only here one more night."

"You want to bring him to the opening of my play?"

"No, Helen. That's not what I'm asking."

He left it to me to say the words. "You're not going to come."

"I knew you'd understand. I'll make it up to you, I promise. You'll get to know King, if he makes the team." He misunderstood the look on my face. "I know it's unlikely, but I don't want to crush his dreams. The best he can hope for, really, is a spot on a minor league roster, but who knows? The Newark Bears are just across the river." He smiled with the half of his mouth that wasn't wounded. "You'll like him, Helen, I promise. I've told him all about us."

We heard the sound of the taxi's engine coming up the quiet street. Albert adjusted the dragonfly brooch pinned to my lapel. "Break a leg tonight, darling."

The play started out all right, the audience impressed as the curtain rose to the haunting blast of a train whistle. Harrison had insisted we rent an organ to produce the sound, and though I'd argued against the expense, he'd been right. Coupled with the cutaway set, the sound design gave an uncanny verisimilitude to the stage. The clapping after the first act lifted my spirits a bit. Then in the second act, I watched from the back row as everything I'd worked toward unraveled like a ball of yarn dropped down a flight of stairs.

I was confused when the actor playing the girl's father retreated upstage until I remembered Harrison had changed the blocking so the audience could better see how the doctor treated her. As Charles Gilpin stretched out his hands for the examination, I saw what was about to happen, but there was nothing I could do to stop it. The lighting, calibrated to illuminate Gilpin's dark complexion, had washed out the girl's satin gown so that it looked as if he were touching her naked skin. The audience reacted with a mass intake of breath, followed by hisses and jeers. I heard someone call out, "Don't you touch her!" Gilpin, consummate professional though he was, found the reaction jarring. When the father jumped forward to deliver his line — "Get your black hands away from my girl!" — the audience broke into unexpected applause. Gilpin struggled to regain his composure. "You are condemning your daughter to death, sir," he said, exiting the stateroom with a regal bearing meant to convey his rejection of irrational prejudice. After having been insulted in this way, he refuses to treat the girl, who is seen thrashing in exaggerated death throes while the doctor, in the parlor car, resolutely ignores the entreaties of his fellow passengers — and the increasingly disruptive heckling from the audience.

During the intermission, Richard Martin was overwhelmed at the ticket window by theatergoers demanding their money back. Afraid they'd start a riot, I told him to go ahead and refund the tickets. The mood of the audience that remained after intermission was combative. When the father finally apologizes to the doctor in order to save his daughter, someone in the audience actually stood up, proclaimed he was a doctor, and offered to treat the girl himself. The cheers stopped the show for nearly a minute. In the closing scene where the girl's mother thanks the doctor for saving her daughter's life, the older actress sank to the floor as she had in every rehearsal, the movement meant to show her extreme relief. But the actress lost her balance and Gilpin held out his hand to steady her, so that it seemed as if she were lowering herself to her knees at his command. The chorus of boos sounded like cows herded into a barn for milking.

There was a pathetic smattering of applause as the curtain came down. The disaffected audience got to its feet and hastily exited the theater. When Harrison came onstage, expecting accolades for directing such a daring play, he was met with an empty house. The only people left lingering in the lobby were reviewers. Richard Martin found me to say he was already getting telephone calls from people canceling their tickets for future performances. As the bad news piled on, I reached, instinctively, for Albert's hand. My fist closing on empty air reminded me it was King he'd chosen to be with tonight, not me.

"Heathens. Ignorant heathens." Harrison was fuming, his lit cigarette a hazard in his wildly waving hand.

"The play is wonderful, Harrison, we both know that. The audience just didn't appreciate it. Let's wait and see what the critics have to say."

He snorted and dropped the cigarette, grinding the ash with the toe of his shoe. "I'd better go try to charm the reviewers, then."

My mother gave me a supportive hug, but even she couldn't put a polish on the disaster that had just unfolded. When she asked where Albert was, I told her he'd fallen down the subway stairs and was recovering in bed. "Oh, the poor boy. Do you want me to check on him?"

"No, Mom, promise you won't. He's resting. And anyway, aren't you coming out with us?" I glanced through the lobby doors to see the line of taxis Pipsqueak Productions had paid for, ready to whisk us up to Harlem. I'd booked the Sugar Cane Club, where Clarence worked, for our opening night party. It was a black-and-tan, the only sort of speakeasy we could go to with an integrated cast.

"I'm too tired, dear. I'll see you at home later on."

"Don't wait up, Mom. It'll be dawn before the reviews come out."

"Buck up, Helen." Harrison sidled up to me, dropping his voice to a whisper. "I just had a heart-to-heart with Alexander Woollcott from the *New York Times.*"

"Did he say he liked the play?" A good review was my only hope. The production could survive a slow start, but anything less than a full run would ruin us.

"You know how those critics are, air of mystery and all that. But remember how he raved about *The Emperor Jones*? This role showed Gilpin to much better advantage." He reached over and tucked my hair behind my ear. "Come on, Helen, everyone's waiting for us."

Harrison and I got into the last taxi to pull away from the curb, joined by the set designer and her husband. The two of them prattled together as if they hadn't a care in the world, and I supposed they didn't. The set designer had already cashed her check; the reviews would make no difference to her. The actors had twelve-week contracts, which had to be fulfilled even if the play closed early. I'd already paid the Olde Playhouse for the length of the run — Bernice Johnson's books would balance, at least. No, it was me and Harrison who'd be left holding an empty bag if the show was panned. As far as Pipsqueak Productions was concerned, the only way out of our debts would be bankruptcy.

The taxis pulled up to an unassuming

storefront on 135th Street. Clarence, posing as a loiterer, was doing door duty that night. At our arrival, he pulled a chain that lifted a cellar door, sending a beacon of light streaming upward. One by one, the cast and crew descended into the Sugar Cane Club. It didn't offer the extravagant performances of Small's Paradise or the segregated voyeurism of the Cotton Club — neither of which I could have afforded to rent for even an hour, let alone the night. At the Sugar Cane Club, a three-piece band provided the entertainment while the kitchen put out only one dish: the best fried chicken in New York City. Thanks to Clarence's influence, I'd negotiated a comprehensive price with the owner that included all the food we could eat, all the whiskey we could drink, and a fat bribe to the cop on the beat to guarantee we'd be left in peace.

Clarence seemed so alone out on the sidewalk that I let everyone else go down ahead of me. "Isn't Bernice coming tonight?"

He dropped the cellar door shut while we talked. "No. She doesn't mind me working here, but it's not the kind of place she enjoys. Where's Albert?"

I'd been holding so much back for so many hours that his simple query threatened to unleash a torrent of tears. I took a deep breath and dammed them up again. "He hurt himself, but he'll be fine. Will you be coming down later?"

"I usually stay until the place closes."

I wondered when he ever slept. "We're waiting up for the morning papers. You can't sit out here until dawn."

"In that case, I'll come down before the night is over," he said, pulling the chain and raising the door for me.

In the club, Harrison was rallying the cast, leading loud rounds of toasts in honor of each and every performance. His optimistic mania soon pervaded the party, and the mood I'd expected to be funereal became instead ecstatic. The young actress who played the dying girl had invited a dazzling group of bright-eyed friends who never seemed to stop dancing. The electricians and stagehands of the Olde Playhouse were determined to make the most of the free food and drink. Charles Gilpin held court, reciting soliloquies from Shakespeare. The woman who played his fiancée turned out to be as fine a singer as she was an actress. She joined in with the band, and soon had everyone singing along.

A whiskey mixed with Coca-Cola was put into my hand. I drank it quickly, as eager to forget about Albert and King as I was to numb my anxiety over the play. There weren't enough chairs in the place to seat us all, and as the only space in which to stand was the dance floor, I found myself being passed from man to man as everyone from the set designer's husband to the property master claimed a dance. At one point Harrison pulled me close, his hand sliding up and down my back with the rise and fall of the music. In one ear the drummer's cymbals hissed and sizzled. In my other, Harrison's big heart boomed.

As the hours wore on, the stagehands and crew members wandered home to their beds. Those of us who remained arranged ourselves in a bedraggled tableau around tables littered with half-eaten plates of chicken, half-empty glasses of whiskey, and half-smoked cigarettes. Clarence came down, off duty now, and helped the waiters clean up. Around four o'clock, Gilpin sent his wife home and asked for a pot of coffee.

Finally, the boy we'd paid to wait out on the corner came running in with an armful of morning papers. I blearily looked over Harrison's shoulder as he opened the theater page to Alexander Woollcott's review. My eyes were unable to focus on the text swimming before my eyes. "Read it aloud,"

447

I said, resting my chin on my palm.

Harrison's sonorous voice filled the quiet club. "Joseph Harrison's new play at the Olde Playhouse entirely disregards the talents of Charles S. Gilpin on a tasteless display of propaganda." He stopped, cleared his throat, continued. "Gilpin is, of course, the Negro actor whose powerful and imaginative performance in *The Emperor Jones* was honored by the Drama League at their annual dinner last year. As the darky convict who sets himself up as ruler of a jungle island in O'Neill's prize-winning play, Gilpin proved himself capable of invoking both pity and terror in a role so dominant it was essentially a dramatic monologue. In this new effort, he portrays an arrogant physician whose pride is worth more to him than the life of a helpless child. In *The Emperor Jones,* Gilpin's race brought a crucial element of authenticity to the role. Joseph Harrison, on the other hand, might as well have blackened the face of a white actor with burnt cork to portray the cartoonish doctor. The scene in which the doctor examines the dying girl was staged with so little regard for decency that the audience was rightly scandalized. As Jones, Gilpin's genius was on full display as he transformed from a pompous and unscrupulous ruler into a broken and half-crazed creature. In this play, Gilpin is no more than a foil to the aggrieved father, played with admirable intensity by —"

"Enough!" Charles Gilpin rose from his seat, snatched up his hat, and stalked out of the club, regal as any doomed monarch. Harrison got up to follow him, but I grabbed his sleeve.

"Finish reading."

Standing, Harrison continued. "The supporting cast executed their parts well enough, and the excellent set design deserves mention, but Charles Gilpin is wasted in this new play, and theatergoers will be wasting their time and money seeing him in it."

The Sugar Cane Club was silent as a tomb until Harrison unleashed a stream of curses at the critics for their vindictiveness, at the audience for their ignorance, and at Eugene O'Neill for simply existing. His anger spent, he pulled a flask from his pocket and knocked back a shot, then passed it to me. "Go on, Helen, you deserve it."

One more swallow of alcohol was the last thing I needed, but I did as he said. The liquor stung my throat and brought tears into my eyes. When my vision cleared, I noticed the club had all but emptied. "Come on, dear." Harrison hauled me to my feet as the room spun. "Let's go commiserate together."

The sky was shifting from gray to lavender. I was carrying my coat, and a keen wind raised gooseflesh on my exposed arms. The sidewalk felt unstable beneath my feet, like the beach at Coney Island when the surf pulls away the sand. I grabbed Harrison's hand to steady myself. He snaked his arm around my waist. A taxi pulled up. He slid in first, pulling me practically onto his lap. He was reaching across me to shut the door when Clarence grabbed the handle.

"You don't mind if I share a ride, do you?" He got in without waiting for an answer. Soon we were speeding down the early-morning avenues, swerving around delivery trucks and dodging the occasional streetcar. I groaned as my head and my stomach revolved in two different directions.

"You know what we should do, Helen?" Harrison dropped his voice to its most seductive register. "Go out to California, get into the movies. That's where all the really creative people are nowadays, and all the money, too. Damn these snobbish New York critics. Can you imagine what we could accomplish together, Helen, me directing and you producing?" He put his hand on my cheek. "It was incredibly brave of you to commission this play. It's not your fault if we both go broke over it, but I'll be damned if I give Broadway another ounce of my blood. Oh, Helen." He nuzzled my neck, his whisper warm in the coil of my ear. "If only I'd realized what a treasure you are, I never would have let you go."

The taxi stopped. "Here we are, sir."

I lifted my head, expecting to see my apartment building, but we were at Harrison's place instead. He opened the door on his side of the taxi. I found myself being drawn out along with him. "Come up with me, Helen. We have so much to discuss."

I wanted nothing more in that moment than to be carried off and tucked into bed. Which is where Albert is right now, I thought — in bed with King. I tried to remember, from my reading of Havelock Ellis, just what it was two men did in bed together, but I was too drunk to sort out the hodgepodge of limbs and lips my imagination conjured.

"Your mother's expecting you, isn't she, Helen?" Clarence said. I'd forgotten he was there. Beneath the coat draped over my lap, Clarence's hand had found mine, his fingers cradling my palm. He wasn't holding me back — he was offering me a lifeline. It was up to me to take it.

"Go ahead, Harrison. I'll see you tonight at the Playhouse. We'll talk about everything then. I'm too tired now."

Harrison shook his head slightly, as if I were a child who'd written the wrong answer on the blackboard. "You don't mean that, dear." He gripped my arm and tugged.

"The lady has said no, Mr. Harrison." Clarence's voice cut through the fog in my brain with the clipped authority of a military command.

With a disgusted grunt, Harrison tumbled out of the taxi and into the street, crossing in front of the cab so the driver had to suffer his glare before we could be on our way. Clarence gave our address. I let my head drop to his shoulder, pretending to have fallen suddenly asleep, as I used to do when I was a girl and wanted my father to carry me to bed. Clarence wasn't fooled. "I don't know how you can stand to let that man touch you, Helen."

I didn't open my eyes. "Why do you hate him so much?"

His hand tightened around mine. "You almost died because of that man. Isn't that reason enough?"

It was true, I'd almost died. My head swam in a circle around a single question.

"How did you know?"

Clarence lowered his voice. "My mother does your laundry, remember?"

For the full tick of a second, I wondered what my laundry had to do with anything. Then I understood. I hid my face against his chest. "I'm so ashamed."

"Shush." He kissed my forehead, briefly, lightly. "You survived, Helen. That's something a person should never be ashamed of."

The taxi let us out at our shared address. We walked up to our building, our clasped hands hidden under the fabric of my coat. Together we crossed the lobby, stepped into the elevator. He pressed the button for my floor. The jolt of the car tipped me against him. He put his arm around me. I reached up and touched the back of his neck. The elevator stopped but neither of us made a motion to open it. Instead, I lifted my chin. Our mouths met with the inevitability of magnets.

We'd been sitting on the fire escape outside my kitchen window that spring afternoon. We were in eighth grade and I'd just turned fourteen. Since we were eleven years old, Clarence and I had been seated in the same row in every classroom we shared, the alphabet of our names never separating us by more than a desk or two. That year, there'd been no desk between us. For months I'd been seated behind him, free to stare at his neck, which I found unaccountably fascinating. There were days I wouldn't remember a word of our history teacher's lecture, I was so mesmerized by the way his neck would stretch and sway as he bent his head forward to take notes. That's why we were on the fire escape. We were studying for the history test. He was chiding me for having such incomplete notes. He pointed to one particularly blank page and asked me where my mind had been. I blushed so hard I thought I had a fever. There were no words I could put to the way I felt. Instead, I leaned across my notebook and kissed him.

That day, my mother had driven us apart before our tongues could touch. Now there was no one to stop us. A hollow place I hadn't known existed opened up inside of me, hungry to be filled. I thought of his converted storage closet in the basement. His cot was narrow, but the room had a door and he had it to himself. The drinks I'd had at the Sugar Cane Club made me brave, or reckless, was there a difference? I stretched my arm out and blindly felt the row of buttons, pressing the lowest one.

The elevator descended, then stopped. We broke our kiss and met each other's eyes.

We could move to Paris, I thought. He could teach me French. He'd learned to speak it, during the war. Even in my own imagination, I had to transport the idea of me with Clarence to another country in order to picture it. Because when I thought of the two of us here, those stories from *The Crisis* leaped off the page. A sentence I'd read typed itself across my mind's eye, except that I saw Clarence in the tortured man's place, blinded by those hot iron rods.

He reached out to open the elevator. A few steps would bring us to the cot in his room. It didn't matter if my skin was only a few shades lighter than Bernice's. She was black, and I was white, and in America that meant my hand on Clarence's arm put a target on his back. I wanted to burrow into him, his body a sanctuary from the disaster of the play and Albert's betrayal, but soon the sun would rise and then what? We were on a runaway train. I found the words to pull the brake.

"Won't Bernice mind?"

He jerked his head back, as if I'd slapped him. "Of course she'll mind. It'll break her heart. Why, won't Albert mind?"

"No." My tears came with such force they splattered him. "He won't mind at all."

"Oh, Helen." The pity in his voice as he

said my name snuffed out the heat between us. I sobbed and he held me, but it was as a favor to a friend. The elevator started up again. When it stopped at my floor, he pressed a flat palm against my collarbone and slowly straightened his arm. I stepped back, alone, into the hallway.

I stared at the elevator until it completed its descent. A neighbor put out her empty milk bottles and saw me standing there. I turned away before she could greet me, digging out my key to let myself in.

Chapter 31

I came in with the Sunday paper tucked under my arm, still amazed to find King in my bed. It had been like a dream, these past (I counted them) thirty-eight hours. To miss any of them would have felt like time wasted except for the way he held me while we slept. Now it was nearly noon. His train for New Orleans departed at five o'clock. Whether, or how often, we'd see each other again was an open question I hadn't dared ask.

"There you are." King stretched his arm from under the blanket. I shed my clothes and slid in beside him. "Where've you been?"

"I went out for the paper, and I picked up some rolls from the bakery. The percolator's plugged in, coffee'll be ready soon."

"Hallelujah." He took my chin in his hand and turned my face to examine my eye. "You look like you've been kicked by a horse. How bad does it hurt?"

"It looks worse than it is." I'd seen, when I stopped in the bathroom, the bruise that ringed my eye, the swollen lid dark as a ripe plum. Apparently, it was even more shocking in color than it was to me in the mirror. King told me he'd never seen such a sickly shade of green.

The percolator sighed. "I'll get it," King offered. I watched him walk naked from the room, his chest thicker than I remembered, his shoulders broader, but his waist just as trim. Disabled soldiers littered the sidewalks of New York, but King had gone to war and come home without a scratch. I thought of telling him about the protective spell I'd cast by religiously looking for his name on the lists, but I feared that speaking of it would destroy the magic, like Houdini at a false séance.

I was opening the *New York Times* to the theater pages when he came back carrying two cups of coffee, both with milk. "What are they saying about Helen's play?" I scanned the columns until I found Alexander Woollcott's review. I read it to him, the cup of coffee tipping precariously in my hand until King rescued it from my negligent grasp. "Poor Helen," he said, when I'd gotten through the review's devastating final line.

I looked at him, stricken. "I should go to her."

He set the paper aside. "Maybe you could see her after I'm gone?" He took my face carefully in his hands and kissed me. "We have so little time as it is."

I glanced at the clock. I'd only have King for a few more hours. After that, I could devote myself to Helen, go with her to the play every night this week if she wanted me to. I got up to call and tell her so while King fried some eggs in the kitchenette. I put my hand on the receiver, but I couldn't make myself pick it up. I was afraid I wouldn't be able to resist the pull of her voice if she asked me to come, which of course she would, as she had every right to. I was her boyfriend, her best friend, her only friend as far as I could tell. I lifted the receiver but instead of speaking into it I left it off its hook. A few more hours wouldn't make much difference to her, I told myself, but they might be all I got with King.

I saw him off at Pennsylvania Station, and why not? No one would think twice about me being acquainted with a player. Mark Roth, Rex's boss, came over to us. "Whad'ya do, Kramer, try to catch a fastball?"

I raised my hand to my eye. "Not exactly."

He laughed. "Had a few too many and hit the deck, eh? Haven't you heard there's a prohibition against alcohol?" I introduced King. "Right, you're that new recruit." He checked his clipboard, handed King a ticket, nodded at the satchel in his hand. "That all you've got?"

King lifted the battered leather bag we'd retrieved from a locker at the bus station. "Change of clothes and my glove, what else do I need?" He was wearing his khaki trousers with a shirt I'd rinsed out for him, a fresh collar I'd given him, and one of my linen jackets (on me it was fashionably loose; on him the fabric strained at the seams, but he didn't have anything else suitable for New Orleans). His uniform was stuffed into the satchel, buttons and all.

Roth cuffed him on the arm. "A man after my own heart. The Colonel needs a stateroom just for his wardrobe, isn't that right, Kramer?" We laughed at his joke, but he had nothing to complain about. Whenever the Colonel traveled to New Orleans, he had his private car attached to the Crescent Limited, and it was Mr. Nakamura, not Mark Roth, who managed his luggage.

"Give my regards to Rex when you see him."

"I'll do that, Kramer. Say, here comes Waite Hoyt, finally."

While everyone's attention was focused on the Yankees' star pitcher, I turned to King and took his hand. "Good luck."

He kept my hand in his for a long time. "Say, Albert, if I make the team, think you could get me an apartment in that brownstone of yours?"

My mind started to whirr. The poet in the attic had been talking about going out to Hollywood to try his hand at the movies. Maybe I could persuade my neighbor on the second floor to take his vacant apartment? I still had that hammer hidden away in a drawer somewhere. I imagined taking it out and prying open that secret door between my apartment and the next, pictured King walking through it. But no. That passage had belonged to Felix. I couldn't open it for some other man. "I've been thinking of moving, actually."

King lifted his eyebrows. "Really? Well, let me know if you want a roommate."

The conductor whistled all aboard. King finally let go of my hand. "Hopefully I'll be back in April for opening day." He pursed his lips a tiny bit to let me know he'd have kissed me if he could, then jumped up as a hiss of steam jolted the train forward. I

461

forced myself to walk away before he could lean out a window to wave. I didn't trust myself not to chase after the train as it pulled out of the station.

I considered the taxi stand on Eighth Avenue but decided to walk up to the Olde Playhouse instead. I hardly felt the sidewalk beneath my feet as I headed uptown, preoccupied as I was with half-formed plans and speculations. It would do me good to move, I thought. I'd stayed put at the brownstone in the vague hope that Felix might one day return, but I'd known for a long time now that such a day would never come. An apartment in a modern building, with two bedrooms and a real kitchen, that I could furnish as I liked — the idea was so appealing I wondered why I hadn't done it sooner. A couple of bachelors sharing an address wouldn't raise any suspicion, and what could be more natural than the Colonel's secretary splitting the rent with a player on the Yankees' payroll?

At the Playhouse, I found Helen huddled in the office with Miss Johnson, who was helping her figure out the financial implications of their disastrous opening night. I placed my hands on Helen's shoulders, the beginning of a comforting embrace, but she shrugged me off. It was Miss Johnson who addressed me. "My goodness, Mr. Kramer, you look worse than I thought. Miss Winthrope said you'd had a fall."

So that's what she was telling people. "Yes, well, you can see why I missed the performance. I read the reviews this morning, though. I'm so sorry, Helen."

"It might not be as bleak as it seems." Miss Johnson pressed a key on the adding machine, which spewed out a roll of paper. She tore it off and pointed to the results. "Don't forget, Mr. Kramer, the *New York Times* isn't the only newspaper in the city. The *Amsterdam News* had a very favorable review. I was telling Miss Winthrope that the flight of white theatergoers might well be made up by ticket sales to Harlemites."

"Not only that." Richard Martin appeared in the office doorway, crowding me farther into the small space. "I just got word O'Neill himself will be attending tonight, in support of Gilpin."

"Really?" Helen looked up then, her eyes bloodshot from lack of sleep and crying. "Do you really think things might turn around?"

"Anything's possible, Helen." Richard patted her arm. "I better stay by the telephone, just in case."

"And I'll be going home now, Miss Winthrope." Bernice Johnson covered the adding machine and smoothed her skirt. "My parents are expecting me and Clarence for Sunday dinner."

Left alone in the office with Helen, I knelt at her feet and spun her chair to face me. "I'm really so sorry, Helen. Whatever you need, I'm here now."

The way she looked at me — like I was someone from her past whose name she couldn't quite remember — curdled my stomach. "I needed you last night."

I opened my mouth to explain, again, how unexpected King's appearance had been, but she moved her eyes away from my face to a spot on the wall. I didn't need to be a mind reader to know what she was thinking. She'd accepted me, loved me, given me her friendship and her heart. In return, she didn't expect romance or marriage. My presence, my support, my open arms — these were all she asked of me and I had failed her. What did normal men do when they made their women cry? Bouquets of roses, boxes of chocolate, presents from Tiffany's? If that's what it took to get Helen to smile at me again I'd buy them all. But those offerings would feel false coming from me. The gifts were less the point than the lovemaking that followed. A normal man could placate his woman's hurt feelings with passion. My passion had been spent on King. If only I could explain to Helen she had nothing to fear. The part of myself that belonged to her and the part of myself that responded to King were so different, it was impossible for me to play either one false with the other.

But I didn't get the chance to explain. The telephone on her desk rang. It was the Colonel, tracking me down. I thought guiltily of the phone in my apartment off its hook while King and I spent the afternoon in bed. I envied, in that moment, Mr. Nakamura's sacred Sundays off. I couldn't remember the last time I'd been inaccessible to the Colonel for more than a handful of hours.

Helen stepped out to go to the ladies' room while we spoke. I found her in the lobby after. She'd splashed her face with water and combed her hair. I tucked an errant strand of it behind her ear. "He wants me to come see him right away, but I'll be back tonight, I promise. I won't let you down again, darling."

The Colonel opened his door elegantly attired in white tie and tuxedo. I remembered there was a charity event for the Liederkranz

465

Society on his calendar that evening. It must have been a struggle for him, I thought, to bathe and dress himself without Mr. Nakamura's ministrations.

"By Gad, son, what happened to you?" He led me through the apartment to the library, the Persian Saruk Helen and I had picked out cushioning our footsteps. In the two years since he'd moved in, the apartment had been elegantly furnished, but he so enjoyed the light in the library that he'd decided against curtains. He brought me toward the window so he could examine my eye, the evening sun making me squint. "You look like you lost a boxing match."

"That's not far from the truth, sir." Since he'd already recognized my black eye for what it was, there didn't seem much point in lying about the rest of it. "I was caught up in a police raid Friday night." I told him about King coming to New York, that I'd taken him out on the town, how we ran into the police.

"You mean that soldier who rushed the field at the Polo Grounds? I remember him. A strapping young man. It's up to Huggins, of course, but let's wish him luck." We sat on wingback chairs pulled up to a low table on which a silver tray held a carafe of schnapps and two fluted glasses. Tilting back my head to drink brought a painful rush of blood into my bruise. "So, Kramer, about this play of Helen's. You read Woollcott's review." It was a statement, not a question. He finished his drink and lit a cigarette. "The play will be closed by tomorrow. Tonight will be the last performance."

"I wouldn't be that pessimistic, sir. The *Amsterdam News* had only good things to say. Helen thinks they might be able to make up their losses, given enough time. Perhaps it will start to catch on —"

"You're not understanding me, Kramer. I am telling you to shut it down."

"Shut it down?" How exactly was I supposed to do that, I wondered?

"I want you to dissolve the company. You're the president, after all. I'm calling in my loan. Honor all the contracts first and make sure there are no outstanding liens. I'll take whatever's left and write off the loss. And get in touch with Martin Beck tomorrow. Tell him the Olde Playhouse is his if he still wants the property."

I was stunned by the swiftness of his decision. "But, sir —"

He leaned forward, planting his elbows on his knees. "I can't have this kind of publicity, Kramer. Not so close to opening day."

I knew he was nervous about Yankee

Stadium. The press hadn't yet caught wind of the fact that he was buying Huston out, once construction was complete. The man was down in New Orleans enjoying one last spring training with the players. The opening day program featuring the two Colonels would be the last souvenir of their partnership. I couldn't see, though, what that had to do with Helen's play. "But, sir, a person would have to look up the incorporation papers of Pipsqueak Productions to even know you were an investor."

"Exactly. On April eighteenth, I'll be standing beside dignitaries, introducing the world to the greatest stadium since the Coliseum in Rome. I will not risk having my name associated with an indecent theatrical. Especially not one produced by a young woman whose clothes I pay for."

Now I understood. The press could easily twist the Colonel's support for Helen and her family into something scandalous. Not that the reporters would necessarily put their insinuations into print. How many nights had they watched Babe Ruth stumble into a hotel with a woman not his wife on his arm, and never a word in the morning papers? Even so, a reporter with dope on a man was a dangerous thing.

"I hate to crush her dreams like this, Kramer, but it's best you get it over with. Tell her tonight."

"You want me to tell her?"

"I have plans, as you can see." With a sweep of his hand he indicated his tuxedo. "You are attending the performance tonight, aren't you?"

I nodded, too dispirited to speak. I'd already let her down, and now I'd be the bearer of bad news. Perhaps it was for the best, though, that I be the one to tell her. I could spend the entire night with her, if she wanted, now that King was on his way to New Orleans. A picture of him in the sleeper car on the train flashed into my mind. I felt the shiver of it through my whole body.

The Colonel was talking. I'd missed some of what he said. "Assure her I'd value her help."

"With what again?"

"The party at Eagle's Rest. The architect tells me the mansion is ready to receive guests. Once the Yankees have barnstormed their way up to New York, I want to host a reception before the start of the season for the team managers and some of the players. Ruth, of course, and Waite Hoyt. Not Carl Mays, obviously." I took out my notepad and a pen, but he waved it away. "I'll give

469

Osamu the guest list. The point is, I can't very well have their wives asking my butler for, well, whatever women ask for. So, you'll come up, the two of you, and Helen can play hostess. Take her to Macy's for a new spring outfit. She's been wanting a fur coat, hasn't she? Not mink, though. Something respectable. Seal, perhaps."

Our interview seemed to be over. He stood and smoothed the creases from his tuxedo. "Let her down gently, Kramer. Remind her she knew the risk she was taking as a producer."

"Maybe she'll go back to managing."

"We'll see." He walked me to the foyer. "Did you know, Kramer, I have an apartment here in this building, a two bedroom in the back on the ground floor?"

"Really?" My thoughts immediately flew to King — a bedroom for each of us, perfect for two bachelor roommates.

"I bought it as an investment, but I think you should live in it. It's unfurnished, and the maintenance will be more than the rent at that place you have now, but it's about time I raise your salary. And it will make things easier for me if I can always find you."

"That's very generous of you, sir."

"You need looking after, Kramer." He stepped close to examine my eye. I thought

470

he might recommend I see a doctor — the bruise had been getting nastier as the day wore on. Instead, he gently took my jaw in his hand and turned my face to the side. I could smell the schnapps on his breath as he brought his lips to my eye and kissed it.

It seemed to be the sign I'd been waiting for, the signal that we were alike, two queers playing it straight for appearance's sake. But what if I was wrong? I hadn't grown up with a father. For all I knew, this was how a man might reassure his injured son.

The Colonel's voice was a whisper in my ear. "I want you to stay out of trouble from now on, Kramer. Men like us, men with secrets, we cannot afford to be compromised."

CHAPTER 32

I wiped mist from the windowpane to look out at the Hudson River. Daffodils, taken by surprise by the Easter cold snap, wilted in their flower beds as peacocks dragged their emerald feathers across the frosted lawn of Eagle's Rest. Down along the riverbank, the first train of the morning snaked its way toward Albany, people already up and about their business.

I had no business to be about. Pipsqueak Productions was dissolved. The night of our second performance, Albert had insisted on coming up to my apartment with me after the play. For a moment, I thought he would kiss me in my living room the way I'd seen him kiss that man. But no, when he sat me down on the couch and took my hand, it was to deliver the news that Jake was calling in his loan. The performance we'd just attended turned out to be the last of my career.

A flurry of activity had followed as the costumes and props were auctioned off to pay our debts. Poor Richard Martin suffered a relapse as he scrambled to rescue every historically significant scrap of paper from the Olde Playhouse. We sent him back to Montauk while the archives of the theater were bundled up and tossed out with the trash. Bernice Johnson helped me close our accounts: contracts with the cast settled, severance checks to the crew issued, debts cleared. Jake more than made up for his loss on our loan with a real estate deal that proved the building had been the smarter investment all along. A wrecking ball now presided over the empty lot where, for nearly a century, the Olde Playhouse had stood.

When Jake asked me to help him organize this reception for the Yankees, the last thing I wanted to do was throw a party, but how could I refuse him? At least it gave me something to think about besides my failures. The team was barnstorming up the coast — last I heard from my brother, they'd reached Maryland — and in a few days they'd arrive here at Eagle's Rest. I'd been relieved, when Mr. Nakamura reviewed the guests with me, to see that King Arthur, a walk-on recruit who wasn't even signed yet, hadn't made the list.

"Helen, are you ready?" Albert's voice followed his knock on the pocket door.

"Yes, come in." I'd unlatched my side once I finished dressing in the adjoining bathroom, which was stocked with a selection of ladies' toiletries chosen, I assumed, by the salesgirl at Macy's. The closet, too, had been filled with outfits appropriate for the varied activities of country living. There were flannel trousers and sturdy shoes for walking around the estate, smart outfits for lunching in the dining room, and a cocktail dress for evenings in the parlor. When I pulled open a drawer and found silk pajamas and cotton underwear, I could imagine the chain of command that resulted in them being there: Jake telling Albert to make sure I had whatever I'd need; Albert informing the salesgirl to put together a complete ensemble; Mr. Nakamura unwrapping the delivered packages; the laundress ironing out the wrinkles and putting everything away.

The door slid open and Albert appeared, dressed and ready for the day. "Mr. Nakamura's bringing up breakfast. Well, good morning Pip! Have you been out yet today?" Albert crouched to pet the silly dog, who was turning pirouettes on his tiny hind legs.

"I had him out earlier. It's still freezing, can you believe it, and April already?" I placed my fingers on his cheek where, a month ago, King's fist had landed. "You're just about good as new, Albert. I can hardly see it anymore."

He put his hand on mine, kissed my palm. "The Colonel just said the same thing."

In Jake's room there was a breakfast table by the bay window on which I found plates of eggs and baskets of bread and jars of jam. I took my place in the chair Albert pulled out for me. Jake was in his dressing gown and slippers, an informality that had surprised me my first morning at Eagle's Rest but which I'd now come to expect. Beneath the table, Pip and Princess conspired to cadge pieces of sausage. Mr. Nakamura hovered in the background while we leafed through newspapers and watched the morning sun melt the frost from the lawn. Our plates were whisked away so unobtrusively I only realized they were gone when Jake and Albert lit cigarettes and leaned back in their chairs. The smell of tobacco was delicious, but I knew Jake would disapprove of my asking for one.

I'd never been so fussed over as I was at Eagle's Rest. All this luxury should have made me feel special but instead I felt diminished by comparison. The way Jake lived was a testament to family, inheritance, and success. For family, I was down to a widowed mother, our only inheritance my father's life insurance checks. I'd failed first at being an actress, then a manager, and now a producer. I'd never bear a child, couldn't even adopt one on my own. The future I imagined for me and Albert was impossible as long as King was lurking in the wings. Albert kept saying what good friends we'd be, the three of us, but I wouldn't be able to stand it, watching him give someone else what he couldn't give me.

It was bad enough now that Bernice had come to live in my building. I'd assumed that losing her job managing the Olde Playhouse would delay their marriage, but she'd recalculated. Instead of splurging on a big wedding, Clarence and Bernice had settled for a small ceremony at Saint Benedict the Moor before taking over the second bedroom in the custodian's apartment from Clarence's sister. With her light skin and letters of reference, Bernice had no trouble finding a new position balancing books for a bank downtown. But she had bigger plans now, Clarence told me: to save up enough to purchase their own building, where Clarence would be custodian and Bernice the manager. Lately, I couldn't cross the lobby without seeing one or the other of them, gold bands bright on their fingers.

It made Harrison's offer all the more tantalizing. I had the letter he'd sent from Los Angeles folded in my pocket. The movie business was booming, he wrote. They were in dire need of producers and directors — and he'd met women doing both. I knew better than to think he was hinting at marriage when he said what a good team we'd make. Still, his proposition was enticing. *Throw your lot in with me, Helen, and the sky's the limit for both of us.* Even if all I got from Harrison was a few introductions, I figured that would be enough to land me a job. In California, I'd have a fresh start on my own two feet. My mother hated the idea, of course, and not just because she'd be left living alone. She was convinced Jake's interest in me was an opportunity I couldn't afford to pass up. But when he'd closed Pipsqueak Productions, I'd seen how vulnerable I was to the whims of a millionaire.

"Are you ready to be dressed, sir?" Mr. Nakamura's question signaled that breakfast was over. Albert went to his room to catch up on the Colonel's correspondence while I reviewed with the cook the menu for the reception. The kitchen, a large space of tiled walls and steel counters, was situated out of sight in the basement, and why not? Jake had no plans of ever setting foot in it. I thought it dreary but the cook preferred it, she said, to the cramped kitchen at Jake's apartment in the city. When I asked if there'd be enough ice for the cocktails, she showed me a walk-in freezer stacked with blocks wrapped in burlap.

Next I surveyed the seating arrangements in the dining room. It was a wonder there was any oak left in the forest after every inch of the room's walls had been paneled. A carved mantel, imported from some demolished Bavarian castle, overshadowed the table, while dark beams crisscrossed the ceiling. The cook was planning to prepare asparagus, but I was afraid the green stalks would look unappetizing in such a brown room. I was wondering what yellow vegetables might be in season when Albert found me.

"I've finished my work for now, Helen. I thought we could take a walk." He'd brought my new coat with him and I put it on, though the day had begun to warm a bit. I'd give it to my mother, I decided; I wouldn't need a seal fur in Los Angeles.

Pip was thrilled to be outside again. He bounced and barked after the peacocks, which screamed and spread their tail feathers until he slunk away, whimpering. We decided to go see the monkey house, following a slate path through a patch of woods to the zoo. There was a scrim of ice on the stone. When my foot slipped, Albert took my hand and held it. How much like lovers we must have looked as we strolled the grounds of Jake's princely estate.

"King would love it here," Albert said. "Did you know he spent his summers on his grandparents' farm in Wisconsin?"

"How would I know that?" I yanked my hand away to pet Bulgari, who had come down from the kennel to greet us. She'd lost her swagger since Oh Boy died last year, and Jake hadn't shown her at Westminster that winter. I was wiping drool from my hands when she lifted her massive head and barked to greet her master.

"There you two are," Jake said. "Kramer, I just had a call from Huston. There's a problem with the easement for the subway station on 161st Street. Equitable Trust won't sign off on it because of an outstanding lien, but it turns out that lien is their own mortgage! I need you to get on the telephone and straighten it out."

"Yes, sir. Should I speak to Huston first?"

Jake nodded, his neck dipping into the

mink collar of his coat. "Tell him he need not attend the reception if he'd rather stay in the city to supervise."

"You won't mind scratching him off the guest list, will you?" I asked as Albert hurried away.

Jake shrugged. "The man can be useful. I'd never have gotten the financing for the stadium on my own. But an organization needs one person at the head, otherwise it pulls itself apart going in different directions. Once we get past all the hoopla on opening day, it'll be a relief to have the Yankees to myself."

We continued past the dairy barn and the duck pond to the monkey house. A coal stove in the corner kept it warm and I shrugged off my fur. The smell was awful, despite the fresh straw and sawdust. Half a dozen capuchins swung themselves across the bars of their enclosure like trapeze artists, while a pair of rhesus monkeys sat in a corner of their cage peeling bananas imported all the way from Nicaragua. Pip clawed at my leg, wanting to be picked up. His nose wriggled and his little head swiveled back and forth as he acquainted himself with these strange creatures. I wondered what they thought of their change in circumstances, transported from the jungles of the

Amazon to a manicured estate along the Hudson River. Was it a relief to have their food provided daily instead of scavenging through a hostile forest? But no, I realized, as they chirped and screeched. Even an easy life was not a fair exchange for freedom.

"My zookeeper tells me the rhesus pair will breed. Won't that be something, Helen, to watch them rear a little one?"

One of the capuchins reached out a dexterous hand and grabbed hold of Pip. Its grip was surprisingly strong and I struggled to bend back its fingers. With a yip, Pip jumped from my arms and scampered out of the monkey house.

"I've been meaning to thank you, Helen, for organizing this reception."

"Are you happy with the arrangements?"

"I am, yes. It will be so helpful to have you as hostess. The wives will appreciate it, I'm sure." I hadn't realized I was meant to host the party as well as plan it. "I know it was a disappointment for you," he continued, "losing the production company."

"Yes it was. I've been thinking of going out to California to try my hand at the movies. Joseph Harrison, the director, he went out last month and he's already got himself a project."

Jake looked as mystified as if I'd just told

him I was planning to fly to the moon. "But, Helen, you can't go to California. We need you here."

"I'm sure Mr. Nakamura could have planned this party in his sleep, Jake. There are more opportunities for women in the movies than there are on Broadway. If I'm ever to find my footing again, I need a fresh start in a new industry."

"Why keep chasing this idea of a career, Helen? So many of us depend on you. Your mother, for one. You know I lived with my mother until the day she died. And then there's Kramer."

No there isn't, I wanted to say, not for me, not as long as King was around. "What about Albert?"

"I need you to help me with him, Helen. You're a good influence. Together we can keep him out of trouble."

The pair of rhesus monkeys, having finished their bananas, began to groom each other. One bent its head forward while the other combed long fingers lovingly through its fur. If you want to keep Albert out of trouble, I thought, you can start by keeping him away from King Arthur. I didn't realize I was thinking out loud. Hearing Jake respond startled me.

"Why's that, Helen?"

"Oh, well, he's the one who gave Albert that black eye."

"Kramer said they'd gotten mixed up with the police at a speakeasy. He didn't tell me it was King who started the trouble." Jake cocked his blocky head to the side. "I've got enough headaches with Ruth and his shenanigans."

A minute ago, I thought the only way for me to take charge of my destiny was to relocate to the opposite edge of the country. Now I was being given a chance to change the course of things right here. My mouth went dry. I spoke so softly it was practically a whisper. "I wonder if King might do better on one of your farm teams."

"That's not a bad idea, Helen. I don't usually interfere in these decisions, but I could put in a word with Huggins. I seem to remember him saying the Newark Bears could use a good batter."

Newark was just across the river. There were ferries every hour. "Didn't you just acquire a minor league team out in Missouri?"

"Yes, in fact, I did." He lured the female rhesus away from her mate with a peanut. She reached through the bars and plucked it from his palm with her clever fingers. "Kansas City might be just the place for that soldier. But what about you, Helen? Will you give up this idea of going out to California?"

I realized Jake was offering me a trade: my career for Albert's safety. With King out of the picture, everything could go back to the way it had been between Albert and me. I knew Albert loved me, he'd said so himself often enough. As for his perverse desire for King, really, I thought, what good could come of it? Police raids, arrests for indecency, blackmail. There was no happiness at the end of the road for men like that — society wouldn't permit it. I'd be saving Albert from scandal, and Jake, too. He'd built that pocket door between our rooms to protect me from rumors. What rumors would swirl if word got out that Colonel Ruppert's personal secretary was a pansy? "But what will I do with myself, Jake? I'm a grown woman. I can't live off my mother."

He had his solution all cued up. "Work for me, Helen. Kramer does, why shouldn't you? You'll help me when I need you. When I don't, you could teach a class, maybe. Aren't those settlement houses always looking to enrich the lives of poor children? You'll have your account at Macy's, and I'll make you an allowance. Anyway, you don't need money in your pockets up here at

Eagle's Rest."

"What if I get married someday?" The slightest glimmer of hope was enough to rekindle my vision of the future with Albert.

"If you marry, you'll become your husband's responsibility, of course. But marriage isn't for everyone. Look at me. What have I missed that married men have?"

Children, I would have said. Romance. Companionship. But Jake had nephews to carry on the Ruppert name and nieces to spoil with presents. Perhaps in his youth there had been someone who stirred his passion, but at his age I supposed he no longer craved that sort of thing. And he'd have us to keep him company, me and Albert, if only I agreed.

"I guess I'll give up on California for now." Jake gave the monkey another peanut and brushed off his hands. "I'm glad we understand each other, Helen. For Albert's sake."

"Yes, for Albert's sake." I believed the words were true, but saying them put the taste of soap on my tongue.

CHAPTER 33

The wind was at our backs as Helen and I stood on the High Bridge, looking down the Harlem River toward the tip of Manhattan, the spire of the Woolworth Building poking up through the distant haze. Closer, the rival ballparks faced off across the river. The Colonel had wanted to outshine the Giants, and he'd certainly done it. The muscular facade of Yankee Stadium rose twice as tall as the squat horseshoe of the Polo Grounds. We could just make out the flags, tiny as toothpick decorations, fluttering from the top of its stands.

On the roads below, an endless line of automobiles carried thousands of passengers toward the ballpark. Trains were running every couple of minutes, crammed with fans eager to tick through the stadium's forty turnstiles. The Colonel was expecting to fill sixty thousand seats for opening day at Yankee Stadium. It would be the largest assembly of persons to ever witness a game of baseball, the entire population of some small cities converged around a four-acre wedge of grass.

The Colonel's limousine was reserved for dignitaries that day, so Helen and I were making our own way to the stadium, a pair of tickets tucked securely in my jacket pocket. Mrs. Winthrope would be watching the game with Rex from the clubhouse, but the Colonel wanted me and Helen out in the stands, the better to report back to him, he said, on the atmosphere among the fans. To avoid getting stuck in traffic on the Macombs Dam Bridge, we'd decided to take the subway up to 168th Street and walk across the High Bridge to the Bronx. It was a day so long anticipated we both wanted to savor it at a pedestrian's pace.

I'd reviewed the Colonel's schedule with him last night while Mr. Nakamura laid out a double-breasted coat of melton wool with a black velvet collar. There would be a band concert on the field and fireworks to announce the start of play. Photographers from all the papers would be jostling for shots of Colonel Ruppert with Tillinghast Huston and Harry Frazee (how fitting that the first game to be played in Yankee Stadium should be against Boston). A parade to dedicate the stadium would feature the high commissioner of baseball, the Bronx borough president, the mayor of the city, and the governor of New York. The restaurant and refreshment stands were ready for business, the bleachers had been improved to support twenty-one thousand fans, and Babe Ruth had promised Huggins a home run against the Red Sox to inaugurate his new playground.

I jammed my hat farther down on my head. A chill wind was making me second-guess my decision to drag Helen across the High Bridge. I'd been nostalgic for those Sunday afternoons when I'd pass the time up here while Felix was at his trustees meetings. When the history of the Yankees was written, I supposed the abandoned effort to locate the stadium in Harlem would be, at best, a footnote easily overlooked.

"Should we move on, Albert?" Helen asked, my reverie having lasted longer than I realized.

"Sure." I held out my arm for her, our steps easily falling into sync. "It's too bad King's not on the roster. It would have been something to see him on the field today, wouldn't it?"

"But you said yourself it was a great opportunity for him to play in Kansas City."

488

"Oh, it is. The Blues are a competitive team. King was lucky to land a spot with them." He'd sent me a postcard from Maryland, which was as far north as he'd gotten on the Yankees' barnstorming trip up the coast. It was only a few words to tell me he'd been signed to the minor league club in Missouri. He wished we could have met again, he wrote, but he was being put on a train in Baltimore and sent directly out west. *Look me up if you're ever in Kansas City! Maybe next year New York?*

King's postcard had dashed my silly hopes of the two of us sharing that apartment the Colonel had offered me. I'd tried talking to Helen about it, but every time I mentioned King's name she managed to change the subject. Instead I'd gone down to Antonio's. Jack tried to buck me up, reminding me of the couple of great days (and nights) King and I had shared. But I wanted more than just a night or two. I wanted more than the stolen hours Paul's benefactor gave him, more even than the furtive way I'd lived with Felix. What I wanted, I realized, as Helen and I strolled arm in arm across the High Bridge, was something I could never have with a man — the kind of relationship I had with her. Out in the open. Without secrets.

Men like us, men with secrets. The Colonel's words ran through my mind like tape through a stock ticker. When I'd talked it over with Paul, he said it was obvious what the Colonel meant: that he was a man who preferred pansies. It wouldn't have damaged his reputation back in the 1890s, when slumming trips to Greenwich Village were de rigueur for wealthy men like Jacob Ruppert. The Colonel had been so handsome in his youth, the fairies would have flocked to him like fireflies. But he'd always been afraid of scandal. Now that he was the famous owner of a baseball team whose every decision was scrutinized by the press, I could understand why he'd be at pains to keep his past a secret.

If that was, indeed, the secret he meant. We may have both been men with secrets, but what if they weren't the same ones? I might have been reading too much, all these years, into that incident of the red bow tie. Perhaps he thought my secret was something else entirely. He may have learned that my father had committed suicide, or maybe he thought Helen was my mistress. I should have simply asked him, while his lips were still on my black eye, what he meant by his remark. But the moment had passed, my doubts crept back in, and now I didn't know

490

how to put the question to him.

"I'm so glad the weather held." Helen pointed appreciatively at the patches of blue showing through the fast-moving clouds.

"Me too. The Colonel would have been apoplectic if the game had been rained out."

On such a promising afternoon, it was to be expected that we weren't alone on the High Bridge. Clusters of men hurried past, the snippets of conversation I overheard suggesting they, too, were heading to the stadium. Ladies promenaded over the old aqueduct. An artist had set up her easel at a picturesque spot. A family was approaching us, the mother pushing an empty pram while the baby took unsteady little steps grasping its father's outstretched hand. They made a pretty picture, and I lifted my hand to the rim of my hat to acknowledge them as we passed. Then the father raised his chin and I saw the face his hat had hidden.

It was Felix. My legs would have buckled if I didn't have Helen to hang on to. She bore me up, thinking, I supposed, I'd simply stumbled. Perhaps she hadn't spotted him, didn't remember him. Surely he was as eager for us to pass by without comment as I was.

Helen stopped. "Mr. Stern, hello."

"Hello, Miss Winthrope, Albert. How nice

to run into you both. Let me introduce you to my wife. Rebecca, this is Mr. Kramer, who I've told you so much about, and his friend Miss Winthrope."

I wouldn't have thought it possible for me to be shaking the hand of Mrs. Felix Stern, but it was happening. Helen knelt in front of the baby. Felix let go and it toddled into Helen's arms. "May I?" she asked, looking up at its mother.

"Of course, Miss Winthrope. Aaron loves to meet new people."

While the women played with the baby, I stepped back to the railing, afraid I might be sick. Felix trailed after me. He put his hand on my back. Even through my coat, I felt its warmth between my shoulder blades. "Are you okay, Albert?"

"I'm surprised to see you, Felix."

"But not a bad surprise, I hope. I figured you might take this way to the stadium."

He'd arranged it, then, this accidental rendezvous? I focused my eyes and took him in. He looked exactly the same, except more neatly dressed. The silk of his tie and the wool of his coat were of a higher quality than I remembered him wearing. Stepping back, his hand fell away and I saw a new watch on his wrist, its crystal face unblemished. He was being taken care of. I looked over his shoulder at the baby Helen was holding, its chubby fist batting at her face. Maybe they'd adopted him. After all, he had an entire orphanage at his disposal. "Is it really yours?"

Felix glanced at his family, pride evident in his expression. "Yes, he is. Aaron Stern. He just had his first birthday."

"And you got married."

Felix briefly met my gaze then looked out over the river. "After I got back from Vienna, yes."

"So it worked, then?"

I watched his profile as he swallowed, the Adam's apple riding up his throat. "I learned how to cope with it. Rebecca is a remarkable woman. She's a wonderful mother. It's such a relief, Albert." He looked at me now, a sheen of moisture magnifying his dark eyes. "You know how desperately I wanted to be a father."

His desperation, yes, that was something I knew all too well. "Does she know?"

"Only that I had a nervous breakdown. Not why. No one knows why, except you."

I shoved my hands into my pockets to keep them from reaching for him. "I'm happy for you, Felix."

He filled his fist with the fabric of my sleeve. "Are you really? Because it would mean so much to me if that were true. If we could be friends again, meet sometimes. I —" His eyes darted to his family then settled back on me. "I've missed you, Albert. Are you still at the brownstone? Can I come see you?"

I pried his hand from my sleeve and held it to my chest. Another man with a secret. Another man with his eye on the clock, counting down the minutes until he'd be expected at home. It would only be a matter of time before the strain of his lies led to another breakdown. Where would they ship him off to next, some ashram in India?

"Actually, I'm about to move out." I hadn't been able to save him before. This time, I was saving myself, too. If scandal didn't find me, heartbreak would. Instead, I would follow the Colonel's example. Stay out of trouble. Avoid blackmail or arrest. With Helen, I could live in the open, honestly, without fear of being compromised. It was just as well, I thought, that King was all the way out in Kansas City.

Helen was placing the baby in its pram. How unfair that she'd never be able to have one of her own, even if I could have given it to her. I remembered our visit to the orphanage, how badly she'd wanted to save that little boy. I'd wanted that, too. Maybe that was something we could, one day, do together.

I made my choice. "Go on, now, Felix, your wife is waiting."

We watched, for a while, as the little family made its way back toward Manhattan. I flapped my hands to dispel the current of electricity Felix's touch had sent through me. Helen caught them. "You're cold as ice, Albert. What's wrong?"

"I forgot I was afraid of heights." I linked my arm in hers and turned our steps toward the Bronx. "I'll be better once we get to the other side of the bridge."

■ ■ ■ ■

1928

■ ■ ■ ■

CHAPTER 34

My nerves were shot as the Cardinals took the field at the top of the seventh inning, up two runs to one on the Yankees. We were ahead three games to none, but the World Series was best of seven, and anything could still happen. For two scoreless innings, I'd been gripping the arms of my chair with every at bat announced on the radio.

"I suppose Colonel Ruppert won't be too upset to lose this one, will he, Helen?" Bernice said. "He'll make more money if the Series comes back to New York for another game."

I was too astonished to reply. Clarence reached into the washtub of ice and extracted a Coca-Cola. He pried off the top with the opener on his key chain and handed it to his wife. "You're thinking like a bookkeeper, honey. A true sportsman wants to win every time, no matter the cost."

"He's right." My mother shook her head

no when Clarence offered her a soda. "Jake won't take a deep breath until his team has won. It isn't good for his health."

I pictured Jake at Sportsman's Park in St. Louis, certain he had his jacket on despite the heat wave that was forcing spectators into their shirtsleeves. "Shush now, let me listen."

That afternoon Clarence had helped us carry our radio downstairs for a listening party in the lobby. His mother joined us, too. A widow now, Mrs. Weldon kept her hands busy with mending during the game. Some cousins or nephews came by — I couldn't quite keep track of the various relatives who seemed to cycle in and out of their basement apartment. And, of course, there was Clarence and Bernice's son, James.

James was four and a half years old that October, and already as precocious a boy as I'd ever known. Compared to the unfortunate children who participated in the plays and pageants I directed for the settlement house, James was a positive prodigy. Though he'd never yet set foot in a schoolroom, Bernice had taught him his numbers, and under Clarence's tutelage he'd learned to sound out a newspaper headline. It was thanks to me, though, that he could recite poetry from memory. James was just a baby when Bernice had gone back to work, determined to keep adding to their savings. Clarence and his mother were always around to watch him, but to give them a break I'd offered myself as an occasional sitter. My mother complained they took advantage of me by leaving James in my care, but it was just a few hours a day. It wasn't as if I had much else to do. The classes I taught at the settlement house only took up a couple of my afternoons. My evenings were free to spend with Albert, and we often went up to Eagle's Rest with Jake for days or weeks at a time. Besides, I told my mother, every hour I got to spend with James was precious to me.

That afternoon, James raced around the lobby, jumping on and off laps and playing with Pip, whose little legs were getting stiff with age. His dark hair was softly curled, his complexion more gold than brown, and his eyes — well, no one agreed as to which side of the family those green eyes came from, but they leaped out of his face like emeralds from a riverbank when he looked at you, as he was looking at me right now.

"Aunt Helen, will Babe get another home run do you think?"

"I think it's a safe bet, Jimmy, but you're not a betting man, are you?" I tickled him and he ran over to his father. Clarence, I knew, had a considerable wager on the outcome of the game. Bernice didn't approve, of course. She invested nearly every cent they earned in stocks she researched herself. Unable to deny her husband his small measure of fun, though, she'd allotted a fixed amount for him to take his chances.

I didn't need a betting slip in my pocket to tie my fortunes to the outcome of the game. Albert had gone out to St. Louis with Jake, leaving me on deck, as it were. Jake had already planned a reception at Eagle's Rest to commemorate the end of the season. If the Yankees won the Series, it would be a party and he'd want me to be there to play hostess. If they lost, he'd be in a sulk and he'd need me and Albert to lighten his mood. Either way, my bag was packed for the trip up the Hudson.

"And the pop fly is caught, that's one out for the Yankees. Now Babe Ruth, the playboy of baseball, makes his way to the plate. Will he drive in another home run? No! Wee Willie Sherdel throws a strike. It's a battle of wills now. The only run Sherdel's given up came in the fourth when Babe smacked an impossible inside curve out of the park — impossible for any other player, that is. Now Babe lifts the bat, ready for the next pitch. Another strike!

Babe turns to have a word with the catcher and — oh no! Sherdel throws a sneak pitch over the plate. Babe has struck out! But wait, the umpire refuses to call it! An illegal pitch, that's what the ump says, and now the entire roster of the St. Louis Cardinals is pouring onto the field in protest."

Every one of us jumped out of our chairs, as if being on our feet would make our ears more capable of hearing the announcer, who was momentarily drowned out by the raucous booing of the Missouri crowd.

"What's happening, Aunt Helen?"

"I'm not sure, Jimmy."

The announcer's voice won the battle of the radio waves and cut through the clamor. *"It's no use, folks. The umpires have closed ranks. The call will stand! The Cards lumber back to their bench as Babe locks eyes with Sherdel on the mound. It's still two strikes on the Babe, and here comes the pitch. A curve-ball on the outside. Wee Willie's still shaken by all the excitement it seems."*

I squeezed my mother's hand, her rings digging into my fingers, as another ball was thrown wide of the plate. Clarence lifted James into his arms to quiet the boy. Even Pip stopped his antics and stood stock-still on four little paws, the triangles of his ears cocked to the announcer's voice.

"Here comes the pitch. It's a fastball over the plate." As far away as Manhattan, we heard the pop of that ball meeting Babe's bat and recognized the sound. We were celebrating even before the announcer confirmed it. *"The Sultan of Swat connects! It's an easy swing but the ball keeps rising. It's over the roof and still it sails on! Some lucky pedestrian would be well advised to look up at the sky right about now. The Babe is rounding the bases, triumphant. The crowd is too stunned to give him the ovation he deserves. He waves a mocking hand at the spectators as he's welcomed back to the Yankees bench, a hero returned from battle."*

We were still cheering for Babe when Lou Gehrig hit his homer. Sherdel was yanked off the mound after that, but the damage had been done. We were limp with relief in the ninth when Babe caught the winning fly and ran it in, arm held aloft like a torch of victory.

The thrill of another World Series win for the Yankees turned our listening party into a celebration, Clarence discreetly pouring shots of whiskey into our bottles of Coca-Cola. Finally the party broke up, everyone pitching in to bring the radio and the empty plates of eaten sandwiches up to our apartment. James scooted between our legs and plopped himself on our couch, opening up a book of children's poems. "Aunt Helen, can I stay here and read with you?"

"It's about time you had a nap, Jimmy," Bernice said, but Clarence overruled her.

"Let him stay a while. I've got to go out and collect on my bets before the bookies run out of cash. Why don't you come with me, honey? I'll take you out for dinner on my winnings."

"He can sleep on the couch if he's tired, Bernice. We don't mind, do we, Mom?"

My mother shrugged. She tried to hide it, but I knew she had a soft spot in her heart for James. When I sat beside him to see what poem he'd picked out for us to read, I noticed one of Clarence's betting slips sticking out of his pocket. "Your dad will need that, Jimmy. I'll be right back."

They were in the hallway, waiting for the elevator. Opening my door, I heard their conversation before they saw me. "If she wants a child so much," Bernice was saying, "why doesn't she marry Albert and have one of her own already?"

Clarence circled his arm around her waist. "Let's not worry about anyone else, honey. Just look how lucky we are." The elevator arrived. Pulling it open, Clarence glanced back and saw me, tears on my face and his betting slip in my hand. "I just remembered Jimmy was playing with my slips. Go on, honey, I'll be right down." Sending her to the basement without him, he came and touched his handkerchief to my wet face. "I'm sorry, Helen. She doesn't know what she's saying."

"Do I spend too much time with Jimmy?"

"No, that's not it. She just works so hard, is all." He looked down the hallway of my apartment to see James on the couch, proudly reciting a poem to my mother. "You and Jimmy, you're good for each other. Don't you worry about it."

As predicted, James soon fell fast asleep, the book of poetry clutched in his little hands. When Clarence came by after dinner to collect him, I placed a kiss on James's forehead, the boy a ragdoll in his father's strong arms.

My mother and I were getting ready for bed ourselves when a Western Union messenger rang our bell. "It's a telegram from Rex," I said, giving the boy a quarter for his trouble. "Sent from St. Louis Union Station."

"Read it, Helen."

WE WON STOP BOARDING YANKEE SPECIAL ARRIVING GRAND CENTRAL TOMORROW NIGHT

STOP TELL MOM STAY HOME WILL BE MOB
SCENE STOP TICKET READY FOR HELEN
10AM TRAIN TO EAGLES REST WILL JOIN
YOU FRIDAY STOP ALBERT SAYS HI STOP
REX

I was disappointed, as the evening wore on, that no telegram came for me from Albert, but he must have had his hands full. Mr. Nakamura had been left at home — game three had been played on Sunday and not even a trip to the World Series, Jake complained, could convince the man to give up his day off — which meant Albert was both butler and secretary. I could only imagine the riotous scene unfolding on the train as the players celebrated their win. There was a reception planned at the Biltmore Hotel for their arrival Wednesday night, and there'd be celebrations in the city on Thursday, too. I guessed I wouldn't see Albert until he arrived at Eagle's Rest on Friday with everyone else.

That night in bed I propped a pad on my knee and began making notes. This would be Jake's third time celebrating a World Series victory. I knew he'd want me to plan something special, but first I had to figure out who to expect. Miller Huggins would be eager to get home to his sister's place in

Florida, but he wouldn't refuse Jake's invitation. Tony Lazzeri, I guessed, would be going straight into surgery for his injured arm, while Bob Meusel was heading out to California, but Ruth and Gehrig and Hoyt would certainly be coming. I wouldn't know which other players would be invited until I got the final guest list. And what about the women? Mrs. Hoyt would come, of course, and Rex's boss and the Yankees' business manager would both bring their wives, too. Gehrig was still single, so I assumed he'd be on his own, as Jake didn't countenance girlfriends at the estate. Babe Ruth, however, hadn't been seen in public with his wife for a couple of years now. I wondered, given his exceptional performance, if Jake would ease up and allow Babe to impress a lady friend with an exclusive invitation to Eagle's Rest.

I found out the answer to that question on the New York Central next morning, where I was seated across from an attractive woman in an otherwise empty compartment. She was dressed well without being flashy, her dark hair swept fashionably to the side. Her toothy smile was a tiny imperfection that only made her face lovelier. We greeted each other as the conductor's whistle blew and the train lumbered out of the station.

"You must be Helen Winthrope," she said, extending a gloved hand. I wasn't used to being recognized, and my surprise must have shown on my face. "Rex told me to look out for you. He arranged my ticket, too."

She seemed far too sophisticated for my brother, not to mention older than he was, though for a woman this good-looking, Rex might not let a difference in age deter him. "I'm sorry, but my brother didn't mention you."

"No, no one does, if they can help it. I'm Claire Hodgson. Rex must have figured putting me on the train with you would keep my picture out of the papers when Babe comes home tonight."

I nodded, the mystery solved. "I knew you were out of my brother's league."

"Rex? Oh, he's adorable, and so are you, Helen. I'm proud to know you both. But I'm with Babe. Have been for a while now. Don't worry about Mrs. Ruth, though. She's shacked up with a dentist in Massachusetts." Claire shrugged her shoulders. "Doesn't matter. I'm a widow, and I've been an actress, so it's not as if I'm worried about my reputation. You're an actress, too, I hear?"

"I was, for a while." Claire's congeniality was catching; already I felt as if we were dear friends rather than strangers. "So you're coming up to Eagle's Rest, too?"

"Might as well. Babe won't have a moment to himself the next couple of days."

"He was magnificent. We listened on the radio. My heart was in my throat the entire seventh inning."

By the time the porter came around to take reservations for lunch, there was no question we'd be sharing a table. She was so slender I expected her to have a salad bowl and half a grapefruit, but was pleasantly surprised when she ordered the Spanish mackerel with lemon butter. I asked if she'd met Albert. She said she'd seen him but hadn't yet been introduced. "Rex tells me you and Mr. Kramer are — ?"

"Together, yes." I noticed her eyes dip to my ringless left hand as I stuck my fork into my chicken pie. "We've known each other for ten years now."

"Well, marriage isn't all it's cracked up to be. Babe's a darling to me. Have you met his daughter, Dorothy? She's just a few years older than my own girl." Her mood was bright as polished silver, but I caught a hint of melancholy in her voice. "We'll all be together as soon as ever we can."

To that I merely nodded. It was accepted fact Babe Ruth's Catholicism would never allow him to divorce his wife as long as she lived. Which put me and Claire Hodgson in the same boat: women in love with men incapable of being our husbands.

Not that there was much difference, anymore, between me and Albert and a married couple. We spent nearly every evening together, having taken subscriptions to a number of theaters, and there was always a new movie to see, talkies replacing the silents more and more. Sometimes my mother cooked us supper, and Jake often invited us to join him if he found himself dining alone. There were days I practically lived at Albert's apartment, heading home only to sleep. I wouldn't have bothered to do even that — Albert had set up the second bedroom for me, with a closet I kept some clothes in and a chaise lounge I could sleep on — but my mother insisted I not give the doormen at Jake's building any reason to gossip. Then there were our days at Eagle's Rest, which felt to me now like a second home. Albert and I were there every April for the reception before opening day, and each October for the party to close out the season. Jake only attended away games during the postseason, so when the Yankees were on the road the three of us would often head up the Hudson together. Pip had even made friends with one of the monkeys, the female rhesus, who reached out gleefully from her cage whenever she saw him.

Planning parties for Jake wasn't much of a career, but he'd been right, it turned out I didn't really need one. I felt a twinge of regret at what I'd sacrificed whenever I saw Joseph Harrison's name on the screen at the movie theater, but then again, I might have been as big a failure in Hollywood as I had been here in New York. I hadn't given up much, not really, not compared to what I'd gained. Whenever I saw Albert's face in the audience at one of my settlement house plays, smiling as the children bumbled through their lines, I knew I'd been right to steer him clear of King.

For years now, Albert hadn't been in a lick of trouble — no black eyes, no police raids. He'd become indispensable to Jake, who'd raised his salary to the point we could have easily afforded a little house of our own on a leafy street in Brooklyn. But we didn't need a house, living as we did. We only needed each other. Like Claire and Babe, we were bound together in every way that mattered. He called me darling, said he loved me, kissed my lips now instead of my cheek. Never mind that his kisses were fluttering things. I'd managed to forget, over the years, the kind of kiss he was capable of giving.

CHAPTER 35

The train was holding its departure for us, but even though they'd dubbed this extra run of the Southwestern Limited the "Yankee Special" it wouldn't wait forever. Rex was on the platform, clipboard in hand, checking off players as they jumped aboard. "You're late!" he shouted at the last couple of stragglers. He scanned his list then shoved his pencil behind his ear. "That's all the players. You've got the Colonel squared away, don't you, Albert?"

I did. His luggage was stowed in his private stateroom, my own suitcase in the butler's berth adjacent to his own. I had a new respect for Mr. Nakamura after this trip. It really was a full-time job keeping the Colonel perfectly attired. "Did you send a telegram to Helen?"

Rex nodded. "Arranged for her ticket up to Eagle's Rest tomorrow, too. I put her next to Babe's friend, Claire. Figured two gals could gab their way up the Hudson together. We'll meet them there on Friday. I told Helen you said hi." Rex and I clambered onto the train as the exasperated conductor finally blew his whistle. "Oh, Albert, I almost forgot. Miller Huggins had me add a Kansas City player to the manifest. Remember that game we went to at the Polo Grounds, back when I was in school? I'll never forget the first time I saw Babe Ruth hit a homer. Anyway, it's the soldier we met that day. Huggins wanted to bring him out to New York to make him some kind of offer."

It was like trying to make out the spoken words in a silent film. I saw Rex's mouth move but couldn't trust I'd understood his meaning. "King Arthur is on this train?"

Just then, Babe Ruth came hooting and hollering along the corridor, leading a pack of celebrating players in a drunken parade as he reenacted his winning catch. Rex and I flattened ourselves against the wall to avoid being trampled. "He's here somewhere, but good luck finding him."

The idea that King and I were both rocking over the same stretch of track made me light-headed. There had been plenty of nights, over the past five years, when I'd be going happily along with Helen on my arm, not thinking of him at all. Then some man's blue eyes would pop out at me from the drab world in which I lived and the hairs on my arm would stand at attention, expecting his touch. He'd sent a couple of postcards that first year he was in Missouri, but he was a terrible correspondent. We'd lost touch during the off-season, when he'd sailed for Cuba to join a ragtag exhibition team. He could have come to New York if he'd wanted to, I told myself. If he'd missed me, he would have. But he didn't, and I didn't go visit him, either. When the Yankees played the Cardinals in '26, King must have guessed I'd be in St. Louis. For all I knew, he was in the stands. Between pitches I looked for him, my eyes scanning those thousands of hatted heads for a glimpse of his fair hair.

But moments like that were few, with months or even years between. Ever since I'd made my choice on the High Bridge, Helen and I had lived a charmed life in the Colonel's employ. I'd never had someone care about me as deeply as Helen did, or depend on me as completely as the Colonel. There was hardly an idle hour during which I might fall into a lonely melancholy. And if I did? There was a time I would have dolled myself up and dragged myself down to

Antonio's, hoping to catch some man's eye for a furtive encounter that would leave me lonelier afterward than I'd been before. Now I simply gave Helen a call. Before I knew it, we'd be seated happily at a restaurant or in the audience of a show. I had no flashes of panic, no dread of arrest or ruin. I'd have sworn I had no regrets, either — until I heard King Arthur's name and that stubborn part of me I'd thought was long forgotten insisted I seek him out.

King may have been on this train, but Rex was right when he'd said good luck finding him. We'd all been in such a rush to get to the station that the exhilaration of winning the World Series was still pounding through everyone's blood. I'd looked through two cars of rioting players, and all I had to show for it was a torn sleeve and a bruised elbow. I gave up and shoved my way back to the Colonel's stateroom just as Babe's parade charged past me again.

"You'd think his arm would get tired," I said, locking the door to keep them out.

"We can't begrudge Ruth his antics tonight, Kramer, not after the way he snatched that ball out of the air to win me the Series." The Colonel changed out of his suit and into the silk pajamas I laid out for him. He must have been the only member of the Yankees organization determined to get some sleep that night. I was still in my shirtsleeves, the underarms sour with perspiration after that hot afternoon in the stands. How the Colonel had the fortitude to keep his jacket on throughout the entire game was beyond me.

"That catch was truly a thing of beauty, sir." Any other player would have hobbled off the field and stuck his sore knee in an ice bath, but not Babe Ruth. He leaped over benches like a steeplechase horse as he took that caught ball on a victory lap around the locker room. His elation carried him right to the train station. Since then, gulps of gin had served the double function of numbing his knee and elevating his mood so that the carousing was still going strong.

The Colonel and I were talking over the game when the door to the stateroom suddenly shook under an assault of pounding fists. He cautiously approached. "What is it?"

"Come on out here, Colonel, and have a drink with us!" Babe's booming voice was buoyant as a circus barker. "We wanna toast ya!"

"You go to sleep now, Ruth. We have a big day tomorrow when we get back to New York." The Colonel turned to me with a smile on his face, satisfied with his response. Then the door of the stateroom was blasted to splinters as a big fist came smashing through the wood. The diamond on Babe's pinky ring glittered as his arm reached for the Colonel. Did Babe think he could haul the man through the hole he'd punched in the door? His hand closed around a handful of silk, then his arm pulled back, tearing the Colonel's pajamas and leaving him half-naked. A tremendous whoop echoed along the corridor. "I got the Colonel's pajamas!" Babe cried, as if that piece of silk were as significant a catch as the winning ball of the World Series.

I expected the Colonel to be livid, but instead he giggled hysterically, the excitement of the moment overcoming his usual reticence. "I'm lucky Ruth loves winning as much as I do, Kramer."

"Should I get you a fresh pair of pajamas, sir?"

"No, you go on to bed." He caught his breath as his giggles turned to sighs. "Send a porter back to fix this door before you turn in."

I did as he asked, then decided to take one more walk through the train before attempting to sleep. But King wasn't in the club car with the cheering players. He must have already bunked down for the night, the curtain around his berth drawn shut. I was surprised at the depth of my disappointment. The word *lovelorn* came to mind. I was making my way back to bed when the parade of rioting players burst through the coupling between the cars. Babe held the torn piece of pajamas in the air, the others following like hounds on a scent, their howls barely human. At the end of the corridor was a washroom barely big enough for a man to stand in. Fearing I'd be crushed or mauled, I reached for the handle and tried to open the door but it stuck. Babe's eyes were wild, his face red and sweating as he lurched along. What would they want to tear from me? I wondered. I shoved the door hard. It gave way. I stumbled in and slammed it shut, turning the lock as the riot raged outside. Only then did I realize why the door had been so difficult to open — the washroom was occupied.

I spoke over my shoulder. "I'm sorry, I'll get out in a second. You see what's happening out there?"

The commode flushed and I heard the sound of the lid being closed, a zipper being pulled, a belt being buckled. I considered pivoting to address the man, whoever he was, but that would have put us face-to-face, close enough to kiss — a thought that made me blush. Instead I pressed myself forward to make as much space between us as possible.

"Albert, is that you?" I turned around. King's face materialized as if by magic. "I've been looking all over this train for you."

It took me a moment to adjust to the reality of a world with him in it. I would have thought I was making him up if it hadn't been for the weight of his hands on my shoulders. "I've been looking for you, too."

"Have you really?" He'd been drinking, I could see that from the sheen in his eyes, but he wasn't crazed. The train rocked along the tracks, swaying us against the walls of that narrow room. He must have been dizzy because he sat down on the closed lid of the commode and pulled me onto his lap. "Where have you been hiding?"

I pushed the hair back from his forehead, let my fingers trace the curve of his ear. "I was in the Colonel's stateroom."

"I should've known to look for you there." He placed a palm on my cheek, curled his fingers around my neck. Someone pounded on the locked door, jiggled the handle, gave up and moved along.

I meant to tell King how many times I'd picked up a pen to write him, how often I thought of him, how I still had that button from his uniform among my keepsakes. Instead, I said this: "I always forget how blue your eyes are."

"I never forget you." He switched off the light, leaving only the glow coming through the frosted glass to illuminate his expression. His eyes drifted shut as he brought our mouths together.

Since last I'd seen him, the only kisses I'd known were fleeting ones on Helen's closed lips. I hadn't minded. I'd figured the chambers of my heart she was able to fill were the necessary ones. Yet all it took was a single kiss from King to reveal the fatal flaw in my reckoning. The scent of his sweat filled my nostrils as I succumbed to the irrefutable logic of desire.

"Rex said you've got a meeting with Miller Huggins?" We'd stayed in that washroom long after the rioting in the corridor ceased. We were standing now, the motion of the train swaying us like a dance. He helped me get my shirt back on. I put a knot in his tie and snugged it up to his collar.

"Yeah, on Thursday, at the Yankees office. Do you still live in that brownstone?"

"No, I have an apartment in the Colonel's building, but the place'll be overrun with reporters. Let me see if I can't get you invited up to Eagle's Rest. A bunch of players will be going. One more won't matter."

Though we were on the same train for another nineteen hours, I didn't see King again. I thought I caught a glimpse of him when we got off at Grand Central Station, but there was such a mob of fans and reporters I couldn't be sure. At the reception with the governor at the Biltmore, I took Rex aside, he squared it with Huggins, and next thing I knew King Arthur's name had been added to the list of players who'd be coming up to Eagle's Rest.

CHAPTER 36

Eagle's Rest may have had fifteen bedrooms, but it was a puzzle how to fit twenty-three people into them. I was run off my feet finalizing menus and inspecting deliveries, so when Claire volunteered to take over the room assignments I gratefully handed her the guest list. After all, she knew better than I did which players got along and which couldn't stand each other. Officially Claire was rooming with me, but really she'd be sleeping in Babe's room next door. She put the married couples and Miller Huggins in the guest bedrooms on the second floor. Upstairs, four of the eight rooms were occupied by staff. Rex had already volunteered to double up with the Yankees' publicity man, so Claire paired off six players into the remaining three rooms. She and I were passing each other in the hallway Friday morning when she caught my arm.

"There's a new recruit I don't know who

just got added to the list. Do you think Mr. Kramer would mind taking him in? The only other option is to put him with the butler."

I thought of that bell in Mr. Nakamura's room, how Jake rang for him at all hours of the day and night. "It wouldn't be practical for the butler to share. I don't suppose Albert will mind."

"I didn't think so." She flashed me a knowing smile. "He must not spend much time up there anyway."

Around noon I heard the honk of a horn as a car rolled up the gravel drive. I was getting up to see who it was when Claire came racing down the stairs and right out the door. Babe Ruth stepped out of a brand-new DeSoto Coupe and caught her up in his arms. He'd left Manhattan ahead of everyone else, and I soon understood why. Claire led him up to his room, and it was a full two hours before they emerged, both freshly bathed and dressed for dinner. They made themselves at home in the parlor, mixing drinks from Jake's extensive stash of liquor.

The limousine arrived next, Schultz at the wheel and Mr. Nakamura beside him. Albert and Miller Huggins had ridden in back with Jake. Out of consideration for me, they'd brought my brother with them, too. Rex ran up and lifted me off my feet. "We won the Series, Helen!"

"I know, Rex, I was listening. Go on inside, Babe is mixing drinks."

Jake cut a jaunty figure in his tan suit and straw boater, the joy of his team's victory visible on his face. "Is everything ready, Helen? The players will be arriving any minute." He nodded to Schultz and the limousine drove off, followed by the caretaker in his truck, to meet the train.

I had my eye on Albert as I told Jake we were prepared for all of his guests. "Claire Hodgson has been a tremendous help. It was kind of you to invite her."

"After the way Ruth played in St. Louis, I couldn't refuse him." He patted my arm before going inside, followed by Miller Huggins. From the dejected way he shuffled along, no one would have guessed he'd just won the World Series.

"Helen." Albert was strangely elated, hugging me like we'd been apart years instead of just a few days. "Have you seen the guest list?"

"Excuse me, Miss Winthrope." Mr. Nakamura had been left stranded in the drive with a pile of luggage. "Where am I taking these, please?"

I gave Albert a kiss. "I'd better help him. Babe and Claire are in the parlor. Go ahead, I'll join you in a minute."

Everyone else arrived while I was sorting out the suitcases. I found Jake in the foyer, welcoming his guests with hearty handshakes. "Helen, there you are. Mrs. Hoyt was asking for you." The first time Waite Hoyt brought his wife up to Eagle's Rest, she'd thought I was Jake's housekeeper until her husband set her straight. I was Mr. Kramer's friend, he told her, because that's how they all knew me. Mr. Kramer's friend and the Colonel's hostess. "Stay with me, Helen," Jake whispered, pinching my wrist. "The women like to see you when they come in."

I received his guests as if his mansion were my home, too. When it seemed we'd come to the last of the arrivals, Jake followed them in, leaving me momentarily alone in the foyer. But he'd gone too soon. There was one more player coming through the door.

"Hello again, Helen."

I refused to believe my eyes. It was impossible, I told myself, yet here he was, King Arthur at Eagle's Rest. Though his fingers were warm, I felt a cold shiver at their touch. I hadn't yet managed to speak when Albert came trotting out of the parlor to greet him. They explained how they'd run into each other on the train back from St. Louis. Their words seemed to come from a great distance, drowned out by the whoosh of blood in my ears.

"I hope you don't mind sharing." I thought Albert was speaking to me. "All the other rooms were full so Helen put us together." But I hadn't, I wanted to say. It was Claire. If I'd seen King's name, I would have rerouted the roads to keep him away.

I moved through that evening like a somnambulist, making inane small talk over drinks and forcing food into my mouth at dinner. Babe's assault on Jake's stateroom was a general topic of conversation. Instead of joining in, I watched Albert gaze at King, who was seated across the table in the extra chair I'd squeezed in for the new recruit. I cringed to see how his eyes feasted on the sight of the man.

Jake's attention, fortunately, was elsewhere. When I made the seating chart, I'd put Claire to his left because I wanted him to know what a lovely woman she was. She'd been studying Jake's antiques and commenced to dazzle him with her knowledge of his Emma Stebbins bas-relief depicting the purchase of Manhattan. "I believe she used Charlotte Cushman as a model for that woman who stands behind Henry Hudson in the sculpture," Claire said. "They were lovers, don't you know."

"Charlotte Cushman and Henry Hudson?"

Claire playfully swatted his wrist. "You're teasing me, Colonel Ruppert. No, Charlotte and Emma, of course."

After dinner, Claire insisted she and Jake go look at the sculpture together. I excused myself, too. I told Albert I'd hired some extra help from the village and that I needed to have a word with the girls before they embarrassed themselves fawning over Babe Ruth. I came back up from the kitchen to see everyone gathered in the parlor, music from the player piano filling the room. Jake was showing Claire a vase from his collection of Chinese porcelain while Babe and Gehrig talked over plans for their exhibition tour, set to commence tomorrow afternoon at Dexter Park in Wood Haven. Albert was talking to King and Rex, the three of them making a casual group in a quiet corner of the room. I thought about joining them — what would be more natural than approaching my brother and my young man? Except Albert wasn't really mine, was he, not while King was here.

"Is there anything you need, Miss Winthrope?" Mr. Nakamura was at my side, an ice bucket in his gloved hands.

"No, thank you. If anyone asks, tell them I went up with a headache, would you?"

"Shall I bring you some aspirin, miss?"

I shook my head. "I'm sure I'll be fine."

I shut my curtains and curled up on the bed, awash in self-pity. I wished I had Pip to comfort me, but I'd left him at home with my mother. The thought reminded me of Princess, who'd died a few years back. Jake had replaced her with a feisty descendant of one of Pip's littermates. I supposed she was sleeping in the wicker basket Jake kept at the foot of his bed. I was considering going to get her when my door opened, a wedge of light widening across the ceiling. Albert, I thought, come to reassure me that nothing could come between us. King's appearance was an aberration, he'd say. As soon as the party was over and the guests had gone, we'd go back to being ourselves again, me and Albert and Jake, the three of us cozy around the breakfast table, the dogs playing at our feet.

"Helen, are you okay?" Claire sat on the bed beside me. "Here, I brought you some Saratoga water."

I sat up and accepted the glass she put in my hands. "I'm fine, just a headache."

"I saw you come up and then I noticed Albert disappear, too. I figured I'd better move my things over to Babe's room now, before you two wouldn't want to be disturbed."

Of course that's what she would assume. For years, I'd let people believe that Albert and I were lovers. I secretly savored their knowing looks, though the truth was we had nothing to be ashamed of. But tonight he really was someone's lover, just not mine.

I started sobbing. Claire held my hand and asked no questions. She must have been acquainted with plenty of reasons for a woman to cry. "Let me get you a cold washcloth for your face. You won't want Albert to see you like this."

I closed my eyes as I listened to her cross the room. But instead of hearing the door to the bathroom creak, I heard the pocket door sliding open. Too late I sat up. "Not that door, Claire."

But she had seen, through the opening, Mr. Nakamura in Jake's room, laying out his pajamas on the bed. I could practically hear the gears in her mind whirring as she slid the door closed. I knew what conclusion she must have jumped to. The idea of a washcloth forgotten, she hastily gathered her things before I could find the words to set her straight. At my door, she stopped and faced me. "What I don't get, Helen, is why Albert goes along with it." Then her beautifully arched eyebrows rose to the top of her lovely forehead. "He was right. Babe, I mean. About Albert."

"Right about what?"

"He's a pansy, isn't he? I should have known. I was an actress long enough to recognize the type. I guess it was seeing him with you that threw me off. You three have got it all worked out, haven't you? Albert covers for your affair with Ruppert, and you cover for him."

"No, Claire, it isn't like that, not at all. Let me explain."

"Oh, don't worry. Nothing shocks me anymore, not since Babe told me about Dorothy. She's his, you know, with another woman. Can you believe he convinced his wife to adopt his own daughter?" She shook her head. "It's a wonder we women have any pride left at all."

"Claire, wait —" But she'd slipped into the hallway. I was getting up to follow when I heard Mr. Nakamura's gentle knock on the pocket door. It was the same knock he gave every morning, the knock that asked if I was dressed and ready to join Jake for breakfast. It had never sounded so corrupt before.

"Is everything all right, Miss Winthrope?"

"Yes, Mr. Nakamura, everything's fine. Good night."

"Good night, miss."

He locked the door from that side, as usual. You see, I wanted to tell Claire, I couldn't have crept into Jake's room even if I'd wanted to. Claire had projected her own compromised situation with Babe onto my innocent one with Jake. I'd speak to her in the morning, make her understand how wrong she was about us.

But that night, as I curled myself around a pillow in an otherwise empty bed, I wondered if Claire wasn't right after all. I did cover for Albert. He didn't have to worry about being pegged for a pansy with me by his side. But why shouldn't I shield him from suspicion? It wasn't as if Albert wanted to be the way he was. I'd never seen him so distraught as the night he confessed his condition. He couldn't help it, any more than he could help his color-blind eyes or his damaged heart. It was a perversion of the sexual instinct, Dr. Havelock Ellis wrote, that attracted men like Albert and King to one another. It wasn't normal. You couldn't build a life on it. I doubted you could even call it love.

Claire was right about me, too. Being with Albert explained my presence in Jake's household. Without him, I knew how people would think I earned my place. Jake wouldn't abide a scandal, of that I was certain. Where would it leave me, if Albert paired off with this baseball player? An unmarried, unemployed, ex-actress living with my mother. What do you call a Bachelor Girl who forgot to get married? A spinster. That's how the joke went, and it would be on me. I was thirty-one years old. I'd let my chances slip through my fingers. A future with Albert was all I had to count on now. If I didn't hold fast to him, I'd be left empty-handed.

CHAPTER 37

King held my head to his chest. "How fast is my heart beating?"

I listened to the pulsing of blood through the muscle. "Not as fast as you think."

He eased his legs down, stretched out his hips. "Don't lie to me, Albert. You were perfect." He kissed the top of my head. "I can't believe you've never done that before."

"When would I have done that? I'm a pansy, remember."

He arched his back and shifted me to the side. "That doesn't really matter, Albert. It didn't matter in Berlin, anyway." We were face-to-face on the pillow, our noses touching. "You say we're different, that I'm normal and you're a pansy, but don't you see? We're really the same. We're both men who love other men."

I only half-listened as King went on to explain Dr. Magnus Hirschfeld's theories on homosexuality. Let him have his Ger-

535

man ideas, I thought. Just hearing him use the word *love* filled my heart with helium.

"Let's have a smoke," I said. We sat up in my narrow bed, the cot that had been brought in for him neglected on the far side of the room. I had the lights off and the windows open, inviting a breeze without exposing us to any guests who might look up from a nighttime walk on the grounds. All they'd see, if their vision was keen, were the red dots of two cigarettes floating in the darkness.

"It was good of Helen to put us together like this," he said. "It must be wonderful for you to have a friend like her."

It was. Helen was more like family than my own mother had ever been. She was the sister I never had. I was closer to her than most men were to their wives. To King I said simply, "I can't imagine my life without her."

King frowned. "The question is, does she leave any room in your life for me?"

"Why, are you planning our wedding?" I was joking, of course, but even so I embarrassed myself.

He didn't laugh at me, though. "I went to a wedding like that, at Hirschfeld's Institute. They didn't have a license, of course, but there was a ceremony and rings. Cake, too."

I sometimes wondered if he made them up, the things he told me about Berlin. Anyway, I assured him Helen would be happy to include him in our circle. King's mind must have still been on the subject, because he asked me why the Colonel had never married. "Is he queer, too?"

"I wonder about that myself." I narrated to him the episodes that formed the basis of my speculations: the red bow tie, the Hamilton Lodge Ball, the kiss he'd placed on my damaged eye.

"But that was five years ago. You've never just asked him, in all this time?"

The moment had never been right, I explained, and besides, what if I were wrong? I'd be exposing myself by simply posing the question. What I had been puzzling over, since the last time I'd seen King, was the connection between the Colonel and Helen. "He treats her like a mistress, but that's not at all how it is between them. It was one thing when he was backing her professionally. Even opening an account for her at Macy's made sense, since he wanted her to be well dressed to accompany him places. Since her production company failed, she's been on his payroll, but I'm not sure as what. She helps out with these parties, but that's just a couple times a year.

She's such a smart woman, I'm sure she could make a success of herself if given half a chance."

King bit into one of the apples I'd brought up, knowing how he got hungry in the night. "Didn't you say the Colonel was friends with her father?"

"The man died in his arms, he told me."

"Well, maybe that's it, then."

"But twenty years is a long time to feel guilty for an accident."

"Not guilt. I mean love."

I took his apple and bit into the flesh. "I told you, he's not in love with Helen."

"Not Helen. Her father. Don't you see? He might be taking care of Helen for her father's sake, if they'd been lovers."

I couldn't believe I'd never put it all together before. Helen's father could have been like Felix — a man like us who managed to marry and father a couple of children. I told King about Felix's proposition on the High Bridge, how that treatment in Vienna hadn't worked after all.

"But you turned him down?" King put the core of the apple on my nightstand and pulled me back under the blanket.

There was no moon at all that night, just a faint glimmer from the patio lights below. Still, those blue eyes swam up through the

538

darkness. "It wouldn't have ended well, for either of us. I decided I'd rather just be with Helen."

"But doesn't she want more from a man than you can give her?"

Maybe it was that operation she'd had that left her devoid of sexual desire, I thought. Besides, it wasn't the same for women. From what I understood, they mainly tolerated sex because it led to children. She couldn't have any, so why would she bother? "No, she's fine."

King slid his hand along the side of my body, following the ridges of my rib cage to the rise of my hip bone. "But you aren't fine, are you?"

"I love Helen, I do. When it's just the two of us, I forget all about this." I placed my hand on the flat of his abdomen, walked my fingers up to his clavicle. "Then you show up and remind me."

"Not just me, I hope. It isn't healthy, Albert. Hasn't there been anyone else?"

There's only you, I wanted to say, but didn't. Five years hadn't seemed like so many while they were going by, but now I didn't want to wait another day, let alone a month or a year, to be with King again. "Do you think Huggins is going to call you up from the minors?"

"I hope so. He's looking at me for a pinch hitter. Babe and Gehrig both came out of the World Series on fire, but the rest of the team was in a slump." He settled my head on his shoulder, preparing for sleep. "Are you still in the market for a roommate?"

I think I murmured yes, but I might have already been dreaming. The last thought I had before falling asleep was that I'd have to move Helen's things out of my second bedroom. I didn't think she'd mind. After all, she never stayed the night.

Chapter 38

"Good morning, Helen." Jake was at his breakfast table, feet slippered and dressing gown knotted around his waist. His Boston terrier bounded over to me, whimpering and yapping. I picked her up and took a seat, the little dog squirming on my lap. I hadn't dressed yet, but with a robe over my nightgown I was covered from neck to ankles. It was a domestic scene, sure, but not a romantic one. I wished I could send Mr. Nakamura to invite Claire to have coffee with us so she'd see it for herself. "The reception was a success, thanks to you. I'm glad you sat me next to Claire Hodgson. What an engaging woman. I'm surprised she puts up with Ruth's nonsense."

"I think he's been behaving himself since they got together." I sipped gratefully at a cup of coffee. It had been a restless night, with sleep coming only toward morning. If Mr. Nakamura hadn't knocked on the pocket door, I'd have still been in bed with my eyes closed.

Jake looked up from his newspaper. "Where's Kramer? His eggs are getting cold. Osamu, ring for him, will you?"

Mr. Nakamura and I locked eyes for a moment so brief I wasn't sure it happened. Then he bowed his head slightly, leaving it to me, it seemed, to make some excuse for Albert's absence. "He was up late drinking with the players. Let's not wake him this morning, Jake."

Downstairs, the cook had put out a breakfast buffet for the guests, who knew better than to expect their host to join them. If anyone noticed my absence they'd assume I was with Albert, not Jake. Except for Claire. I should have dressed, I thought, and gone down to speak with her. But it was too late now, I realized, when Mr. Nakamura excused himself to coordinate the exodus of people needing rides to the train station.

"Is everyone leaving already?" I asked.

"Ruth and Gehrig are heading out to start their exhibition tour," Jake said. "I think the other players all have tickets for the ten o'clock train, isn't that right, Osamu?"

"Yes, sir." He let himself out, balancing a tray laden with our breakfast dishes.

"Where is Kramer? I wanted to go over

my schedule. I have a lunch meeting with Huggins to review next season's roster. He's anxious to finish up our business so he can go fishing in Florida." The newspaper rustled as he folded it. "It'll be nice to have Eagle's Rest to ourselves again, won't it, Helen? I'm thinking of spending a few weeks up here. I want to savor winning the World Series in peace and quiet. You and Kramer will stay, won't you? We can invite your mother up, too, once everyone else has gone away."

"Of course I'll stay, Jake." I placed the puppy, sleeping now, in her basket and went over to the bay window. The sill, wide enough for a seat, was furnished with throw pillows. I made myself comfortable and looked out over the lawn and down to the river. What was it about the Hudson, I wondered, that made it so gorgeous?

An engine started up. I saw Babe and Claire get in the DeSoto. Gehrig, hitching a ride, was crammed in the rumble seat with their luggage. My brother and the publicity man were climbing into the caretaker's truck, while Schultz loaded bleary-eyed players into the limousine for the trip to the train station. Mrs. Hoyt, looking up, saw me and waved good-bye. I automatically waved back before worrying what conclusion she, too, might come to, seeing me in this window.

The rumble of engines faded away until the only sounds were the screams of peacocks and the distant chirps from the monkey house. Two men appeared on the lawn. Albert and King. They were jacketless, their shirts open at the collar and sleeves rolled up above their elbows. Where could they be going, dressed so casually? King stopped but Albert kept walking until they were some distance from each other. The casements were closed, so I couldn't hear what they were saying, but I could see clear as day that Albert had a baseball glove on his hand, King a ball in his. He threw it and Albert made the catch, thanks more to the accuracy of King's aim than Albert's eye. His return throw was dismal. King had to jog halfway across the lawn to pick it up. They tried a few more tosses with similar results. Then King walked over to Albert. He stood behind him, put his arms around Albert's shoulders, circled his wrists with his fingers. I couldn't believe what I was seeing. Did they think they were invisible, embracing so openly in the broad daylight?

But no, King wasn't embracing Albert. He was instructing him in how to pitch, turning his shoulders and manipulating the bend in Albert's elbow.

Jake sat beside me and lit a cigarette. "I'm not sure how that player got himself invited to Eagle's Rest. I didn't even know Huggins was bringing him to New York. He's thinking of calling him up from the minor leagues. Huggins says he's never caused any trouble in Kansas City."

Though I'd never smoked in front of him before, that morning I took the cigarette from Jake's fingers and inhaled deeply as we watched King teach Albert how to handle a baseball. Their two faces were cheek to jowl, as if dancing a tango. I saw Albert's eyes close, for just a moment, as he tilted his head back against King's shoulder. King pursed his lips and kissed Albert's temple. It happened so fast I doubted Jake had noticed. But there was no misunderstanding the joy on Albert's face as his eyes blinked back open.

Jake pressed his handkerchief into my hand. "Don't fret, Helen. I'll tell Huggins to leave him in Missouri if you think he's still a risk."

They separated, jogging away from each until they both turned, like opponents in a duel — except, instead of bullets, a baseball traveled the distance between them. It sailed easily through the air now, each soft toss followed by a sweet catch. "Couldn't you trade him away somewhere?"

"Why, you don't think sending him back to Kansas City will be enough?"

My mouth didn't open. There were no words I could be accused of saying. But I knew what I was doing as I shook my head from side to side.

"I seem to recall one of our scouts had his eye on a player with the San Francisco Seals. I suppose we could arrange a trade."

California. I'd once hoped the state would be distant enough for me to start a new life. Now, I only hoped it would be far enough to keep King away. "The Pacific Coast League plays a long season, doesn't it?"

"Over two hundred games a year." Jake put his hand on the back of my neck, bowing my head. He placed a single kiss on my crown. "I'll tell Huggins to make the trade."

We stayed in the window seat together, my head on Jake's shoulder, watching Albert and King have a catch. If Claire had seen us like that she never would have believed we weren't lovers. But the man I loved was down there on the grass, his heart a plaything in my hands.

1939

CHAPTER 39

The only sounds in the bedroom of Jake's Manhattan apartment were the thin hiss of the oxygen tank and the soft rustle of newsprint. Through the plastic window of the therapeutic tent, Jake's face was so pale and slack I wondered how we'd know the difference when he died. Albert and I sat beside the bed, leafing through the paper, looking for a story we thought he might like to hear. Not that we could tell if he could hear us anymore. He'd been drifting in and out of consciousness since yesterday, when the priest gave him last rites and Dr. Schwerdtfeger warned us the end was imminent. They'd done all they could for him at Lenox Hill Hospital to treat the phlebitis in his blood. The only thing left, the doctor had said, was to make him comfortable at home, among his family and friends.

For the moment we had the room to ourselves. The nurse was eating her lunch in the kitchen with Jake's cook. George Ruppert had gone out to telephone Jake's nieces and nephews. I wasn't sure where in the sprawling apartment Mr. Nakamura had gotten to, but experience taught me he'd materialize the moment he was needed.

I turned the pages of the *New York Times,* but nothing in the news that day seemed appropriate. Jake was upset enough about the state of affairs in Germany. He wouldn't want to hear about Jewish refugees stranded in Czecho-Slovakia or Neville Chamberlain's trip to Rome to appease Mussolini. Displaced Negro sharecroppers protesting along the highways of Missouri was no sickroom story. There was the news out of Washington — Congress's vote to cut funding for the Works Progress Administration, the Senate's filibuster of antilynching legislation — but Jake had stopped following politics months ago. "How about the preparations for the World's Fair in the Bronx?"

Albert shook his head. I realized it would be cruel to speak of something Jake would never live to see. He pointed to a different article. "Read about Lincoln Ellsworth's flight over Antarctica. The Colonel always wished he could go on that kind of adventure."

"Oh yes, he'll like that." If it had been up

to Jake, he'd have set out himself across the ice to rescue Admiral Byrd from his lonely outpost. As it was, he'd had to settle for funding the expedition. The closest Jacob Ruppert had ever come to Antarctica was when the supply ship they'd named after him delivered its load of dogs and equipment to Little America. Throughout the 1930s, he could never tear himself away from the Yankees long enough to go to Europe, let alone to the bottom of the world. He'd sponsored expeditions across the globe, but in all his seventy-one years, Jake had never so much as gotten his passport stamped.

A twitch of his eyelids was the only sign he heard us. Albert finished reading the article while I opened the curtains. Across the street in Central Park, bare tree branches made a dark pattern against the gray January sky. It seemed heartless to me that the traffic along Fifth Avenue continued to flow as if a life were not about to end fourteen stories above. Albert joined me at the window. "Think it will snow?"

"The weatherman on the radio is predicting it." I hadn't heard Mr. Nakamura come in. He was exchanging the untouched water glass on Jake's nightstand for a fresh one. "Babe Ruth is on his way up."

"Really?" I was surprised. Jake hadn't spoken to Babe since he'd unceremoniously traded him away to the Braves. "I thought he was still in the hospital."

"He was released this morning, I believe. Colonel Ruppert's brother took the call."

Indeed, at that moment George Ruppert entered, accompanied by the nurse, who worried the room would be too crowded once Babe arrived. "We'll go," Albert volunteered, but George caught his arm. He wanted Albert to stay, in case he had to step out to welcome his nieces, who were expected any minute. "We'll need a witness to give the reporters a quote, if Jake says anything to Ruth. But, Helen, perhaps you wouldn't mind waiting in the library?"

"Of course not." During the months Jake had been ailing, I'd gotten used to being shunted off to the library whenever his nieces or nephews or sister came to visit. Jake had long ago explained his preference for keeping his family and his employees separate. In all the years, his brother George was the only relative I'd spoken to directly. I went to the bedside and reached under the oxygen tent to take Jake's swollen hand, gently stroking the knotted veins. I told him I'd be back soon. I felt a slight pressure as he attempted to grip my fingers. The weakness of the gesture broke my heart. I fled to the library, temporarily blinded by my tears.

I spent the next half hour alone with Jake's aging Boston terrier. Her hearing was diminished and her eyes were clouded with cataracts, but sensing my presence she stepped out of her basket and teetered toward me on stiff little legs. I lifted her onto my lap. She made me miss my Pip, dead seven years now. Jake had offered me another one of Princess's progeny, but I'd refused. My sweet Pip was irreplaceable.

The cook brought me a sandwich, which I shared with the dog, her appetite unaffected by her age. It was no wonder Babe wanted to see Jake so urgently, I thought. Healing the rift between the two men would erase a sour footnote to Babe's legacy. I suspected it had been Claire's idea rather than his own. She always did have a keen instinct for appearances, especially since becoming Mrs. Ruth. Babe's daughter, Dorothy, had luckily been away at boarding school when his first wife was killed in that house fire. Along with Claire's daughter, the four of them were now the very picture of a happy household. Dorothy still had no idea that the family friend who occasionally visited was her real mother.

I put the dog back in her basket and

crossed the library. There weren't many books, but the shelves were heavy with porcelain vases and bronze sculptures and silver-framed photographs. I examined the pictures one by one. Jake's parents at Linwood decades ago. Jake as a young man, handsome and dashing. The Ruppert children lined up by a Christmas tree lit with candles. It must have been taken around 1880, I thought, estimating Jake's age to be twelve or thirteen, his face recognizable across all the years. Of the three sisters and two brothers posing with him, only two were still alive. Their brother Frank had died of typhoid years ago, and their sister Anna had recently passed. Then, of course, there was Cornelia. Though her face in the photograph was only the size of my fingernail, there was a familiar line to her mouth and jaw. I rummaged through the frames and was surprised to find what I thought for a second was a photograph of myself. But no, it wasn't me, but rather another woman posed in a similar way to that portrait I'd had done when I was in drama school.

"You won't believe what happened." George came into the library and dropped into a chair. "I never thought I'd hear my brother's voice again, but he actually opened his eyes and said 'Babe.' I don't know how he managed it. Anyway, Ruth has gone to give his story to the papers." He saw the photograph in my hands and grew pale. "Cornelia. You remind me of her sometimes, Helen. It's the great regret of our lives, the way our parents reacted when Cornelia ran off with Franko. Jake was devastated to lose her."

I sat on the ottoman near his feet. "Tell me about her."

How she died I already knew, though George's telling added pathos to the story. She'd insisted on marrying Nahan Franko, a divorced Jew, over her parents' absolute opposition. He'd even converted to Catholicism, George said, but still their parents refused to attend the wedding or so much as speak to their daughter once she became his wife. It frightened them all, especially Jake, to see their sister shunned. Only when she was on her deathbed did their parents relent, but by then it was too late.

I said that Jake had told me her appendix burst. George nodded. "She'd been operated on just the day before. Jake never had the chance to see our sister alive again. Our parents were so remorseful they bribed a gravedigger to exhume her body from the plot Franko had chosen, so she could be buried near our family." He took the photograph from my hands and gazed at it. "The Bachelor Circle used to host an annual ball at the Liederkranz Society. Jake would always take Cornelia. I'll never forget watching them dance together. They were the two most beautiful people in the entire ballroom." He handed the picture back to me. I wouldn't have said beautiful, exactly, but there was character in her face.

When Albert came in, George got to his feet. "Why don't you two go home for a while, get some rest. I doubt there will be any change tonight."

Albert wanted to stay, we both did, but there was no denying the exhaustion we each felt. It was late in the evening by the time we left. Albert said no one would gossip if I slept at his apartment, given the circumstances, but I'd promised my mother I'd come home to update her on Jake's condition. Albert hugged me for a long time while the doorman went out to hail a taxi.

"I don't know what happens next, Helen. What will we do without him?"

"We'll cross that bridge when we come to it, darling."

By the time I got home, my hands were so cold my mother insisted on making me a mug of chocolate. We sat together on the couch, our shoes off and our legs tucked up under us. "Did you know about Cornelia Ruppert, Mom?"

"Oh yes, that all happened while I was working at Linwood." I imagined my mother back then, her blond hair pinned up, a prim uniform snug around her tiny waist. If I'd been casting the role of housemaid, I would have rejected her as too pretty for the part. "They were all up at Linwood when Cornelia ran off to get married. Not one of the siblings was permitted to attend. It upset Jake terribly. I know because I was serving dinner when he and his father had a fight. Jake wanted to be the one to give his sister away, since their father refused, but he threatened to cut Jake off, too, if he so much as sent a bouquet. A year later she was dead." My mother gazed into her mug of chocolate, as if reading tea leaves. "Poor Jake. He was inconsolable. That summer she died was the last I worked at Linwood."

I slept on the couch, wanting to be near the telephone in case Albert called. As I closed my eyes, I thought about the ways in which our losses held us in such thrall. The death of my father thirty years ago had done more to shape me than the lifelong companionship of my mother. Jake had obviously been capable of love. He could have married, had children, hosted family holidays at

Eagle's Rest rather than business receptions. Instead he'd kept his heart close all his life, unwilling to risk another hurt as devastating as the loss of his sister.

CHAPTER 40

I stretched out on the sofa in my shirtsleeves and trousers, jacket and shoes at the ready. Though I wanted desperately to be holding the Colonel's hand when he took his last breath, I welcomed George's suggestion of sleep. I was still unnerved by Babe Ruth's excitement over his dying words. "He said my name, he called me Babe. You heard it, didn't you, Albert?" I told him I did, though it was little more than a bleat, the sound he made. He could have been saying anything, but it didn't matter. Babe was happy, the newspapers would love it, and the Colonel always did appreciate good publicity.

After Babe walked out with the Colonel's brother, I'd sent the nurse away, too, saying I needed a moment with him in private. I was hoping he'd have saved some consciousness for me, but as I lifted the therapeutic tent and crawled in beside him, he seemed to have fallen into a coma. My lungs relaxed in the oxygen-rich air. I smoothed the white hair back from his forehead and stroked his sunken cheeks. I murmured in his ear the words I'd never taken the chance to say, not in the twenty years we'd been together. Because we had been together, he and I, in our own way. We were more to each other than employer and secretary, more even than friends. We'd never been lovers — that one kiss he'd placed on my eye had never been repeated — and yet we had been in a kind of love. I put into words, for the first time, what each of us had known silently all along. That we were alike, he and I. Two of a kind. We'd kept each other's secrets, and for the sake of everything we'd shared, I assured him that his would remain safe with me as long as I lived. I kissed his dry lips. Though it had been days since he last ate, I would have sworn I tasted a trace of peppermint.

When George suggested Helen and I get some rest, I'd asked her to stay with me, but she'd promised to go home to her mother. I hugged her close before she left, uncertain of what would become of us. For so long, we had orbited around the Colonel like moons around the sun. I didn't know what we'd do once his light burned out. Helen said we'd cross that bridge when we came to it, and I supposed she was right. Tomorrow would arrive one way or another.

Tired as I was, I couldn't sleep. I reached for a book and was disgusted to see I'd picked up that copy of *Mein Kampf* I'd borrowed from the library. I hadn't wanted to pay for the horrid thing but it seemed important to know what Hitler had planned for Europe. Because Chamberlain was living in a dream if he thought Hitler would be satisfied with a slice of Czecho-Slovakia and the Sudetenland. At least, that's what Felix said.

I'd contacted him last fall, when the Colonel instructed me to arrange a fundraiser to support the German Jewish refugees. It felt good to work with Felix again. When we met to plan the event, for a moment I wondered if he'd taken up with a very young man until he introduced the sixteen-year-old with him as Aaron, his son. I shook his hand, ashamed of my assumption. There had been no other children, I learned, this one boy bearing all the burden of his parents' expectations. I hoped he had the strength for it.

We organized a charity exhibition game at Yankee Stadium that raised thousands of dollars for the Joint Distribution Committee. I thought he'd simply turn over the money, but Felix insisted on traveling to Paris himself to deliver it to their headquarters. His wife had expected him home in a month's time, but then there'd been that terrible violence in Berlin, the *Kristallnacht* the German papers called it, and Felix stayed on to facilitate visas for the Jews clamoring to get out of Germany. I could only imagine the strain he was under. Shouldering the responsibility for relocating a thousand orphans had led to his last collapse. How would he withstand the onslaught of hundreds of thousands of desperate people?

I closed Hitler's book, unread yet again, but there was no muting the news pouring out of Germany. Hateful speeches at every torch-waving rally. Priests arrested, Jews rounded up, politicians murdered, pansies carted off to concentration camps as if their mere existence was dangerous to the Reich. What would King think of his beloved Berlin now? I wondered.

I'd last written to King back in 1933 after reading about the raid on that institute he'd told me about. It had been ages since we'd last corresponded. There'd been a flurry of letters after he was traded to San Francisco, plans for a holiday visit that never materialized. We spoke long-distance a couple of times, but I never knew where to call him. The Pacific Coast League had their players on the road practically year-round and I missed more calls than the operator was able to connect. Eventually I stopped expecting to hear his voice at the other end of the line when I answered the telephone. Weeks turned into months, and before I knew it a year had passed, then two, then ten. I was certain he'd found other companionship. In any place they played, there was sure to be some small-town pansy desperate to catch the eye of a man like King.

Back when Huggins was planning to trade him away, I'd reminded the Colonel of that long-ago day at the Polo Grounds when he'd wished Huggins could find him a strapping player like King. "You know I never interfere in those decisions, Kramer," was all the Colonel said. I never brought it up again.

It hardly mattered. I was too old now to attract a man with a glance. Besides, it wasn't safe out on the streets of New York anymore. There'd been a couple of years, after the stock market collapse, when performers like Jack suddenly became all the rage. Speakeasies competed to feature pansy acts, and Jacqueline had moved uptown to a swanky club with a grand piano and a proper stage. The Pansy Craze, as they called it, lasted only a couple of years, but Jack earned enough to retire by the time the police, needing something to do once Prohibition was lifted, started cracking down on immorality. I reminded myself to give Jack a call. Paul said he was like a bouquet of roses left to dry in a vase — still lovely, in a way, but withered and without fragrance.

It had been years since I'd seen anyone from my old life in the Village. For the Colonel's sake, I'd led a circumspect existence. There was not a whiff of scandal to taint his memory. To all the world Helen and I seemed to be a couple, and we were, in every way but one. We lived like millionaires, she and I, and though technically we were the Colonel's employees, I knew he thought of us as family. We'd made a contented threesome, Helen and the Colonel and me. How would it throw the two of us off balance to lose the third leg of our stool? I wondered.

It was a question that was swiftly answered. I'd drifted into sleep, for how long I had no idea, when the telephone woke me. It was time, George said. I rushed upstairs, my shoelaces untied, my jacket forgotten, to be part of the small circle around his bed when Colonel Jacob Ruppert died.

CHAPTER 41

Why me? That was the question shuttling back and forth across my brain. Why did Jake give more to me than to his own family? A week after his death, I came home from the reading of his will too stunned to know what to feel or think. My mother was waiting in the doorway of our apartment. At the sight of my shocked face, she asked, "What is it, Helen? Didn't he leave you anything?"

I hugged her tight, bracing her for the astonishing news. "No, Mom, that's not it at all. He left me the most of anyone, more than his own relatives."

It seemed as if my mother had been holding her breath my whole life, the way she let the howl fly from her throat. I practically carried her to the couch, she was so hysterical. "You see," she kept saying. "You see, Helen? Hasn't it all been worth it? Didn't I tell you it was your chance?"

"Calm down, Mom. Don't act like you predicted twenty years ago Jake would make me an heiress." Saying the word out loud started me shaking. *Heiress.* Three hundred thousand dollars, the lawyer had said. Why, the interest alone was as much as Albert's entire inheritance, and I'd collect it every year for as long as I lived. It was enough to run the estate, if I wanted to keep Eagle's Rest. And that wasn't even all of it. I dropped down next to my sobbing mother, my own heart palpitating as the enormity of it sank in. Along with Jake's two nieces, I was owner of the New York Yankees. Besides Effa Manley, we'd be the only women owners in all of professional baseball. Then there were the rest of Jake's holdings: the realty company, the office buildings, the brewery. For decades he'd lived large on the profits of his empire. My share was sure to outshine any success I could have achieved on my own.

My mother was calming down, but her hysteria proved infectious. Now I was the one sobbing and shrieking, my heart beating so fast I felt faint. "Put your head down, Helen. I'll go make us some hot milk and whiskey."

I did as she said, resting my head on the arm of the couch while she went into the kitchen. I recalled a lung exercise someone once taught me and used it to settle myself down. I was almost calm by the time Albert knocked on the door.

At least, we assumed it was Albert. That's why my mother pulled the door open without bothering about the chain. With a clamor of shouts and stomping feet, a dozen reporters barged right into our hallway, brushing past her until they reached me in the living room. I stood up, speechless, when I was blinded by the flash of a camera bulb. They commenced to shouting at me the same questions I'd been asking myself for the last hour. Why? Why you, miss? Why did Colonel Ruppert leave you a fortune?

"Get the hell out of my way." Clarence's commanding voice shut them up. He pushed through the commotion until he reached my side. "Are you all right, Helen?" When I nodded, he turned to face the reporters with his arms outspread. Summoning all the fearlessness he'd learned in the trenches of France, he forced the dozen men back on their heels and shut the door behind them. My mother was left with two empty mugs hanging from her hands, the spilled milk and whiskey a puddle at her feet. She looked at the two of us. "I guess I'll make three mugs this time."

Clarence led me back to the couch. My knees were bouncing so fast he actually held them down. "Tell me, Helen, is it true what they're saying, that you're a millionaire now?"

"I don't know about that, but I did inherit a fortune." I winced at the word. *Fortune.* Why should I have so much of it while Clarence had so little? It was tragic how the collapse of the stock market had brought such misery to his family. Over time, Bernice's investments had grown until they were nearly enough to purchase the apartment building she'd been dreaming of, a modest walk-up on 121st Street. Smart as she was, though, Bernice hadn't been immune to the frenzy of speculation that had every housewife and stenographer placing her savings in the hands of a stockbroker promising instant wealth. When the market collapsed, the brokerage called in her margin, and her investments evaporated. All those years Bernice had left James at home with his grandmother, or with me, so she could work and save for their future seemed suddenly a disastrous waste. Clarence had reassured her they were better off than most, he with a steady job and their family with a decent place to live despite the Depression that followed in the wake of the collapse. But Bernice blamed herself, the guilt of it weighing her down until she couldn't lift her head high enough to see the oncoming streetcar that ran her over. Her death wasn't counted among the Wall Street suicides that made the news, but her life was lost to the Crash just the same.

Jake, on the other hand, sailed through untouched. He'd learned his lesson speculating on the Florida land boom, he often said, advising anyone who would listen to steer clear of the market. Most of his wealth came from bottles of beer and baseball games, both of which only got more popular as Prohibition ended and the Depression dragged on. His good judgement left all the more for me to inherit.

For all her ambitions, Bernice had left Clarence flat broke and a widower, to boot, but for James's sake he'd set aside his grief and set about raising his son. Jimmy was fifteen now and smarter, Clarence claimed, than his two parents combined. If things kept on according to plan, he'd be graduating high school early and starting college next fall — though how Clarence would pay for it was a mystery to me. The solution popped immediately into my mind: I'd sponsor James's education. I was just opening my mouth to say so when my mother

came running in from the kitchen, scream-
ing. We jumped up to see what had frightened her. An enterprising reporter had
clambered up the icy fire escape and was
tapping at the kitchen window.

"Just give me a quote for the paper," he
shouted through the frosty glass. "Give me
a quote and I'll get the rest of them to leave
you alone."

Clarence picked up a frying pan to
threaten the man, but I grabbed his arm.
"Just open the window. Let's get this over
with."

"Are you sure, Helen? I'll call the police if
you don't want me to handle it myself."

"I need them to go away." I turned to the
window and shouted, "Will you really leave
me in peace if I give you a quote?"

The reporter crossed his heart, then
plucked his pencil from behind his ear and
held it poised over his pad. I nodded at
Clarence and he pushed up the window.

"Just tell me why, Miss Winthrope, why
did the Colonel leave you such a fortune?"
He leaned so far over the sill he nearly fell
into the kitchen. He was asking the right
question, I thought, but I didn't have the
answer. "When did you first meet the Colonel?"

"I met him when I was just a girl." I

looked back at my mother, who was hovering in the kitchen doorway. She encouraged me with a nod. "My late father was his mechanic."

"His mechanic? Here, in Manhattan? When was this?" The reporter's pencil was flying across the page of his notepad.

"Just say they were friends and leave it at that," my mother interrupted. "That's enough about your father, Helen, don't you think?"

"How did you and the Colonel spend your time? What sorts of things did you do together?"

"I used to go to the Polo Grounds with him sometimes, and I was there for the opening of Yankee Stadium in the Bronx. For a while he owned the theater I managed, and he brought me to the kennel club shows at Madison Square Garden, back when his dogs were competing."

"Weren't you with the Colonel when the ship he funded for Admiral Byrd set sail for Antarctica?"

I nodded, recalling that day. Jake had fantasized about accompanying the expedition, but his health was in decline and his doctor wouldn't allow it. He'd settled for supplying it instead. The dock at Bayonne was so hectic with stevedores, the deck of the ship so overrun with sled dogs, I became worried about him being jostled. A cameraman caught the two of us together just as I took his arm. Nobody knew who I was then. The picture ran in the paper without spelling out my name.

"And I heard you spent a lot of time at his Hudson River estate." He struggled to turn the page of his notepad with a gloved thumb. "Eagle's Rest. He left it to you, isn't that right? Did you two go up there alone?"

Clarence lifted the frying pan again, ready to thrash him for being fresh, but I answered him plainly. "No, of course not. Mr. Kramer was always with us, and many others, too."

"So what was he to you, then, miss?"

"A friend." The reporter's skepticism lifted his eyebrows. "It's true. He never even took me dancing. He was —" I searched for the right word to describe my relationship with Jake. "He was like a father to me."

"That's enough now." My mother stepped forward and took my arm. "You got what you came for, now get out of here before Clarence throws you out."

The reporter looked down the icy fire escape. "Can't I at least come through and take the elevator?"

"We're done here." Clarence shut the

window and watched as the reporter began his precarious descent. When he was certain he wouldn't be climbing back up, Clarence said he better get back down to the lobby. In the doorway he turned to me. "Listen, Helen, I think you should get out of town for a while. Once this gets printed in the paper, every long-lost relative you never heard of will come crawling out of the woodwork with a sob story, asking for a share of your prize."

"I suppose you're right, but first you have to promise me something."

"Anything you need, Helen."

I spit into my hand and held it out. He looked skeptically at my palm, shiny with saliva. "What am I agreeing to, exactly?"

"You have to promise first, Clarence."

He spit into his hand, too, and we shook, the two of us eleven years old again. "Okay, tell me."

"You have to promise you'll let me pay for Jimmy's college. Please."

He hesitated. I hoped he could see this was friendship, not charity. I wouldn't let go of his hand until he agreed, which he did, for Bernice's sake, he said, and James's, too. "Thank you, Helen. You couldn't love that boy more if he were your own son, and don't I know it." The green flecks in his eyes were magnified by the shimmer of water gathering in them. "Lock this door now, and don't open it without the chain on."

I did as he told me. Looking down at my palm, I saw it was still wet from our mixed spit. I was about to wipe it off on my blouse, then stopped. Glancing quickly down the hallway to make sure my mother wasn't looking, I lifted my palm to my mouth and licked.

CHAPTER 42

The Colonel's will had only been read a couple of hours ago but already there was a scrum of reporters in front of Helen's apartment building, shouting and shoving and stabbing their pencils in the air. Through the glass door I saw Clarence in the lobby, his soldier's shoulders squared as he struggled to keep them out. I put my head down and pushed my way through their jabbing elbows, hoping not to be recognized. It didn't work.

"Look, boys! It's Albert Kramer, Colonel Ruppert's secretary." The throng closed on me, their questions a cascade of words crashing in my ears. Why did he leave her a fortune? What was she to him? I shouldn't have been surprised at their eagerness. The Colonel's fame as owner of the Yankees made his bequest a headline story. His wealth was rumored to be one hundred million dollars, much of it safely invested in real estate, making him one of the few millionaires who hadn't been wiped out in the Crash. I knew a proper accounting would shave that sum considerably, not to mention the taxes, but even so, Helen would be a rich woman for the rest of her life. It was a change in station as sudden as a fairy tale. No wonder the reporters were clamoring for a scoop. I imagined the front pages of tomorrow's papers were all being reset, new type put in place to announce the news of Helen's inheritance. But no matter how many questions they asked, or how many articles they wrote, I swore to myself the one story the press would never get was the real reason the Colonel made Helen his heiress.

When her bequest had been announced at the lawyer's office, I'd thought it would be so glaringly obvious that everyone would guess the Colonel's motivation. But no one put it together, the way he placed Jerry Winthrope's children on a par with his own relatives — Rex and his nephews given jobs, Helen and his nieces inheritances. More than that, though, was the cash gift that advanced Helen ahead of his own flesh and blood. To me, who knew the Colonel's secrets, it was conclusive evidence of his devotion to Helen's father, the dear friend who'd died in his arms, the man he once had loved. I imagined if Felix and I had reunited, I'd have come to feel the same way about his son, Aaron. It was as close as we could come, men like us, to being fathers ourselves.

I told the reporters I had nothing to say, but that short sentence was like tossing chum to sharks. My hat was knocked off in the frenzy. Clarence reached out to pull me from their grasping hands, dead-bolting the door to keep them from following me into the lobby. My heart was hammering as he handed me my hat.

"Have they gotten to her?"

He nodded regretfully. "I was in the basement when the first ones came by. They barged right into her apartment before I could get up there to help. They had a photographer with them, too. He got a picture before I hustled them out. One of them climbed up the fire escape. He promised they'd go away if she gave him an interview, but you see for yourself that was bogus."

I looked back at the chaotic scene outside. The reporters' mouths gaped all the wider as the glass door muffled their voices. "I better get upstairs." I shook Clarence's hand, fortifying myself with his strength.

"Call the police if you have to."

At Helen's apartment I steadied my breath, knowing it wouldn't help for me to arrive agitated. Her mother peeked around the chain before opening the door. "Thank goodness it's you. She's terribly upset." She called over her shoulder. "Helen, Albert's here."

I was still shrugging off my coat when Helen threw her arms around my neck and collapsed against me like a drunken dance partner. I maneuvered her into the living room and onto the sofa. "I shouldn't have let you come home by yourself." I looked past Helen to include Teresa in my apology. "It was a mistake for me to stay behind."

Helen nodded tearfully, but her mother said, "You had that business to finish at the lawyer's office." She sat down and asked me about the outcome of my meeting with Ruppert's relatives.

"The nieces have filed letters of no contest. No one in the family wants to see this dragged into probate court. Helen won't have any opposition."

She sighed with relief and patted Helen's hand. "You see? No one resents your inheritance."

Helen rested her head on her mother's

lap. "What am I going to do with it all, Mom?"

She smoothed back Helen's hair. "Good, I hope."

"I told Clarence I'd pay for Jimmy's college." She looked at me, a tentative smile on her face. "That would be a good start, wouldn't it, Albert?"

"I'm sure the Colonel would have liked that."

"But I still can't figure it out, Albert. Why did he leave so much to me?"

I was tempted to tell her, but how could I help Helen understand the place she occupied in the Colonel's heart without staining the memory of her father, a memory she and her mother both held in such reverence? I wondered if Teresa Winthrope had ever suspected; Felix told me his own wife had no idea. I supposed she thought the Colonel had left her daughter a fortune out of the simple goodness of his heart.

Helen lifted her head from her mother's lap. "I think I'll go lie down for a while." She put her hand on my arm as she passed my chair. "Albert, you'll stay, won't you?"

"Of course I will, Helen." I clasped her hand in mine. "As long as you need me."

"We'll keep each other company while you rest," her mother said. "We've been drinking hot milk and whiskey. Come on, Albert, I'll make you one."

We sat at the kitchen table. Her hair had gone white these past few years, but even in her sixties it was easy to see how beautiful Teresa Winthrope once had been. "I didn't think she'd be this upset, Albert. An inheritance should be good news, shouldn't it?"

"Helen's overwhelmed is all. It's a lot for her to take in."

"But you'll help her. I can't tell you how often I've thanked God for you. Jake was worried I might not approve, when he told me what you were, but it just made you all the more perfect as far as I was concerned. Can you imagine if she'd married?" Teresa shook her head. "You know how Jake was. He believed a married woman was her husband's responsibility. He would have left her something, I'm sure, same as he did you, but nothing like this. She wouldn't have had so much time to devote to him, either, if she'd had a husband. That was thanks to you, too, Albert. How could she have met someone else when the two of you spent so much time together? And you brought her to his attention. Once he got to know her, I knew he'd see how special she was." Her words caught in her throat.

"Helen always was her father's pride and joy."

My head spun from the rush of Teresa's words. I figured Helen must have explained to her mother about me at some point, but no, it was the Colonel who'd told Teresa I was a pansy. Yet she didn't mind, quite the opposite. I wondered if it was possible she knew the whole truth. "The Colonel was very fond of your husband," I said, testing the waters.

"Oh, Jerry and Jake would have done anything for each other. He would have raised his daughter like his own if I'd asked him to, but I never did, you know. He couldn't have loved her more if she'd been his own flesh and blood. I didn't see the point in saying anything, not while he was alive." She drew a handkerchief from the front of her blouse and blew her nose. "I guess you've known about Helen's father for a while now, haven't you, Albert? I assumed Jake told you the truth at some point."

"Not in so many words, but yes, I figured it out, about the Colonel and your husband."

She sighed. "Good. I'm glad we got that out in the open. It'll make it so much easier for me if you could break it to Helen. After

581

all these years, I don't know if I have the courage to tell her the truth about her father."

"Of course, if you want me to." I reached across the table and took her hand. "She won't think any less of him, I'm sure of it."

"I hope not." Her lips started to tremble as the tears returned. "I wanted him to tell her himself, while he was still alive, but he'd lived with the lie for so long I suppose he just couldn't do it. Or maybe he figured she already knew. Do you think Helen does?"

I'd lost the thread of her words. "Does what?"

"Know Jake was her father." She choked up saying it. I helped her complete the thought.

"Her father's lover, you mean."

Teresa's face scrunched up as if trying to read type too small to see. "What on earth are you talking about, Albert?" Then she looked at me like I'd walked into her house with shit on my shoes. "What, you think Jake was like you, that he did this for Jerry? They weren't perverts, Albert. They were normal men, both of them. After Jake got me pregnant, I married Jerry so fast he had no idea Helen wasn't really his. Jake didn't believe in marriage, that's true, but he was no queer."

I sat in stunned silence as the movie of my life spooled backward through my mind. Every assumption I'd made, every conclusion I'd come to, had been wrong. The Colonel had recognized me for what I was while I had reinvented him in my own image. That kiss he placed on my black eye wasn't to show me we were the same, but to keep me in line. We each had secrets, sure, but they were entirely different ones. For years I'd imagined us sharing a silent understanding, a bond so deep it didn't need to be put into words. It seemed impossible that I had been such a fool. I wouldn't believe it, not entirely, without hearing her say it one more time.

"You're telling me, Teresa, the Colonel was Helen's natural father?"

A glass shattered, shards skittering across the kitchen floor. I swung around in my chair to see Helen in the doorway, her hand still in the shape of the glass she'd been holding.

CHAPTER 43

I knew it was true as soon as I heard the words. I stumbled backward, my arms outstretched, as if finding my way blindly through an unfamiliar house. I shut myself in my bedroom, locking out my mother, whose pleading voice seeped through the keyhole. "Give me a chance to explain, Helen," she begged. But there was only one question I wanted the answer to.

"Did Daddy know?" I rested my ear against the closed door to hear her answer.

"No, Helen, I swear to you. But even if he had, he would have loved you just the same. Now let me in. I need to talk to you."

I told her to go away. There was nothing she could say that would change the fact my whole life had been a lie. It was so obvious now, I felt like an idiot not to have figured it out before. But I hadn't been looking for the truth because I had no idea I was being deceived by my own mother. By both of my parents, I corrected myself. I felt sick, as if my own skin were an ill-fitting suit that itched and pinched. The room was stifling. I had to get out of there. I gathered some garments from the dresser drawers, threw them willy-nilly into a suitcase, and yanked open the door. My mother fell forward, and I had to catch her. I remembered how I used to look up to her, when I was a girl. She seemed so small now. I pushed her aside and grabbed Albert's hand. "Let's go."

The reporters had finally gone. We were able to get to the curb and into a taxi without being mauled. "Just drive through the park for a while," I told the cabbie. I stared out the window as streets and sidewalks gave way to meandering walkways where pigeons pecked at snowbanks and squirrels scurried across bare tree branches. Jake had given me so much, while he was alive and in his will, too, but in that moment I imagined trading it all in for the chance to call him Dad. I turned to Albert, looked him square in the eye. "Did you know?"

He rolled up the partition so the driver couldn't hear us. "No, Helen. I had no idea the Colonel was your father. I thought — well, I thought something else entirely. I'm as surprised as you are."

"They lied to me, both of them. But why, Albert?"

"I don't know, Helen. He lied to me, too. At least, he let me believe a lie." Albert seemed shell-shocked. "I hardly know which way is up anymore."

"What's the use of finding out now, when it's too late to do anything about it?" I thought of those anniversaries my mother and I would observe, the date of Daddy's death magnified in our memory. She saw what it did to me to have lost him. How could she not have said I had another father waiting in the wings to understudy the role? But Jake was the one who'd chosen not to play the part. "Maybe I wasn't good enough to be known as his daughter."

Albert took my hands. "That's impossible, Helen. You were wonderful to him. If anything, he's the one who didn't deserve to be your father."

The taxi circled Harlem Meer and emerged onto Frawley Circle. The cabbie knocked on the partition. "You want I should go around again?"

We were stopped for the moment at a red light. I turned to Albert. "Let's get out of town, go up to Eagle's Rest. It's as much yours as it is mine, I hope you know that."

586

He said it was a fine idea, but that there'd be lots of legal matters requiring my signature in the coming weeks. I simply couldn't stand the thought of sticking around Manhattan. "If I gave you my power of attorney, would you take care of it for me?"

"Of course I would, Helen, if that's what you want."

We had the taxi take us back to the lawyer's office. By the time all the necessary papers were signed, the short winter day had turned dark as night. I hadn't eaten since breakfast. Neither had Albert. Without having to discuss it, we went to our favorite restaurant. The maître d' had never asked us who we worked for or how we knew each other. As far as he was concerned, we were just that nice couple who'd been coming into his place every month or so for the past twenty years. He must have observed that neither of us wore a wedding band. I supposed he thought we were just friends. Either that, or we were having the longest affair in the history of the world.

It was too late by the time we finished dinner to catch a train to Eagle's Rest. Instead, I went home with Albert. I carried my suitcase into the room we both thought of as mine. He brought me a blanket and a pillow for the chaise lounge and we said our good nights. As I changed into the night-gown I'd packed, I studied myself in the mirror. There it was, written all over my face. The shape of Jake's chin. That same crease around the mouth. His jaw. No wonder I'd mistaken that photograph of Cornelia for my own. Was that why he'd made me an heiress, because I reminded him of his sister? But no, I realized — when it comes to inheritance, daughter trumps sister.

I stepped back, considered the length of my body. No one would mistake me for a young woman, but I'd aged well. Never having birthed a child had kept my hips from spreading and my breasts from sagging. I'd always been vigilant with a tweezer, and lately I'd been having my hair colored at the salon at Macy's — charged to Jake's account, of course. Even so, my body wasn't what it had been back when Harrison took me to bed. But that wouldn't matter to Albert.

I let myself into his room. His light was on, but his eyes were closed in sleep, a book tented on his chest. I moved it aside, switched off the light. He woke as I got under the blanket. I lifted his arm and settled my head against his shoulder. There was warmth where our skin touched but no heat. I pressed my ear to his chest and listened to the throbbing of his heart, its murmur a little hiccup between each beat.

In the dark, Albert's whisper was so quiet I could only think he hoped I wouldn't hear him. "I could try, if you want me to."

I nuzzled against him. "Don't worry, darling. This is all I need."

He relaxed and placed a careful kiss on the crown of my head. "Sweet dreams, Helen."

I wished him the same. I felt the weight of his arm increase as he fell back to sleep. A soft rasp in the back of his throat accompanied each breath, rhythmic as a lullaby. For the first time in all my life, I slept through the night in a man's arms.

My picture in the morning papers wasn't terrible, but still I hated to see my face staring at me from the front page. At least I wasn't recognized at the train station, the early-morning commuters too caught up in their own concerns to notice me standing on the platform, my suitcase hanging heavily from my hand. Albert promised to join me once all the legal matters were settled. He worried about me up at Eagle's Rest all by myself, but I reminded him I'd hardly be alone: besides the caretaker and his wife, there was the zookeeper and his family, not to mention all the animals. I'd have to hire a housekeeper, too. I never had learned to cook for myself, and the last time I'd done laundry I was just a girl.

It was strange being at the estate in winter. The caretaker hadn't been expecting visitors, and the furnace was stoked low. There was enough heat circulating through the radiators to keep the pipes from freezing, but it would be a few hours yet, he told me when he picked me up at the station, before the mansion felt warm. Even with my coat on, my joints ached as I wandered from room to room. The chandeliers, draped in sheets of linen, hovered like ghosts over the dusty furniture. I felt like an intruder. I had to keep reminding myself Eagle's Rest was mine, that my father had given it to me.

Father. My mind still went to an image of Daddy in his garage when I thought of the word. I forced myself to picture Jacob Ruppert in his place. But no, Jake could never replace him. I may have only had him for the first eleven years of my life, but Jerry Winthrope had stamped me as his daughter as clearly as if I'd been molded from his own flesh. He'd encouraged me, included me, valued me, praised me. Somewhere inside myself I still carried that little girl who believed she could fix everything, do anything, become whatever she wanted to be. Jake had supported me, sure, but as the years went on he'd weaned me from my career, narrowing the scope of my ambitions until he was the center of my life. He didn't need to trick me like that, I thought. If I'd known what he was, I would have gladly devoted myself to him. But he hadn't given me the choice. Instead of letting me be his daughter, he'd shortchanged us both by casting me in the role of employee.

The caretaker's wife brought me a hot lunch from her own kitchen. She lingered while I ate, pretending to keep me company but really satisfying her curiosity about Jake's funeral. "I read in the paper there were fifteen thousand people at the procession. Is that true, Miss Winthrope?" I told her there might have been even more. People lined Fifth Avenue from 93rd Street all the way down to St. Patrick's Cathedral, spilling into Rockefeller Center. "And his coffin carried by Mayor La Guardia and Senator Wagner, and our old governor Al Smith."

"Mr. Kramer was one of the pallbearers, too," I reminded her, but she wasn't impressed.

"It was no more than the Colonel deserved, I'm sure. I can take that if you're finished, miss." She picked up my plate and cleared her throat. "If you don't mind my asking, miss, do you know what's to become of the estate?"

"Didn't Mr. Kramer explain when he telephoned to say I was coming up?"

"Just that you'd be arriving and would be staying for a while."

Apparently the morning papers hadn't made their way to the caretakers' cottage yet. "Colonel Ruppert left it to me. Eagle's Rest is mine."

"Yours?" There was disdain in the gaze she swept over me. "Why would he do that, miss?"

I knew what she was thinking. I opened my mouth to tell her the truth, but the words never got past my lips. All his life Jake had kept me a secret, even when I was standing right next to him. Was that why his nieces acquiesced to his wishes and left me an uncontested heiress — to protect the Ruppert name from scandal? My God, I thought, had his family known all along? My uncle and aunt, my own cousins, all of them closing ranks and paying me off to maintain the mystery of my paternity. It was horrible to think of it this way, but unless I wanted to ruin Jake's reputation and antagonize his family, I'd have to get used to people assuming I'd been my father's mistress.

The mansion was warming up, steam clanging through the radiators. I went upstairs, entering Jake's room straight from the hallway instead of through the pocket door. In his dressing room I opened every drawer and closet. Three-piece suits in gabardine, shirts of Egyptian cotton, enough silk bow ties to stitch into a quilt. I ran my hands along the fabrics, dipped my fingers into dozens of pockets. I gathered a jacket in my arms and hugged it, imagining what it might have been like to have embraced the man who wore it, knowing he was my father. He'd denied me that chance, and for what? Scandal never touched the summers we spent at Eagle's Rest. In these rooms we had our own little world, our play within the play. If only there had been a fairy to dab Jake's eyes with magic juice so I could have heard him say he loved me once before he died.

I stepped back from the wardrobe. They were nothing to me now, these empty rags. What would I do with them all? I wondered. The answer came easily. There were thousands of men lining up at soup kitchens all over New York, their once fine clothes worn to tatters. I'd simply contact the local relief agency. By tomorrow, Jake's tailored wardrobe would be on the backs of a hundred hobos. I picked out a few things to save: a bowler hat he often wore, a coat I thought Rex might like, a set of gold cuff links I wanted Albert to have. In Jake's bathroom I smelled his soap — he'd never worn cologne — and lifted the lid on a jar of peppermints he kept on the windowsill. It wouldn't do to make a museum of his room, I decided. Once I'd cleared it out, I'd move in myself. Albert could have my old room, and between them we'd always keep the pocket door open.

When I heard the telephone ring, I knew before I picked up the receiver it would be my mother. I cut through her apologies. "Tell me, how did it happen, Mom?"

The line was silent for a long time before she began to speak. "Do you remember on your visit to Linwood, Helen, seeing the cove by the old mill? Such a beautiful place. I used to swim there on my mornings off. Jake did, too, it turned out. He was in the middle of the cove when I swam out to him." I imagined them circling each other in the water. Was there romance, I wondered, talk of love? Had the woman who was my mother and the man who was my father created me from their irresistible but forbidden passion? "You know how these things go, Helen. He needed comforting. I needed to be noticed. I was young, but I wasn't a virgin. We met there every morning for a month or so. He was so handsome back then. It's surprising, really, you weren't more of a beauty."

I hung up. She'd call again, I knew, that night or the next day, though I could already piece together most of the story she'd tell. When my mother realized she was pregnant, she was smart enough to know Jake would never marry a Protestant housemaid, not after the way his parents had disowned his sister for marrying a divorced Jew. She'd taken care of it by finding a man who would make her his wife, and count himself lucky for it. One thing I'd never fault her for was her choice. Jerry Winthrope was as kind and good a father as any girl could wish for. If he'd lived, my mother might never have told Jake I existed. But Daddy hadn't lived. I remembered, now, how she'd taken Jake aside after his funeral, how they'd turned to look at me. Jake always takes his responsibilities seriously — that's what she told me, and hadn't I seen the proof of it a thousand times over the years.

The winter light was beginning to fade. A

truck from the Bronx Zoo would be coming for the monkeys in the morning, so I put on my coat and went out to say good-bye to the rhesus female who'd been so fond of Pip. They never did breed, that pair. She extended her hairy arms, beckoning me closer. I let her hug me, our foreheads touching through the space between the bars. Unaccountably, I started to cry. What had been the point of capturing them from their jungle home? I wondered. Jake had caged them here for years so he could occasionally be amused by their antics, and now they were off to another set of cages. I supposed that's how he thought of me, too: a prized part of his collection. I hadn't known my value while he was alive, but he'd shown me with my inheritance what I was worth to him.

I went back past the barn. It was a lonely place now that the Saint Bernards were gone. Lonely, but big. Bigger than the Provincetown Playhouse had been. I couldn't help but imagine how easily a stage would fit at the far end, how many rows of seats the barn could accommodate. I let out a hoot to test the acoustics. Not bad, I thought, as my voice came bouncing back to me from the rafters. I hadn't taught drama at the settlement house for years now, the administrators having deciding it was more important to focus on nutrition and hygiene while this Depression dragged on. "You can't eat art" is how they put it to me when my classes were canceled. You may not be able to eat it, I thought, but still a person is starved without it.

Turning the barn into a theater was a fanciful notion, but the idea reminded me I needed to get a handle on the running of Eagle's Rest. I called Albert and asked him to send up the accounts for the estate so I could go over them.

"Are you really going to keep it, Helen?"

"Yes I am. I want us to live here, me and you."

"But what do we need with a fifteen-bedroom mansion?"

"We could start a school, or an orphanage, or turn it into a hotel. We can do whatever we want, Albert. There's no one and nothing to stop us anymore."

I ate another lackluster meal alone. The caretaker may have been happy enough to subsist on his wife's cooking, but I didn't want to. When my mother called, I had to stop myself from asking what she'd made for dinner that night. Again, she apologized. Again, she explained. "I would have told you, believe me, Helen, but there was so much at stake."

"But why was Jake's reputation more important than telling me the truth? You could have trusted me to keep quiet."

"Of course I trusted you. But he insisted. Everything was conditional on me never telling a soul."

"What everything? Do you mean the hospital bill he paid?"

"Not just that. What do you think we've been living on all these years?"

I thought we'd been living on Daddy's life insurance because that's what my mother had told me. But no, she said, there'd never been any life insurance. "Jake supported us, all three of us, even though Rex wasn't his responsibility. He set it up through his lawyer. Every month I got a check, and once a year he'd give me a call. Until he talked to you, Helen. That's when he took an interest."

It was exhausting, this constant rewriting of my life's story. "I'm hanging up now, Mom."

"Helen, wait. You'll have to forgive me eventually, you know. The checks are bound to stop now, and it's only a matter of time before I'm evicted."

"Evicted? Don't be so dramatic."

"Do I have to spell everything out for you,

Helen? Ruppert Realty owns this building. We've never paid rent since the day we moved in."

The relief agency was thrilled, the next day, to accept my donation of Jake's clothing. While I sorted through it all, I sent the caretaker to the station to pick up Mr. Nakamura. He'd asked Albert if he might come up to get some personal things and offered to bring the accounts for Eagle's Rest. The Bankers Box he set on the table in Jake's bedroom would keep me busy for a week. It would be a welcome distraction, having this problem to keep me occupied.

"There was also some correspondence." Mr. Nakamura handed me an envelope addressed to Albert, care of Colonel Ruppert. It had been delivered to Jake's apartment, he said.

I saw that the stamp had been canceled in Bradenton, Florida. "Why not give it to Albert, why bring it to me?"

"I noticed the name of the sender. It was my impression that this was a person of particular interest to Colonel Ruppert and yourself."

I turned the envelope over, read the name written on the flap. What could Mr. Nakamura possibly know about King Arthur? I put the letter in my pocket, unopened. "You knew Jake very well, didn't you?"

He bowed his head. "You'd be surprised what a man reveals about himself when he forgets the servant in his room is a person, too."

It was getting late. Already the sun had set, the moon a black dot casting no light on the dark river. "The caretaker's wife made a mushroom soup. After you pack up your things, would you have supper with me?"

"Thank you, Miss Winthrope." Mr. Nakamura was grateful enough for the invitation, but when we sat down to eat I saw his nose wrinkle as he brought the soup to his mouth.

"Tell me how you came to work for Jake."

He seemed glad for an excuse to put down his spoon. Removing his spectacles, he polished the lenses as he spoke. He'd come from Japan to attend an American university, he told me. His father was in business and wanted his son to have an international education. "But Oregon only tolerated Japanese as migrant laborers. It was no place for a respectable *hi-imin* like me. After one year of college, I came to New York to work and save money. I got a job at a Rolling Ball booth at Coney Island." I knew the kind of place he meant. It was a simple game, but for some reason the workers were all Japanese, their foreignness adding an exotic flavor to the simple fun of knocking down pins to win a prize.

"It was a terrible job, late hours and so hot all summer. The others spent every dollar they earned, as if they were men of leisure in the pleasure district of Tokyo. I saved, but when the time came to return to school I found I'd lost my ambition. Instead I found work in a tailor's shop. He had a little room where I could sleep, so my expenses were few. I learned to sew — women's work, my father would have said. I was ashamed of my failure at college and gave up on the idea of returning home. When Colonel Ruppert came in to have his suits fitted, he noticed me. He'd had a Japanese valet at the hotel where he lived in Washington while he served in Congress. He thought it would be fashionable to have one for his own household, so I moved into the Ruppert mansion. I started as his valet in 1909, then became his butler. He was a good employer, and I became complacent."

Mr. Nakamura kept his face clean-shaven and his hair was still black; how could he be old enough to have worked for Jake for thirty years? I was ashamed to realize that, in all the time I'd known him, I'd never so much as wondered where he'd been born. Osaka, he told me when I asked.

"What will you do now?" In addition to Jake's five-thousand-dollar bequest, it sounded like he had quite a nest egg built up somewhere.

"I might return to Japan for a visit. I have a bride there I've never seen."

I didn't know what was more surprising — that he was married, or that he'd never seen his wife.

"She was a picture bride," he explained. "I made my selection and sent a dowry and money for her travel, but before she could embark, the new immigration law was passed, and she was no longer welcome in America. She waited, hoping the situation would change, until it was too late for her to marry anyone else. I've supported her, modestly, of course, but she has lived with dignity. She brought my mother great comfort in her later years." He stood and cleared our plates. "I'll bring these down to the kitchen. Thank you for inviting me to supper, Miss Winthrope. I have to go now, if I'm to catch the last train."

I'd allowed his story to distract me from King's letter. I took it out of my pocket, pushed it across the table, pulled it back toward me again. It wasn't addressed to me. I had no business opening it. But Mr. Nakamura had seen King's name and known it should be placed in my hands, not Albert's.

It had been years since I thought about how I'd conspired with Jake to get King traded out to that team in San Francisco. I'd felt cruel at the time, but Albert couldn't have minded so very much. I didn't remember him ever mentioning King in all these years. I picked up the letter and sliced it open.

Dear Albert,

First of all let me say I'm sorry about not writing more. I'm not exactly a man of letters as you know. But I just saw in the paper about the Colonel dying and figured you must have taken it hard. I always admired how loyal you were to the man. But now that he's gone I wonder if you might be planning to travel and see something of the world for yourself? I got released from the Seals a while back. I'm coaching in the Grapefruit League now. Florida is nice this time of year. What would you think about coming down to Bradenton?

I know we've spent less than a week

together if you add it all up, but it also feels as if I've known you my whole life. Do you know what I mean? Maybe you do. I hope so. Maybe you feel that way, too. So now you know where to find me if you ever wanted to. Find me, I mean.

Yours, King

Chapter 44

I'd concluded Helen's business by St. Valentine's Day, but then George Ruppert asked me to help him settle the Colonel's personal accounts as well. St. Patrick's Day was around the corner by the time I walked through his empty apartment for the last time. Mr. Nakamura, who'd overseen the packing of the Colonel's possessions, was also leaving. He handed over the keys to the real estate agent who'd be representing the sale and picked up the two suitcases that held the entirety of his possessions. As we took the elevator down together, I asked him about his planned trip to Japan.

"That was my intention in January, Mr. Kramer, but things have changed since then."

"But Helen said you had a wife to go home to."

"A bride, not a wife. But Japan hasn't been my home in so long, I'm afraid I'd be a stranger there. Even so, it's my American wife who's causing the problem."

"You have another wife?" I'd spent decades in Mr. Nakamura's company without ever suspecting him of such a complicated personal life.

"Not legally. The judge we stood in front of wouldn't marry a white woman to a Japanese man. We should have tried again, but somehow we never did. I thought she'd be willing to let me go for a visit, but she worried I might never come home. We're leaving the city, though. Colonel Ruppert left me enough to purchase a small house in Maryland, near our son."

"Your son?"

His face flashed with pride. "He completed the education I never finished. He works in Washington as a translator for the Japanese embassy."

He only had Sundays free; how had Mr. Nakamura managed to live an entire secret life in just twenty-four hours a week? For years I'd believed we were three celibate bachelors, the Colonel and his butler and his secretary. Now it seemed every man but me had a wife or children, or both. I asked if the Colonel knew about his family. He shook his head. "Colonel Ruppert preferred to imagine I only existed during the hours I was in his presence."

Out on the curb, I helped him load his suitcases into a waiting taxi. "Good luck to you, Albert." He'd never before called me by my Christian name.

"Same to you, Osamu," I said, realizing I had no idea of his religion.

I couldn't leave the city without saying good-bye to Jack. Across Manhattan, police now patrolled the docks and infiltrated the movie houses, luring men like us into arrest and ruin. But Jack was safe in the little eyrie he'd created for himself, the four walls of his studio apartment papered in chinoiserie and objets d'art perched on every window-sill. A pair of pretty parakeets chirped in a silver cage as he poured us jasmine tea. When I'd asked for a drink, Jack told me he'd given up alcohol completely on the advice of his doctor. Though he hid it well, I wondered if there wasn't a touch of jaundice beneath his makeup.

"The Colonel lied to me, Jack. At least, he let me believe a lie. I thought we had an understanding, the two of us. I thought we were alike. Now I don't know what to believe."

Jack lit a cigarette and placed it in an ivory holder. "It seems to me you've got nothing to complain about, Albert. He knew you

607

were a pansy and kept you on all these years regardless. And he did leave you a tidy sum. Nothing compared to Helen, though."

"The reporters all assume she was his mistress, no matter how much she denies it." I shifted a pillow, trying to get comfortable on his Victorian divan. "Anyway, the family didn't want any of it coming out in probate court. They still haven't forgotten the scandal of Cornelia's elopement."

"But that was last century." Jack crossed his ankles, Turkish slippers peeking out from the velvet folds of his dressing gown.

"It's all about appearances with them. The Astors can get away with anything, they're old money, Protestants, real Americans. For all their wealth, the Rupperts were strivers, foreigners, Catholic beer brewers for God's sake. They never felt American enough to live down a scandal."

"But it's a new world nowadays, Albert. No one cares about that kind of thing anymore. When you thought he was queer, well, that was a secret worth keeping. But a baby with a housemaid? That's a story as old as Abraham."

I let our visit linger as we caught each other up on our mutual friends. Toni and Edith had sold Antonio's to some mobsters and moved out to Provincetown, Massachusetts. Paul's benefactor had signed over the deed on Waverly Place before he and his wife decamped for France, where they lived modestly on the small income they had left after the Crash. We both agreed it had been good of the man to set Paul up like that, but even though he had the deed free and clear, a dancer couldn't afford property taxes on a Manhattan town house any more than he could afford rent. Needing to find a way to make the house pay for itself, Paul had partnered with Geneviève to open the Greenwich Village Academy of Dance. Their marriage, though, had been a shock.

"I'll tell you, Albert, of all our friends, Paul's the last one I'd have picked to marry a woman. It was sweet of them to invite Jacqueline to sing at the wedding."

I finished my tea. "Do you miss being her?"

"I can't say that I do, really. She had a good run. She paid for all this." He waved the cigarette holder around the room, as lovely as the inside of a jewel box.

When Paul proposed to Geneviève it was just business, but that business now bound them together more closely than most married couples. They slept in separate bedrooms, of course, and they each had romantic affairs with other men (even, occasionally, the same man), but the town house was their home, the Academy of Dance the fruit of their partnership. It made me think of Helen. She'd already given me her power of attorney and invited me to live with her. It was a small step from there to the legal bonds of matrimony. Maybe that was why, when I called my mother to tell her I was canceling my telephone number, I asked her to send me my grandmother's wedding ring, a gold band set with diamonds and rubies. I had it in my pocket when I finally closed my apartment and headed up to Eagle's Rest.

Helen met me at the station in the caretaker's old truck. She was wearing flannel trousers with boots and one of my old sweaters, which hung boyishly on her frame. I teased her that she looked more like a farmer than an heiress. The caretaker had been teaching her about gardening, she said, and she'd been learning to cook. "My mother calls and talks me through the recipes. I guess I'll have to move her up here eventually, if you don't mind, Albert. She hasn't been evicted yet, but Clarence thinks it's only a matter of time until someone at Ruppert Realty notices there's no income from our apartment."

Turning through the gates of the estate, we passed between the two enormous eagles perched on either side of the drive, their metal wings outspread. I remembered going out to that junkyard in New Jersey with Helen to purchase the statues, salvaged from the old Grand Central Terminal. The Colonel had them hauled up here on a barge, four thousand pounds of cast iron apiece. They were more intimidating than welcoming, but I couldn't imagine it would ever be worth the effort to have them carted away.

We pulled up to the mansion, the lawn dotted with crocuses, the river winking and sparkling in the sun. Helen switched off the engine. "Welcome home, Albert."

The next day we drove into Carmel to file the papers that would give Helen title to Eagle's Rest. The registrar of deeds was out to lunch when we arrived, so we wandered the oak-paneled hallways of the courthouse to pass the time until he returned. "You two must be looking for a marriage license," a helpful clerk said. "Follow me." Before we could explain, the clerk had ushered us into a room and handed us a form. "Did you bring your birth certificates?"

"Darling, you have them in your handbag, don't you?" I looked at Helen, my expression as serious as I could manage.

"But, dearest, I thought I saw you put them in your pocket."

"Did you?" I patted my jacket. "Oh, but I changed jackets when you said it might rain. I'm so sorry, we'll have to come back another day."

"I'll bet you're a professor from the college, aren't you?" the clerk said. "They're so absentminded. Come back soon, there's a three-day wait after I issue the license before you can marry. If you get your blood tests today, you'll have the results by then."

If that was all it took, I thought, why shouldn't Helen and I get married? There was no one else in my life, and it would be a shame for her to end up a spinster. We'd have a partnership, like Paul and Geneviève. Together at Eagle's Rest we could carry on as before, living in the Colonel's mansion and spending his money, but instead of serving him we'd dote on each other. We could even adopt a child, once Helen was Mrs. Kramer.

We found the registrar returned from lunch and concluded our business. As Helen drove us back to the estate, I said, "Why don't we?"

"Why don't we what?"

"Get married."

She stared at me so intently she swerved into a ditch, stalling the engine. "Do you mean that, Albert?"

I took her hand, suddenly emotional. "I can never be everything you'd want in a husband, but you know I love you, don't you, Helen?"

She put her hand on my cheek. "I love you, too, Albert. I can't imagine my life without you."

My heart ballooned in my chest. "Is that a yes?"

She nodded and we hugged each other. A passing truck blared its horn at us, half on and half off the road.

That night over dinner (Helen had attempted pork chops) I patted my pocket nervously, wondering when would be the right moment to present her with the ring, which I figured could do double duty as both engagement and wedding band. I'd been thinking about the ceremony. We wouldn't want anything fancy, not at our age or in our circumstances. I was sure a justice of the peace here at the estate would suffice. I supposed Helen would want her brother there, but Rex was a baseball scout in Cuba now and I didn't want to wait for him to book passage from Havana. My own mother had told me, when we'd spoken on the telephone, that she didn't want to travel, saying she'd prefer me to visit later with my bride. Just Helen's mother, then, though that seemed a small party. Perhaps we could invite Mr. Nakamura and his American wife. It crossed my mind to ask Jacqueline to sing, but I nixed the idea. Marrying Helen meant leaving that life behind forever.

I fingered the ring in my pocket. "Helen, darling, let's talk about the wedding." My voice echoed off the tiled walls of the basement kitchen.

"Let's not, Albert, not yet. I've decided I want to go to St. Petersburg while the Yankees are still at spring training. Now that I'm an owner of the team, I think Jake would have wanted me to at least see them play."

"But they'll be leaving soon to start barnstorming up the coast. Why not wait and see them in the Bronx?"

"I'll be hounded by reporters if I show my face at Yankee Stadium, you know that." She put a gnawed bone on her plate. "I went ahead and booked us a sleeping compartment on the Silver Meteor tomorrow. We'll have to get up early. It leaves from Pennsylvania Station at ten thirty in the morning, but that'll get us to St. Petersburg by the following afternoon."

I bit into a piece of gristle. Between our two inheritances, we could travel anywhere in the world — Casablanca, Alexandria, Constantinople. "Wouldn't you rather take a honeymoon after the wedding?"

She got up to clear the table. "No, Albert, I've given this a lot of thought. We have to go to Florida before we get married."

Up in New York it was barely spring; in St. Petersburg, palm trees swayed in the breeze against a fiercely blue sky. The sun was so bright Helen had to squint to see the road. We'd hired a car and were driving to the Don CeSar, an elaborate castle of a hotel where the Yankees used to have a contract. Helen hadn't made a reservation, but this deep into the Depression most of their rooms were empty. Perhaps that's why the hotel clerk, when we admitted to not being married, insisted we take separate suites. It didn't really matter. Helen was just next door, and anyway, ever since the idea of marriage had been introduced she'd gotten superstitious about sleeping in my bed. Once we were husband and wife, I supposed we'd keep each other warm every night for the rest of our lives. But we hadn't set a date yet, and my grandmother's ring remained at the ready in my pocket.

The Yankees were playing the Brooklyn Dodgers the next afternoon. Helen wore a white cotton dress, I was in a linen suit, and we'd both purchased sunglasses and straw hats. The humid air teased Helen's hair into unruly curls, but I told her she looked lovely and it was true. I liked being at a ballpark again, the thwack of ball meeting bat, the soft pop of a catcher's mitt. Unlike the New York fans, the crowd here was relaxed, cheering and groaning in lighthearted unison. The Yanks lost, Gehrig's hit the only highlight of a lackluster game. Afterward, as he lingered on the field to sign autographs, he looked up and recognized us in the stands. He jogged over, a little slower than he once was, the hair at his temples showing some gray in the unforgiving Florida sun. We talked for a while, the three of us. Gehrig said he wouldn't have held out so long last year if he'd realized it would be the Colonel's last.

"You men don't mind playing for a woman, do you?" Helen asked.

"It's our pleasure to play for you, Miss Winthrope, you and the Colonel's nieces. He did you a great honor, leaving you the team and all."

"Poor Lou, he looks terrible, don't you

think?" Helen said on our way back to the car.

"I guess the old Iron Horse isn't as young as he used to be."

We turned the trip into a vacation, relaxing on lounge chairs and swimming in the Gulf of Mexico, the salt water delicious on our sun-starved limbs. On the beach, we listened to the waves and rubbed suntan oil on each other's skin. I read poetry in German while she paged through magazines, a waiter from the hotel appearing with a fresh mai tai as soon as the ice in our glasses began to melt.

The visit to Florida was slated to last a week. The afternoon of our last day, Helen said she wanted to take the ferry across Tampa Bay and explore Longboat Key, so we drove the hired car onto the Bee Line. For the next hour, we walked the deck under a hot sun, the spray cooling our faces as we searched the water for manatees. When she took the wheel and eased the car off the ferry, I didn't think she had any particular destination in mind. I was surprised when we ended up at McKechnie Field for an exhibition game between the local Grapefruit League team and the Tigers. "You didn't get enough baseball from the Yankees?" I asked.

"You don't mind, do you, Albert? Being at the ballpark helps me think about Jake. We'll have dinner at the oyster bar out on Anna Maria Pier after the game, okay?"

I agreed, thinking that would be a perfect moment to present her with the ring. I imagined asking a waiter to hide it in an oyster, pictured her surprise at finding the gold band in the shell. Her eyes would fill with tears as I dropped to my knee and asked for her hand. Because why shouldn't I do it up right? I knew how much she'd be sacrificing, marrying me. She deserved whatever I could give her.

We found seats in the stands. Helen fanned her flushed face with the programs. I asked if she wanted me to get her a lemonade.

"No, I'm fine, Albert. Look, here come the players."

They jogged out onto the field, their names blaring through a loudspeaker. I paid no attention until the coaches were announced. I must have heard wrong, though. It was too much of a coincidence for it to be true. I squinted but couldn't see him. I dragged my gaze away from the field and settled it on Helen. "The announcer didn't say King Arthur, did he?"

"I think so," she said, her expression

inscrutable behind those sunglasses.

"But that can't be. He was out in California last I heard." I craned my neck, but I was unable to see into the shaded dugout.

"I don't remember you mentioning him in all these years."

"We used to keep in touch, when he first went out to California, but he's a terrible correspondent. You remember how he was during the war, don't you? Neither one of us got so much as a postcard."

Helen adjusted the brim of her hat to keep the sun off her face. "Not a man of letters, you might say."

What a peculiar turn of phrase. It reminded me of something King once said. What if it really was him? My pulse began to race until I reminded myself that in a few days I'd be a married man.

Marriage. The institution suddenly seemed as flimsy a fantasy as a Hollywood set. What had I been thinking, to propose to Helen like that? Of course she'd expect more from me than I was able to give. Never mind about the sex. There was a corner of my heart — I felt it stirring at the mere notion that King and I were in the same ballpark — that would never let her in. She said it was enough for her, what I was able to give. But it shouldn't be enough, not for either of us.

There was a dispute on the mound after an inside pitch grazed the batter. The Bradenton coach emerged from the dugout to argue with the umpire. He threw his cap dramatically to the dirt and there he was, King Arthur, his hair just as blond, his eyes — we were sitting right behind first base — just as blue as I remembered them.

Helen stood up suddenly. Her white dress must have caught King's attention because he looked in our direction. He saw me and smiled, unsurprised, as if he'd been expecting me to turn up. King pointed at me, a fleeting gesture, but I could read his message as clear as if it were posted to the scoreboard. *Stay there. I'll find you.*

My heart stopped and started up again. It was twenty years ago and we were back at the Polo Grounds. I was writing down my address on the back of the Colonel's business card. If I'd known King would be waiting on my stoop, I'd have skipped dinner for the extra hour it would have given us together.

Helen's hand touched my shoulder. Looking up, I hardly recognized the happy face I saw reflected in her glasses.

CHAPTER 45

There it was, the look in Albert's eyes I'd waited all these years to see, and it wasn't for me. How stupid I was to have brought him here. I'd wanted to see for myself he was over his infatuation with King before I let him marry me. Now I wished we'd never come. I locked myself in a smelly stall in the ladies' room and covered my face with a handkerchief. We could have been happy, Albert and I. We had everything we could ever want: money, the estate, each other. Except I never really had him. I'd convinced myself it didn't matter to me, what we couldn't share. What I hadn't credited was how much it might matter to him.

King came over to us during the seventh inning stretch, shook my hand before taking Albert's. He said how glad he was to see us both, asked if we'd wait for him after the game. Those last two innings were the longest of my life. Albert couldn't stop talking about what a coincidence it was, us running into King here, in Florida, when he thought he'd been in California this whole time. Finally, he calculated the impossible odds of it all. "This wasn't an accident, was it, Helen?"

I figured he'd hate me, but I was fed up with falsehoods. "There was a letter. Mr. Nakamura delivered it to me by accident. I should have given it to you. I'm sorry, Albert."

"No, don't be sorry, Helen." He held my hand as he looked out over the green field. "I'm grateful. I might not have had the courage to come, if you'd left it up to me."

Would the universe never get tired of playing tricks on me? I wished I could go back in time and tell Mr. Nakamura to get that letter where it was meant to go. Albert might never have mentioned it. We'd be married by now, at home at Eagle's Rest, sitting down to a supper my mother had cooked. But if I started down that road, where would it end? Would I go back to the day I saw them together on the lawn, when I asked Jake to trade King away? Or to the time I warned Jake against signing King to the Yankees? Or to that afternoon at the Polo Grounds, when King asked for Albert's address? But if I did have the power to spin the world backward on its axis, wouldn't I use it to go back to the moment when Colonel Jacob Ruppert spotted that motorcycle in Daddy's garage?

There'd be no end to my regrets if all my thoughts were of the past. The only moments in my life over which I had any control were the ones in front of me now, today.

King rejoined us, face washed and hair combed, wearing khaki pants and a polo shirt open at the neck. We small-talked awkwardly until I swallowed hard and invited him to join us for dinner. I handed King the car keys, saying the sun had gotten to my head and would he drive, he must know the way better than I did? From the back I watched as he stretched his arm across the seat, his fingertips brushing Albert's shoulder.

We crossed the Cortez Bridge and went up Gulf Drive, passing a line of little resort hotels along the beach. Half of them were out of business, pathetic FOR SALE signs tacked to their boarded-up doors. Albert turned around to talk to me. "I bet those places are going for a song. What do you think, Helen, of investing in Florida real estate?"

"You can't be serious." Jake had lost

thousands when the Florida land boom went bust. But Albert had his own money, and the Depression couldn't last forever. I imagined tourists would flock back to the Gulf Coast one of these days. Albert asked to pull over so he could jot down some information. We'd only traveled a few miles with King in the car and already our visions of the future had diverged.

We parked on Bay Boulevard and walked out onto the pier, pelicans perched on every piling. I was in a daze all through that dinner of shucked oysters and cold beer, the three of us huddled around a table overlooking the water. Albert made a point of including me in the conversation. Occasionally he placed a hand on my knee below the table. But these were conscious gestures. Between the two men was an unforced flow of words.

"Here, try it with hot sauce." King shook a red dash from a tiny bottle onto an oyster and brought the shell to Albert's lips. Albert stretched out his neck as King tipped the slippery meat into his mouth. A line of seawater ran down Albert's chin. King dragged his fingers across Albert's face to wipe it away.

It was like losing my father all over again, how alone I felt. I excused myself and went out to watch the sunset. There was a commotion happening on the pier. A fisherman had hooked something special. A hammerhead shark, about a yard long, thrashed its prehistoric head, the fisherman's hook piercing its lower lip. I watched it swim in circles around one of the pilings, tangling the line and frustrating the fisherman. It turned on its side and its strange eye stared up at me. All it wanted was to be free. If I'd had a knife, I would have gotten on my belly and reached over the side of the pier to cut that string, but the shark didn't need my interference. With a brave jerk of its head it tore out the hook and swam away. I knelt on the wood planks to catch my breath.

"There you are, Helen." Dinner over, they'd come to find me. King drove us to the ferry landing and handed me the keys, asked when we were heading back to New York. Albert looked at me. "Not for a few more days yet, isn't that right, Helen?" He knew very well we had tickets for tomorrow afternoon.

The ferry arrived. Cars were starting their engines. "Listen, Albert, why don't you stay? It's early yet. Keep the car. I'm exhausted, all I want to do is crawl into bed. I'll get a taxi when we dock and go back to the hotel." The car behind us in line honked. I waved them around, gave Albert the keys.

"You better move the car."

"Go ahead, Albert," King said. "I'll see her on board."

King brought me to the gangplank then pulled me close. "Albert told me you did this." I felt faint as I readied myself for his accusations: how I'd sent him away, sabotaged his career, denied them their chance. "You read my letter and brought him to me, even though you knew this might happen." King hugged me then, that broad chest of his pressed against my breasts. "You must love him more than I imagined, to give him up like this."

Had I given him up? Was it all decided? It was ridiculous of me to be surprised. I'd seen them kiss all those years ago. I knew what there was between them. Whether it would make them happy I had no idea. Dr. Havelock Ellis painted a bleak picture of life for men like Albert and King, but what the hell did he know? I'd seen the look in Albert's eyes when he spotted King on that ballfield. It wasn't perverse, or indecent, or abnormal. The only word for it was love.

The cars had all been loaded. The ferry blew its whistle. I stepped back and stumbled. King grabbed my arm, saving me from falling in the water. Over his shoulder I saw Albert. He'd parked the car down the road and was walking back. They stood there together in the circle of light at the end of the dock as the ferry pulled me back across the bay.

I wasn't sure I'd ever see him again, but Albert returned to the Don CeSar the next afternoon in time to drive me to the train station in Sarasota. I'd spent a sleepless night thinking of all the things I wanted to say, but sitting beside him in the car none of the words seemed to matter anymore. He offered to wait with me on the platform but I didn't think I could stand it. I told him to go ahead, resenting how easily he agreed. I made him promise to write and to call and to visit. He made me promise the same. "You'll be our first guest when we open our hotel, Helen."

When had it become "our" hotel, I wondered. I didn't know if King planned to give up baseball to become a hotelier, or if it was simply that everything was already "we" with them.

We kissed good-bye, his closed lips pressed briefly to mine. "Here, Helen, I have something for you." He reached into his pocket and drew out a gold band set with diamonds and rubies. "It was my grandmother's," he said, sliding it onto my finger. "There's no one else it could ever belong to, I hope you know that, darling." He meant to be kind, but the ring was a tragic reminder of all I'd never have. I watched him drive away, the rooms in my heart that had been furnished for him empty and forlorn.

I was temporarily blinded under the arched portico as I moved from full sun to deep shade. I was waiting for my eyes to adjust when a small figure ran toward me from out of the gloom, a little boy whose mother had just noticed he was no longer at her side. Afraid he'd dash out into the street, I grabbed him and lifted him off the ground, his feet churning in the air. His laughing face came into focus. It was astounding, how much he looked like James: same softly curled hair, same golden skin, same green eyes.

"Thank you so much, ma'am. I told you to stay right by me, Horace." His mother was neatly dressed in a linen suit, her flat-brimmed hat trimmed in blue ribbon to match her blue handbag. Her complexion was more richly brown than her son's, but up close the resemblance was unmistakable. She seemed eager to get back to her suitcase and basket, abandoned some yards back under the portico.

The boy was heavy in my arms but he had

calmed down, distracted by the dragonfly brooch I always wore. He tried to pluck it from my lapel and his mother swatted his little hand. "Oh, he's all right," I said. "He reminds me of —" What word could I use to convey to this woman the place Jimmy held in my heart? To say he reminded me of my custodian's child wouldn't come close to the truth. I thought of what Clarence had said, that I couldn't have loved him more if he were my own. "He reminds me of my son, when he was this age."

"Your son, ma'am?" Her eyebrows pulled together as she looked me up and down. My tanned skin was nearly as dark as Bernice's had been. I wondered if this woman would make the assumption that I belonged on her side of the color line? She flashed me a quick smile as her eyebrows settled back into their natural shape. "I'm Mrs. Glenn," she said, holding out her hand.

Shifting Horace's weight to my hip, I managed to extend my left arm, the gold ring a surprise on my hand. I'd have to introduce myself as Mrs., but I hesitated to use my own name, fearing she may have read about me in the papers. Glancing down at the monogram on my suitcase I blurted out the first name that matched. "I'm Mrs. Weldon. Pleased to meet you, Mrs. Glenn. But you,

Horace" — I tickled him and made him laugh — "you call me Aunt Helen, you hear?"

He suddenly became shy. "Yes, Aunt Helen."

I set Horace on his feet as we crossed the portico. Mrs. Glenn picked up her case in one hand and her basket in the other. I kept hold of Horace's hand as we moved into the station. They were going to Maryland, Mrs. Glenn told me. "How far are you traveling, Mrs. Weldon?"

I'd been dreading the isolation of my empty compartment, the ordeal of being seated alone in the dining car. They wouldn't be good for me, those solitary hours. "To New York, but perhaps we can travel together as far as Washington?"

Mrs. Glenn gave me another long look. "You'd be more comfortable on your own, I'm sure, but if you'd rather have our company it's fine by me."

"Next." The ticket agent called Mrs. Glenn forward. I glanced up and realized we were at the COLORED window. I'd been about to offer them the empty place in my compartment. I'd forgotten that, down south, Horace and his mother wouldn't be allowed aboard the first class sleeping car.

"You two traveling together?" Apparently,

standing in the wrong line was all it took for the white agent to see me as black. My ticket was in my pocketbook. If I bought a new one here, I'd be giving up a comfortable bed, drinks in the lounge, restaurant service — but at least I wouldn't be alone. "Yes we are," I said.

We boarded the car immediately behind the diesel engine, picking our way past luggage racks to sit beside one another on a hard bench. I felt like an imposter as the other passengers all gave me a second glance. None gave me a third, though, and I began to relax. For the first hour or so, Horace was content to kneel on the bench and stare out the window, but as the views became familiar he took a pad of paper and a box of crayons from his mother's basket and settled himself cross-legged on the floor, contentedly drawing colorful scenes. When he said he was hungry, my stomach growled in sympathy. There was only one table on this side of the kitchen to serve the entire colored compartment, and it was booked solid. I hadn't thought to purchase anything on the platform when we'd stopped in Gainesville, and it would be another two hours before we arrived at the next station.

"I brought along plenty, Mrs. Weldon,

we'll be happy to share, won't we, Horace?"
I agreed, but only after she promised to let
me treat the two of them to a late supper
during our layover in Jacksonville.

Once his stomach was full, Horace fell
asleep, stretched across our two laps. Mrs.
Glenn twirled locks of his hair with her
fingers. Whispering, she said, "Horace's
daddy is bright like you. Didn't his parents
throw a fit when he brought me home! After
two generations of careful marriages, they
were counting on passing their grand-
children off for white. No chance of that
with me for a daughter-in-law."

"Mrs. Glenn, I hope you won't be offended, but I have to be honest, I'm not
black. I just didn't want to travel by myself."

She gave me a sharp look. "Well, it hardly
matters what you started out as, Mrs. Weldon. If you're married to a black man, the
white world won't want anything to do with
you, am I right? Why don't you tell me how
you met this husband of yours."

Since I'd claimed Jimmy as my son and
stolen Clarence's name, it seemed easiest to
use a true story from my childhood. Telling
it was like traveling back in time. Our last
names both starting with the same letter
meant that Clarence and I were always
seated near each other in school. In sixth

grade, he was in front of me and a Polish boy named Wronski was seated behind me. "On the very first day of school," I told Mrs. Glenn, "that horrid Wronski boy took one of my braids and dipped it in his inkwell. When I bent over my desk, my braid rolled right around my shoulder and ruined my new school blouse. I was too afraid of the teacher to raise my hand so I just sat there, crying. Well, Clarence saw what happened. He didn't say anything to me, but when we were walking home he pulled that Wronski boy into an alley and gave him a punch to the gut. No one ever bothered me again, I can tell you."

Mrs. Glenn smiled, satisfied with my fairy tale. "And you've been in love ever since. You two were lucky to be living up north. Even so, I can't imagine it's been an easy life."

It wouldn't have been an easy life, she was right about that, but for the first time I realized it wasn't inconceivable. There were no laws against it, not in New York anyway. I'd always assumed my mother's horror at catching me and Clarence kissing had been because of his race, but it occurred to me now it was my parentage she was thinking of, not his. Even then she must have hoped Jake would one day recognize me as his daughter. No wonder she'd sacrificed her life savings to bribe that surgeon. She'd calculated Jake would never be so generous to a girl who'd had an abortion — let alone a girl in love with a Negro. She must have been thinking of my inheritance more than the color of Clarence's skin when she forced that bar of soap between my teeth. Sweat chilled my palms as I realized how the course of my entire life had been scripted to prepare me for the role of heiress.

My hands were shaking as I picked up one of the magazines the porters had given out. It was the most recent issue of *The Crisis*. Idly flipping through the pages, I looked for an article to occupy my thoughts. I started reading about the new Harlem Community Art Center. It sounded like a wonderful place, an interracial effort to bring all kinds of arts to the neighborhood. I should have volunteered to teach there instead of the settlement house. It was too late now. When I'd called from Florida to say I was returning without Albert, my mother told me the eviction notice she'd predicted had finally arrived. I was only stopping in Manhattan long enough to help her pack. She'd be moving up to Eagle's Rest with me. We'd make a sad pair: a scheming widow and a bitter spinster in a dead bachelor's mansion. Now there's a Dickens novel, I thought.

But maybe I could write a different story. I'd told Albert we could do whatever we wanted with Eagle's Rest. Why not start an art school of my own? The barn was big enough for a theater, and the parlor could be a classroom. The view of the Hudson would make a fine landscape for painting. Goodness knows there were enough bedrooms. If the children bunked together in groups of four or five, I could enroll fifty students and still have rooms for staff. I shifted Horace off my lap so I could take some paper and a pencil from my pocketbook. I'd need supplies — I started a list that quickly grew to be two pages long — and teachers, too, for academic subjects as well as the expressive ones. I'd need someone to supervise the cooking and cleaning and ordering. My mother, I thought, would be perfect for the job. It occurred to me I'd never wondered before what career she might have pursued if she'd been given a choice and a chance.

But where would I get the students? I picked up *The Crisis* again, leafing through the back pages. There were advertisements for all kinds of courses and degrees — sewing, teaching, agriculture, bookkeeping, secretarial — but there wasn't one for a school of the arts. I looked at Horace's drawings. They were wonderful. Perhaps he'd be my first student.

When we disembarked in Washington, I asked Mrs. Glenn for her address so we could correspond. Horace presented me with one of his drawings and I said I'd treasure it. There was a layover at Union Station while the train reconfigured, the colored car uncoupled and sent back south, the remaining black passengers integrated according to their class. I got back on board using my original ticket. It was strange, but I felt more like an imposter being fussed over by the porter in my private compartment than I had riding in that segregated baggage car. I spent the three hours to New York writing Albert a long letter detailing my plans for turning Eagle's Rest into an art school, determined to show him he wasn't the only one with a vision of the future.

James was in the lobby when I walked into my apartment building. I'd so recently been remembering him as a little boy it disoriented me to see how close he was to becoming a man. He surprised me by throwing his arms around me. "Dad told me you're going to pay for my college. I don't know how to thank you, Aunt Helen."

"Just do your best and make us proud, that's all I ask."

"I hope I can make him proud. He's already gotten the books for some of my courses from the library so he can study along with me, in case I need his help."

I'd been seeing Clarence with a mop in his hands for so many years, I'd almost forgotten he held a teaching degree. "I bet you won't have a single professor who's smarter than your father, Jimmy."

"That's the truth. It's too bad he ended up wasting his life as a custodian."

But it wasn't a waste, I told him, and anyway, his father was only forty-two years old, the same as me. His life wasn't over yet. Neither was mine, I thought, as Clarence came walking toward us. There was a dusting of gray in his hair now, a certain sag of skin beneath his chin, but he still moved with the posture and purpose of a soldier. It had never been possible, before, for me to imagine a world in which he and I might be together. But I was an heiress now. Three hundred thousand dollars, an estate on the Hudson, a third of the Yankees: it straightens a woman's spine, having all that to call her own.

"Has Jimmy told you he's set his sights on

Howard University instead of City College? I'm not sure that's what you had in mind, Helen, him going away to school."

"You go anyplace you like, Jimmy, and don't worry about the cost. We'll call it the Colonel Ruppert Scholarship, how about that?"

He hugged me again then ran off to tell his grandmother. Clarence and I were suddenly awkward together. I didn't understand why until he took my hand, pinching the ring Albert had given me. "You've finally done it, then? You've married him?"

Across the lobby, the elevator opened. My mother stepped out, saw us together, stopped. I read the disapproval in her eyes, but I was done letting her stage-manage my life. I'd be doing my own directing from now on.

"No. Albert's staying in Florida, actually. He gave it to me as a keepsake, is all. It was his grandmother's."

"I'm glad to hear it, Helen." He twisted the circle of gold until my finger was free of it, then placed it in my palm, closing my hand around it. "I was afraid it might be too late."

But it wasn't too late, not for any of us. Stepping closer, I rested my forehead against his rib cage. Inside my heart, a new room opened, folding back the shutters from its windows.

AUTHOR'S NOTE

On January 21,1939, the front page of the *New York Times* proclaimed the surprising news that an unknown ex-actress had inherited a fortune from the millionaire owner of the New York Yankees. While this true historical circumstance was the inspiration for *Bachelor Girl,* and while Colonel Jacob Ruppert was a real person, this book is a work of fiction. The novel does not pretend to reveal the truth behind the mystery of why the real Jacob Ruppert left a fortune to a woman who was known as, and only ever claimed to be, his friend. The mystery was, to me, not a puzzle to be solved but an enigma that sparked my imagination.

Many of the historical details related to the character of Jacob Ruppert in the novel are true — for example, the real Colonel Ruppert, a lifelong bachelor and president of his family's brewery, had an estate on the Hudson River called Eagle's Rest, built

Yankee Stadium, and signed Babe Ruth. He really did live in a mansion at the corner of Fifth Avenue and 93rd Street in Manhattan, employed a Japanese valet, owned a stable of racing horses, showed prize-winning Saint Bernard dogs at Madison Square Garden, kept a zoo of exotic animals, and sponsored an Antarctic expedition. His sister Cornelia really was shunned by her parents for marrying Nahan Franko, a divorced Jewish musician; after she died of appendicitis, her parents took possession of the coffin containing her body without her husband's knowledge or consent. And on January 30, 1921, the *New York Times* really did report that Jacob Ruppert had picked the Harlem site of the actual Hebrew Orphan Asylum to build Yankee Stadium.

I have used these historical details fictitiously to invent the character of Jacob Ruppert you meet in the novel, whose thoughts, words, actions, and motivations were all invented by me. While I conducted extensive research as part of my process for writing this novel, I had no access to (nor any knowledge of) any diaries or letters or personal papers related to Jacob Ruppert or the Ruppert family. I often left out or re-arranged biographical details related to the real Jacob Ruppert to better serve the fictional story I am telling.

The characters of Helen Winthrope and Albert Kramer are creations of my imagination who occupy the historical spots once held by real people about whom I know very little. The only connection the characters of Helen and Albert have to any real person is their first name and their position relative to Jacob Ruppert: one as his heiress, the other as his personal secretary. Like Helen and Albert, Felix Stern, Teresa Winthrope, Clarence Weldon, Bernice Johnson, and many other characters you meet in the novel are fictional.

The historical characters you encounter in the novel, including Babe Ruth, Claire Hodgson, Miller Huggins, Charles Gilpin, George Ruppert, Eugene O'Neill, and Lou Gehrig, are all used fictitiously. The story of Babe Ruth's adopted daughter, Dorothy, is based on Dorothy Ruth Pirone's own 1988 memoir *My Dad, the Babe: Growing Up with an American Hero.* Yankees fans will know that the baseball game depicted in chapters five and six is a fictional one; I have attempted to depict subsequent games accurately.

The novelist's job is to create a world that the reader can experience as real, whether that world is in the future on another planet or in the historical past here on Earth. The verisimilitude of the novel's world allows the reader to believe in the characters who live there, to care about what they do and what happens to them. In turn, caring about fictional characters allows readers to practice a powerful kind of empathy by making friends of strangers and inviting them to inhabit our minds and hearts. Thank you for inviting the characters in *Bachelor Girl* into yours.

ACKNOWLEDGMENTS

Infinite gratitude to Mitchell Waters for believing in this story since it was a mere paragraph, and to Steven Salpeter and everyone at Curtis Brown, Ltd., for making me feel so at home. Abundant thanks to Tara Parsons for seeing the potential in these pages, and to the entire team at Touchstone for supporting the novel in such spectacular fashion.

I am indebted to the many friends and family members who read and gave feedback on the novel in progress, including Anna Drallios, Jennifer Glenn, Marie Hathaway, Alex Hovet, Mariel Martin, Nancy Middleton, Rita van Alkemade, and Petra Wirth. Particular thanks to my colleague Neil Connelly for his keen eye and generosity of spirit.

Thanks also to Saint Basil Academy in Garrison, New York, for giving me an extensive tour of Eagle's Rest; to Linwood

Spiritual Center in Rhinebeck, New York, for allowing me to wander the grounds; to William Krattinger, Historic Program Analyst at the New York State Office of Parks, Recreation and Preservation; to the archivists at the New York Public Library and the National Baseball Hall of Fame; and to the librarians at Shippensburg University for supporting my research.

I gladly acknowledge the profound influence of historian George Chauncey's groundbreaking book *Gay New York: Gender, Urban Culture, and the Making of the Gay Male World, 1890–1940* on my conceptualization of this novel. The short story that inspires the play Helen produces in the novel is "A Chance to Make Good" by John L. Harrison, which was published in the NAACP magazine *The Crisis* in August 1918.

If you'd like to know more about the many historical sources that informed and inspired this novel, I invite you to explore my "Footnotes" blog at www.kimvanalkemade .com.

ABOUT THE AUTHOR

Kim van Alkemade is the author of the historical novels *Orphan #8* and *Bachelor Girl.* Born in New York City, she earned a BA in English and history from the University of Wisconsin–Parkside, and an MA and PhD in English from the University of Wisconsin–Milwaukee. She is a professor in the English department at Shippensburg University of Pennsylvania, where she teaches writing.

The employees of Thorndike Press hope you have enjoyed this Large Print book. All our Thorndike, Wheeler, and Kennebec Large Print titles are designed for easy reading, and all our books are made to last. Other Thorndike Press Large Print books are available at your library, through selected bookstores, or directly from us.

For information about titles, please call:
  (800) 223-1244

or visit our website at:
  gale.com/thorndike

To share your comments, please write:
  Publisher
  Thorndike Press
  10 Water St., Suite 310
  Waterville, ME 04901